I looked out over an unfamiliar city, a toothed skyline of brick-and-stone buildings in a flat landscape. A brown river wound through, bound with iron bridges. A train rumbled and whistled. Factories poured black pollution out of tall smokestacks.

As I watched, I saw an enormous spray of energy, colored like the rainbow, fall into view from high above. It blotted out the sun and filled the sky. Bright spots of colored light swarmed like wasps, hot and vibrant, tearing the sky apart. I could see the black of outer space and stars shining, cold pinpricks of light as the sky withdrew like the water in a tidal wave. It rolled back and back, leaving the city naked, exposed to the blazing tide of death that swooped down to light every building with the flare and flash of all the colors in the spectrum.

With a roar the blue sky rushed back in and washed the rainbow colors away. The buildings on the skyline glowed with an evil violet glare. As the sunlight faded into night, I smelled rotting meat, the overwhelming, gagging stench of corpses.

The living room reappeared around me. The white plaster ceiling looked oddly close at hand. It occurred to me that Ari might be carrying me in his arms. I checked, and yes, he was.

"Nola? Are you back?"

"Sort of."

"Are you ill? You've gone pale."

"Just terrified. That's all."

He carried me to the couch, set me down, then sat next to me and slipped his arm around my shoulders. "You went into another of those sodding walking trances."

"Yeah, sure did. It was quite a vision."

"Of what?"

"The death of Interchange. . . ."

KATHARINE KERR

APOCALYPSE TO GO

A NOLA O'GRADY NOVEL

DAW BOOKS, INC.

DONALD A. WOLLHEIM, FOUNDER

375 Hudson Street, New York, NY 10014

ELIZABETH R. WOLLHEIM

SHEILA E. GILBERT

PUBLISHERS

www.dawbooks.com

First Printing, February 2012
1 2 3 4 5 6 7 8 9

DAW TRADEMARK REGISTERED
U.S. PAT. AND TM. OFF. AND FOREIGN COUNTRIES
—MARCA REGISTRADA
HECHO EN U.S.A.

PRINTED IN THE U.S.A.

In Memoriam
Martin H. Greenberg
a lover of the short story,
but his should have been longer.

Acknowledgments

Many thanks to Howard Kerr, Madeleine Robins, Amanda Weinstein, Karen Williams, and Cliff Winnig for putting up with reading this book in ever-changing pieces. Thanks to Max Kahn for his thoughts on the effects of power stations. A special thanks to Kate Elliott and Jo Kasper, who suffered through revising the opening with me.

Chapter I

MY FIRST SATURDAY OFF WORK in a long time—
and it had to go and rain. I sat in the front room of my
flat and stared out the bay window at the gray sky, which
was busy drizzling water over my view of drab houses and
an apartment building. I'd been hoping for a day in the
park or on the beach with the guy I live with.

Ari Nathan, my partner in a number of senses of that
word, was slumped down on our old blue couch with his feet
up on the coffee table and his laptop balanced on his midsec-
tion. He's macho gorgeous, to my way of thinking, anyway,
with his wide dark eyes and softly curly dark hair. He works
out a lot, too. It shows, particularly when he's wearing tight
jeans and a thin white T-shirt as he was that afternoon.

I was contemplating seducing him for recreational purposes when someone or something downloaded itself into
the room. I turned cold, and my hair, which is not quite
shoulder-length, lifted away from my face in what felt like a
blast of wind. Not far from where Ari sat, a blue shape appeared on the landing of the stairs that led down to our
front door. The way it shimmered and throbbed in a pool of
blue-violet light obscured the details, but it looked vaguely
human overall. Psychically, I felt it as female. Something
metallic gleamed around her neck. A hint as to her identity
objectified itself as the faint smell of cat urine.

Ari went on typing; he'd noticed nothing, which meant the phenomenon was purely psychic. I got up and walked toward the shape. As I got closer, I could see black tattoos all over her neck and bare shoulders—roses, maybe, though I couldn't be sure. When I raised one hand to draw a Chaos ward and try to banish her, she shook her head as if to say, "No, don't!" and held up a glittering blue-violet sphere about the size of a billiard ball.

"Stolen property," the shape said to me. "Where are they?"

"Where are what?" I said. "I don't understand."

"What are you? A fence?" She hissed like a giant cat and disappeared.

Ari had heard me speak. He looked up with eyes that drooped in martyred resignation. "What is it now?"

"I don't know," I said. "Some kind of apparition."

"Has it gone?"

"Yeah, though she wasn't really here. Just a projection, I think, probably from a deviant world level."

"That's all? Oh, well, then, I shan't worry about it." He speaks like a Brit with a classy accent, because he learned his English in London.

"No need for sarcasm. Huh. I wonder if she's a were-leopard? I think such critters exist, anyway."

Ari sighed and hit a few keys. When I glanced at the laptop screen, I saw a solid mass of Hebrew letters.

"Working at your second job?" I said.

"None of your sodding business."

Which meant that yes, he was. He's an Interpol officer first and foremost, but he's also an Israeli national and, let's face it, a spy. "Secret agent" sounds nicer, but whatever you call it, he funnels information to his government that they wouldn't otherwise have.

Oh, well, no one's perfect.

My name is Nola O'Grady. I can't tell you the name of the government agency I work for. Our funding depends on our staying top secret, not because we have bureaucratic enemies but because most Americans would consider us a waste of tax monies. Your average citizen has no idea that the forces of unbridled Chaos threaten civilizations daily throughout the multiverse. My agency's mission: stop them from destroying ours.

I'm the head of our San Francisco bureau, or as we're known in the Agency, the Apocalypse Squad. It sounds impressive, but as squads go, ours is pretty small game. I have two full-time staff members and a part-timer who happens to be my younger brother, Michael. Ari, my bodyguard, is technically not on Agency staff, merely on loan from Interpol "indefinitely."

"Uh, Nola," Ari said, "about this were-leopard."

"Yeah?" I said. "What?"

"Is she going to come back?"

"How would I know?"

"I was afraid of that." Ari paused to glower. "Could you make a guess?"

Before I could answer, his laptop beeped at him. Ari stared at the screen as if it had committed a crime. I waited. A minute passed. "Say what?" I said.

"Sorry." He looked up. "Another e-mail from AOS Fourteen. Do you remember who he is?"

"The guy who must be another Interpol agent, but you couldn't find him in any of your outfit's online directories."

"Right. He says that Javert told him you've apprehended the suspect we're calling Belial. He wants to know if you'll remand to his custody."

"Tell him you can't share that intel until he identifies himself. And ask for his need to know."

Ari sat up straight and put the laptop onto the coffee table. He spent a few minutes fiddling with the machine, because he had to detach the Hebrew keyboard in order to attach the English version.

"Did you ever hear back from your in-house security people?" I said. "If Mr. Fourteen can use the e-mail system, they must have some kind of password or something for him."

"Not necessarily. Conceivably he could have authorization to edit the system log."

"The what?"

"Never mind."

"How am I ever going to understand this stuff if you won't tell me?"

"You don't need to understand it. You have me for that."

While we waited to see if AOS14 answered, I ran the psychic procedure that the Agency calls Scanning the Aura Field or SAF. This particular function has a number of uses, depending on how the operator focuses her mind. In this instance, with an SAF: Links I let my mind roam around what little data I knew about AOS14, who had appeared, via e-mail only, at the very end of my last case, the arrest of the aforementioned Belial.

For good measure, I included the apparition, which had appeared only moments before Spare's e-mail. Synchronicity means a lot in my line of work. Almost immediately I saw a memory image of another thing that had recently appeared: a graffito that someone kept painting on the front of the building where we lived. About eighteen inches high, it was a solid black circle from which emerged seven black arrows, three on the bottom half, four on the top. Although it looked like a highway symbol for a multiple exit interchange, it signified the opposite of orderly procedure.

"That's weird," I said. "AOS14 must be connected to the Chaos magic symbol, the unbalanced version, I mean. The graffito you keep washing off our front wall."

"Interpol agents are vetted," Ari said. "We don't hire magicians."

"I said it was weird."

"All of your psychic impressions are weird."

"I can't argue with that. The real question is, are they accurate?" I let my mind roam a little further. "Wait, I get it now. It's just because of his initials, AOS. The guy who invented the Chaos magic system was a Brit named Austin Osman Spare."

Ari started to reply, but the laptop beeped at him. He glanced at the screen. "An answer," he said and hit a few keys. He read, he scowled, he swore in Hebrew.

"What's wrong?" I said.

"He just told me that his name's Austin Osman Spare."

I gaped. "Look, it could be some kind of pseudonym."

"If you'll wait a moment, I'll tell you what he says." Ari

cleared his throat. "I assure you that's my real name," he read from his screen. "I come by it legitimately, though of course I'm not the world-famous British artist."

"World-famous?" I said. "I'd never call him that."

"Do you mind not interrupting?" Ari glared at me, then continued reading. "The fourteen is an integral part of my name. I'll explain at some point should you wish to meet."

"His family must be crazy for genealogy," I said, "if he goes around telling everyone he's the fourteenth in his line."

"Will you shut up?" Ari snarled, then continued reading. "I would like to discuss a matter that should interest you greatly. I have some information of interest to O'Grady as well and a request to put before her." He looked up. "He goes on to say that he wants to know if he can contact you directly via e-mail."

"What about?"

"He doesn't say."

"Um, would you mind asking him?" I considered. "And ask him what his position is in Interpol. He may be the guy at the NCB level who wanted you here in San Francisco."

Over the next half hour or so, encrypted messages rode the airwaves between Ari and the mysterious Mr. Spare14. In the end they made an exchange. Spare14 learned one of my e-mail addresses, secure but separate from the Agency system. In return he handed us a piece of information that twisted my mind like a kaleidoscope.

"I do operate at the NCB level," he admitted, "but in a custodial position for a world with severe problems. I believe that O'Grady's brother has visited it."

After Ari read this bit aloud, I found the implications so difficult to process that I couldn't speak. Ari watched me for some seconds.

"What's wrong?" he said. "I can tell that you've got the wind up about something."

"I just put a few weird things together, and I don't know what we're going to do about them."

"That seems to be normal for our situation. He must be referring to the deviant world you call the Interchange."

"Yeah, for sure. But how does he know about it?"

Ari answered me. I saw his lips moving, but I heard nothing. I felt myself get up and go to the window. Instead of the usual view of our Sunset district neighborhood, I looked out over an unfamiliar city, a toothed skyline of brick-and-stone buildings in a flat landscape. A brown river wound through, bound with iron bridges. A train rumbled and whistled. Factories poured black pollution out of tall smokestacks.

As I watched, I saw an enormous spray of energy, colored like the rainbow, fall into view from high above. It blotted out the sun and filled the sky. Bright spots of colored light swarmed like wasps, hot and vibrant, tearing the sky apart. I could see the black of outer space and stars shining, cold pinpricks of light as the sky withdrew like the water in a tidal wave. It rolled back and back, leaving the city naked, exposed to the blazing tide of death that swooped down to light every building with the flare and flash of all the colors in the spectrum.

With a roar the blue sky rushed back in and washed the rainbow colors away. The buildings on the skyline glowed with an evil violet glare. As the sunlight faded into night, I smelled rotting meat, the overwhelming, gagging stench of corpses.

The living room reappeared around me. The white plaster ceiling looked oddly close at hand. I could smell witch hazel, Ari's usual aftershave. It occurred to me that he might be carrying me in his arms. I checked, and yes, he was.

"Nola? Are you back?"

"Sort of."

"Are you ill? You've gone pale."

"Just terrified. That's all."

He carried me to the couch, set me down, then sat next to me and slipped his arm around my shoulders. "You went into another of those sodding walking trances."

"Yeah, sure did. It was quite a vision."

"Of what?"

"The death of Interchange."

Ari's eyes narrowed in puzzlement, and his lips parted as if he were about to speak. He closed them again and merely stared at me.

"I don't know how I know," I said. "But I know."

A memory image from a Tom and Jerry cartoon rose in my mind, of a Swiss cheese with holes big enough for the mouse to crawl through. Oddly enough, the image meshed with the vision. The rainbow horror had turned a world into Swiss cheese, maybe by accident, maybe by design. Sometimes my visions can be in really bad taste. A lot of people died, maybe millions, and what did I see? A cartoon mouse.

"I feel okay now," I told Ari. "I'd better record this vision and check in with my handler."

"You'd best not go into another full trance until you've eaten something."

"I wasn't planning on another trance. Don't worry. I'll just log on and send him e-mail like a normal person."

Not, of course, that I sent him normal e-mail. The Agency has its own heavily encrypted system, TranceWeb, that exists "in the cloud," as it were, but a cloud of its own, Cloud 9 as we call it for laughs. Besides describing our earlier visitor and then the vision, I had a crucial question to ask Y, my handler. Should I turn the Belial entity over to this Spare guy if he really did work for Interpol?

I'd captured Belial (him or it, I wasn't certain about the gender) on my Agency authority, but since the Agency had no official liaison with any police force, I had no idea of what to do next. Suppose I'd gone to the local police and told them that I had a criminal in custody who happened to be a sapient extraterrestrial squid. Would they have believed me? Yeah, exactly—especially when I went on to say that I had custody of only his consciousness, stored on an old-fashioned flash drive, not of his physical body.

When I finished sending the message, I logged off and shut down the system to derail possible Chaos hackers. I swiveled around in my computer chair to see Ari standing nearby. He held out a plate topped with a slice of cold pizza.

"You never ate lunch," he said.

The pizza stared at me with olive slices for eyes.

"I didn't want lunch, that's why," I said. "There's an awful lot of calories on that plate."

"The doctor said you need to eat more." Ari fixed me

with a grim stare. "You need to join the gym and come with me when I work out. Then you won't worry about a few sodding calories."

"I was raised to believe that ladies never sweat."

"Ladies, perhaps, but how does that apply to you?" He stepped back out of range before I could kick him. "Nola, you've got to eat more."

We locked stares. He won.

While I ate the pizza, Ari paced back and forth by the window and talked on his cell phone in two different languages. The Hebrew I could recognize. I thought the other might be Turkish. I knew better than to ask questions, but when he finished, he volunteered some information.

"According to a couple of highly placed people I have access to," Ari told me, "Spare's a legitimate member of my organization. I never mentioned deviant world levels, of course. Neither did they."

"But then, they wouldn't even if they knew."

Although I checked a couple of times that afternoon, I never received an e-mail from the mysterious Mr. Spare14. I did a little more research online about Chaos magic but found nothing I didn't already know. At one time I'd done some serious research into the subject. I'd organized the results in a notebook, and fortunately I remembered where the notebook was.

Some years previously I'd cached some loose papers over at the house belonging to my Aunt Eileen and her husband, Jim Houlihan, when I'd moved out of town on Agency business. When I called her, she had no objections to my coming over to hunt.

"Stay for dinner, dear," Aunt Eileen said. "Tell Ari I'm making lamb stew with poppy-seed noodles to go under it."

"That will seal the deal, for sure. Thanks. We'll be glad to."

Ari put on a proper shirt and his gray sport coat. I changed into a pair of trouser jeans and a red-and-white-print cotton blouse. Before we left, I placed a couple of Chaos wards on every door and the downstairs windows. When I finished, Ari activated the elaborate electronic security system that he and his buddy Itzak Stein had installed in the building and the garage out in back. Ari and I had leased the entire building in which we lived, two flats out in San Francisco's fog belt, to ensure that any danger our jobs might bring would target only us, not an innocent neighbor. At the moment the bottom flat stood empty except for my father's old desk, but I didn't want anyone prowling around in it, empty or not.

My Aunt Eileen and her family, which at that time included my younger brother, Michael, and his girlfriend, Sophie, live in the sunbelt, that is, the southeast side of the city. The house stands in the Excelsior district, partway up the hill that's topped with the blue water tower. It's an odd misshapen house on a double lot, three stories at one end, two at the other, but only one in the middle section: a long living room that the front door divides in half.

In one half of the living room, a pale orange brocade sectional sofa stands under a portrait of Father Keith O'Brien, my uncle on Aunt Eileen's side of the family, in his Franciscan robes. I've never seen anyone sit there. The family clusters at the other end of the room, where there are shabby armchairs and recliners arranged near the TV, when, that is, we're not in the kitchen.

It was in the kitchen that we found Aunt Eileen that afternoon, sitting at the round maple table and reading the newspaper. She wore one of her usual retro outfits, a pair of leopard print capris and a pale blue cotton shirt with rolled sleeves. She had new pink fuzzy slippers with bunny faces, complete with long ears.

A large pot of stew simmered on the stove. Wisps of herbed steam rose from the surface. Ari inhaled deeply and smiled. I sat down at the table a couple of chairs over from hers. Aunt Eileen folded the newspaper and laid it down.

"Ari, dear," she said, "you can take off that jacket. It's awfully warm in here."

"That's quite all right," he said. "I don't mind."

"You really don't have to hide your gun. I mean, honestly, we all know you're a police officer."

I snickered. Ari winced, but he did take off his sport coat to reveal the Beretta in its shoulder holster.

"He never leaves home without it," I said.

Ari shot me a scowl, then draped the jacket over a chair and sat down next to me.

"Where's everyone else?" I said.

"Well, Jim's at work," Aunt Eileen said with a sigh. "There was more trouble with the L Taraval line, and so of course they called him in."

"That happens too much," I said, "his boss taking his weekend, I mean." My uncle worked for Muni, the San Francisco public transport system, which exists in a state of perpetual decay.

"It's the budget problems. Since he's on salary, they don't have to pay him for overtime."

"Makes sense, but very irritating."

She nodded her agreement. "Brian's team is playing today. High school basketball's over for the year, so now he's on the baseball team. I don't know about Michael and Sophie—upstairs probably, and I don't really want to know what they're doing. Let's hope it's schoolwork."

A lesson in human biology, maybe, I thought, but I kept the thought to myself. Apparently Ari was thinking along the same lines.

"You've been quite generous to both of them," Ari said. "I can have a talk with him about proper manners when you're living in someone else's house."

"You're a darling," Aunt Eileen said. "It's wonderful how he listens to you. Just make sure you knock before you open the door."

Ari left the kitchen by the back stairs that led to the bedrooms on the floor above. Aunt Eileen waited until he was well gone.

"I hate to admit this," she said, "but I'm beginning to think your mother was right about Michael."

"That he's an out-of-control juvenile?"

Eileen held out a hand parallel to the table and waggled it to indicate she could go either way. "At times he's fine. At others, he's really hard to handle," she said. "Jim makes things worse, bellowing at him, usually after he's downed a couple of glasses of whiskey. Jim has the whiskey, that is, not Michael. I've never seen Mike touch any kind of alcohol, which is just as well."

"Yeah, it sure is! What's the problem? Too much lewd conduct with Sophie?"

"No, it's his schoolwork. He doesn't do any, and here he's got the chance at that scholarship for college. If he doesn't get into college, the scholarship won't do him a bit of good."

"I'll have Ari press home a few salient points. There's something about being lectured by a man packing a Beretta that should make Mike sit up and listen."

We shared a laugh, but I worried. When Michael was born, I was ten, and I thought he was the best doll in the world. Since my mother had seven children total to take care of, she was glad to let me play mommy with the new baby. Once my father disappeared a few years later, and she needed to work outside the home, I became Michael's second mother. Since I was just a teenager, my parenting skills were minimal.

"I think the real problem," Aunt Eileen said, "is that Michael's talents are blossoming. They always come in like teeth and make a person just as irritable as teething makes a baby. That's why I'm trying to ignore his behavior with Sophie. It calms him down."

"As long as she doesn't get pregnant."

"I got her to Planned Parenthood. She's really glad to have the birth control." Aunt Eileen paused for a sigh. "Just don't mention that around Father Keith."

"Another thing to hide from him, huh? Like my own visits there."

Aunt Eileen rolled her eyes at the memory. When I turned sixteen, I started pouring out Qi like a lighthouse, and boys became the moths. I'd had no idea why they all started ignoring my awesomely beautiful younger sister to swarm around me instead. Not all of my would-be suitors were boys my own age, either—unfortunately. It was a period of my life that I did my best to forget.

"I'm just glad Ari's taken an interest in Mike . . ." She hesitated with a quick drum of her fingertips on the table. "And speaking of Ari, I've been wondering. I know he's here to be your bodyguard. Does this mean that someone's threatening you? I'd really hoped that when that awful man Johnson was killed, you'd be safe."

"Yeah, so did I. But I honestly think that this bodyguard business is just an excuse. I'm really not sure why he was attached to the Agency. It doesn't seem to be the way Interpol usually operates."

"Jim's been saying the same thing."

"He's right. Of course, if the State Department asked for Ari, that would count for something, but no one will tell my boss if they did. I do know that somebody very high up in Ari's chain of command wanted him here." I shrugged. "Ari doesn't know who."

She sighed with a shake of her head. "I do wish you'd get another job. Something safer, where people would tell you things if they were important."

I smiled as vaguely as I could. Eileen got up and poked viciously at the stew with a long wooden spoon.

Michael and Ari came downstairs a few minutes later. Sophie, Mike informed me, was going to take a shower. Although Ari sat down at the table, Michael hovered near the doorway. He shoved his hands into his jeans' pockets and put his back against the wall, mimicking the way that Ari often stood. He was a skinny kid, just about my height, 5'8", though with long legs that promised more growth later. We look a lot alike, black hair, fine features including the slightly tilted Irish nose, but his eyes are blue whereas I have hazel eyes that tend toward green.

"I need to find something in the upstairs storage rooms," I said. "Mike, why not come with me? I'm going to need your help to move cartons around."

"Oh, okay." He groaned the words rather than speaking them and peeled himself off the wall.

Ari cleared his throat. Mike glanced at him, then turned to me. "I don't mind helping," he said.

"Great!" I said. "Let's go."

At the extreme north end of the Houlihan house is a stack of three small rooms where Uncle Jim's mother, Nanny Houlihan, had lived before she passed away. Eileen had turned them into storage areas, though recently she'd cleared out the ground-floor room and stashed its contents elsewhere, because it housed the psychic gate to the deviant world level known as Interchange. Uncle Jim had padlocked the door into that room and hammered a couple of boards across it to keep it shut. We climbed the stairs up to the door of the second storage room. On the landing Michael paused and turned to look at me.

"I'm real sorry about the bad grades," he said.

"So am I. If you want to go to college, you'd better bring them up in summer school."

"That's what Ari said, too. He told me I was hella lucky to have a chance at college." He reached for the doorknob. "School would be seriously better than going into the army like he did."

Michael opened the door and held it to let me go in first. Since an old venetian blind covered the room's only window, I flipped on the overhead light. The antique steamer trunk in which I'd stored my college notebooks and other souvenirs sat against the farthest wall of the square room. Big storage cartons and a treadle sewing machine blocked the path. Michael began moving things out of the way, then stopped and turned toward the window. He frowned and seemed to be listening to a distant noise. I heard nothing.

"What is it, bro?" I said.

"This is totally whack," he said. "I'm not sure—just let me—" He took a couple of steps toward the window, then stared at it. "There never was a gate here before."

"Is there now?"

"Yeah. I can feel it, but it's not on right. I mean, it's sort of skewed or hanging weird, like a door that's off one of its hinges." He looked over his shoulder at me. "I'm thinking I could pull up that blind, and then we could see what's over there."

Over on the other side of the trans-world gate, he meant. I ran an SM:D and felt nothing but the usual low hum of suffering inherent in earthly existence.

"Okay," I said. "Let's give it a try."

It took us a couple of minutes to clear a path to the window. I stood at one side of it and Michael, at the other, where he could reach the pull cord to open the blind. As soon as he touched the cord, the blind made a clattering noise and melted away.

Sunlight flooded my vision and made my eyes water. I

could smell fresh air, scented with damp earth and manure. I blinked hard and squinted to look around me. We were standing right on the edge of a flat roof, looking down at a vegetable garden edged with mutant morning glory plants, ten feet high, some of them, supported on poles. We'd come through to Interchange.

"Oh, shit!" Michael said. "I forgot."

"Forgot what?" I said.

"That the house is different here. It's only got one room at this end. Nola, step back, a big step, and then turn around. Okay?"

"Okay." I followed orders.

I bumped into a pile of cardboard cartons. Dim electric light replaced the sunshine. I heard Michael whistle in relief, and I let out my breath in a sigh. We were back in the storage room at the Houlihan house.

"Sorry 'bout that," Michael said. "That was hella stupid of me."

"Well, it's not like you knew what was going to happen."

"Yeah, that's the problem, isn't it? I'm having to learn how to world-walk on my own, and sometimes I seriously mess up. I wish Dad was here. It's gross that he got busted like that."

"Yeah, I have to agree."

Michael scowled at the venetian blind. "It's weird about this gate opening up. I helped Aunt Eileen carry some stuff up here just last week, and it wasn't open then, the gate, I mean."

"Huh." I considered the problem. "Well, I know even less about this stuff than you do, but let's look at it logically. There's a couple of possibilities. Dad opened the original gate downstairs a long time ago, but he's in prison. So, maybe someone else opened this one."

"They did a fail job if they did."

"The second possibility is that it opened itself. Do you think gates can expand themselves? Sort of like a leak in a packed earth dam, where the water keeps washing away the dirt once the leak gets started. The hole gets bigger and bigger."

"Maybe." Michael sounded doubtful. "But why now?

Dad must have made that other gate what? Thirty-five years ago?"

"About, yeah."

"And it never spread in all that time."

"That's true. Maybe it's spreading now because you've found your talents. You're another world-walker in this house. Do you think the gate has some kind of property that would sense that?"

"Maybe. I might be sending out, like, vibes, and I was using the gate downstairs hella often for a while. But—I dunno."

We looked at each other in utter confusion.

"It might have something do with Dad," I said. "In that letter he smuggled out, Dad mentioned being paroled. He also said he was thinking about us a whole lot. Maybe he's out, and that had an effect on the gate. This whole process takes place on some deep level of your mind, after all."

Michael's eyes got very wide. "If that's true," he said, "we could go get him."

"We could—if only we knew exactly where he is and how to reach the place. And of course I might not be right about the parole. I'm just guessing. For all we know he's still in Moorwood Prison, whatever world that's on. I'm willing to bet it's not on Interchange. That would be too convenient."

"Too dangerous, you mean, with all the rads."

"That, too, yeah. If he's still in jail, we can't even visit him. The authorities would want to know where we came from. You don't want to end up in the cell next door for the same crime."

"Yeah, guess it would be the same, if I brought you along. Transporting someone across world borders. I keep forgetting it's illegal. Well, it is there, anyway, wherever there is."

"Exactly." It occurred to me that Austin Osman Spare14 had to know something about world-walking. "Now, look, I may be in a position to find out more about this situation. I don't know yet if I can or not, but I'm going to try. Getting Dad home is high on my priority list these days."

"It would sure be easier to concentrate on stuff like

school if I could, y'know, talk to him about world-walking."
Mike sounded sincere. "I just get seriously confused sometimes, trying to read my school stuff, and trying to figure out
what the hell I'm doing with these gates."

"Yeah, I can see that. Unfortunately, I also have Agency
work to do here. I can't go haring off across the worlds until
I know what I'm doing and have the time to do it in. Understand?"

"Yeah, I do. Y'know, there are other gates in San Francisco, like the one that over-there police squad used to take
Dad away. I've been thinking about making a map."

When I did a scan around this idea, I felt only a distant
and faint chance for danger. "The Agency could use something like that. They'll pay you for it."

"Cool!"

Michael glanced back at the window. "We better get the
stuff you wanted and go back downstairs," he said. "This
room's starting to give me the creeps."

When I opened the trunk, I had to rummage through a
lot of notebooks as well as shoe boxes full of things friends
had sent me, like Christmas and birthday cards, the kind of
paper junk that somehow you never want to throw out
even though there's no reason to keep it. I did find the material about Chaos magic about halfway down the layers, as
well as an old college notebook from a class on Jung's psychological theories. On impulse I grabbed that, too, and we
left.

As we walked down the hall toward the living room, I
heard women's voices, arguing. Aunt Eileen was one, and
the other—

"Oh, shit!" Michael said. "It's Mom!"

He turned and ran back to the stairs. The miserable little
coward had gotten halfway up before I mentally registered
the news. I was tempted to follow his example. Instead, I
squared my shoulders and walked on into the living room.
Why hide? Mom had already figured out that I was in the
house.

"Oh, there you are," she said. "Condescending to say
hello to me, are you?"

Deirdre O'Brien O'Grady, five foot two, slender, her

graying hair dyed a tasteful auburn, set her beringed hands on her hips and glared at me with cold blue eyes. Yet she was smiling with the little twist of the upper lip, the flare of one nostril, that we all called her sneer. She was wearing a boxy pants suit in powder blue, with matched pearls at her throat.

"Hi, Mom," I said. "I thought you never wanted to see me again. Just trying to do what you asked."

"The one time you ever did." She made a girlish giggling sound—I wouldn't call it a laugh—and went on looking me over with the cold stare, her usual minute assessment of my hair, clothes, body. "At least you've finally lost all that weight," she said eventually. "But you could get some better clothes now that you can fit into them."

Aunt Eileen was hovering, watching her sister, glancing now and then at me. I was determined to avoid a screaming fight in front of her, and in front of Ari, too, who was standing on the other side of the room, his eyes narrow, his mouth slack in disbelief. I noticed that he'd put on his jacket, probably to hide the shoulder holster.

"I was just introduced to your boyfriend," Mom continued. "The latest one, I suppose." Her eyes flicked his way, then back to me. "How many does that make, anyway? Five? Six? Or do you even bother to keep count anymore?"

My good intentions vanished. "What's wrong?" I said and smiled. "Envy's a sin, you know."

Mom caught her breath. From somewhere upstairs a sharp cracking noise rattled through the living room. The windows trembled and boomed, but the glass held unbroken.

"Oh, come on!" I said. "Why can't you just say it instead of sounding off in the aura field?"

"What? Do you honestly think I did—it must be Michael and his damn firecrackers again."

One section of the brocade sofa lifted about three inches off the floor, then dropped with a groan.

"He's not hiding under there," I said. "Why the hell can't you just admit you're as talented as the rest of us? This stupid charade—ever so middle class, are we? And for the wife of a man in the building trades! Crap, look at you! The way you're dressed! Do you think you're the bloody Queen of England?"

Mom stared at me openmouthed. I realized that I'd just hurled all the insults Dad used when they were fighting on the same theme. I squelched a temptation to apologize. Mom turned to Aunt Eileen.

"I'm leaving," she said. "I don't have to stand here and be insulted."

"No, you don't." I found something original to say. "You can be insulted anywhere you go. It's your hobby, isn't it? Indignation."

An invisible hand grabbed a thick bunch of my hair and yanked. I yelped. Mom smiled at me, turned on her heel, and stalked out. She slammed the front door behind her so hard that the windows rattled again, this time from natural causes.

Aunt Eileen let out her breath in a long sigh. Ari stopped lurking in the hall and hurried over to me. He slipped an arm around my shoulders and hauled me in to rest against him. I leaked a few tears onto his chest, then pulled myself together.

"She dropped by unannounced," Eileen said to me. "I'm so sorry, dear."

"Well, I'm sorry I lost it." I wiped my face on my shirtsleeve. "Ari, will you forgive me for being a jerk?"

"What makes you think you acted badly?" Ari said. "She has to be the most appalling woman I've ever met."

I decided that falling in love with him had been one of my better decisions.

"She really was responsible for those—" Ari hesitated. "Those phenomena, I suppose you'd call them?"

"Yeah," I said. "Behind every so-called poltergeist lurks someone just like my mom."

"I really wish she'd married again," Aunt Eileen said. "She was very beautiful when she was younger, you know. That's where Kathleen and Sean get it from. Deirdre had her chances, even with everything."

"Everything," I glanced at Ari, "means all of us kids, with Pat's lycanthropy thrown in as a bonus."

Aunt Eileen nodded in sad agreement.

"Why didn't she marry again, then?" Ari said.

"She was staying faithful to my father like a good Catholic widow should." I tried to keep my voice level, but Aunt Eileen winced at the sarcasm. "I just don't understand that." I turned to her. "I'm sorry."

She shrugged and gave me a watery smile.

"But now we know he's not dead." Michael came strolling into the living room as calmly as if he hadn't run for his miserable life a few minutes previously. "Why won't she believe us?"

"Because it only hurts worse, dear," Aunt Eileen said, "knowing he's alive but can't come back. Do you remember what he wrote about having to wear that StopCollar thing?"

"Well, yeah." Michael frowned down at the rug. "Y'know, I feel lousy about this. Maybe we never should have shown the letter to her."

"Maybe so," I said, "but it's too late now. We did."

CHAPTER 2

ARI AND I LEFT MY AUNT'S around eight o'clock that night with my notebooks, enough leftover food for two dinners, and a special family photo album and scrapbook that Eileen had put together for us. As usual, I insisted that I drive. Unless you've been a passenger in a car driven by a macho Israeli guy, you don't know what "fear of death" means.

We'd just turned onto Sloat Boulevard for the last leg of the trip home when Ari's shirt pocket began to beep. He pulled his cell phone out of the pocket and glanced at it.

"Drive faster," he said to me. "Someone's trying to breach the security system." He pressed a couple of buttons on the phone. "I've alerted the police."

As I tapped the accelerator, I thanked Whomever that Ari wasn't doing the driving. If he'd been behind the wheel, we would have careened through the streets at eighty— needlessly, thanks to our souped-up Saturn's interesting features. Whenever we approached a red light, I pressed a button on the steering column, and the light turned green. Turning corners at fifty—no tipping, no screeching, no problem. We made it back to our pair of flats in record time.

As I turned off Noriega onto 48th, I saw a squad car pulled up in front of our building. I parked in front of the building next door. Before I could turn off the engine, Ari had opened the door and gotten out. He ran down the sidewalk ahead of me and joined the pair of uniformed officers who were standing under the streetlight. I locked up the car in case someone was lurking nearby. I caught up with Ari just in time to hear an officer say, "No sign of forced entry."

"Good." Ari was holding his Interpol ID out where they could see it. "Do you think we could have a look through the front window with your torch? Er, flashlight."

As they went up the front steps, Ari returned his ID to his inner jacket pocket. The second officer nodded at me to indicate that he knew I was there, then walked over to lean against the squad car and look up at the top flat windows. Apparently, I was supposed to feel protected.

Thanks to the streetlights I could see up and down 48th. Down by the corner on Moraga a man was standing, hands in his jacket pockets, watching. I sketched a surreptitious Chaos ward and sailed it his way. When it hit, nothing happened. One of the neighbors, I assumed, being curious. He proved my assumption right after a minute or two by taking keys out of a pocket—I heard them jingle—and letting himself into the building on the corner.

Ari and the other police officer came trotting down the steps. I heard the cop saying, ". . . get a tech out here if you want."

"I'll dust for any prints," Ari said. "But I'm assuming he was wearing gloves."

"Yeah, probably so," the officer said. "If there's any more trouble, Nathan, call us."

"I will, and thank you."

The officers returned to their squad car and drove off. Ari glanced my way.

"Is it safe to put the car in the garage?" I said.

"Yes," Ari said. "When the officers turned onto 48th, they saw someone hurrying down the front steps. He had a motorcycle in the side drive. He took off up Moraga before they even reached the building. They had no real grounds for pursuit."

"Okay." I paused to look up at the top floor. "Let me run a quick SM:L."

The search mode turned up nothing of interest in the top flat. "The front door into the bottom flat," I said, "has had its Chaos wards erased. The guy knew what he was doing when it came to that kind of surveillance. Not so much with electronics, huh?"

"No. I take it he was no ordinary thief."

"No, 'fraid not. He must have sensed your alarm going off. I can't tell if he felt it psychically or if he had a gadget."

"Did he get inside?"

"I doubt if he could have opened the door before he sensed the alarm. Erasing a Chaos ward takes time."

We did a second thorough check of the building and the garages in the rear before I drove the car in. Ari held the leftovers, my notebooks, and the photo album while I stood under the porch light and placed new Chaos wards on the downstairs door. He watched my hands as I did.

"Would someone have to touch the wards to erase them?" Ari said.

"Nope. It's all done with Qi."

"Then I wonder what set off the alarm."

"The Qi, probably. It's a biomagnetic force. If you know how to use it, you can set up an energy field or channel it into something approaching a beam. How sensitive is the system?"

"Very. It can respond to a listening device aimed its way, for instance. Qi, is it? I'll take that under advisement."

Before we went in, Ari reset the alarm on the lower floor by pressing buttons on his cell phone, which was not, as you've probably guessed by now, a standard issue model. When we arrived upstairs, I turned on a few extra lights. The idea that some Chaos operative had been hanging around my home base left me nervous. We searched the flat but found nothing disturbed. We both settled down to check our inboxes, Ari on his laptop, me at my desktop in the corner of the living room. I'd received nothing from AOS14, but while we'd been at Aunt Eileen's, Y had answered my question.

"Before you turn the flash drive over to Spare," Y said, "vet him and get back to me."

His caution made perfect sense. Neither of us wanted

Belial, that murdering Chaotic cephalopod, turned loose into the multiverse by an accomplice.

"Nola?" Ari said.

"Yes?" I left the trance state and turned in my chair to look at him. He was sitting more or less upright on the couch with his laptop on his lap.

"I was just checking the records for the security system," Ari said. "It says that an energy release by an unknown device triggered the alarm."

"Okay. It was the Qi discharge, then, I bet, when he erased the wards. Say, while you're there, would you see if that cat-person apparition left a trace? It was around one o'clock when she appeared."

Ari nodded and clicked on a few icons. "Yes," he said. "Unknown device energy discharge at thirteen dot oh four o'clock, security node seven." He frowned at the screen. "Accompanied by a one second spike in ambient level of background radiation."

"A big spike?"

"No, just a blip." He glanced at me. "Nothing dangerous, I'm glad to report."

All of this data told me that the apparition had been produced by some sort of device rather than being a purely psychic phenomenon. Yet Ari had heard and seen nothing when it first appeared. I had another puzzle on my hands, one that the SAF:L I'd run earlier had linked to the Chaos magic symbol. I opened a new file and made a few notes.

I returned to answering my e-mail. When you're part of a large bureaucracy, even a secret one like the Agency, you end up spending a lot of time on e-mail. The Apocalypse Squad got its share. Thanks to multiple encryption systems, it's just plain safer than cell phone calls. Since all the big phone companies archive cell messages on their server network, my agency, like the CIA, forbids its agents to use texting even for personal communications. A careless message might reveal where an agent lives, for instance, or other dangerous fragments of data.

When I finished, I swiveled around in my computer chair to see what Ari was up to. He'd put his laptop on the coffee table.

"You know," he said, "I've been thinking about the unpleasantness with your mother. Is it because of her example that you won't marry me?"

I sighed. "I don't see why you're so obsessed with the idea of marriage."

"You're like the roadrunner in those cartoons, always speeding away from me. That makes me the coyote. Of course I want to catch you. Not for my dinner, though."

"Gee, thanks! Meep meep!"

He smiled and patted the cushion next to him.

"I am not coming over there if you're going to keep talking about getting married."

His smile vanished. "Why are you so dead set against it?"

"I don't want to be married. It's not you. It's the institution. I don't want to be in an institution."

His glare deepened.

"That's a joke," I said. "The institution part, I mean."

"I understood that. I merely resent you joking about this."

My brain finally spat out the information that I'd hurt his feelings.

"I'm sorry," I said. "This discussion makes me really anxious. I don't mean to trivialize the subject."

He softened the scowl to exasperation.

"Look," I went on, "why can't we just have some kind of modern committed relationship without all the legal hassles?"

"Because as far as I know, you're not committed to anything. Especially not to me."

I started to reply, then realized that I'd never told him I loved him, not once, not even in bed.

"For all I know," Ari continued, "you're hoping I'll be sent back to Israel, and you'll never have to see me again."

"That's not true."

"What is true, then?"

I felt my aura shrink and harden into a shell of Qi around me. I longed to cower inside it and throw wisecracks his way, but I refused. I walked over to the couch and sat down beside him.

"Well?" he said. "Do you want me gone?"

"No. Don't be stupid!"

"That's something, I suppose. A sign of affection in its own way."

"Oh, stop it! Ari, I love you. I love you a whole lot, and I can't even imagine being with any guy but you ever again."

The way he smiled, with a wave of relief and joy mingled together, shattered the aura shell. When he held out his arms, I slid over and cuddled up. I rested my head on his chest and heard his heart pounding.

"You're shaking." He kissed me on the forehead. "You need to marry me for your sake as well as mine, you see. That way you'll know I'm never going to leave you."

I pulled back so I could see his face. He was grinning.

"You never give up, do you?" I said.

"Of course not. Why should I? I'm right."

"You're lucky I love you, or I'd kick you so hard—"

He laughed, then kissed me for real. I felt the Qi begin to flow between us. He nuzzled the side of my neck and slid one hand down to my lap.

"Do you want to work anymore tonight?" he said.

"No." I felt my desire as Qi warmth, a sweet, troubling warmth wrapping around both of us. "Let's just go to bed."

"Hmm." He let go of me and moved a little away. "I don't know."

"Say what?"

"Perhaps I should hold out for marriage. No more sex until you—"

"You wouldn't dare!"

"No, actually, I wouldn't." He grinned at me. "But you sounded appalled at the very thought."

He was right, damn him, but I refused to admit it. When I started to get up, he caught my hands and pulled me back down. Before I could object, he kissed me again. I did my best to stay cold. Two can play at that game, I thought. Which is possibly true, but I wasn't one of the two. At the next kiss I melted right into his arms.

My research ended up waiting until the next morning. I logged onto the desktop first and brought up a page that described the original Austin Osman Spare. I even found a couple of pictures.

"Huh, listen to this," I told Ari. "The guy I know as A. O. Spare had a dad who was a London police officer. I wonder what he thought of his son turning into an artist and a magician?"

"Rather a lot, I should think," Ari said. "None of it favorable, at least as far as the magic's concerned. I take it he didn't join the force like his father."

"No. He seems to have had a really miserable life, poor guy. One of those great British misfits. His magical studies were what was important to him."

Ari rolled his eyes at that. I logged off and turned to my old notebook, which I'd filled with tiny writing in violet ink, a habit I'd dropped when I was nineteen. The sight took me back to my teens, a place I didn't want to go. I concentrated hard on the matter in hand.

Spare had started with Crowley's concept of magic as a system of producing changes in consciousness. He took it several steps further by refusing to endorse any one system of magical or spiritual practices. By conflating various systems of ritual magic, meditation, and shamanistic techniques, he aimed to produce artificially what my Agency and I would call genetically determined psychic talents. Whether or not a practitioner could use this magical smorgasbord safely was another matter. I was glad I'd never tried it.

The second notebook, written in sensible black ballpoint, dated from my years as a psychology major in college. As well as the usual lecture notes on the psychological system and therapy methods of Carl Jung, it held a wealth of material on the early Christian beliefs that scholars lumped together as Gnosticism. Along with alchemy and other magical beliefs, the Gnostics had fascinated Jung, who'd been far more open-minded than most medical doctors are.

As I looked over my sketchy descriptions, they began to fascinate me as well. Although I didn't know why, this material struck me hard as being important to the case at hand. The Collective Data Stream had prompted me to retrieve that notebook, but as usual it had omitted the reason why I needed it. That's the trouble with having psychic talents: ambiguity is our way of life.

"This all looks interesting," I told Ari, "so it wasn't a wasted trip."

"It's never a wasted trip when your aunt offers us dinner." He was hovering in the doorway into the hall. "I want to go to the gym. Come with me. Working out's much better for you than starving yourself."

"Thanks to you I get plenty of exercise in bed."

"That's not enough. Sex doesn't elevate your heart rate for a long enough period of time."

I stared. "You mean someone *measured*?"

"They must have." Ari quirked both eyebrows. "Hadn't thought of it that way before."

"Health nuts have no shame. I hate gyms! I don't want to go today. Maybe next time."

"There never will be a next time at this rate."

"That's the idea, yeah."

"Besides," he went on, "I don't want to leave you here alone, not after our prowler last night. We know now that someone wants a look at our flat. I don't want you alone in it if he comes back."

There he had a point.

"I wonder if he was searching for Belial," I said. "It's a good thing I keep him in the wall safe."

"That thought had occurred to me." Ari considered for a moment. "I don't know why our would-be intruder even wanted to get into the downstairs flat. It's obvious that the front rooms are empty. The only thing of interest he could have seen would have been your father's desk."

"Which is empty, too." My mind twitched. "Not that our burglar would have known that."

I turned in my chair and glanced at a pair of innocuous-appearing cardboard cartons sitting on the floor near the TV. When my sister had given me Dad's old desk, she'd packed up the things inside it and sent them along, too. I reminded myself that I really needed to go through the papers soon. With one last reproachful glance in my direction, Ari turned away to head for the bedroom and his workout clothes. As soon as he'd taken two steps, I felt the ASTA.

"Uh, this is going to sound dumb," I said, "but I have to

reverse my opinion. You'd better not go. Someone's out there waiting for you to leave."

Ari raised a hand to the place where he usually wore his shoulder holster. He muttered under his breath, then trotted on down the hall to fetch the gun. I ran an SM:D and felt it like a stab of ice to the heart. Dimly I could sense a car and a threat inside it—no details, however, came to me. Ari returned, armed. He sidled along the wall to reach one of the side panels of the bay window. He pushed the lace curtain back a few inches so he could peer out.

"See anyone out there?" I said.

"Just the usual cars. I've been keeping track, you see, of the neighborhood vehicles ever since we moved in. Most people try to park in the same spot. None of the cars seem out of place." He glanced over his shoulder. "Can you locate the threat more precisely?"

I slid open the wide drawer of my desk and brought out the pad of newsprint paper and box of crayons I keep for running Long Distance Remote Sensing attempts. I leaned back in my chair with the pad on my lap and the crayons right to hand and went into SM:D again. My hand grabbed a gray crayon, scribbled, set it down and repeated the process with blue, green, yellow ocher, more gray. I stared out into space and thought of next to nothing.

At last my hand threw a spurt of black into the picture and told me that we were finished. I closed down the SM:D and looked at what I'd drawn.

"He's on Moraga," I said, "in a black car parked in front of that blue house on the corner across the street from the Great Highway."

"Very good," Ari said. "That means he can't see our building."

"Not with his physical eyes."

Ari said a single word in Hebrew, not a nice one, judging by his tone of voice. "Very well," he continued in English. "Let's give him what he wants. We're going to leave, but we're only going to drive around the block and see if we can take his license number."

To throw our suspect off a little further, I drove several blocks south on 48th before doubling back. We were assuming that he'd wait to approach the building until he was sure we'd gotten far away, but apparently he valued speed over caution. As soon as we turned onto the frontage street by the Great Highway, I saw that the black car had left the scene.

"Back we go," Ari said.

I spun around the corner onto Moraga and sped up to 48th in the oddly silent Saturn. It never roared at high speeds. Ari's mystery mechanics really knew their business. I turned onto 48th but saw no sign of the black car.

"He must have parked around back," Ari said. "Pull up on the street."

I followed orders and parked in front of the neighbors to the north. Just as I killed the engine, I saw someone rushing down our front steps, a slender man wearing tan slacks, a black turtleneck sweater with the neck pulled high, and a wool watchman's cap pulled down low on his forehead. He had black tattoos on his cheeks, but I couldn't identify the design. Ari slithered out of the car and drew his gun as he stepped onto the sidewalk.

"Police!" he called out. "Stop! You're under arrest!"

By then our would-be intruder had reached the sidewalk. For a moment he hesitated. I realized that he was holding something in his right hand. A gun? The man yelped and starting running south.

Ari barked out the command again, "Police! Stop! Drop your weapon!" and braced the Beretta in both hands.

I flinched in fear, but before I could slide down in my seat for shelter, the intruder threw what he was holding to the sidewalk. A metallic blue-violet sphere hit about five feet in front of him. Yellow light flared like bright fog, but I heard no explosion, saw no flames or smoke. The man raced into the fog of light and disappeared. So did the light. Ari lowered the gun and stared, merely stared openmouthed with the Beretta dangling from one hand. Ordinary gray sidewalk stretched out empty in front of him.

I felt not the slightest trace of danger, not an ASTA, not a SAWM, not an SM:D, nada, zip, jack. I got out of the car and joined him.

"He's gone, all right," I said. "Way gone."

"I got that impression," Ari said. "I suppose that the object he threw has some sort of transport function."

"Good guess, yeah. The only other alternative I can think of is that there's a world-walker's gate right in the middle of the sidewalk, and somehow I doubt that."

"Seems unlikely, yes."

"The apparition had a sphere just like his."

"How very odd." Ari started to holster the gun, then hesitated. "Is it safe to go round back to look for his car?"

I ran a quick SM:L. Nothing. "Yeah," I said. "It is."

He holstered the Beretta. Together we walked down the driveway and saw the black Toyota sedan parked sideways in front of our garage. It carried ordinary California license plates. Scrape marks in the paint just below the latch of the hood indicated that someone had pried it open recently. When I looked into the driver's side window, I saw a single generic-looking key in the ignition.

"It must be stolen," I said.

"Yes." Ari took his cell phone out of an inner jacket pocket. "I'll call the police."

"What are you going to tell them?"

"That someone's blocking our garage. They won't believe what just happened. I'm finding it hard to do so myself."

"Me, too. While you talk things over with the police, I'm going upstairs. I want to start going through those boxes of papers. I wonder if that's what this guy is looking for."

"If he was, wouldn't he have tried to take them from the Donovan house?"

"With an eighteen-foot fence to get over and Kathleen's pack of dogs waiting on the other side?"

"Right." Ari winced at his oversight. "I'll come round with you to let you in the front. You're sure no one's upstairs?"

I did a quick check. "Positive."

Before I went upstairs, I checked the back doors to both flats. The Chaos wards were still in place. Ari saw me safely inside, then returned to the garage to phone and file his complaint about the blocked access.

I went into the living room and considered the cartons

of papers from Dad's old desk. I was oddly afraid to begin looking through them. I suspected that my father, my wonderful Dad, whom I'd loved so dearly, had shot two British soldiers to death when he was in the IRA. Dad might have written something that would give me a definite answer. I wondered if I wanted to know the truth.

I sat down on the floor by the first carton and methodically took everything out of it. The box mostly contained papers, typed and handwritten both, all of them in Irish. I'd forgotten half of what I knew of that language, but from deciphering a few phrases here and there I realized that most concerned his job in the contracting business.

On the rest he'd made notes about us kids, our progress in school, our music lessons—nothing that related to the IRA, and nothing that would interest a follower of Chaos. At the very bottom lay the certificate proclaiming my sister Maureen an honors student for her junior year of high school. I remembered how proud of her Dad had been. He'd been taken away from us a couple of weeks later.

I saw why I'd been afraid to open those boxes. Memories flooded back, all painful, of his disappearance and its aftermath. At least I now knew why he'd gone and where he was, and that he'd never wanted to leave us.

I heard the front door open. Even though I knew it was most likely Ari, I took no chances. I got to my feet and began to summon Qi between my hands with a slow stroking motion, round and round, wrapping the heat into a ball that I could, if necessary, turn into a weapon. Footsteps thumped on the stairs; then Ari's voice reached me.

"The police will be here in a bit," he called out. "The neighbors tell me that they've never seen that car before."

"Okay," I called back.

I let the Qi scatter itself harmlessly into the air. Ari walked into the living room.

"Are you all right?" he said. "Have you been weeping?"

"Yeah." I wiped my eyes on the sleeve of my blouse. "But I'm okay now. Just old memories."

He sat on the couch to watch when I pulled over the second carton and opened it. On top lay more ordinary papers. Under them, though, I found the surprise.

Four rows of small cardboard boxes, each a different color, four boxes to a row, covered the bottom of the carton. The arrangement ranged from red in the upper left-hand corner to violet in the lower right. In between, the colors roughly followed the order of the spectrum.

"It looks like Kathleen arranged these for some reason," I said.

"Frankly," Ari said, "I'm surprised she knows how the spectrum goes."

I gave him a dirty look. "Kathleen's not real bright, but she is my sister, and I don't like to hear her dissed."

"Sorry."

Ari leaned forward on the couch. I picked out a dark green box and held it on the palm of my hand. It was about four inches square and amazingly heavy for its size. I took out the blue-violet version and found it just as heavy.

"You know what?" I said. "These don't have lids. Every seam's glued down. To open it you'd have to slice along one of the edges." I ran a fingernail down one side of the blue-violet box to demonstrate.

"Don't!" Ari snapped. "Just put it down slowly, back into the carton."

"Say what? Do you think it might explode?"

"Why take the chance?"

I swallowed heavily, took a deep breath, and returned the two boxes. The case of nerves made me put them in the wrong locations. Before I could correct the order, it corrected itself. The boxes never moved, but their colors changed places with a rainbow colored ripple. I yelped. Ari swore in both English and Hebrew.

"Well, I guess Kathleen didn't arrange them," I said. "Come to think of it, Kathleen packed all this up, and then Jack tossed it into the SUV and drove over here with it. You guys carried the cartons upstairs and dumped them onto the floor. Nothing blew up then."

"True. I suppose I'm conditioned to think every unknown object might be an IED."

"You know what's more likely? Remember that thing our visitor threw onto the sidewalk? That wasn't any ordinary hunk of dynamite."

"Right." Ari's eyes drooped, and his British accent grew thicker. "Silly of me, to think they might be something I might understand. I—" He paused, listening. "Here are the police. I'll just go down."

He left the room and stomped down the stairs. He banged the door behind him when he went out, too. I got up and trotted over to the window to look out: sure enough, a squad car had pulled up at the curb. I watched Ari greet the officer. They walked around the side of the building.

I glanced at the boxes again and remembered something else. The female apparition had held up a blue-violet sphere. One of the boxes was the exact same color as that sphere. So was the sphere our would-be thief had used to escape. I took my cell phone out of my jeans pocket and punched my brother's speed dial number.

Instead of Michael, Sophie answered the phone. From the abundance of background noise I could tell that she was sitting in traffic, probably in my uncle's old Chevy truck, since he let the boys borrow it on occasion.

"Can you hear me?" I said. "It's Nola."

"Oh, hi, Nola!" she said. "Mike and I are just sort of cruising around." Her voice dimmed. "It's your sister."

"Ask Mike," I said, "if you guys can come over here to my place. I've got something to show him."

"Sure," she said. "He's been thinking he should call you anyway. He says it's mental overlap."

"That's the family name for it, yeah. See you in a few."

I clicked off and returned to contemplating the array of brightly colored boxes. In about five minutes, Ari came back upstairs.

"That car was reported stolen," he said. "The officer's sent for the city tow truck to take it away. Someone will call the owner tomorrow."

"Why not have the poor guy just come get it now?"

"It's not proper procedure. He'll have to pay the towing fees and the like."

"Yeah, but if he just came and got it, there'd be no towing fees."

Ari considered this, then shrugged. "There needs to be a procedure," he said, "and it needs to be followed."

The principle of Order on the hoof, that's my Ari. I didn't bother arguing any further.

I kept watch out the front window for Michael, though I heard the ancient red truck grumbling along before I saw it. I went downstairs and reached them just as he was parking across the street. Sophie hopped down from the passenger seat, a pretty blonde girl in tight jeans and an oversized blue sweater. She was wearing a pair of black orthopedic shoes, one especially made for her clubfoot, and on her normal foot, a thick-soled version to compensate for the height difference. Stylish, no, but she could walk without lurching like a drunken sailor.

"It's great to see you," she said. "I hope we get a chance to, y'know, talk."

"Is something wrong?"

She glanced in Michael's direction. "I don't know."

Something between them, maybe, I thought. I arranged a sympathetic expression, and we let it go at that.

Jingling the keys, Michael led the way across the street. I happened to glance at the apartment house that stood next to our building. The neighbors both upstairs and down were lurking at the corner windows that gave them a good view of our building's front. I waved. None of them waved back. I was beginning to get the feeling we weren't real popular in the neighborhood.

"Before we go inside, bro," I said, "I'd like you to take a look at something." I pointed to the place on the sidewalk where the break-in artist had thrown his device. "See that little nick in the concrete?"

"Yeah," Michael said. "What about it—oh! Jeez." He took a few steps toward it. "This is seriously weird. There was a gate here, but it's gone."

"It was a temporary arrangement only."

He frowned and stretched out a hand toward the place where I'd seen the yellow light. "I can almost see something, a kind of fog, and then someone moving, but it's blurry and faded. Y'know?"

"Yep. That's called a scar on the time stream. We'll see how long it lasts. Come upstairs, and I'll tell you more. I think it concerns something that Dad kept in his desk."

As soon as we walked into the living room, Michael spotted the carton that held the array of boxes. He had just started to say hello to Ari when he let his voice trail away and stared at the papers and other clutter on the floor.

"What is that?" Mike's voice was nearly a whisper.

"Papers from Dad's desk," I said.

"Don't mean those." He walked over and squatted down by the open cartoon. "What are these?"

"I don't know. We were hoping you'd have some ideas."

"Not ideas. Just a feeling." Michael reached into the carton. "God, they're hella beautiful."

When he laid a finger on a yellow box, it sang one pure note, starting out loud, then fading away. Sophie caught her breath with a gasp. Ari and I exchanged a look.

"They didn't sing for you," Ari said.

"Nola's not a world-walker," Michael said.

"Yeah," I said. "Well, we just saw someone throw a blue-violet sphere onto the sidewalk. It created light and smoke, and when he ran into the smoke, he disappeared. Gone. Totally gone."

"Whoa!" Michael whistled under his breath. "Stinky nasty!"

"Is that good or bad?" Ari said.

"Good." Michael grinned at him. "Real good."

"What I wonder is, are there spheres inside those boxes?" I said. "I'm afraid to just cut one open to look."

Michael picked up the blue-violet box and hefted it in one hand. His expression turned dreamy, distant, as if he focused on some other view.

"I think they're spheres, all right," he said. "Orbs. That's the name they like. Orbs."

A cold frisson rippled down my back. I walked over to the carton and looked down as Michael put the blue-violet box back in its place. Each box appeared to be a little taller than before, as if they were straining upward toward my brother's hands. At moments I saw a flicker of glow from one or the other of them.

"Mike," I said, "move away from the carton for a minute.

I want to see what happens when you're some distance away."

Michael stood up and walked out of the living room to the head of the stairs. The boxes seemed to shrink. The flickers of glow disappeared, only to reappear when Michael returned.

"I don't suppose you'd let me have these," Michael said. "Looks like a complete set."

"You're right. I wouldn't. No unauthorized experiments, buster."

"Yeah, I figured. You'd better put them somewhere, like, y'know, you can lock. Seriously."

"I couldn't agree more." For one thing, not that I said this aloud, I wondered if they were the female apparition's stolen property. If so, I didn't want her taking them back again before we figured out what they were—and who she was.

Ari had bought and installed a sizable wall safe in our bedroom as part of the upper flat's security system. I'd hung a framed print over the door, one of Monet's water lilies sequence. Inside, we kept extra items from Ari's weapons collection as well as some of his gadgets. I'd packed up the flash card containing Belial's consciousness in a special antistatic wrap and put it inside as well.

To this peculiar collection we added my father's boxes. Since the carton was too large to fit, I let Michael take them out and place them on the floor of the safe. No matter which box he placed next to which, the colors rippled and changed to preserve the spectral order. As they did so, they sang to him.

"I gotta wonder if the colors stay the same inside." Michael looked at me with begging eyes. "Could we open just one?"

"It isn't Christmas Eve."

We shared a smile. As kids, we'd all been allowed to open one present on Christmas Eve, which gave our parents some extra sleep on Christmas morning.

"Yeah, I figured," Michael said. "But I had to try."

I shut the safe door with a click and spun the combination lock to scramble the numbers. As I was putting the print back in place, I heard a faint whisper of music from inside, a fragment of a sad melody in some minor key.

"Did you hear that?" Michael said. "I don't know what it is, but I bet it came from those boxes."

"So do I. Let's hope they're still there the next time we look for them."

"They will be. They've been waiting for Dad to come back all these years, haven't they?"

"If you say so, they probably have." I shrugged. "I wouldn't know."

With his hand on the doorjamb, Michael paused and looked back at me. "I do know," he said. "They've been waiting, and they know I'm his son, too. Y'know, this is all hella strange. Seriously."

If understatements could get the Nobel Prize, that remark would have won him a medal.

For our late lunch, Ari and Michael decided to go fetch take-out food from a nearby deli, which gave me a chance to talk privately with Sophie. In the time that she'd been living at Aunt Eileen's, she'd put on a few much needed pounds, though her thin little face still showed her history. She'd been born on Interchange, then been abandoned by her mother. As a child she'd starved on and off for years. We sat down together on the couch.

"So what's the problem?" I said.

"I dunno, and that's part of the problem." She gave me a weak smile. "Last month, I started feeling really weird, and it wasn't female stuff, y'know?"

"Okay. Weird, how?"

"I wanted to go up the hill to the big park and run around through the grass and trees." Her face colored a delicate pink. "Naked."

"Uh-oh. I've heard that symptom before. When was this, right before the full moon?"

"Yeah. Mike was teasing me about it. He howled, kind of like a dog."

"He's heard the symptom before, too." I remembered a detail from Dad's letter. "Can I take a look at the palm of your hand?"

Sophie held out her right hand. I took it and looked at

the pattern of lines. In the center of the palm, where a lot of people have Ms and Ws, she had a deep letter F. Otherwise her hand looked perfectly normal to me. I let go of it.

"Well, I guess that doesn't mean much," I said. "Unless—" The CDS came to my assistance. "Fenris. Odin's wolf."

Sophie began to tremble.

"Do you ever dream about wolves?" I said.

"Yeah." Her voice was barely audible. "I did last month, anyway."

"At the full moon?"

She nodded. Her eyes filled with tears.

"I think you know what I'm working up to," I said.

She nodded again. "I don't want to be a werewolf," she whispered. "Not here, not where everyone's so nice to me. I'd have to go back to Interchange."

"Why? Even if it's true, you don't have to go around biting people. That's a choice some lycanthropes make. Others fight against the tendency and live reasonably normal lives. Father Keith can help you. You can trust him on that."

"But I'm so scared," Sophie's voice stayed at the whisper level. "If I lost Michael, I'd just die."

I could remember feeling the same about my first real love. Fortunately, her relationship with my brother had a much better chance of lasting than my first affair had.

"You won't lose him," I said. "Sophie, haven't you figured out just how weird our family is? If you do have lycanthropy, it means you'll fit right in. Our brother Pat had it. It's nothing new to the O'Gradys."

She covered her face with her hands and wept in an overflow of relief. I got up and hunted down a box of tissues in the bedroom. I brought them back and set the box down next to her on the couch.

"You might not have it, anyway," I said. "It usually manifests much earlier than this. You're what, sixteen?"

"Yeah, as far as I know." She grabbed a couple of tissues and snuffled into them before she continued. "I don't know when my birthday is, so I might be seventeen already."

"Then you should have started making the change a couple of years earlier. Unless the radiation on Interchange has an effect on lycanthropes, but you'd think that if anything it would make them more common."

"There were some around. Not many, and when the cops found one, they took them away somewhere. Poof! and the person was gone. I dunno if they shot them, but I bet they did."

"Well, nobody's going to shoot you here. Ari won't let them."

She managed a weak smile at that.

"Let me think about this," I went on. "I'll see if I can come up with an answer for you."

But Sophie provided the answer herself, when Mike and Ari returned with bags of deli food. Although the two men would have eaten right out of the cartons, I insisted on putting the meal out on proper plates. I brought out utensils, too. Fingers are not good enough for potato salad, no matter what some males of our species think.

Sophie came into the kitchen to help me carry the food out to the living room. When she saw the platter of pastrami and corned beef, her big dark eyes grew wide.

"Look at all that meat," she said. "I guess I'm still not used to it, yet, all the stuff there is to eat here."

"You didn't get much meat back on Interchange, huh?" I said.

"Almost never, yeah. It was so expensive there, but Aunt Eileen cooks some almost every day."

My mind poked me. "I bet that's why you're developing your talent late," I said. "And furthermore, I bet it's why I keep seeing more and more lycanthropes around here, too. The amount of meat we all pack away must trigger the gene or activate the virus."

We decided to reveal Sophie's secret right away. I figured that the family needed to know before her first change. Pat's lycanthropy had taken us all by surprise. The uproar that followed had injured him psychologically even beyond the normal stress of discovering that he had werewolf genes. Sophie sat down next to Michael on the couch.

"I've got something to tell you," she said. "Nola figured it out. When I felt so weird, y'know? You were right to howl."

Michael turned to her and grinned. "Are you telling me that you're—"

"Yeah." Sophie's voice returned to her near-whisper. "Nola thinks I might be. I'm just getting it late." She was staring at Michael in honest fear, waiting for his reaction.

Michael grinned at her. "That's so cool," he said. "I mean, like, it's just so cool!"

"It is?" Her voice became steadier by the word. "You like it?"

"Sure. Y'know, I wanted to be a werewolf once myself." He held out his arms. "That's great!"

Sophie nestled against him and began to snuffle once again.

"You're a werewolf?" Ari sounded utterly confused.

Sophie nodded and wiped her eyes on a tissue.

"Oh," Ari said. "For a bit there I thought you were going to say you were pregnant."

Everyone laughed, even Sophie. Michael looked as if he was struggling against the impulse to kiss her right in front of us.

Ari and I retreated to the kitchen on the pretense of bringing in the rest of the food only to find that someone had gotten there ahead of us, a little blue smelly meerkat-like being. Or-Something, Michael's tame Chaos critter, was standing on the counter by the sink and chowing down in the cardboard container of coleslaw. When I yelped, it raised its wedge-shaped head. Strands of cabbage hung from its snaggly teeth. When I snapped my fingers, it disappeared.

"So much for the vegetable course."

"What?" Ari was staring at the counter. "I saw the carton moving. And cabbage hanging in the air." He turned to me with a look of sheer exasperation. "What?"

"A Chaos critter." I said. "I told you about those. This one was eating the coleslaw, so I scared it off."

"If these things can eat real food, why can't everyone see them?"

"I don't know. It's one of the questions the Agency's research staff is working on. I'll tell you if they come up with a theory."

Ari started to speak, then merely set his lips together with a sour twist. I threw the remains of the coleslaw into the garbage.

"I got you some artichoke hearts, too," Ari said. "I suppose they qualify as a vegetable, anyway."

"Barely, but thanks."

Before Michael and Sophie left, Michael admitted to me that he'd started working on the map of gates.

"Sean's helping me find them," he said.

"He can find anything," I said.

"But he can't actually open them."

A little sibling rivalry there, I thought. "Have you actually spotted other gates?"

"One, yeah, in a cemetery down in Colma, but it doesn't go to Interchange. I dunno where."

"Both of you be careful, will you?"

"You bet. Sean wants to talk to you. He's uptight about when we get Dad back. I mean, he's gay, and he remembers Dad being hella down on that."

I said an unladylike word. I remembered it, too. It also occurred to me that the Dad I was remembering would be less than thrilled to find me living with a man I wasn't married to. "I'll call Sean. Let's not worry about this stuff until we actually have Dad home again."

"Yeah, it's not a sure thing." Michael paused for a gloomy interval. "I'll call Father Keith tomorrow about Sophie."

"Good. Ask him about a group called the Hounds of Heaven. I think she'll find them interesting."

CHAPTER 3

BY THE TIME MICHAEL and Sophie drove off, the time stream had washed away all traces of the thief and his temporary escape gate. I spent a few minutes trying to pick up traces of the energy but found none. The sidewalk was only a sidewalk with a little chip missing where the guy had thrown the blue-violet orb.

I went back upstairs and called Sean, but I only got his answering service. I left a message and clicked off. While I called, Ari paced up and down in the living room, but he stopped before he drove me crazy.

"I was thinking of going to the gym," Ari said. "But I don't like the idea of leaving you here alone. There's not much chance that our would-be thief will come back right away, but one never knows."

"That's true," I said. "I'm real glad you're staying home."

"All right. I can do a few sets of push-ups and the like here." He sounded genuinely pleased at the prospect, a tone of voice that brought back grim memories of high school gym teachers.

"How many do you do?" I said.

"Three sets of fifty each. One hundred fifty for each exercise, that is. Sit-ups, push-ups, and the one whose English name I never can remember. You start standing, drop to a crouch, do a plank, then back to a squat and up."

"No wonder you can't remember the name. Your brain's bruised from slapping against your skull a hundred fifty times."

Ari set his hands on his hips and scowled at me, just like the gym teachers used to do. "It's actually quite invigorating."

"The very thought makes me feel faint. That's what I used to do in gym class, faint. Constantly. It was real embarrassing."

"You probably fainted because you were starving yourself."

He had a point, not that I was going to admit it.

"Have fun," I said. "I'm going to sit here and read my notebooks."

"You could at least try a few—"

"No." I may have snarled.

Ari gave me one last scowl, then stomped off to the bedroom to change into gym clothes. I put on a Lady Gaga CD loud enough to cover the sound of him repeatedly dropping to the floor.

Later that evening we had unexpected visitors. I was catching up on routine Agency business at my desktop, and Ari was watching a basketball game on TV, when the front doorbell rang. I started to go downstairs to open the door, but Ari stepped in front of me.

"I don't feel any danger," I said.

"I don't care. Just wait."

He picked up the new TV remote he'd acquired recently, a shiny black model, not the pizza-stained gray one I used to own. When the doorbell rang again, Ari clicked a couple of buttons. On the TV screen an image appeared of two men standing on the porch.

"It's just Sean," I said. "And Al. His boyfriend, y'know?"

"Oh," Ari said. "I'll go down and let them in."

When he set the remote down, the basketball game reappeared onscreen. I followed as he strode to the head of the stairs, where we kept a waist-high metal filing cabinet. I'd been planning on putting flower arrangements on top to brighten up the space. Ari opened the top drawer and took out a pistol I'd never seen before, a blue-gray thing that looked less lethal than the Beretta but lethal enough.

"Ari!" I snapped. "It's my brother."

"I know, but I'm taking no chances. Someone might be lurking behind them."

I followed him down the stairs. When he opened the door with his left hand, Sean and Al both saw the gun in his right and put their hands up with a theatrical flourish.

"Er," Al said, "if you're busy or something, we could just leave. You don't need to fire warning shots across our bow. Honest."

"I just wanted to make sure it was really you." Ari lowered the gun to point at the floor. "Next time, give us a ring before you drop by, will you?"

"You bet," Sean said. "Can we put our hands down now?"

"Yes." Ari cracked not a trace of a smile. "You've been vetted."

We all trooped back upstairs, Ari first, for which I was grateful. I'd been afraid he'd herd us at gunpoint.

Al Wong and my brother Sean made a handsome couple, though Sean was so preternaturally beautiful, with his perfect features, wavy dark hair, and blue eyes, that Al tended to be ignored in the equation. In any other context people would have noticed him immediately, because he was as good-looking as any Hong Kong movie star. As it was, he got shoved into the background, which, luckily, he preferred to being on display. He tended to dress in flannel shirts and jeans, while Sean went for tailored slacks and beautifully cut shirts in fancy fabrics. That night Sean was wearing an emerald-green silk shirt with fawn slacks and a brown suede jacket cut like a sport coat. The color and sheen of the silk made his eyes glisten like sapphires.

"What brings you to our neck of the woods?" I said.

"The friends we were hanging with," Sean said. "They live pretty close by. And so when I got your message, I thought we'd just see if you were home." His voice shook as he continued. "Next time I'll call ahead for sure. I know he's a cop, but jeez!"

By the time we returned to the living room, Ari had put

the gun away. He flopped back down on the couch and turned on the TV sound. When Al noticed the basketball game, he shrugged out of his beaten-up canvas barn jacket, dropped it onto the floor, and flopped down next to Ari to watch.

"The Warriors," Ari announced, "are losing badly."

"They usually are," Al said. "I wonder if Don Nelson will ever win that six hundredth game."

Sean and I left them analyzing the team and went into the kitchen to talk. Sean took off his suede jacket and hung it over the back of his chair before he sat down.

"Mike told me you were worried," I said.

"Yeah," Sean said. "I used to get so damn scared when Dad would lecture us on how awful gays were. 'Homos,' he called us. I knew even then he was talking about me. Like, from the time I was maybe six I knew what I was. I was sure I was going direct to hell." He forced out a smile. "Probably even before I died."

"Well, Dad had a lot of strong opinions about a lot of things. That doesn't mean he still does."

Sean tilted his head to one side and blinked at me.

"We haven't seen him in so long," I continued, "that we tend to think of him as being exactly the way he was when he was arrested. But prison changes people and their opinions. Who knows what Dad's like now?"

"Oh." Sean considered this for several long moments. "I can see that, yeah. He's had all these years away, and we won't know what they've done to him till we get him home. Well, if we can get him home."

"It's going to be kind of a crap shoot."

"I'll just have to deal with it. If we do find him, we can't leave him there."

"Right. Besides, there's Mom. They'll have a lot of stuff to work through."

"That'll keep him busy!" His grin turned wicked. "Ari's a lot like him. You're involved with a guy who's just like your father. How Freudian can you get?"

I crossed my arms over my chest and glared at him. Sean displayed his survival sense by changing the subject.

"Mike must have told you I was helping him with that

map," Sean said. "It's taking both of us to do it, and it took us forever to find one gate. Now that we've got one, though, I know how they feel, or I should say, how I feel when I sense one. We can focus in on the vibes, which means we should be able to find the others faster, well, if there are any."

"I don't understand. You guys knew about the gate in Aunt Eileen's house already."

"That's what Mike and I thought, that we could use that one to zero in on the others. We couldn't. It's different than the others. We know Dad made it, right? Well, someone else made the others. So the vibe's different. Y'know?"

"No, actually, I don't, but I'll take your word for it."

"Okay." Sean shot me a grin. "And because I'm helping, I was wondering if you could take me on as a stringer for the Agency."

"What? You? Looking for gainful employment?"

"I know I'm a slacker."

"Self-knowledge is the beginning of wisdom." I folded my hands piously. "Learn, my child, and grow wise."

Sean stuck out his tongue at me. "Well, I deserved that," he went on to say. "But will you? You're the head of the bureau now, aren't you?"

"Yeah, and if you weren't my brother, I could hire you tonight, but I don't want to be accused of nepotism. I'll ask my boss about it. They put Michael on stringer status, and my boss mentioned a while ago that they might be interested in recruiting more O'Gradys."

"Thanks. It wouldn't kill me to earn a little money now and then. Al's birthday is coming up, and I don't want to buy him a present with his own credit card."

The guys left when the basketball game ended. Al had to get up in the morning to go to his government job. I locked up, then sat down next to Ari on the couch. He turned off the TV and looked at me.

"Ari, there's something you need to think about," I said. "You genuinely scared my poor brother when you were waving that gun around."

"I never wave a gun around. That's irresponsible."

"Well, okay, sorry. Just seeing it scared him anyway. You

don't know what he's like when he gets into full panic mode. It could take hours to calm him down."

"I needed to make sure that it was them and only them. After all, it's my job to keep you safe."

I don't know what got into me, the Devil, maybe, but lines from *The Tempest* floated to the surface of my mind. "Ariel, thy charge exactly is perform'd, but—"

Ari growled. I don't know what else to call it but a growl, and his face changed to a dangerous lack of expression. "I hate that sodding play," he said, and he sounded on the edge of growling again. "And my sodding name, and that sodding playwright, too."

I stood up and took a couple of steps sideways to get clear of the coffee table. He got up with the Qi of pure rage swirling around him like the tempest in question. I moved to put the coffee table between us.

"I'm sorry." I made my voice as calm as I could. "Ari, I didn't realize it would bother you so much."

He took a deep breath, then another, and shoved his hands into his jeans' pockets—to keep them safely confined, I figured, like they'd taught him in anger management class. For several minutes we stood on that knife's edge. Finally, he sighed and forced out a thin smile.

"I'm sorry, too," he said. "Every summer when I visited my mother in London, I was teased about my wretched name, and that sodding Shakespeare play always came into it. Airy spirit! Too delicate for—" He stopped, cleared his throat, and breathed deeply yet again. "Well, no need to go into all of that."

"There's not, no. You actually make me think of Ariel Sharon, not Shakespeare."

That got me a genuine smile. "Thank you," he said. "That's very flattering."

"I'll never mention the play again."

"And I'll try to stop making an ass of myself." He frowned down at the floor. "I'm honestly surprised I reacted the way I did."

I metaphorically bit my tongue to keep myself from bringing up *Midsummer Night's Dream*. "It's getting late," I said instead. "We're both kind of tired."

"True." He looked up, back to his usual controlled self. "Almost time for bed. I'm going to go take a shower, I think."

"Good idea." I grinned at him. "I'll come take one with you."

And, as I figured, the logical development from that activity calmed both of us down.

Monday morning arrived too soon, and with it e-mail, the timesink from Hell. When I logged on, I found a ton of it, most of it about administrative details. One e-mail, however, stood out from the rest.

It arrived on my non-TranceWeb e-address from AOS14. "I would very much like to meet with you about a matter of some interest to those you work for. Would you be willing to discuss a link between our respective agencies? We can offer you the police and justice capabilities you lack." That was all it said. It was enough.

I logged off, got up, and charged into the bedroom, where Ari, dressed only in a pair of baggy gray shorts, was changing into his workout clothes. He caught my mood and took a step back, which put him up against the bedroom wall.

"You bastard," I said. "You've blown the Agency's cover. You made some kind of report about us to Interpol, didn't you?"

"No, I didn't." He sounded perfectly sincere. "They had rumors of your existence before I entered the picture. Why else would they have sent me to your State Department in the first place?"

"They sent you to the State Department, not direct to us."

"Yes, thanks to the rumors, and where did State send me? Oh, come now! I wouldn't be here if my higher-ups knew nothing about the Agency. They couldn't assign me to an entity they'd never heard of."

"That's true, but when did the rumors become recognized fact?"

His face never changed, but his SPP winced.

"It's one thing," I went on, "to send an agent to a point of contact within the State Department in the hopes said contact can link him to someone farther along the line. It's quite another to know all the details."

"Who says they know all the details?"

"You're weaseling, Nathan."

He picked up his T-shirt from the bed and put it on before he spoke. "I'm going downstairs to do my workout."

I shut the bedroom door and leaned against it with my arms crossed over my chest.

"I can carry you," Ari said. "If I wanted to just move you to one side, I could."

"Not if you were ensorcelled."

He sighed and began to study the pattern on the blue paisley bedspread. I could read a resigned sense of defeat in his Qi as well as his SPP. He looked at me again.

"Will you forgive me?" he said. "I was under orders to file that report. It's only accessible by two people, the two I phoned about AOS14."

"One of them told AOS14."

He blinked a couple of times. "Oh," was all he said.

I considered what to do next. Step One: raise hell at the Agency, which would raise hell with State, which in turn would raise hell with Ari's superiors. Step Two: announce I could no longer work with Mr. Nathan, who had proven himself untrustworthy. Step Three: wave good-bye to Ari as he was hauled back to Israel by the outfit he worked for. Step Four: hear that he'd been killed in Iran because he'd returned there to spy for Israel one time too many.

Love really sucks when it gets in the way of your job. I considered what other course of action lay open to me. Step Two would be: hear what AOS14 had to say. I took Step One immediately.

"Okay," I said. "I forgive you. But after this, I want to know when and where you're passing intel about me and my Agency. You owe me, Nathan."

"I realize that." He hesitated. "Very well, if it happens again, I'll tell you." Again, the hesitation. "I had no idea that they would give that report to a third party."

His SPP told me that about this detail he was speaking the truth. I also had the odd intuition that he, too, was thinking that love sucked when it got in the way of one's job.

"Should I go live in the downstairs flat?" For that one brief moment he sounded not weak, never that, but vulnerable.

"No," I said. "Don't be a jerk, Ari."

He smiled and walked over to kiss me.

It took us a while to heal the breach, as it were. Once we had, we got dressed, and he went downstairs to work out. I returned to my computer desk, only to find the landline answering machine blinking. The message came from the realtor who handled the building we leased.

"The neighbors have phoned me twice now," Mr. Singh's voice told me. "They complain about graffiti, guns, car thieves, and firecrackers thrown onto the sidewalk. Please call to enlighten me." He left his business number.

I thought of several jokes about long-distance enlightenment, canned them all, and came up with a good lie when I returned the call.

"The firecrackers were the work of the local teen gang," I told him. "They're really mad because we keep removing their graffiti. When Ari caught one at it, he tried to arrest him, but the kid got away."

"Ah, I see." Mr. Singh sounded relieved. "Of course, your partner is a police officer. I shall tell the neighbors this. They will be relieved that the gun they have seen is a legal weapon."

I returned to the day's business affairs. Although I offered to videoconference with Mr. Spare14, he preferred to leave the discussion in e-mail. After a few rounds, we had arranged a meeting for Tuesday, the next day. I decided that it would be professional courtesy to let Spare14 know that I knew about Ari's double-dealing. When I asked about including Ari in the meeting, Spare14 answered that he'd be welcome.

"I thought he would be," I typed. "This way he'll be able to write up the meeting for his superiors."

Spare14's answer came back, "*Peccavi*. Sorry."

"I have sinned" covered too much ground to be an honest admission. Had he badgered the information out of the two higher-ups to whom Ari had originally sent his report? Or had he come by it some other way? I'd have to wait to answer that question until we met.

When Ari came back upstairs, I logged off and shut down my computer. The strangest communication of the day arrived at that point, not in e-mail, but on the dead black screen. I'd seen IOIs on a powered-off screen before, but this one came from outside my own mind.

As I watched, the screen brightened to pale gray. A black circle appeared, fringed with seven stylized arrows, four toward the top, three at the bottom: the symbol of an unbalanced form of Chaos magic. The face of a white guy with a shaved head, blue eyes, and an unsettling resemblance to some of my relatives formed in the center of the circle—the entity I called Cryptic Creep. He'd been contacting me against my will ever since we'd moved into the flat. The graffito that so bothered the neighbors, that very same Chaos symbol, was his work.

Although he looked like the O'Brien side of my family, his voice reminded me of no one I'd ever known: high and fluting. I heard it as if it came from outside my mind, but since Ari paid no attention at first, I knew it was a psychic communication. I, however, answered him aloud rather than risk opening up my mental language level to someone I didn't know.

"Nola," he said, "you've been ignoring me."

"Yeah," I said. "Why not? You always deliver the same old message."

"The message is important, that's why. Find the Peacock Angel. You know about the good news he brings to the world."

"I've got angels of my own, and their church has been claiming to bring good news for a couple thousand years."

"For their sheep, perhaps. This angel speaks to the elite few. He'll speak to you."

I suddenly realized why I needed those old college notes. "Manichees?" I said. "Valentinians? Sethians? Which flock of sheep do you belong to?"

"Oh, come now, you know better!" He laughed, a dry little mocking mutter, and disappeared.

The circle lingered a moment more, then faded away. I swiveled the computer chair around to look at Ari. He was staring at me with loving sadness.

"Who were you talking to now?" he said.

"I don't know," I said. "But I don't like him much. That I can tell you for sure."

CHAPTER 4

TO MAKE LIFE DIFFICULT for eavesdroppers, Spare14 and I had arranged to meet outside in Golden Gate Park, but well away from the usual tourist areas. To the west of the museums and the Japanese Tea Garden lie the places that we locals use, a string of small lakes and meadows. We picked a grassy picnic area next to Kennedy Drive, just past Spreckels Lake, which would most likely be deserted on a weekday. I debated wearing a business suit, but since we'd be meeting informally, I eventually decided on trouser jeans and an indigo-and-white print blouse with a v-necked rust sweater over it. I carried a leather shoulder bag, into which Ari put a handful of electronic devices. He also stashed a small plastic box in his shirt pocket and another, larger metal box in the inside pocket of his leather jacket.

"This will let me know if someone's focusing a listening device us." Ari tapped his shirt pocket.

"What's the other one?"

"Two extra clips for the Beretta."

"Oh." My stomach clenched. "Are we expecting trouble?"

"I always do. Better safe than sorry."

As usual, I did the driving that afternoon. When we reached the park, I turned into the greenery on a narrow side road that led to the meadow in question. Since it needed repaving, I slowed down, and a good thing, too. From the shrubbery at the side of the road a young boy darted out after a soccer ball—right in front of us. I slammed on the brakes. The car jerked to one side with a squeal and the thump of tires on potholes. Ari swore in Hebrew.

"Did I miss him?" I was shaking so hard I could barely speak.

"Miss what?" Ari snapped. "There was nothing there."

I simply could not believe him. In my memory I could see the boy's horrified face as the car bore down on him. I unbuckled my seat belt and got out to look. No boy, no ball, no nothing lay in the street except for the skid marks of our tires. Ari got out and joined me.

"You saw something?" he said.

"A kid, yeah, running right in front of us." I laid one hand at my throat. I could feel the pulse at that spot pounding merrily away. "I thought I'd hit him for sure."

"Go stand over there." Ari pointed to the sidewalk. "I'll park the car."

I followed orders. Rather than watch his version of parallel parking, I considered what had just happened. If we'd been going fast on a crowded street, I would have swerved right into a nasty accident. I'd seen an image, obviously, not a real boy. The question was its origin—inside my own mind or some kind of sending?

I heard the fluting voice of Cryptic Creep. It came from outside of my own mind, all right, and from a long way away.

I can't protect you unless you join us. That's just a sample of what they can do.

"Who's they?" I said aloud.

You know who must fear you now. Belial's allies.

"Sure, but who sent the image?"

No answer.

"Did you? Why the hell should I trust you?"

Nothing—no answer, no voice, no presence—nothing. When Ari rejoined me on the sidewalk, he held out the car keys. I shook my head.

"When we leave here," I said, "you'd better drive. I have a bad feeling about this."

"Do you think it'll happen again?"

"That's what I'm afraid of, yeah. I don't know anything for sure."

He nodded and pocketed the keys. As we walked off, he caught my hand in his. I clung to his grasp.

In the midst of the sunny green lawn, Spare14 waited for us on a park bench. I recognized him immediately from the photos of the original Austin Osman Spare. Neither tall nor short, squarely built with a squarish face, he had gray hair swept back en brosse and blue eyes. He'd also dressed casually, in a pair of tan chinos, a blue shirt, and a gray cardigan sweater. A battered old-fashioned leather briefcase sat next to him on the bench. He was feeding stale bread to the birds and squirrels mobbing his feet, just another middle-aged man whiling away some time in the sunshine, or so he appeared.

"He sure looks like the artist," I said to Ari. "It's kind of spooky, in fact."

As we approached, Spare14 glanced up and smiled, then scattered the last of the bread for the flock and stood. He crammed the empty paper bag into the briefcase. He stepped carefully around the feeding birds and walked over to meet us.

"O'Grady and Nathan, I believe." He sounded British, middle class, mostly. "I'm Austin Spare Fourteen."

I murmured a "How do you do?" and we all shook hands.

"Doubtless you're wondering about the fourteen," Spare14 continued. "It's a bit difficult to explain, but I'll try as we proceed." He glanced around, then pointed to a nearby picnic table. "This seems to be the best we can do for seating arrangements."

We all sat down, myself and Ari on one bench, Spare14 on the other across the table. He put the briefcase on the bench next to him, then made a tent of his fingers and considered us pleasantly.

"I'm trying to decide how to begin," he said. "I suppose that bluntness is best. Doubtless you realize that I come from a different though parallel world."

"I'd suspected that," I said, "but I couldn't be sure."

"In many ways my world is far more technologically than yours, for reasons that are quite complex. For example, I happen to be a clone. When the great artist died, a number of his cells were harvested with permission from his kin. A full line of clones was developed from them over the years. I'm the last, I'm afraid. Genetic material weakens with time. And that is why I am Austin Osman Spare Fourteen."

Ari's entire body drooped into his look of extreme martyrdom.

"He's not having a joke on you." I'd run an SPP and could speak confidently on the subject. "I can tell he's sincere."

"I was afraid of that," Ari said.

Spare14 smiled, a little ruefully. "I knew this would all come as a shock to you."

Ari nodded. "More so to me than to O'Grady."

"I'll admit to being surprised," I said. "Before we move on, I have a question. In our world the original Spare's work was barely known. He lived in poverty, obscurity, and surrounded by cats. But in your world—"

"He was famous, successful, and quite rich, really. The cats, however, were present in abundance. I have more than a few myself." Spare14 smiled as if the thought of owning lots of cats pleased him. "I'll tell you something I've realized over the years. While doppelgängers, like clones, share their genetic makeup and their basic personalities and talents as small children, how they develop as they grow varies widely, depending on the world around them. To oversimplify, the original Spare fit very well in my world. He was sadly misplaced in yours."

"That makes a lot of sense. Thanks."

"You're welcome. Now, as things worked out, I have only a modicum of my noble root stock's artistic ability, though I did inherit a talent for police work from his father."

"And so you're an Interpol officer," I said. "Not an artist."

"Exactly. I have been for twenty some years now. I'm part of a special unit with top secret status, which is why,

Nathan, you couldn't find my data online. I've been told that you confirmed my standing with two of our superiors?"

"I did, yes," Ari said.

"Good. Your caution is commendable." Spare14 paused to open the briefcase. "Any more questions so far?"

"None that can't wait," I said.

Ari shrugged.

"I have three goals," Spare14 began, "and I hope this meeting will lead eventually to reaching them. First, of course, there's the question of the Belial entity. Second, my unit would like to liaison with O'Grady's agency on an official and permanent basis."

"I'm not quite sure what you mean," I said. "Interpol or your secret unit?"

"The unit, a very specialized part of Interpol." Spare14 glanced at Ari. "It was formed to deal with crimes that cut across deviant world levels."

"I see." Ari's tone of voice implied that he regretted doing so.

"Which brings us to my third goal," Spare14 continued. "Nathan, we'd very much like you to apply to join us. Your weapons skills are first rate. You speak a good many languages. Your relationship with O'Grady indicates a certain openness to new ideas."

Ari opened his mouth to speak, then shut it. Spare14 leaned onto the table on folded arms to get a clear view of Ari's expressions. "You're already a seconded officer, I believe?"

"Yes," Ari said. "I hope you couldn't find the name of my primary agency."

"I couldn't, no." Spare14 smiled briefly. "It's none of my affair, really. If you choose to become one of us, your standing in the unit won't affect your first position. You'll simply move laterally within the Interpol structure."

"Fair enough," Ari said. "This unit is what?"

"Trans-World Interpol X Team." Spare14 bobbed his head in apology. "I'm afraid the acronym comes out to TWIXT. Betwixt and between, you know. More than a bit silly, but there you are. It was established long before I had any say in the matter. They added the X merely to prevent the acronym from turning into TWIT."

I laughed before I could stop myself.

Spare14 sighed. "I'm afraid that some of the persons involved in its creation didn't speak English as a first language."

Ari was sitting very quietly, staring out across the green lawn with an expression I can only call gob smacked. I'll admit to feeling somewhat the same myself. Spare14 rummaged in the briefcase and took out two pieces of paper, ordinary office paper covered with Times Roman printout. He handed one to me and one to Ari.

"I thought it best to give you both some notes on the unit's function. O'Grady, you're going to have to report to your superiors, of course. I know how hard it is to remember this sort of startling information."

"Very considerate of you."

"And, Nathan, you'll need to have the data as well. Please consider our offer carefully."

Ari made a strangled sort of noise that might have been "thank you." I glanced at the printout, which had headings like "Function of TWIXT" and "Considerations for Recruitment," all very ordinary in their odd little way. I folded it and put it in my shoulder bag. Ari glanced at his, then also folded it and slipped it under his jacket into his shirt pocket.

"I see you're armed," Spare14 said to him.

"Oh, yes," Ari said. "Any objections?"

"None, if you think it necessary." Spare14 paused to twist around on the bench and look behind him. "Um, is this a dangerous situation?"

"Not that I'm aware of." Ari said. "I like to be ready in case it becomes that way."

"This particular world level," I put in, "is currently in a state of Chaotic imbalance."

"Yes, indeed it is." Spare14 closed his briefcase before continuing. "That's one reason I'm here. We at TWIXT have been considering liaising with your agency for some time. It's the only possible point of contact with your government that we can see."

"I'll agree with that, for sure," I said. "No one else would ever believe you exist. Do you have linkage with any other governments?"

"No, none directly. Only through Interpol, but even there, only two or possibly three people know. I say possibly because the third person is highly skeptical. We decided that the United States was the logical national entity to approach."

"Why? Because of our superpower status? Or because we tend to believe all kinds of really weird crank ideas?"

"I prefer to think of it as your being open to new possibilities. In return, we can offer your agency something that you must need, that is, a police unit with cross-world capability. We have operational databases we can put at your disposal, for example, and various other support services."

"For instance, taking suspects like Belial off our hands?" I said.

"Exactly, and we can ensure that they come to trial in an appropriate manner on their own worlds of origin. TWIXT operates under the same principles as Interpol. We follow the laws of whatever world or country we work in. We are not loose cannons. Nathan can tell you that."

"True," Ari said. "You'll remember that I had to answer to the NCB back home when I shot Johnson."

"Yeah, I do, and I was impressed. I need to consult with my superiors."

"Of course," Spare14 said. "If they'd like, I'd gladly travel to your main office for a face-to-face meeting."

"All right, I'll take this all under advisement. As to your other goal, I'm afraid I can't hand over Belial without consulting with the higher-ups as well. They've ordered me to proceed with caution."

"No doubt," Spare14 said. "I understand completely. Javert has the suspect's body in custody already. It appears to be in some kind of deep sleep."

I had a sudden twinge of conscience. "I hope they can reunite the two halves. I've got his consciousness saved on a flash card. He deserves a fair trial, not an automatic death sentence."

"You'll have to give them that camcorder," Ari said, "along with the card. Up to them to figure it out."

"Which I'm sure Javert's department can do," Spare14 said. "They have that device that allows them trans-world travel of a sort, after all. Javert assured me that it has some property that will allow them to send the suspect back to his proper body."

"Beam me back in, Scotty," I said.

Both men gave me sour looks. I ignored them.

"I can tell you a little more about this species," Spare14 went on. "We're all very lucky that they live underwater. With their high intelligence and psychic abilities, they'd be a menace to every other world if they could move about freely. As it is, if your superiors decide to remand the suspect, Javert will have to travel in a special vehicle, a mobile water tank, in essence."

"Is his world a deviant level of Earth," I said, "or another planet?"

"I'm not at liberty to give details." Spare14 paused for an apologetic smile. "Not right now, at any rate."

The meaning was clear: only if the Agency agreed to liaison with his unit would he be allowed to share that intel.

"If they're underwater," I continued, "how do they get their devices to work? I know the camcorder's not going to function soaking wet."

"They do have air bubble chambers of some sort." Spare14 thought for a moment. "And many of their machines operate on water pressure and the heat rising from underwater vents. You know, otherwise I don't really know. I've never been there myself. I must ask Javert next time we communicate."

Spare14 delved into his briefcase again and brought out a large paperbound book that looked just like every Civil Service crammer I'd ever seen, except this one had "Security Rating 1: Recruit" stamped in big red letters across the front cover. My hands itched, as they do when I see information I need.

"My dear Nathan, let me urge you to sit the examination."

Spare14 gave Ari the book. I got a glimpse of the title: Examination Preparation, Grade 1, TWIXT. Ari caught me looking and turned the volume over to reveal a blank white back cover. Had we been alone, I would have kicked him.

"I suggest you read this material before you make your decision," Spare14 was saying. "If you decide against joining us, nothing will change or happen to you. No one would believe you if you tried to reveal our existence, but you don't strike me as the sort of man to leak intel to the unauthorized. Neither, of course, are you, O'Grady. Er, that sort of woman, I mean."

Ari glanced my way with a small exasperated snort. I was tempted to indulge in a little aggressive questioning, but when I looked across the lawn, I saw an angel standing about twenty yards away, beckoning to me from among the eucalyptus trees bordering the meadow. I stood up and stared at both Spare14 and Ari as coldly as I could manage.

"I'll let you discuss this in private," I said.

Spare winced, but my sneer had no effect on Ari. "Don't go too far," was all Ari said.

"Just across the lawn." I pointed at the angel. "Over there."

I trotted off. Since I'd just seen the false image of the boy, I was suspicious of this sighting at first. I gathered Qi between my hands and coaxed it into a ball, ready to defend myself if necessary. As I got closer, I recognized St. Maurice, a tall male figure, gleaming white like new marble, in a Roman tunic and breastplate with a gladius, the Roman stabbing sword, slung from his belt. His wings stretched out in greeting, then folded neatly along his back.

"*Ave salveque, magne,*" I said and tossed the gathered Qi aside.

He smiled at the designation of "great one."

"*Salve.*" He held up one hand in the Roman style of greeting, then jerked his thumb in the direction of the bench. "*Quis magus? Et cur adest?*"

Who's the magician? he wanted to know. And why is he here?

"*Non magus,*" I said, then realized that if there was a Latin word for "Interpol officer," I certainly didn't know it. "*Custos populorum—*" I began.

"We can speak English if you prefer," St. Maurice said. "Now that I'm dead, it's all the same to me."

"*Gratias*, thanks. He's an Interpol officer, a policeman. Sort of like the Praetorian Guards. He just looks like the magician Austin Spare."

"Ah, I see. Does he serve the Good and the Highest?"

"I don't know. I'm assuming so. Can you find out?"

St. Maurice shaded his pale eyes with one white hand and studied the two men across the lawn. A flickering sphere of yellow light appeared above the table, then slowly descended to surround them. I saw Ari grab the sensing device from his shirt pocket. Distantly I heard a high-pitched beep. The light disappeared.

"Good enough," St. Maurice said. "*Eo credas et Judaeo etiam.*"

You may trust both him and the Jew. I had no idea how he knew Ari's ethnic identity, but considering that Maurice was both an imperial Roman and a Christian martyr, he was being remarkably open-minded about it. Maybe that, too, came from being dead. It must sort out your priorities for you.

"*Gratias, magne,*" I said.

"*Vale, filia.*"

I wanted to ask him about Cryptic Creep, but he disappeared in a quick flash of silver light.

As I walked back to the bench, I realized that Ari and Spare14 had stopped talking. They were staring at me instead.

"Is something wrong?" I said.

"I look up," Ari said, "and you're standing in the middle of the sodding lawn talking to the empty air."

"I happened to be speaking with St. Maurice."

Ari's eyes drooped in sour resignation. I noticed that he was still holding his gadget.

"Er," Spare14 said, "a vision?"

"No," I said. "His scan set off Nathan's alarm."

Ari muttered in Hebrew and stuffed the gadget into his shirt pocket. Spare14 tried to run an SPP on me, but I deflected it.

"Ah," I said, "you *are* a fellow psychic. I thought so."

"Not a natural one." Spare14 kept his voice level, but I could feel his annoyance at being caught out. "I followed my esteemed rootstock's methods for years before I developed a few paltry talents."

"This past month or so, I've felt someone looking my way, every now and then. Well, I've felt two persons, but one was malicious, and the other one, okay."

"I was the fellow without malice, I assure you. I owe you an apology for spying, but I did need a look at you before I approached you openly."

"Apology accepted. This kind of surveillance—is it how you gained access to Nathan's confidential report about the Agency? *Peccavis*, you told me."

"You're a very clever woman, O'Grady," Spare14 paused for a sigh. "And that's all I'm going to say on the matter."

"Nola," Ari said, "you're the head of the Apocalypse Squad. I want to look into this business of joining TWIXT." He paused. I could feel him gathering himself for a psychological effort. I waited. I knew how much macho pain it cost him when he finally asked, "Do I have your permission?"

"Yes," I said. "If you both agree that I can file a report to the Agency on the matter."

"Most assuredly," Spare14 said. "I understand."

"Nothing would stop you, anyway," Ari said.

Spare14 dug into the briefcase again and brought out a black carrier bag, made of Kevlar or some similar material. He slid the examination book inside, then secured the zippered flap with a small combination lock.

"Here you are." Spare14 passed the bag across the table to Ari. "Do be careful with it."

"Of course." Ari managed to keep from looking my way. "I'll give your offer serious consideration."

"And my dear O'Grady." Spare14 leaned toward me with a smile I can only call unctuous. "I do hope you'll give your agency a good report of our meeting? As I said, I'm quite willing to travel if necessary to lay our proposal before its directors."

"I'll pass everything along," I said. "Not a problem."

We shook hands all round, and the meeting ended. Spare14 returned to his bench in the sunshine. As we walked away, I glanced back to see him taking a bag the size of a throw pillow out of his briefcase. Birds flew down and squirrels came running to flock around his feet as he began scattering popcorn. I began to wonder if the briefcase came from the same workshop as the TARDIS. It seemed a lot bigger on the inside than on the out.

Ari and I headed across the lawn toward the general area of our car.

"So you decided to join the unit?" I said.

"I'll sit the exam at least. I'm too sodding curious not to. It's all your fault, you know. You've infected me with a taste for this sort of information."

"This sort—"

"Deviant world levels." Ari sighed with brief melancholy. "Part of the exam seems to deal with those. But the really important bits are the units on inter-world law and procedures. It's a good thing I have some leave accrued. Holiday time, you know. I'll put in for it so I can study."

"Then there's a lot of data in that cram book."

"It's quite thick, yes."

"It sounds like my kind of intel."

He turned his head and scowled at me. "It's got a security restriction. You don't have clearance."

"I figured that. Why else the lock?"

He smiled.

"Look," I said, "we, and I mean us personally, have had visitors from deviant worlds, first the apparition and then that guy who tried to break into our flat. Every bit of data I can gather about deviant world levels is important. I have need to know, Ari."

"I can run your request by Spare14. That's all I can do."

"Judging from the things he said just now, he'll turn any requests down until the Agency's officially linked up with TWIXT. That'll take months once the bureaucrats get involved."

"Sorry. There's nothing I can do about that."

Ari and his damned procedures! We left the lawn and turned down the narrow side road where we'd left the car.

"Those intruders from other worlds." I tried again. "They're Chaos threats."

"Yes."

"Stopping Chaos threats is my job. I can't do it without more information about this deviant—"

"No, I won't let you read the sodding book."

I knew better than to try giving him a direct order. I did what I usually do when I feel baffled: I got mad.

"Then I'll just have to wheedle it out of you." I kept my voice calm. "You might think of a few things you'd like. Things we haven't tried yet."

At first Ari merely looked puzzled. I sensed his Qi level spark upward when he realized what sort of "things" I meant.

"Nola, don't," he snapped.

"Don't what?"

"Make my life miserable by trying to wheedle access to the sodding book."

"You could just give in now."

"No! I don't care if you're the bureau head. You don't have the clearance to read it."

So that's it, I thought. He'd hated asking my permission to take the TWIXT exam so much that he was reasserting control. All right, O'Grady, I asked myself. Are you going to let him get away with this?

Aloud, I said nothing more until we reached the Saturn. I settled in to the passenger seat, Ari behind the wheel. He held the carrier bag upright between his ankles while he buckled on his seat belt, then picked it up and set it on his lap. I considered tactics. It was just possible that I could read the combination from his mind if I could catch him when he was opening it, but I was willing to bet he'd never open it in front of me. He noticed me staring at the bag.

"I'm going to keep this at the gym," he said. "I have a secure locker there."

He'd left me no alternative but treachery. I spent a moment pondering just what his most intense sexual fantasy might be. I had plenty of hints from the various activities we'd already sampled. The more I pondered, the more obvious it seemed.

"I bet you own a pair of handcuffs," I said. "Maybe a couple of them. You are a cop, after all."

"Yes, I do." He glanced my way. "Why?"

"I bet you've got a pair that would fit me."

I smiled at him, merely smiled, that is. I kept my own Qi under control for fairness' sake, but I felt his Qi level spike.

"Nola, stop it!"

"Stop what? I'm merely thinking out loud. If there are sections in that book that give TWIXT codes, secret stuff like that, I would never read those. You could tape them shut. I only want the background material."

He growled and stared out the windshield.

"Handcuffs and those black stockings you like so much," I went on.

"Let's just go home."

"Is that a yes?"

"No!" He turned the key in the ignition with a macho flick of his wrist.

As we drove home, I stayed alert, watched the road, scanned the sidewalk, kept my eyes moving, but I saw no false images and nothing else abnormal or dangerous. Well, nothing, that is, if you don't count the effects of Ari's driving style, which produced a lot of blaring horns and obscene gestures from the other drivers on the road.

We survived to make it home. Ari settled on the couch with his laptop. I went into the bedroom and took off the sweater, the shirt, my athleisure shoes, and my healthful and utterly non-sexy white cotton socks. That left me wearing a black lace bra and jeans. When I came back to the living room, I noticed that he'd attached the Hebrew keyboard to his laptop and tucked the carrier bag underneath. I stayed standing, just beside the entrance to the hallway with my back against the side wall of the room.

"You don't need to worry about me taking that bag from you," I said. "It won't do me any good without the combination."

"Yes. That's why there's a lock." He punched a couple of keys, then looked up. "I'm thinking of going to the gym. I can't do my weights routine here. Run scans, will you? I don't want to leave you alone if it's not safe."

"Okay. I'll just be in the bedroom. After I run the scans, I'll go through my underwear drawer."

He said nothing, but I saw his jaw tighten.

"When you came back from Israel," I went on, "I bought some new things that you haven't seen yet, a black lace garter belt and stockings. They'd look good with this bra and the handcuffs."

Ari winced. I felt the Qi begin to flow between us. He hit a few more keys. The laptop shut down.

"I'm going to the gym," he said. "I need to get out of here. If you're not safe, it's your own sodding fault."

"Why?" I leaned back against the wall and hooked my thumbs into the waistband of my jeans. This time I let Qi flow out toward him along with the smile. His face turned pink.

"Nola, stop it! I'm not going to give you the combination, and that's that."

"Okay. Then take the book out of the bag and just give me that."

He set the laptop down on the coffee table, put the carrier bag beside it, and stood up. I let the stalemate hold while I scanned the Qi he was inadvertently releasing: a steady overflow with no hint of his irrational rage. He was annoyed, but he had good reason to be. What did come through was raw desire.

"I suppose," Ari said, "that if I don't let you read the sodding book, I'll end up sleeping on the couch."

"What? Of course not. I'd never do that to you. I'm only bargaining with—well, let's call it refinements." I gave him my best heavy-lidded smile. "Like the handcuffs and the black garter belt. With the stockings. Fishnets instead of lace if you prefer."

"This is utterly unfair of you, and I'm not going along with it." He took a couple of steps toward the hallway, which meant toward me. "I'm going to get my workout clothes out of the dryer and leave."

I had one last weapon. It was my least favorite playtime activity, but damned if I was going to let him keep that book away from me.

"Yes, you should go. I'm being a bad girl." I looked modestly down though I kept him in view through my eyelashes. "I deserve a spanking."

Ari cracked. He walked over, caught me by the shoulders, and kissed me. I laid my hands flat on his chest.

"Just take the book out of the bag," I said. "First."

"But you won't read the TWIXT code section?"

"I promise. Why would I want to?"

"Right." He kissed me again. "I can't believe I'm doing this."

"I can." I rubbed up against him. "It's obvious how much you want to. I've been a very bad girl."

He caught my hands in his, spread them away from my body and pressed me back against the wall. When he kissed me, he was oozing so much Qi that I started to sweat.

"I'll just go change into something cooler." I pulled a hand free and ran my fingers through his hair, also sweaty. "Just bring the book with you when you come into the bedroom."

"You're going to read it right away?" He kissed the side of my neck. "I think not."

"No, I'm going to put it somewhere for safe keeping, where you can't get it back until I'm done with it."

Ari let me go and returned to the coffee table. He twirled the combination lock, then opened the bag and slid the book out. I took it from him.

"There," he said. "You hide it. I'll fetch the handcuffs." He smiled, tight-lipped and tiger-eyed. "And your hairbrush."

Some while later, I got dressed and left him asleep in the bedroom. I took the cram book into the living room, fetched a notebook and a pen, and gingerly sat down on a soft sofa cushion to read through the relevant sections. True to my word, I skipped the chapters on TWIXT legal codes. Oh, all right, I did glance at them. They had nothing I needed, and besides, they looked hideously complex.

The pages of background proved to be invaluable. The material covered the formation of deviant worlds and hinted at travel between them. Although the book supplied a lot of details, the basic principle was simplicity itself. Forget all those sci-fi stories about killing Hitler and changing history. Worlds split and deviated not because of human actions—or the actions of any other intelligent species—

but by mathematically determined transformations inherent in the system of worlds. The multiverse turned out to be one huge fractal pattern, generating replicas and deviants of itself by its inherent nature.

The impetus or energy for this self-generation was still a mystery, according to the text. The astrophysicists on Spare14's level tended to believe that "quantum fluctuation" or "foam" lay behind the deviations. Although the process could be expressed by enormously complex mathematical formulae, the book showed none of those. I guess the authors figured that mathematical geniuses wouldn't want to join TWIXT.

A fractal pattern like the famous Mandelbrot Set only transforms along three axes: Vertical, Horizontal, and Time. In the multiverse, the transformations occur in Time and some unknown number of spatial dimensions. Like Numbersgrrl once told me, they shoot off in all directions. The process can generate splits at varying times in a level's existence. Thus two "cousin worlds" might be strikingly similar if the one had recently been generated from the other, or conversely, surprisingly different if the split lay in the distant past.

The book used an elaborate analogy to explain these principles. It postulated cars of the same brand and model parked one above the other in a multilevel car park. Although the cars were identical when they left the factory, different owners used them for different journeys. They let individual kinds of junk pile up in the trunks and glove compartments as well. In some cases an owner might even have painted a car in some eccentric way. The result would be a set of cars that had most things in common while displaying significantly distinct features.

Gates between worlds would then be like elevators in the car park. No one could simply jump through the concrete floors that separated the nearly identical cars. A person desiring to move from Car A to Car B had to walk up the spiral ramps or take the direct elevator from floor to floor. The analogy broke down at that point because in the multiverse there are no ramps, and the elevators do not stop at every floor.

With time, cousin worlds move too far apart to "continue to share information," as the cram book put it. I took that as meaning they could no longer be reached one from the other. Thus a world-walker could find only recently separated and thus somewhat similar worlds. The information stopped there with a couple of cryptic notes. Recruits had to pass the exam and become sworn agents before they learned how to travel from world to world. Luckily, I already had some information on that subject.

I was just putting my notes away in my computer desk when I heard Ari go into the bathroom. In a minute he came into the living room, yawning, stretching, grinning at me. He'd put on his jeans and a red 49ers T-shirt, both of which showed off his assets. He walked over, caught me by the waist, and kissed me. I laced my hands behind his neck and pulled him down for a second kiss.

"I hope I didn't actually hurt you," he said.

"You didn't, no. You were surprisingly moderate with that hairbrush. Merciful, even."

"Good, though mercy was certainly more than you deserved. Have you taken a look at the book yet?"

"Oh, yeah, I'm done with it. You can have it back."

He pulled back to study my face. "Already?" He sounded strangely disappointed.

"Yeah. I learned in college how to speed read through that kind of material. Why? What's wrong?"

"I was hoping you'd want to bargain for a second look at it."

"Nope. Sorry. No more of that fancy stuff." I was half-sincere, half-teasing him, because the entire experience with the handcuffs and so on had turned out to be much more pleasurable than I'd anticipated. "You'll have to wait until I want some more classified information out of you."

"I'd better do well on that exam, then. Nothing like a little motivation."

"If you pass, will they give you more data?"

"So Spare14 gave me to understand. Which reminds me. While you were off communing with the saints, I told Spare about our burglar and that bluish sphere. He confirmed that the device had transport capabilities."

"Does he think that guy will come back?"

"No. He admitted that the transport type of orb is very rare."

"Which means there are other types."

"I can't confirm that." He was grinning at me. "You don't have the right clearance."

"Very cute, Mr. Nathan."

He laughed, then kissed me. "I love you," he said.

"I love you, too." It felt surprisingly good to say. "I really do."

"Then why won't you marry me?"

I suppressed a snarl. "Because you're a stubborn bastard who doesn't know when to stop badgering me about it."

"That should be a recommendation, not a drawback. It shows I'm sincere."

I groaned and slipped out of his grasp. "Let's get something to eat," I said. "After all that exercise, I'm hungry."

CHAPTER 5

AFTER A BRIEF EXCHANGE OF E-MAIL, I received Y's permission to turn Belial's consciousness over to TWIXT. By contrast, the TWIXT offer of liaison presented difficulties. In a trance meeting late on Wednesday morning, Y tried to explain.

"For one thing, I'm worried about security," Y said, "since TWIXT has psychics. The threat you call the Cryptic Creep is bad enough, and now you tell me that this Spare fellow managed to get information that Nathan thought was classified."

"That's true, but if we liaise with TWIXT, they'll be our allies, not another threat."

Y's trance image crossed its arms, stuck out its lower lip, and sulked, but only for a few seconds. The image blinked out. Hiding your emotions in the trance state sometimes requires an image reboot. In a second or two he returned to his usual august self, a Japanese-American man of middle age, his thick hair streaked with gray, but still a good-looking guy, really, even with his wire-framed glasses.

"Don't forget," I said, "that Saint Maurice vetted Spare14."

"Yes, that's true." Y heaved a dramatic sigh. "At times we must throw the fishing line of truth into the waters of darkness and see what takes the bait. I'll admit to being relieved at having Belial off our hands."

"So am I. And I think you'll find Spare easy to talk to, if you decide to arrange a face-to-face meeting."

"All in good time, Nola." His image betrayed him with a scowl, and he changed the subject. "About this Cryptic Creep person, any more visitations?"

"None so far."

"Good. Where do you get these names, anyway? You must have read comic books when you were a girl. Batman, things like that."

"I did. I was obsessive about the X-Men. But, look, Spare14 will be here in an hour to pick up Belial. What shall I tell him about the liaison?"

"That his proposal is under advisement. We'll be having a top-level meeting about it tomorrow."

With that, Y closed down without even a good-bye. The sulk baffled me until I mentioned it to Ari.

"He's afraid of losing control of his unit," Ari said, "or of having to share the control. I saw a lot of that in the army. It's one of the reasons I didn't want a military career."

"You mean he's jealous of Spare?"

"No, not personally. He merely sees Spare as a threat of sorts to his power base within the Agency. Or so I'd guess. I don't know the man, of course, but it's a common pattern."

"It makes perfect sense," I said. "But at the same time, Spare's offering something Y really wants, that policing capacity."

"True. He must feel torn."

I worried for reasons of my own about one aspect of this sudden involvement with TWIXT. Before Spare14 turned up, Ari had assured me that as an Interpol officer he had no authority to interfere with my efforts to bring my father home. As a member of TWIXT, he'd be duty-bound to stop me and Michael from breaking the terms of Dad's parole — assuming, of course, that he'd been paroled — by taking him from his world to ours. I doubted if we could find out where he was and get him out of there before Ari became a sworn officer of the trans-world police.

"By the way," Ari went on, "speaking of Spare14 and all that, my request for leave's been approved."

"How much do you have accrued?"

"Three weeks. That should be more than enough to study for the exam. The legal material's fairly simple."

To you, maybe, I thought. "One more question. If you get into TWIXT, will you still be my bodyguard?"

"I'll insist on it, though I'm quite sure you're part of Spare's scheme. Through you, he can keep in touch with the Agency whether they officially link up or not."

At one o'clock, Spare14 arrived. He was wearing a blue business suit with a white shirt and a diagonally striped red, blue, and yellow tie. He carried his briefcase. We all shook hands, and he sat down in one of the wood armchairs covered in maroon leather. The briefcase sat on the floor next to him. Ari took the couch, and I stayed standing.

"Nathan," Spare14 said, "I'll send you e-mail with details on the examination as soon as I have them. There's some talk of setting up a special session to speed you through the process."

"Thank you," Ari said. "We'll see how things go, then."

"Just so. And my dear O'Grady, I hope you have some news for me."

"The Agency's taken your proposal under advisement," I said. "The top people will be having a meeting tomorrow."

"Splendid! I hope that your surrendering custody of the Belial entity is just the beginning of our cooperation."

I smiled. "Let me hand over the calamari in question."

I'd already removed Belial in his antistatic packaging from the wall safe. I'd bundled him with the camcorder and a lot of bubble wrap in a box that was about eighteen inches on a side. The box currently sat on my desk, but I picked up a sheaf of printed forms first.

"I have some paperwork to fill out," I said, "concerning the transfer of the suspect to your authority."

"Very good. I have some for you, too."

It took us twenty minutes to finish all the various forms and to make sure that we each ended up with copies of the complete set. Ari signed everything as a witness with official standing. When we finished, I gave Spare14 the box.

"I shall be leaving this world level soon," he said, "to remand the suspect to Javert's custody. He'll arrive on the level you call Interchange in a few days."

"I'd been hoping he could come here," I said. "I'd like to meet him, but I suppose traveling in a water tank's kind of difficult."

"Very, actually, especially since he requires a specially trained world-walker to assist him."

I sat down in the other armchair. Spare14 unbuckled the straps on his briefcase, which was about two feet long and ten inches wide. Its mouth opened much wider, of course, but I was still surprised when he slipped the box inside without any trouble. When Spare14 buckled the briefcase shut, it remained about ten inches wide despite having swallowed an eighteen-inch cube. I tried not to stare. He sat back in the chair and smiled vaguely at me.

"So," I said, "I'd like to ask you about Javert. Is he a seconded officer?"

"He is, indeed, and seconded from a very well-developed police force. Most members of his species are ordinary, law-abiding citizens of their underwater realms. I really should make that clear. The Belials are the exception."

"Every species has its criminals, then?"

"Unfortunately, that's quite true."

"I was wondering if Belial was acting alone, or if he was part of a gang."

"The latter. Javert has been tracking the case for years." Spare14 put his fingertips together and considered me over the arch. "They're thieves, basically, though I've never been clear about what it is they steal. It's very valuable, whatever it is. The name translates as the Silver of the Heart."

Interesting, I thought. The concept of stolen property had just popped up again.

"That's a bit opaque," Ari remarked.

"Yes," Spare14 said. "Translation between any human language and the languages Javert speaks is alarmingly difficult. Their brains are quite different from ours. Their language concepts are, too, or so I've been told. For instance, 'forward' and 'backward' mean very different things to them."

"But psychic communication's possible," I said. "I had a

detailed conversation with Belial, and a brief one with Javert."

"He did mention that." Spare14 gave me his unctuous smile. "Which is one reason, my dear O'Grady, that we're hoping to liaise with your agency. Your group appears to have a somewhat different set of talents from those we have available in TWIXT. Pooling our resources would be valuable to both."

"Oh, I agree," I said. "Unfortunately, it's not my decision to make. Whatever this silver stuff is, I wonder if Belial was hoping to find it here on this world. If so, he'd need human accomplices for the actual heist."

"Just so," Spare14 said. "Javert's planning on getting the truth of that once Belial's two halves are reunited. Plea bargaining for information received is part of their justice system, too."

"I see. If you could relay some of that information once Javert obtains it—"

"Certainly, assuming Belial is forthcoming." Spare14 glanced at the briefcase where said suspect currently resided. "Now, O'Grady, I have a rather nosy question to ask you. Do feel free to tell me to mind my own business. It concerns your brother."

"Ah," I said. "Which one?"

"The youngest, I think. He's the one who must be a world-walker."

"Yeah, that's Michael. Someone spotted him on Interchange, I take it."

"You're quite right. The someone was myself, actually. I realize that he's young, and doubtless needs to continue his education, but we'd be very interested in recruiting him once he reaches his maturity."

"I can see why," I said, "but the Agency has already expressed the same interest. They're offering him a college scholarship in return for a commitment."

Spare14 set his lips in a tight line, then forced out a smile. "I see," he said. "Well, we may be able to match that generous offer. The talents you and your brother display really do seem to be extraordinarily strong. Um, I take it you have other siblings?"

"Yes," I said, "but I can't speak for them."

I smiled; he smiled.

"Very well." Spare14 took a leather card case out of his inner jacket pocket. "Allow me to give you my cards. I meant to do so the first time we met, but your visitation from a saint—Maurice, was it? yes, Maurice—rather startled me, and I quite forgot."

Spare14 studied his surprisingly thick card case before removing any cards. I took two from him, and he handed a pair to Ari. Each gave a different address, one in my San Francisco with a zip code, and the other, in a version of the city called SanFran, with the simple postal code of NE. The interesting detail, however, came after the post code. The address in my San Francisco included the designation "Terra Four," and that on Interchange, "Terra Three."

"Now, about that Terra Three office," Spare14 went on. "You'll notice that I'm not identified as an Interpol officer on that card."

"From what I know of Interchange," Ari said, "you don't want to admit that you're an honest police officer. Very bad for your health."

"Oh, yes. The locals assume that I'm running some sort of exclusive numbers racket. Should you ever go to SanFran, could you kindly keep up the fiction?"

"Not a problem," I put in. "You can count on us."

"Thank you." Spare14 nodded in my direction. "I'll return to my office here after meeting Javert. If I may telephone you when I do?"

"That would be fine, yes," I said. "World-walkers are in demand, I take it."

"They're quite rare," Spare14 said. "People with talents just don't seem to have those big families anymore."

"Is that one reason for cloning?"

"Um, well, yes. But I really can't go into details about that."

"There are some levels, aren't there, where world-walking is a crime?"

"Not so much world-walking in itself, but using the talent wrongly, such as transporting criminals out of the jurisdictions where they're under warrant."

"Is that common?"

"No, certainly not, but it does happen." Spare14 hesitated. "How do you know that?"

"I'm afraid I can't go into detail about it."

He set his lips tight together. I caught Ari suppressing a grin. Now that I knew Michael's talents were so valuable— and I speculated that Dad's collection of boxes would be, too—I could wait to bargain with Mr. Spare14. My father's talent might supply another bargaining point if, of course, he'd agree to work with the police after spending time in prison. I had my doubts about that.

We parted with another handshake all round. Ari escorted Spare14 to the front door. I wondered if the various subjects of our conversation had left Ari wishing he'd been an insurance adjustor. When he came back upstairs, he admitted to feeling stressed.

"I was thinking of going to the gym for my weights routine," he said. "But I shouldn't leave you here alone. Come with me."

I groaned. "No, I'll be perfectly safe as long as I stay inside the security system. Spare told you that our prowler isn't likely to come back, didn't he?"

"Yes, but—"

"Ari, please! I don't want to argue about the damned gym."

He set his hands on his hips and scowled at me. I glared in return. Finally, he said, "Very well, if you're sure you'll be safe."

"I am. Really. I can protect myself, y'know. Besides, I know where the alarm nodes are, and if I have to, I'll punch the panic button and set everything off. The noise alone will send the criminals away screaming."

Ari smiled, but grudgingly. "I'll do a shorter workout than usual. I should be back in about an hour and a half."

On this compromise, he grabbed his sports bag and left.

I sat down at my computer and filed the usual reports and took care of the usual e-mail, then logged off and shut down. Although I waited for a few minutes, Cryptic Creep never appeared on the monitor. I flopped onto the couch to think. Spare14's mysterious briefcase had reminded me of something that had happened years before.

I needed to recover the memory, and at last, it rose. I remembered sitting on my father's lap, which meant I was eight at the very oldest, and laughing when he showed me a secret drawer in his desk, the same one that I now had downstairs. What, I wondered, did he keep in it, and was that something still there? I ran an SM:D and felt no threats in the vicinity. I checked the clock: almost time for Ari to return. I decided, therefore, that I could go downstairs safely, even though I'd have to spend a brief minute outside on the front steps.

I got out of one flat and into the other with no trouble, nor did I see or sense any threat nearby. The downstairs flat, shut up for so long, smelled of dust and damp. I decided against opening a window, just in case a trans-world prowler came around while I was there. Dad's desk, a heavy oak number with drawers on each side of the kneehole, sat in the oddly shaped antechamber, a tiny room with a big walk-in closet on the back wall.

I pulled up the desk chair and sat down to examine the desk. A solid oak slab about an inch thick topped it. Under that, a shallow drawer hung directly over the kneehole. It slid in and out in the ordinary way. It also ran across the entire depth of the desk with no room for a second compartment in back. None of the other drawers allowed for extra space. I got up and examined the back panel just to make sure.

Yet I vividly remembered Dad doing something one-handed underneath that central drawer and pulling out a secret compartment. Maybe someone had dismantled it at some point in the desk's history. I crouched down to look at the bottom of the existing drawer. Not one mark or scuff indicated damage, not a nail hole or chip. I sat back in the chair and let my mind range back to the memory.

"Where is it, Dad?" my child's voice said.

"Not in this world, sweetheart," Dad said.

In the present moment I said aloud a word that my father would have slapped me for saying. At the time I'd thought he was teasing me. Now I realized that he'd told me the simple truth. The drawer doubtless existed in some other world or dimension, a place only he could access. Probably this meant that something very important lay hidden in it, not that it was going to do me one damn bit of good.

Michael, however, might have enough world-walking talent to find the mystery drawer and retrieve the important whatever. I pulled my cell phone out of my jeans pocket and called him. He answered promptly.

"You're not in class, are you?" I said. "I'll sign off if you are."

"Uh, no. Actually uh—"

"You're cutting school."

"Well, yeah. I'm working on the map. I'm failing Civics anyway, so I figured I might as well just cut. It's the last class of the day."

I would have enjoyed yelling and lecturing, but they would have been wastes of time and breath.

"I've got something else in that department for you to work on," I said. "But I don't want to talk about it on the phone."

"Cool! I'll be right over."

"Where are you? What about Sean?"

"I'm up by the Cliff House. I think there's a gate in Sutro Gardens. Sean couldn't meet me today, but maybe he can find it tomorrow."

"You can look after you get out of school."

"Sure. Uh, I'll be right over."

Michael appeared on the covered porch so quickly that I assumed he'd hitched a ride. I let him into the lower flat. The first thing he did was pull out his cell phone and text Sophie to tell her where he was. For an encore, he took off his down-filled jacket and dropped it on the floor. With his jeans he was wearing a short-sleeved orange Giants T-shirt over a long-sleeved red 49ers T-shirt, not what I'd call a successful combination. I picked up the jacket and hung it over the back of the desk chair.

"Sophie'll tell Aunt Eileen," Michael said. "I don't want them to worry."

"Good. Sophie has her own phone now, huh?"

"It's the one Aunt E used to have. She never used it much, because it was too complicated or something, so she gave it to Sophie."

"Well, hey, that was generous of her."

"I thanked her a whole lot, don't worry. And I took out the garbage without her telling me to. A bunch of times."

"Good. Now look, bro, we've got some problems on our hands. One: we can't trust Ari to look the other way if we end up having to do something that's—let's just say dubious—to get Dad home. So say nothing."

Michael nodded and held up one hand like a Boy Scout.

"Two," I continued. "Do not mention gates and stuff like that over your cell phone. All those calls end up stored on some server farm somewhere."

"Ah, come on, no one's going to go over all that shit."

"You never know." I fixed him with a stare one notch above the gimlet eye. "In the Agency we do not take stupid risks."

"Okay, okay. I won't."

"Good. Now, finally, I've got some bureaucratic business to deal with here. I can't leave to go traveling across the worlds, not even to rescue Dad, until this job is finished. If things do work out here, we may be able to get top-notch help for the rescue, but it could take months."

"Months? Jeezus H!" Michael pulled a long face. "I guess you can't tell me what the problem is, huh?"

"You guessed right. There are drawbacks to having a sister who's a secret agent. Sorry."

His SPP radiated a profound sense of self-pity mingled with youthful impatience.

"Now, as to why I called you," I said. "It's about Dad's desk here."

After I explained the problem, Michael sat down in the chair. He laid both hands palm down on the desktop.

"I feel something, for sure," he said. "But I dunno. I mean, hey, wait!"

With his right hand he reached under the central drawer, then grinned. He pulled out a second drawer with the same twist of the wrist and flourish that I remembered Dad using. I squatted down and peered past his knees to see how the drawer hung—on narrow brass runners that had not existed earlier, at least not on this world level.

"There it is," he said. "Epic cool!"

Inside the drawer lay a manila folder. Michael picked it up and handed it to me. "That's the only thing in here."

When he closed the drawer, it disappeared. So did the rails. I shivered, I admit it—me! who should have been the expert on such phenomena.

"Y'know," Michael said. "We could put those boxes in this drawer."

"Very sly, bro. So one fine night you could pick the lock on the front door and come in and take them?"

Michael gave me a grin of the "I'm just a goof don't hit me" variety.

"I know they call to you," I went on, "but you'll have to wait to answer. Now, don't forget your jacket."

We returned to the upstairs flat. While Michael raided my refrigerator, I sat down in one of the armchairs to leaf through the folder. It contained a medium-sized stack of printer paper, slightly yellowed along the edges with age. The printout text, in the old Bunchló na Nod font, was mostly in Irish Gaelic, not that I was surprised. Dad had written notes by hand, also in Irish, all over the margins.

Michael came back with half a pastrami sandwich clamped in one hand and a bottle of turquoise-blue sports drink in the other. He stood next to me and craned his neck to see the paper I was holding.

"Jeez," Michael said. "What is that weird shit?"

"Your ancestral tongue."

"Oh. I guess I shouldn't have called it weird shit, then."

"You got that right." I scowled at the papers. "It's mostly Irish, anyway. I keep finding passages in a peculiar Latin." I waved the bundle of papers in his direction. "It's going to take me a while to translate these."

"Is there anything in there about the boxes? Can you tell that much?"

"Not yet. Let me get my dictionary."

He flopped down in the second armchair while I searched the bookshelves.

With the aid of the dictionary I could pick out meaning

here and there. I could read the notes Dad had written, but the printout presented real problems. The parts in Irish Gaelic were written in a very archaic language, positively medieval in its constant invocation of various saints and dire warnings of damnation to fall upon anyone who misused the information for evil. Worse yet, not all the words were in my dictionary.

I got the general impression that the information in question had originally been part of a book. Nothing gave me so much as a clue of what it was or where Dad had found it.

"Well?" Michael said.

"It's going to take me a long time to work this stuff over." I laid the papers down on the coffee table. "But I think they might have something to do with the gates and worlds. Dad made notes about a passage concerning keys to the doors guarded by angels."

"How long?" Michael popped the last bit of the sandwich into his mouth and mumbled. "Will it take you to translate it, I mean?"

"Don't talk with your mouth full," I said. "A couple of days, maybe. This stuff is dense."

Michael groaned with dire drama and wiped his greasy hand on his jeans.

I was about to suggest he use a napkin when I heard the front door open. I went to the top of the stairs to check: Ari, still damp from his shower. He smiled at me as he ran up the entire flight.

"I can't believe you've got the energy to do that," I said.

"Working out builds energy," he said. "You'd find that out if—"

"No! I'm not going to some smelly icky gym."

He rolled his eyes skyward and strode into the living room.

"Mike!" Ari said. "You came by?"

"Nola had some stuff to show me from Dad's desk. So she called me, yeah."

Ari nodded and trotted off down the hall to put his sweaty workout clothes into the washing machine. I felt a pang of conscience at just how quickly we'd shifted his status to "outside the family." I followed Ari down the hall.

"Well, actually," I told him, "I discovered something weird about Dad's desk. It's got a drawer that's in another world. Sort of like Spare14's briefcase."

Ari stopped pouring liquid detergent into the dispenser and turned to give me one of his reproachful stares. He set the bottle of detergent down.

"You must have noticed the way Belial's box fit into the briefcase," I said.

"Oh, yes," Ari said. "I've been trying to forget it ever since. I take it Mike can open the drawer."

"Yeah. I couldn't. There were some papers in it that might be important."

"Might be?"

"I don't know yet. They're really peculiar."

"Nothing new about that, then."

I returned to the living room to find Michael eating my recently purchased vegan peanut cookies right out of the bag. He was looking through the stack of Dad's papers and scattering the occasional crumb or nut fragment onto the floor.

"What is this?" I said. "Aunt Eileen's stopped feeding you?"

"I jogged over here on the beach," Michael said. "The sea air, y'know?"

"Okay. Can you understand anything in those papers?"

"No. I'm just kind of studying Dad's handwriting. In case I have to, like, forge it on something."

"You're going to be a real credit to the Agency one day."

"Yeah?" He gave me a brilliant smile. "Thanks!"

Before I could explain the meaning of the term "sarcasm," his cell phone let fly with a heavy metal guitar riff. Michael took it from his pocket with the cookie-free hand and stared at the text.

"It's from Sophie," he told me. "I guess I better go."

"How are you getting home?"

"Muni." Michael handed me the bag with the last two cookies in it. "It's kind of a walk between buses, but that's okay."

"Ari and I could drive you."

"No, he just got home and stuff. It's no problem. Honest."

I considered offering to drive him by myself, but the memory of the false image attack stopped me. Michael grabbed his jacket and headed off downstairs. I put the bag on the coffee table, then followed Michael down to let him out. By the time I came back upstairs, Ari was sitting on the couch with my Irish dictionary, and the last cookies had disappeared. So much for my adding extra calories to my diet. Ari looked up from the dictionary and frowned.

"I have never seen a language before," he said, "that requires twenty pages of small print for the pronunciation guide."

"And what's more," I said, "the guide's unreliable. When it comes to pronouncing proper names, you've really got to ask someone who already knows."

Ari shut the book and laid it on the coffee table. He was about to make a remark when my cell phone rang. Aunt Eileen, I thought. It was.

"Has Michael left yet?" she said.

"Yeah, he has. Why?"

"He needs to start his homework. His English teacher's given him one last chance to pass if he can revise one essay and finish another. Oh, wait . . . Here he is now. I'll let you go."

Aunt Eileen hung up before I could tell her that Michael had left my flat a bare five minutes earlier. I stood holding my cell phone and staring at it like an idiot. I could hear Michael's voice in my memory, saying, "It's no problem."

"What's wrong?" Ari said.

"Michael's learned how to shorten the journey, that's what," I said. "Keffir fizz hat rack."

"You mean *kefitzat haderach*."

"Whatever. I don't know if he's found gates or if he's imitating Walking Stewart, but he's already across town."

Ari spoke a few quiet words in Hebrew.

"Say what?" I said.

"Never mind. They're not the sort of words I want you to know." He stood up and brushed a few cookie crumbs

off his shirt. "I've been thinking. If I had decided to become
an insurance adjustor, my life would have been a lot sim-
pler, but then, I never would have met you." He considered
for a moment. "I suppose that's a fair tradeoff."

He moved out of range before I could kick him and
picked up the pile of Dad's papers from on the coffee table.
"Do you mind if I look at these?"

"Not at all," I said, "but good luck in trying to read
them."

Ari sat back down on the couch and frowned at the first
page. "This is very odd," he said. "These Latin passages?
They're filled with transliterated Hebrew words."

"Crud," I said. "That means they're Hisperic."

"What?"

"Early Irish monks thought it was cool to interlard their
Latin with Hebrew. A little Greek, too, because those were
the Biblical languages. Very holy, therefore. The resulting
mess is called Hisperic, but I don't know why."

"I can help you with the Hebrew at least."

"I'd really appreciate that. But the worst thing is, it
means the Irish parts aren't Middle Irish. They're Old Irish,
one of the most obscure ancient languages ever."

Ari sighed and put the sheaf of papers back onto the
coffee table. "Let me know what I can do to help," he said.
"And good luck."

Since by then it was past six o'clock in DC, and the
Agency home staff would have closed down for the day, I
left filing a report on Spare14 to the morrow. After we ate a
scrappy dinner of leftovers, Ari started working, web surf-
ing on his laptop with the Arabic keyboard attached.

Part of his job was keeping a watch on chat, news, and
political sites in Arabic and Farsi, looking for clues that
might lead him to people or groups with terrorist ties. Since
he knew three different dialects of Arabic as well as Farsi,
he could post comments and leading questions. It was too
bad, I thought, that he'd never considered a university education, though an academic life teaching languages and lin-
guistics probably would have bored him to despair. No
guns, for one thing.

I picked up the stack of Dad's printout. Although I had

OCR available, the computer probably would have blown a RAM chip if I'd tried to scan that mix of handwriting and a font of yesteryear. The thought of typing it all over again in Gael AX Unicode did not appeal, but it needed to be done. I moaned piteously but briefly and got to work.

I set the page to double-space to leave room for Ari to annotate the Hebrew on the printout and transferred Dad's handwritten notes to proper footnotes. Working with the material helped clarify the meaning to a small degree. By the time we went to bed, my mind had gotten itself tangled from trying to think in four languages at once. I had, however, deciphered enough to know that I needed to understand the entire thing.

About 4 AM I woke in our dark bedroom. Ari had gotten out of bed. I could hear him moving and cloth rustling.

"Say what?" I said.

"Hush," he said. "Stay in bed. I don't want to shoot you by mistake."

I stayed. I could guess that the alarm had gone off and indicated a breach in the security system. I heard Ari walk barefoot to the bedroom door and open it. Since we left a nightlight on in the bathroom down the hall, I saw by his silhouette that he was wearing his jeans, a sweatshirt, and a gun. He stepped out of the room and shut the door behind him.

Since I was naked, I risked rolling out of bed. If I ended up having to ensorcell an intruder, I preferred to do it clothed. I stumbled over one of Ari's T-shirts on the floor and picked that up. It fit like a baggy tunic and smelled like witch hazel, an oddly reassuring scent given the circumstances. I did get back onto the bed, though. Getting shot by mistake wasn't high on my to-do list.

I sat cross-legged on the mattress and did an SM:L for the building. Ari's presence I picked up as he went down the front stairs. We'd shared so much Qi that his aura registered almost as strongly on my mind as my own aura would have. I felt him pause by the front door, then open it.

I held my breath. Nothing happened, except for Ari going outside and shutting the door. I breathed. Another SM:L put him in the downstairs flat. I could sense him moving from room to room in the front of the flat and actually hear him once he went into the empty bedroom directly below me. Eventually he left the lower flat and returned to the porch. I heard him coming upstairs.

"Nola," he called out. "Turn on the bedroom light."

I leaned over and pulled the chain on the antique brass lamp on my nightstand. Ari came down the hall and opened the bedroom door with his left hand. He had his laptop tucked into his armpit and clamped to his side by his left elbow. He was carrying the Beretta in his right hand but pointed at the floor.

"What's all this about?" I said.

"I don't know." Ari let the laptop slip free onto the bed. Before he said anything more, he squatted down and put the gun away in its holster in the dresser drawer. He locked the drawer and stood up.

"The alarm went off." He gestured at his nightstand and the small gray box lying on top of it. "I take it you didn't hear it."

"No, I didn't."

"I thought we might have a prowler, but everything seemed secure." He picked up the laptop and put it on top of the dresser. "Let me check the system records."

He booted up the machine, then worked a few keys. In a couple of minutes he glanced my way with a frown. "Nothing. The alarm sounded, but the only thing in the record is an unidentified energy flux."

"That's not a good sign, is it?" I said.

"No, it certainly isn't."

My memory nipped me. "Those records," I said, "they show you where the flux happened, right?"

"Well, they indicate the closest security node."

"Okay. Do you remember when Jack brought Dad's desk over? You guys put it in the lower flat, and then there was one of those energy discharges—"

"—in the same room." Ari finished the sentence for me. "Yes, I do remember. Hang on a minute." He hit a few keys. "It's the same node."

"I wonder if it was the ghost I saw there?"

Ari spun around to look at me. "What ghost?" he said.

"The one I saw the day Jack brought Dad's old desk over. I told you about her. I thought she was the ghost of the woman who'd committed suicide in the kitchen."

"Right. I do remember now."

Ari shut down the laptop and left it on the dresser. He sat on the edge of the bed and turned to face me.

"The thing is," I said, "I doubt if she really was a ghost. The apparition looked like a blue figure of a woman, pretty much transparent. She told me that there was another drawer in the desk." My turn for the ripple of shock. "God, she was right!"

"Are you thinking she knew about that secret drawer?"

"Exactly that. So it couldn't have been the suicide's ghost. That poor woman wouldn't have known zip about Dad's desk."

"True. In the usual crazed way of these things, that makes sense. What about that other apparition, the one on Saturday?"

"That one didn't look human, but both images must have come from a deviant world level, or maybe from two different ones. Huh, that first one was plain old blue, but the one on Saturday, blue-violet. I wonder if that means something?"

Ari shrugged. "I'll contact Itzak about the alarms. I wonder if he can sensitize the pickup points to Qi. Well, if you're willing to tell him what Qi is."

"It depends. You can't do it yourself?"

"I don't want to faff around with it. I might break something."

"He's good at this kind of stuff, huh?"

"Yes, too good to be doing the sort of work he does for that sodding bank." Ari looked annoyed. "I don't know why he won't listen to me. I keep telling him."

I made a noncommittal noise, which Ari ignored. He yawned, stretched, and pulled off the sweatshirt, then slithered out of his jeans. He dropped the clothes onto the floor and got back under the covers. I took off the T-shirt, but I tossed it over the bed to join the rest of his recent outfit. Neither of us were demon housekeepers. When I lay down, Ari slid over next to me.

"Just leave the light on," he said.

"Say what?" I said. "I want to go back to sleep."

"It's the adrenaline from the alarm and all that. I'll never get back to sleep now unless we—"

"Oh, great! Now I'm a sleeping pill."

"A bit more than that, as you well know."

And because I did know, I let him kiss me. It didn't take long for me to decide that he'd had a perfectly good idea.

In the morning, after I picked up our mail, I went outside to check for graffiti. Ari insisted on going with me. Sure enough, the unbalanced Chaos symbol with its seven arrows had returned. Although Ari wanted to go question the neighbors again, I told him not to bother them.

"It must take a lot of Qi to transfer the symbol from his world to ours," I said. "That unidentified energy the system picked up? It might be his mode of transfer. Could this be what triggered the alarm last night?"

"No," Ari said. "That thing's appeared here a number of times. It never set off the alarm before." He set his hands on his hips and glared at the symbol. "Sodding bastard! I'll go get the hose."

While I waited for Ari to come back, I decided to see how close I had to get before Cryptic Creep could sense my presence. I walked to the edge of the sidewalk, then turned and slowly, one step at a time, I approached the symbol. The shaved head with the familiar face finally appeared when I stood a mere two feet away.

I got in first. "Tell me something," I said, "are you really human or another squid?"

"As human as you are." His smile was almost pleasant. "Neither more nor less. If you can take my meaning."

"A riddle, huh? I am a child of earth, but my race is from the starry heavens."

"Very good," he said. "What about this one? What has existed from the beginning?"

"The limitless light."

"And Chaos is?"

"The shadow that some call darkness."

"And who created the world as we know it?"

"Yaldaboath out of an abortion produced by the longing of Pistis for herself."

He froze, staring at me, started to speak, choked, and disappeared. I tossed a ward at the symbol, which made no response at all. Apparently, he'd taken his Qi and gone home, just because of a line from my old college notes.

Ari came around the corner of the building with the coil of hose over one shoulder and his hands full of rags. He dropped the rags on the sidewalk in front of the graffiti, then attached the hose to the outside spigot.

"Did your cryptic friend appear?" Ari said.

"Oh, yeah, but he didn't stay long. I scared him off with a line from some Roman guy."

"Some Roman guy? Nola—"

"Okay, okay, an imperial era Gnostic dude named Valentinus. Huh. I wonder if that's significant."

As soon as I said it, I knew that, of course, it was. Ari quirked an eyebrow and waited for me to go on.

"Uh-oh," I said. "I forgot that Cryptic Creep worships the Peacock Angel. The Angel was God's foreman, kind of, and created the world according to God's plan. Right?"

"So we've been told, yes, by the occasional nutter."

"Well, I just branded myself as a heretic, and probably of the absolute worst kind."

Ari sighed. "When my father decided to leave the kibbutz, I thought we were going to leave all the nutters behind. Apparently, I was wrong."

"They're following you, yeah, if you mean Cryptic Creep and the Chaos masters."

"Them, too."

"You don't mean me, do you?"

Ari considered me with sorrowful eyes. "I'll just wash this mess off the wall," was all he said.

I was tempted to say something nasty, but he had the hose ready to go. I prefer my showers warm. I marched up the stairs in a steely silence.

CHAPTER 6

WHEN ARI CAME BACK UPSTAIRS, he took off his jacket to reveal the Beretta in the shoulder holster. "Perhaps I should spend some time in the lower flat," he said. "I might catch our graffito artist at work."

"That's a good thought," I said. "We really should do something about setting up your office downstairs. We've got the desk and the chair that goes with it. You could use it any time."

"True." Which was all he said.

He walked over to the bay window, drew the gun, took up a place just to one side, and began studying the view of the neighborhood. At irregular intervals but at least a dozen times a day, he did just this: checked the garage area in back of our flat and the street out front. With the Beretta in hand, he'd scan for suspicious loiterers. The expression on his face while he did this always frightened me: no emotion, not a quiver of a muscle, just a cold impersonal gaze as if his eyes were lenses for a security camera.

What would happen, I wondered, if he saw a clear threat? A couple of shots, I supposed, and he'd worry about explanations later. The guilt would strike him later, too. I'd seen him in the grip of a nightmare after he'd killed a criminal that most people would dismiss as worthless and despicable. For a few minutes I watched him search the outside world for targets. He's doing it for you, I reminded myself. He was risking his own precarious inner balance to keep me safe. Finally, the silence made every nerve in my body twitch.

"Ari?" I said. "*Are* you still interested in working in the other flat?"

"Yes and no." He holstered the Beretta and turned away from the window. "It would be more comfortable than the kitchen table."

"That's the yes. What's the no?"

"I have to admit that the trans-dimensional drawer in your father's desk bothers me. Will it suddenly appear? Will it swallow things I've placed in the other drawers? Silly of me, I suppose."

"No, not at all. I've wondered the same thing. I wish we could talk to my dad about all this stuff, like those boxes. I guess they were his, anyway. The blue-violet apparition seemed to think they belonged to her."

"The apparition." Ari spoke quietly in a tone that signaled defeat. "I'd managed to forget about her. Right. Blue apparitions. Desks and briefcases with trans-dimensional bits tucked inside." He looked my way and grimaced. "Werewolves, now including Michael's girlfriend. Practically my sister-in-law."

"I know, I know," I said. "You should have been an insurance adjustor."

He rose and with great dignity stalked into the kitchen. In a minute or two I heard the tiny clicking of keys that told me he was working at his laptop. I returned to my own computer, where I found a waiting e-mail from Numbers-Grrl. She wanted to see the inter-level gate. Desperately, she said.

"I've got a bunch of bonus airline miles piled up that are going to expire," she continued. "So I thought maybe I could just fly out if it wouldn't hang you up in any way. I'm sorry, I know I'm being really rude to push like this, but do you think your aunt could let us have a look at the thing? I could be in San Francisco tomorrow. I mean, the miles are going to expire next week. And—oh, yeah—my real name is LaDonna Williams."

I understood. For years she'd studied deviant levels, parallel worlds, and the gates between them as theoretical constructs, as chunks of math, equations no more substantial than fairies and leprechauns. Now she had a chance to check her work, as it were, against reality. Besides all that and the airline miles, I wanted to meet her. A few more exchanges, and we had everything set up.

"Itzak Stein phoned me just now." Ari wandered back into the living room. "He wants to have dinner tomorrow. I told him yes."

"I wish you'd asked me first. We're going to have dinner tomorrow with one of my Agency contacts."

"Can't Itzak come along? You can hardly discuss Agency business in a public restaurant."

"That's true, yeah. I'll just tell LaDonna what she can and can't say in front of him."

For our dinner with Itzak and LaDonna, we chose the Elite, a Cajun cafe on Fillmore Street, because it had private booths, little mahogany cubicles left over from the 1930s. We could, if we were careful about volume, discuss unclassified but delicate subjects without being overheard. We reached the restaurant early, as did Itzak. We found him having a drink at the bar—a stressful day at the bank, he told us, was to blame.

"You should get another job," Ari said.

"Not so easy in these troubled times," Itzak said. "And this one has a great benefits package. Health insurance, retirement, goodies like that."

Ari rolled his eyes.

"Not everyone likes to live on the edge like you do," Itzak said with a grin. "Some of us want to have an old age. That means we have to provide for it."

A waiter appeared and showed us to our booth. Ari insisted on sitting with his back to the wall, and I took the chair next to him. Itzak sat down at one side and put his drink on the square table. He was a decent-looking guy, neither handsome nor ugly, with wire-rimmed glasses and thinning brown hair, which he wore short, probably at the bank's insistence. When he grinned, which was often, he looked not handsome but definitely attractive.

"I was wondering," Ari said, "if you could come over Sunday and look at the security system. The alarm went off the other night, but the record function didn't register the reason."

"Oh, yeah?" Itzak said. "Nothing showed up at all?"

"It simply said unidentified energy flux."

Itzak blinked a couple of times. "Now that's too strange," he said. "Sure, I'll be glad to come over. It'll beat playing WoW all weekend."

"Playing what?" Ari said.

"World of Warcraft. Never mind. I'm not going to even try to explain what that is."

Ari was about to press him for an answer when the waiter appeared in the door to the booth.

"Your other guest is here," he said.

"Thanks." I got up and went to welcome LaDonna Williams.

A slender woman in her twenties, LaDonna wore a cream-colored suit with a red silk blouse and high heels. Since her skin was a gorgeous dark brown, the total effect was stunning. Her dark hair had an auburn overtone, probably the result of the expensive-looking straightening process that let it flow down to her shoulders. She also carried a large brown leather shoulder bag, which she slung from the back of her chair.

Itzak stared while trying not to stare while I introduced them. I could tell from his smile that infatuation hovered nearby. LaDonna greeted him politely and sat down across the table from him. She glanced at Ari when I introduced him and nodded a hello, then turned to me.

"It's good to meet you finally," she said, "after all those e-mails."

"It is, for sure," I said. "I just wish I understood the math better." I glanced at Itzak. "LaDonna's a math expert who does contract work now and then for my outfit. Let's see, you do IT, don't you?"

"Well, a little more than just IT," Itzak said.

Ari looked up from the menu he'd been reading. "His degrees are in computer science, all three of them," Ari said. "Cal Tech, wasn't it, for the PhD?"

"Yeah," Itzak said. "I didn't want to live in the Boston sprawl."

"You were sure right about that," LaDonna said. "I went to MIT. Great school, terrible congestion all around it."

"No kidding!" Itzak smiled at her. "Did you major in math?"

This time LaDonna returned the smile, and they were off, geek to geek, exchanging details of their college careers. Ari looked pleased with himself and went back to reading the menu. It is a truth widely acknowledged, I reflected, that a man who's decided to marry tends to shove his old friends in the same direction. He also had to persuade me, of course, a much harder job.

During dinner LaDonna and Itzak both tried to be polite. They would float a general conversation that Ari and I could join, but sooner or later some tangent would lead them off into Mathland. I began to realize, while the waiter was clearing the main course plates, that LaDonna had an ulterior motive. I rummaged in my memory and remembered that yes, I had indeed told her about the incredible security system that Ari's friend had designed and helped him install. Combined with the advanced degrees in computer science, his gadget lore made his a brain worth picking.

With the dessert their conversation did claim my attention, mostly because LaDonna sounded so sly.

"What do you think of the controversy over fractal geometry?" she said. "Is it anything more than pretty pictures on the computer screen?"

"Of course," Itzak said. "We haven't found its root applications yet, that's all." He smiled his charming grin. "Unless of course it determines the structure of the multiverse. Assuming there is a multiverse."

Judging by her SPP, I thought LaDonna was going to levitate out of her chair in beatific joy. Instead, she turned to her shoulder bag and took out an iPad. She opened the bright red cover to reveal a matching skin.

"Oh, I think that the multiverse could be a valid concept," she said. "Let me show you why."

They shoved plates out of the way and leaned across the

table with the iPad between them. I craned my neck to look at the screen and saw upside-down chunks of math. Their conversation failed to enlighten me. I returned my attention to Ari, who looked more pleased with himself than ever.

"What's Calabi-Yau?" I said.

Ari considered. "A baseball team?"

"Somehow I don't think so."

We shared a grin. He caught my hand under the table and squeezed it. Later, once we'd dropped LaDonna off at her hotel, and Itzak had gone on his way home, we agreed that the dinner had succeeded at something we'd never even planned.

Apparently it wasn't my week for plans. The gate expedition to the deviant world deviated, all right, from the nice, safe experience I'd had in mind. On Saturday morning we picked LaDonna up at the hotel. She was wearing a sleek pair of designer jeans, a substantial red cotton shirt, a jean jacket, and athleisure shoes. I'd dressed similarly, in trouser jeans, a v-necked top in gray with a blue floral placed design, and my burgundy leather jacket. Ari managed to drive reasonably safely, and we got to Aunt Eileen's just before noon.

The house smelled like vegetable soup and cheese biscuits. As I'd suspected, Aunt Eileen insisted we all come have lunch once we finished our look at Interchange.

"There's salad, too, of course." Aunt Eileen gave me a significant look. "For those who might want it."

"Thanks," I said. "And dessert, I bet."

"A chocolate mousse." Aunt Eileen grinned at me. "Now don't stay too long over there with all that nasty radiation."

I led the way down the hall to the ground floor storage room, the one housing the more reliable gate. Michael was waiting for us at the door.

"Where's Sophie?" I said.

"Hiding upstairs," he said. "She's hella freaked, like she thinks José's gonna come take her back or something. I don't get it."

"I can see why she's afraid of Interchange," I said. "And the lycanthropy isn't helping her mood any."

"True." Michael said the word exactly as Ari would have said it. "She's started running a fever. Aunt Eileen said that Pat did, too."

"Yeah, he did, right before the change manifested." More evidence, I surmised, that a virus causes lycanthropy. "Don't rag on her about being afraid, okay? She had a pretty nasty life over there."

"You're totally right about that. Don't worry, I won't." Michael turned and opened the door. "Come on in."

He'd thoughtfully taken the steel safety gate off the window that led to Interchange so we could get back again after our visit. I had a moment's worry that maybe LaDonna's lack of psychic talents would keep her from going through, but when Michael opened the gate, she saw the same view through the window as the rest of us did: the sunny garden edged by the giant mutant morning glories.

"Ohmigawd," she said—several times—in a quiet little voice. "It's real."

"We can climb over if you want to, like, stand on another world." Michael sounded as proud as if he owned the place. "Me and Ari had better go first, though."

Ari had brought his sports bag with him. He unpacked two pieces of a rifle, the red-and-silver number that looked like a toy but was genuinely lethal. While he put it together and added the bullets, Michael rummaged in the bag and brought out a two-pound pack of coffee beans.

"I asked Ari to bring this," he told me, "for the old guy who owns the place."

He climbed through the window, and Ari followed. I helped LaDonna haul herself up to sit on the sill. She hesitated, murmured "ohmigawd" one more time, then swung her legs over and dropped lightly to the ground. I stayed inside. Interchange gave me the creeps.

Maybe I merely had a rational fear of the high level of radiation soaking the place. Maybe. All I knew was that my alarms went off like crazy at the thought of going there— but not only because I sensed danger at that particular time. I never wanted to go there, never ever not.

I leaned on the windowsill and looked out. Under the murky yellow sky the giant morning glories nodded in a light wind. The warty misshapen tomatoes hung thick on their vines. Some were red, but most, a blotchy yellow and brown. From a distance I heard a shrill, high whistle. A pair of big brown dogs dashed through the garden rows toward the house. Well, one ran. The other limped along on three legs. Where the fourth should have been he had a bulge the size of a ping-pong ball.

The elderly man who owned the place followed the dogs. He had a friendly wave for Michael and a nod of recognition for Ari. When Michael handed over the coffee, the old guy grinned his toothless smile and thanked him in a burst of Spanish. He winked at LaDonna, who smiled in return.

During all of this Ari had been keeping watch on the yard, rifle at the ready. Now and then he turned his head in a wide sweep, scanning. I had no idea what kind of trouble he expected to see, but the alarms continued ringing in my head.

"Ari," I called out. "Get everyone back inside."

"Right!" he said. "Mike, help LaDonna through."

Michael laced his fingers together and held his linked hands out at her knee level. She stepped on them with one foot, then pushed with the other to get up to the window like a lady mounting a horse with the help of a groom. I caught her around the waist and steadied her as she slid through into the gate room. Michael followed her inside.

As Ari paused for one last look around, I heard a pounding mechanical rumble overhead. The old guy yelled to the dogs and ran for a nearby shed with the healthy dog rushing after. The three-legged dog scrambled along as fast as he could. Neither barked.

"Ari!" I yelled.

"Coming!" He kept staring up at the sky. "What—a biplane? A sodding biplane, and it's covered with police insignia."

For a moment I had trouble breathing. Ari tossed Michael the rifle through the window and hauled himself up to the sill. Overhead the noise of the propeller grew louder and louder. A burst of machine gun fire rattled. Bullets hit the ground. Plumes of dirt like the tracks of some invisible animal marched toward the three-legged dog. It yelped once, then pitched to the ground, dead and bleeding.

Ari swore in Hebrew, then swung his legs through and dropped safely to the floor. My lungs got back to work as the black-and-white biplane roared overhead and flew onward, away from the garden.

"Ah, shit!" Michael said. "The old guy raised that dog from a puppy."

"Very sad," I said, "but get us out of here!"

"You bet." Michael handed Ari the rifle and swung around to stare at the window.

The piece of old sheet shimmered and turned into Aunt Eileen's crisp white shade. The view outside changed into Uncle Jim's flower beds and lawn. The wallpaper inside bloomed with faded bunches of violets. We were back. La-Donna let out her breath in a sharp sigh.

"Damn!" she said. "Didn't even know I was holding it."

"Yeah," I said. "It got me that way, too."

"That poor dog!" she went on. "I take it that we don't trust the cops on that world."

"No, we don't." Ari knelt down and began to unload the bullets from the rifle. "Cops is a good name for them. I'd never call them officers of the law."

"The law of the jungle, maybe," I said. "Which the place kind of resembles, now that I think about it. It's too bad we don't have a more pleasant kind of world to show you."

"I'm working on that," Michael said. "The map's coming along."

As we left the room, Michael let the others go on ahead but signaled me to hang back. We walked slowly enough to talk in relative privacy.

"That whacked gate upstairs, y'know?" Michael said. "It grew again. It's hit the third floor."

"That's scary," I said. "Do you think it could spread into the rest of the house?"

"I don't know. What if it like swallowed the whole house and took it somewhere? Epic fail!"

"Crud! That's a nasty thought."

"You bet. Seriously. Jeez, I wish I could talk to Dad.

Even if he's still in jail, I'm his son. Do you think they'd let me see him without, like, arresting me?"

"I don't know. Although—" I was remembering a remark of Spare14's. "It depends on which world Moorwood Prison's in. In some places it's not a crime to be a world-walker per se, just to use the talent for criminal purposes."

"It can't be against the law to want to see your dad."

"You wouldn't think so, yeah. Look, I have a new resource person. Let me talk to him and get back to you."

"Okay. When?"

"I don't know. It depends on whether he's in his office. He warned me he might be gone for a while."

Michael groaned and rolled his eyes.

"Tell me something. That dog. Why did the cops shoot it?"

"That's one of their jobs, getting rid of deformed animals so they don't breed. They do the same thing to people sometimes, but only when the people are real bad off, no arms, can't talk, super gross stuff like that."

My stomach clenched hard. If I had eaten recently I would have vomited.

"They call it taking out the trash," Michael continued. "Pretty shitty, huh?"

"Very," I said. "What's that phrase? Epic fail. Yeah—of their humanity."

After the meal we drove LaDonna around to a few of the sights. Like everyone who came to San Francisco, she wanted to see the Golden Gate Bridge and the Victorian houses. I offered to take her out to dinner, too, but she admitted that she was meeting Itzak when he got off work.

"Cool," I said. "Let me guess. You're trying to recruit him."

"The thought had occurred." LaDonna flashed me a wicked smile. "Fred's retiring."

"Who?" Ari said.

"The guy who used to do stuff to stuff," I said, "like that modified camcorder."

"Ah." Ari gave me a sour look. "I suppose one could define that as doing stuff to stuff."

"Well, I don't know what else to call it."

"Device engineering, perhaps?"

"Oh, okay, if you want to be stuffy about it."

Ari did not get the pun. I returned my attention to La-Donna. "Did you want to come over to our flat tomorrow? Ari and Itzak will be working on the security system. You can see if he's qualified to be the new Fred."

"Itzak already mentioned that, yeah. I'd like to. Thanks."

We dropped LaDonna off at her hotel so she could change for dinner, then drove home. I tried to settle down with my research materials, but I felt oddly restless. I kept getting up to prowl around the flat and look out each and every window. I thought maybe I was expecting another vision, but none materialized. I wondered if my brief sight of Interchange had disturbed me more deeply than I'd realized at the time.

While I wandered around, Ari was trying to work at the kitchen table. Finally, he gave it up and shut down his laptop.

"Do you want to go out to dinner?" he said.

"We might as well," I said. "I'm sorry. I know I'm being annoying, but I just can't seem to sit still."

I changed into my black satin-backed crepe dinner suit and a pale gray silk shirt. We decided on the Japanese place up on Noriega, where we both liked the food. Or at least, I liked it enough to be able to get some of it down. I was beginning to realize that if he was hungry, Ari would eat anything put in front of him. How else could he eat his own cooking? As usual, Ari insisted we take a table where he could keep his back to the wall and get a clear view of the front door.

I was crunching along on a tempura shrimp when I felt someone watching me. The sensation had not quite reached the level of triggering a SAWM or ASTA, but it registered an interest stronger than idle curiosity. I dropped my napkin on purpose and used picking it up as an excuse to glance around me. None of the other diners were looking my way. I had a few more bites of food, then felt the sensation again. As casually as I could, I turned in my chair, pretended to stretch my back, and looked behind me.

In the far rear corner of the restaurant a blue-violet figure stood beside an empty table. Someone female—I could pick that much up psychically—stood very still and watched me. Although I couldn't be sure, I thought she had black rosettes tattooed on her neck and bare shoulders. The image flickered once, then disappeared. The sensation of being watched vanished with her. I turned back to a normal position and realized that Ari was watching me.

"What were you seeing?" Ari said.

I leaned forward and spoke softly. "Another blue-violet apparition like the one Saturday. I still can't figure out who or what she is, though."

"Oh, splendid! Perhaps you might tell me when you do."

I wrinkled my nose at the sarcasm and picked up my chopsticks.

I saw, felt, or heard nothing untoward for the rest of our meal. When we got home, I changed into jeans and a T-shirt, then logged onto the Agency site—no new mail. I filed a quick report on what I'd seen in the restaurant, then logged off. Ari took his laptop and a selection of keyboards into the kitchen.

Since there was nothing on TV that I wanted to watch, I returned to my computer. I brought up the file with the Hisperic text I'd found in Dad's old desk. Thanks to Ari's notes on the Hebrew words and Dad's notes on the Old Irish, I'd pieced together entire sentences here and there. The most significant so far was "Each angel has a proper color to its wings that signifies the gate before which it stands." I was willing to bet that those colors also coordinated with the set of boxes in the wall safe.

All through the document I found odd strings of vowels that appeared completely random. Dad had annotated them as "scribal errors? some sort of stupid nonsense." My research into Chaos magic, however, tipped me off to the truth. They were chants, meant to be spoken aloud in a particular way, "intoned," to use the churchman's word, or "vibrated," to use the magician's.

As I looked over the pages containing the vowel strings, I noticed one where Dad had added a note stating that the particular angel's wings were blue-violet, the color of the sphere thrown by our would-be burglar and of two of the apparitions I'd seen. I logged off, shut down the computer, and went into the kitchen.

"Ari?" I said. "I'm going to go into the bedroom and try an experiment."

He answered in Arabic. I took this as a sign that he was working.

In the bedroom I turned on the nightstand light, then shut the heavy curtains over the windows to keep the sound inside. I stood at the foot of the bed and laid my printout down on the paisley bedspread where I could read it. The page defined its chant as "aaaa ooo ee aaaa iii." I spoke in an ordinary voice and tried out various systems of assigning sounds to those letters. The Latinate version produced a slight sense of excitement, so I stuck with that.

I adjusted my stance to let my lungs expand as freely as possible, took a deep breath, and began vibrating each sound the indicated number of times, one letter per time. The first run through gave me a complex sensation: close to sexual arousal, yet my mind seemed clear, not muddled with lust. Qi was flowing, I figured, and tried again. The sensations increased to the point where I was panting on the edge of a mental climax.

I summoned up a memory of the color blue-violet from my work with crayons and ran the chant again. The chant ended in a yelp as the floor fell away from under my feet.

I dropped, then flew, swooping through the air. I looked down and saw below me a nighttime marketplace. The plaza, easily as large as a football field, glowed with tiny lights like strings of white Christmas bulbs. Spindly wood buildings, most three or four narrow stories tall, clustered at the edges of the open space. Moving among wooden booths and tables were people—not humans, I realized, but a species shaped much like us, big-hipped bipedal women.

Bright cloth wrapped their hips but left their arms and breasts bare. Each woman had three pairs of small breasts marching down her chest. They wore their blonde hair so short it looked like fur. It was fur, I realized, mostly blonde but dotted with black spots. In the dim light the scene looked slightly out of focus, but they seemed to have dark rosettes tattooed on their shoulders and necks. I was finally getting a clear look at my apparitions. Leopardlike, all right, but I couldn't tell if they were were-leopards or some species derived from the big cats.

I had no real control over the vision. I'd swoop down, then suddenly rise straight up and twist in a wind that blew only on the visionary plane. When I flew high, I looked around to get a fix on the landscape. The marketplace stood in the middle of a city lit randomly by patches of white lights. At one edge of the city I saw dark water, a bay, ocean inlets. At the other rose an oddly familiar pair of hills. Twin Peaks! I recognized their shapes at last and oriented myself. I was seeing a version of San Francisco.

At one point I sank toward the ground at the edge of the plaza. Just when I thought I was going to touch down, my fall stopped itself, and I hovered some eight feet in the air. A leopard woman saw me. She stood taller than the rest, and around her spotted neck hung a weight of silver chains. Her small, curled ears sat much higher up on her head than ours do. She looked up and opened her mouth in a snarl. I saw her white cat fangs clearly despite the dim light.

"You! Here?"

Her words formed in my mind. She sounded as surprised as I felt. The vision caught me again and spun me around, swept me up and sent me reeling into the sky. I was considering chanting to see if I could bring it under control when an alarming truth occurred to me.

"Crud! I don't know how to get back."

That break in concentration saved me. I felt myself falling from the interior height and hit the bed that I'd last seen in front of my body. For a moment I stuck, half on and half off the mattress, then slid to the floor onto my knees with my face pressed against the bedspread, an inelegant end to the trance.

I looked up to see a horrified Ari staring at me from the doorway.

"Are you ill?" he said. "Why were you moaning?"

"Was I moaning?" I scrambled to my feet.

"I heard this ah ah oh oh sound. I don't know what else to call it."

"Chanting. Vision-inducing chanting."

My knees threatened to give way. I sat down on the end of the bed. Ari walked over to stand in front of me.

"Are you sure you don't need to see a doctor?" he said.

"Yes. I'm fine."

"You're drenched in sweat."

"That's from Qi, not a fever." I realized that my shirt was sticking to my body. My damp hair hung in tendrils around my face. "I shouldn't have tried that experiment. Should have done more research first."

Ari sat down next to me on the end of the bed. The lamplight gleamed on his dark hair and turned his eyes into pools of shadow. I could feel his body warmth and smell his clean flesh, but I wondered if I wanted to kiss him or bite him. He would taste good, I figured, salty warm raw meat. Ape: Nature's perfect food.

"Why are you looking at me that way?" Ari raised a suspicious eyebrow and moved over a couple of feet. "You're drooling."

I wiped my mouth on my sleeve and reminded myself that you should never eat the one you love. I put my hands on my breasts to check: yes, only two. Inadvertently, I'd made a psychic link with the species I'd glimpsed. Perhaps the woman who'd spoken to me had forged it. Whatever else those ladies were, they were carnivores to the max. When I looked at Ari, I fixated on the pulse throbbing in the big vein in his throat.

"Nola," Ari said, "answer me!"

I wrenched my gaze away and held up one hand for silence. I took a deep breath and began counting backward from a hundred. The link remained strong. Ari moved farther away to the corner of the bed. I could feel that he was ready to spring to his feet. I visualized a flaming torch and saw it circling my body. The link flared and died. I gasped for breath, then steadied.

"Are you back?" Ari said.

"Yeah."

I'd spoken the truth—almost. I'd destroyed the direct link. Yet a trait of their species resonated with an archetype buried deep in my own psyche and brought it to the surface. I found myself thinking of the Bacchantes. The ancient Greek chant echoed in my mind: IAO, ee ah oh.

"The way you were looking at me—" Ari said.

"Yeah, I know. Not nice. I'm really sorry."

"You were in full trance?"

"Till I fell to my knees. And then I got stuck in a lesser trance. Kind of a hyper phase out."

"Are you going to drift off again?"

"I hope not. I feel light-headed and kind of weird, like my body's a helium balloon." I raised my arms over my head, then let them fall back to my sides. For a moment I lost track of my hands. The skin on my back felt icy cold.

"Is there anything I can do to help?" Ari said.

"Well, there's sex."

He stared. Perhaps I'd been a bit abrupt.

"I feel like I'm not really back in my body yet," I said. "If you made love to me, it would help."

He continued to stare.

"Well, you asked," I said with a snarl. "Is this any worse than you wanting sex to get back to sleep?"

"No. Sorry. It just seemed like rather an abrupt change of subject."

He smiled. I laughed, but my face seemed to belong to someone else.

"We could do something special," I went on. "I don't suppose you have any classified information I need to wheedle out of you."

Ari shrugged and stood up. "I could invent some," he said. "It's almost dawn in Damascus, anyway. I'll go shut the laptop down."

"Okay." I found myself wondering how it would feel to sink my nails into his shoulders. I could lick the blood as it flowed. "Uh, darling, while you're at it, why don't you get those handcuffs?"

His smile deepened to a grin. "Very well," he said. "You liked that, did you?"

"Yeah, but that's not the point. It's for your own good. Why take a chance on my self-control? Once we get started, I might not have any."

"Oh? Are you telling me that making love to you to-night could be dangerous?"

"Yeah, I am. So if you don't want to—"

"Quite the opposite, actually." His Qi level spiked along with his grin. "I'll just go get the handcuffs."

I should have known.

While I changed into the black thigh-high stockings, I concentrated on the details of my current reality: the solid wood floor under my feet, the cool air on my body as I stripped off my sweaty clothes, the mesh of the stockings and the pinch of the garters on my skin, the pool of lamp-light in our familiar room. I'd made a good start on regaining body consciousness by the time Ari came in.

He tossed the pair of steel cuffs onto my pillow, then caught me by the shoulders and kissed me. At the touch of his mouth on mine, the leopard woman archetype sank farther into the depths of my mind. He picked me up and carried me to the bed, then sat down next to me and kissed me again. I felt my body respond—my body, not someone else's. My humanity came back stronger with every kiss and caress he gave me.

The vision, the voices, the Chaos attacks—everything disappeared as my world shrank down to Ari's lovemaking. If I was his sleeping pill, I realized that night, he was my drug of choice.

CHAPTER 7

B Y MORNING THE DRUG HAD worn off, but the city of the leopard women had faded from an emotional threat to a detailed memory. I lay in bed and thought about the woman who'd spoken to me. I wondered about the weight of her jewelry. I'd seen no one else in the marketplace wearing those silver chains, so possibly they marked some kind of status in her society. At the least they probably meant she was wealthy. Be that as it may, she'd made it clear that she disliked me. The feeling had become mutual.

Ari insisted on feeding me, though I drew the line at his favorite breakfast: a peanut butter and chopped pickle sandwich. Instead, he set a plate in front of me with one overcooked fried egg and a couple of pieces of cold, greasy, British toast. When he spread jam on them, I was too depressed to argue.

"It would be Sunday," I said. "I won't hear from anyone in the Agency till tomorrow. About the apparitions, I mean."

"I'd prefer it if you didn't do any more research on your own." Ari rubbed the side of his neck. "I'll admit that being bitten was a new sensation, but there are limits."

"Oh, come on! I didn't even break the skin."

"This time. That's what I mean about limits."

I smiled and forced myself to start eating the egg.

While we were cleaning up after breakfast, my sister Kathleen called. Our mutual friend, Mira Rosen, had finally delivered her baby the night before.

"It's a boy, just like she thought," Kathleen said. "Ten pounds, two ounces."

"Oh, God!" I said. "No wonder she got so big!"

Ari looked at me with a raised eyebrow. When I clicked off, I relayed the news and explained my remark.

"I remember her from that party," Ari said. "The therapist."

"That's right, yeah. You've got a good memory for people."

"It's part of my job." Ari paused to shut the dishwasher door. "Do you want children someday?"

"No."

"Why not?"

"Because our jobs are too dangerous. Some philosopher guy said that having children means giving hostages to Fortune. If we had kids, they could end up being just plain hostages. I'd be worried sick about them all the time."

"True." Ari pounced. "But you're thinking in terms of having my children. If *we* had kids, you said. You're beginning to come round."

I snarled; he grinned.

"Oh, yeah?" I said. "Why do you think I'm going to break down and agree to marry you?"

"Because you're too intelligent not to. Obviously, I'm the perfect man for you. You must see that. So why not marry me?"

"I never knew that arrogance was part of perfection."

"I didn't say I was perfect. I said I was the perfect man for you. There's rather a difference."

"Yeah? Well, tell me, Mr. Perfection, do you want kids?"

"No, for the same reason you don't. See? We even agree on that."

I stomped into the living room and sat down at my computer desk. I had my Gnostic research to distract me from both the leopard women and Ari's obsession with marriage, but Ari followed me.

"I'm going to go downstairs and do my exercises," he said. "Are you sure you won't—"

"Very sure."

"We've got some rope in the trunk of the car. Did you jump rope when you were a girl? You might find it enjoyable—"

"No, nyet, nein."

Ari sighed and set exasperated hands on his hips.

"My beloved darling," I said, "I'm sick and tired of you leaning on me like this. I'm an adult. I don't have to go back to gym class. Please just drop it."

"Well, for the love of God, I've got to do something for you." He spoke quietly, but the words ached with frustration. "I can't get at those spotted bitches or that sodding priest, either, the one who keeps bothering you."

I sat there stunned. Ari turned and started to walk away.

"Wait!" I got up and hurried after him. "I'm sorry. I misread that totally. I thought it was just—well—controlling behavior."

He considered this with a complete lack of expression. When I put my hands flat on his chest, he forced out a twisted smile.

"Do you know what's wrong with you?" he said. "You don't know how to trust someone."

"Say what? I'm trusting you with my life, aren't I?"

"Are you? Physically, yes. You know perfectly well that if someone tried to harm you, I'd stop them or die trying. That's not what I mean."

"Let me guess. I bet this is leading up to, if I really trusted you, I'd marry you and give you my whole life."

"Exactly." His smile turned genuine. "You do see it, then."

"Oh, go do your damned push-ups!"

He muttered a laugh and left the room. I snarled at his retreating back.

Around noon LaDonna and Itzak appeared at our front door, a perfect distraction. Itzak carried in a couple of steel tackle boxes containing, he said, not fishing gear but tools, materials, and diagnostic devices. For hours that afternoon the three of them did various elaborate and arcane things to and with electronics, while I sat in an armchair in the living room and read books the old-fashioned way: by sunlight. One project I did understand. Itzak put a lock on the gun drawer in the file cabinet at the head of the stairs. He installed a digital gadget keyed to Ari's fingerprints.

"No one else can grab the gun and turn it on Ari, huh?" I said. "Not unless they had a blowtorch or chisel or some such thing."

"Before they got it open that way," Itzak said with a sunny smile, "Ari would have killed them. I could put your print on the pad, too. It'll take multiple IDs."

"No, thanks. I have my own weapons access points."

"I'm so glad you and Ari found each other. You'd both be hell for anyone else."

I had to laugh at that, mostly because it was true.

"Ari's insisting on putting detectors on the roof," Itzak continued. "Pray for us."

He squared his shoulders like a soldier going to battle and stalked off toward the back of the flat. I heard him speak to LaDonna as he passed her in the hall. She strode into the living room and flopped down on the couch.

"I am not going up on the roof with those two idiots," she announced.

"You strike me as a wise and sensible person." I closed my book. "I've been meaning to ask you something, anyway. Do you know if Seymour ever looked at the vision I sent him? I'm kind of wondering what he made of it."

"He's on vacation as far as I know."

"Vacation? Since when do we get vacations?"

"When you work in the home office, you do. Maybe you should transfer over."

"DC's not my kind of town." I shuddered at the very thought. "Do you know when Seymour's coming back?"

"Soon, I think. But you could try his assistant. I-C's his handle. He's been trying to find an astrophysicist we can trust to look over your data."

"Astrophysicist?"

"Look, I'm no physicist, just a math head. I do understand parallel world theoretics, but that's because it's been my hobby since high school. I won my first science fair with a project on the subject." She smiled at the memory. "Anyway, thanks to your brother, it's part of my job now. But that's my limit. Mr. Spock the all-knowing scientist only exists on TV."

"That's true. I guess you don't have a tricorder."

She laughed, and I grinned.

"I did read over your report on that vision," LaDonna went on. "Seriously horrible, but all I can say is the multicolored spray must have been some kind of radiation from beyond the Earth's atmosphere. And you knew that already, I bet."

"Yeah, even I could figure that much out."

I was going to continue our discussion, but from overhead came footsteps and the sound of hammering. We both looked up as if we could see through the ceiling. The thumping continued, punctuated now and then by muffled voices.

"I'm not having any premonitions of impending deaths." I spoke quite loudly.

"Good." LaDonna spoke the same way. "I was about to ask."

When my landline phone rang, I answered it. Mr. Singh, the realtor, said hello.

"Let me guess," I said, bellowing. "The neighbors want to know what Ari's doing on the roof."

"That is precisely it," Mr. Singh bellowed in return. "They are worried because he appears to be wearing a firearm on his chest."

"That's called a shoulder holster. He's not going to shoot anything. He's just fixing our security system."

"Ah." Mr. Singh paused and sighed. "Very well. I shall tell them."

We hung up. Eventually the noises stopped, and the members of my private Geek Patrol returned to the living room. Itzak sat next to LaDonna on the couch, and Ari took the other armchair.

"All right," Itzak said. "Someone's directing an odd kind of energy at these flats. That much I know."

"You don't have any idea what it is?" I said.

"No, but it doesn't much matter. I've identified the multiple frequencies they're using, so I can block them, and that'll work for now. I've set it up in the system records as Q—Ari's suggestion, Q for query, because we don't know what it is. LaDonna told me earlier that your employer's research arm will take the problem from there. The real question is who's sending it and why, but I've been told I shouldn't ask that."

"That's right." I softened the words with a smile. "Don't ask it. Forget you ever knew about it, even."

"It's probably Ari's fault, whatever it is."

"Always," Ari said. "My enemies are everywhere."

We all laughed, even Ari.

"How long will you be staying in town?" I asked La-Donna.

"I have to go back tomorrow," she said. "Tzaki took the day off, and he's driving me to the airport. He'll see me off."

"Reluctantly," Itzak said. "But I've been promised that I'll get e-mail."

"About Fred's old job, of course," LaDonna said.

They shared a smile. The smile and the way she'd used his nickname gave LaDonna away. She had a little more than recruitment on her mind, but then, so did Itzak. How often does one hypergeek find another, after all, that magic someone who can actually understand what they're talking about? Race and religion present big problems for normal people, but hypergeeks know one another when they meet, and that kind of love conquers—well, not all, but an awful lot.

As they were leaving, I had a chance at a private word with LaDonna while Ari and Itzak were teasing each other about some incident in their shared past.

"Thanks for the help," I said, "and e-mail me if I-C tells you anything interesting."

"I will for sure. That energy beam's pure Qi, not that I could tell Tzaki that."

"Not yet, anyway."

We giggled.

Ari and I spent a quiet Sunday evening, or at least, I did. He put in a couple of hours of push-ups and other forms of self-torture. We went to bed early, and a good thing, too. On

Monday morning, my cell phone chimed and woke me at 6:15, an hour that signaled bad news. I grabbed the phone from the nightstand and mumbled a hello.

"Nola? Thank God I reached you."

The panic in Al Wong's familiar voice brought my mind online fast.

"Al? What's happened?"

"Sean's disappeared and Michael with him. Eileen just phoned me to let me know they never came back last night. She's damn near hysterical. So's Sophie. Al paused. I could hear him sucking in a deep breath. "So am I."

I could guess. "They went off looking for Dad," I said. "Didn't they?"

"That's what the note said."

"What note? Look, can you start at the beginning? Like, please?"

"Okay." Al paused again, and when he resumed, his voice sounded steadier. "Yesterday afternoon we went over to Eileen's to have lunch with your mother. I know you and she don't get along, but Sean does love her. So I figure I can put up with her now and then."

"You're a brave man."

"Thanks. When Deirdre left, Michael and Sean went upstairs to get some CDs Sean was going to borrow. I didn't think anything of it, but they must have planned this then. We went back to our place, but a couple of hours later, about six o'clock, I guess it was, Sean realized he'd left his wallet at Eileen's, because he'd taken it out to lend Michael twenty bucks." Al paused for another deep breath. "'*Oh, shit,*' Sean says, and he sounded so damned innocent that I should have known he was lying. '*I must have left it in Mike's room. I'll just drive over and get it.*'"

"Without a driver's license?" I said. "Doesn't he keep that in his wallet?"

"That occurred to me, yeah, but way too late. So he went over and never came back. I called over there around nine in the evening. Eileen was shocked. They'd left at seven, told her that they were driving back to our place, Sean's and mine, I mean."

"Wait! Eileen didn't have any kind of premonition—"

"No advance warning, but when I called, she felt that something really bad had happened."

"A danger alert? That kind of thing?"

"Worse than that."

"Crud."

"Yeah, exactly." Al paused again to steady his voice. "So first we did the ugly routine of calling the police, the hospitals, that kind of stuff to see if they'd been in an accident. We couldn't find anything. Finally, she searched the house and found the note tacked up to the door of the first-floor storage room. I wanted to call you right then, but it was almost midnight, and so I figured we'd better wait."

"Oh, yeah? I wish you'd called me right then. It's been hours now." I stopped myself from delivering an angry lecture about time stream scars and how fast they fade. Al was stressed enough without me barking at him. "Anyway, this note, what did it say? Can you tell me?"

"I've practically got it memorized. *Dear folks, sorry. We didn't tell you because we didn't want to argue about it.*"

"The little swine!" I said.

"Yeah," Al said, "though swine is too nice a word. Anyway, they went on to say that you'd know what this all meant. They were going back to some place called Interchange because they'd been there a couple of times and found the gate that leads to your father's location. They want to scout it out, according to the note."

"Crud." It took me a moment to go on. "Yeah, I do know what it means."

"It's dangerous, isn't it?"

"Very dangerous. When I get my hands on that little brat Michael, I—" I stopped because he was too big to spank, and there's no use in making empty threats. "Well, I'll chew him out but good."

Al groaned for a comment. By this time Ari had woken up. He was watching me narrow-eyed. I mouthed, "I'll explain in a minute," in his general direction.

"Al?" I said. "Still there?"

"Oh, yeah," Al said. "Is there anything you can do to get them back?"

"No, not at the moment." At that point I woke up enough

to remember that I was talking on my cell phone—an unwise move. My end of the conversation was secure, but his wasn't. "Look, I'll call you right back. I have to switch phones. This one's not as secure as the landline. You guys have a landline, too, right?"

"Yeah. For my elderly relatives."

"Give me the number, and I'll call you back on that in a couple of minutes."

I took the chance to duck into the bathroom as well as put on my jeans and a pale gray Western-cut shirt before I called Al back. He answered on the first ring.

"Okay, look," I said. "I'm not sure where they've gone and how they got there, but it wouldn't matter if I did. I can't use those gates. I can't follow them. Al, do you understand the concept here? Like, they're on another world than ours, something called a deviant world level?"

"Sean told about all that a couple of days ago." Al's voice hovered on the edge of tears. "I thought he was kidding. Making up an elaborate story, you know? With Michael like maybe they did when they were kids."

"Unfortunately, he was telling you the cold truth."

An awake and clothed Ari walked into the living room. "I'll go start the coffee," he said. "I don't know what this is all about, but I can tell we'll need coffee."

For about ten minutes more I talked to Al. I did eventually manage to get him to understand about deviant worlds, gates, Michael's abilities, and the reckless egos of teen boys with wild talents. During our talk, Al alternated between periods of calm and fits of anger-laced anxiety. He told me, just before we hung up, that he was going in to work anyway, for the distraction.

Ari had just handed me a mug of coffee when Aunt Eileen called, and I held the same conversation all over again. It ended the same way, too, with me admitting that there was nothing I could do at the moment.

"There's no use in even trying to locate them psychically," I finished up. "You remember, don't you, the first time my miserable jerk of a brother went to Interchange?"

"Yes, I'm afraid I do."

"I tried to sense him and never could."

"Well, maybe I'll dream something useful. I'll take a nap this afternoon. I have to tell your mother, and I'll need a nap after that."

Aunt Eileen hung up with a resigned sigh bordering on martyrdom. I did the same.

"I'll kill him," I said to Ari. "I will strangle him with my own two hands."

"Michael or Sean?" Ari said.

"Whichever one I can grab first." I had a swallow of coffee, which had turned cold. "You get to shoot the other one."

"It's a bargain. Seriously, though, let's hope they can get back again."

"Yeah." The anger ebbed, and I felt like crying. I suppressed the urge. "Let's hope. Damn it, I should have known something was wrong." I paused to think about what I'd just said. "This is weird. When they went through the gate, I should have felt an overlap. I didn't get any warning at all. Neither did Eileen."

"Can Sean or Michael block that kind of thing?"

"I don't know. That's a good guess, though." I leaked a few angry tears. "The little bastards!"

"The only thing I can think of to do," Ari said, "is to bring Spare14 into this. He has access to other world-walkers, and if Michael's broken a law or a regulation, maybe I can gain authorization to go after him."

"You're brilliant. It's Monday, so maybe he'll be in his office."

When I called, that particular hope vaporized. Spare14 had left an automatic message on his telephone system. He was out of the office "for a few days," he said, and would try to get back to everyone later in the week. I left a dispirited message and hung up.

"He's probably gone to Interchange to meet Javert," I said.

"Most likely," Ari said. "I'm going to make you some breakfast, and you're going to eat it."

"No pickles!"

"There's some of those frozen waffles left."

I made a small retching noise. He got the point and allowed me to have a couple of apples instead. I returned to the living room to avoid watching him eat the toaster waffles. He always dumped canned tuna on them. Right out of the can.

I spent a miserable day alternating between fits of worrying and doing research—the safe kind, that is, in books. Despite what I'd told Aunt Eileen, I couldn't stop myself from running scans: LDRS, SM:Ps, SM:Ls, SAFs. Although I used every talent I could think of, I never picked up the slightest trace of Sean and Michael. All day, Ari kept moving from one window to another, all around the flat, to stare out and watch the street in front and the garage area in back. He was always armed.

Aunt Eileen called me late in the day. She'd given my mother the news.

"How did she take it?" I said.

"At first she tried to dismiss it. They're just playing a joke, she says. April Fool's, just late." Eileen snorted in disgust. "I'm afraid I got just a wee bit angry. She began to listen, then."

"Just began to, huh?"

"Well, you know how she is. It all elevatored, or whatever that word is they use for battles. Escalated, I mean. I ended up hanging up on her." Eileen paused to sigh. "Then I really did need a nap."

"Did you dream anything interesting?"

"Not really. Just one image of Sean wearing a necklace. I think it was a necklace. One of those modern things that are just smooth metal, like a narrow collar."

"That's odd."

"Very. By the way, I called poor Al, just to see how he was holding up. He left work early, they told me, and he's taking tomorrow off, a personal leave day. If the boys aren't back by tomorrow morning, I'll invite him over for lunch, and why don't you and Ari come, too? Maybe if we all concentrate, they'll hear us and come back."

Highly unlikely, I thought, but I kept the thought to myself. I had nothing better to offer.

"Sure," I said. "Around noon?"

"That will be fine, dear, yes. I'll see you then."

At sunset Ari brought out a pair of binoculars with night vision built in, or so he told me, and resumed his window trek. As the night darkened outside, I could see his reflection in the window glass—and that gave me an idea. Although the full chant-trance procedure had proved itself too dangerous to play around with, I had other lore to draw upon. All the research I'd done on magic over the years had just come in handy. I turned off my computer and got up.

"Ari," I said, "I'm going to try to get some more information on the leopard women."

"What? After what happened—"

"No, no, this is a safer method. I promise."

He growled but said nothing more.

I fetched a piece of white printer paper and my crayons. Once I'd found a blue-violet that more or less matched the color I'd seen on the orbs and the apparition, I drew a large square on the paper and filled it in. I took the paper with me into the bedroom. I opened the closet door to reveal the full-length mirror I'd installed on the back. To make sure it didn't move during the operation, I wedged it open with a shoe. I sat cross-legged on the bed and studied the square of color until I could see the blue-violet as a mental field.

Once again I chanted the proper syllables, but this time I looked into the mirror. My theory: seeing only a reflected image would break the direct connection between me and Miss Leopard-Thing, as I was thinking of her. Surprise—I was actually right. When images formed in the mirror, I felt none of the power that had troubled me so much the night before.

Unfortunately, the images had none of the power, either. They flickered and danced like shadows thrown by a fire. Still, by quieting my breathing and concentrating, I did manage to see in flashes, sometimes clear, sometimes jumbled. Later, I worked with my memory to put together the following like a quick-cut video:

Geographically the place looked the same as San Francisco, even though everything about the city, if you could call the strange sprawl a city, was different—lots of tall trees and tree houses. Rarely did I come across a building made of stone. The hills were heavily built up; the valleys left to natural grass and live oaks. The similarity of the vegetation confirmed that I was seeing a deviant world level, not some utterly different planet.

When I focused on Miss Leopard-Thing, her image appeared. I saw her climbing down a rope ladder from a tree house. In her mouth she carried a canister or stick that glowed with a pale white light—their equivalent of a flashlight, I assumed. Once she reached the ground, she took it in one hand and held it up high to light the way down for another leopard person, a male, obviously, because the only thing he wore was a loose sleeveless tunic that came to his waist. Whoever these people were, their guys had similar equipment to ours. He pretended to bite the back of her neck, very gently, and put his arms around her waist. She opened her mouth and seemed to be laughing, though I could hear nothing. When he let her go, I got a clearer look at him. He seemed familiar—maybe the guy I'd seen on our steps? It was hard to be sure.

Hand in hand they walked down a path between trees. They came to a wooden shed. He opened the door, she held up the light stick, and I nearly gagged. Inside, hanging from big metal hooks, were body parts—whole legs minus the feet, arms minus the hands, chunks of what appeared to be torsos. Since they'd been skinned, I could only guess at which species they belonged to, one with arms and legs, obviously, either apes or other leopard people. Huge racks of ribs must have come from gorillas. I saw a headless body that looked like a skinned chimp—short legs, long torso. Its arms and hands lay on a chopping block nearby.

I felt the urge to vomit so strongly that the sensing process broke down. I got up and walked around the room to shake off the effects. I also ran a Conscious Evasion Procedure by tearing the paper with the blue-violet square into little shreds. Returning to the living room, where Ari was watching basketball on TV, brought me a sense of vast relief at the normality of the scene.

"Are you all right?" Ari said. "You're quite pale."

"Yeah, just grossed out. I don't know why I was surprised that leopard people would be carnivores, but I got to see inside one of their meat lockers. Yuck." I sat down at my computer desk. "I'm going to organize my thoughts and send off a report. These procedures, they don't produce stable data. You've got to write it down before it fades."

Writing the report banished the last of my nausea. Once I'd finished, Ari asked me what I'd seen. I described the flashes of images and gave him more details about the species.

"She has three pairs of breasts?" was his first comment. "They must be rather small."

"Sometimes you're just a regular guy, aren't you?" I grinned at him. "Yeah, they weren't what I'd call big boobs. A pity, huh?"

"I can assure you that I wouldn't want to get anywhere near this female. Especially when I consider the effect she had on you."

"Wise, my darling, very wise. I sure wouldn't be interested in the guy, either, even with the look I got at his junk."

Ari opened his mouth to speak, then shut it firmly. From his SPP, I picked up a strong wave of curiosity.

"Hah!" I said. "You're dying to ask me how big he was, aren't you? Guys always wonder about size."

"Nothing of the sort!" Ari turned as scarlet as a sunset.

I decided to be merciful and changed the subject.

THE HIGH-PITCHED BEEP OF my landline answering machine woke us at eight Tuesday morning. I got up and found that Y's secretary had called and left code on my landline machine. Y was requesting a trance meeting at ten AM my time. Ari insisted I eat breakfast, and I managed to choke down two of his black and crunchy attempts at pancakes. By then it was only nine-thirty.

While I waited for my appointment with Y, I sat down on the couch and noticed, on the coffee table, the photo album that Aunt Eileen had put together for Ari and me. I was leafing through it, looking for snaps of Michael and Sean, when Ari wandered in, wiping his greasy hands on his jeans.

"Family pictures?" he said.

"Yeah," I said. "Aunt Eileen believes in them like a second Bible."

He sat down next to me on the couch, put one arm around my shoulders, and looked at the page I had open: a portrait of my smiling mother who was, at that time, very pregnant with Michael. Opposite were a couple of snaps of myself at ten with my father. Ari reached over and pointed at the photo of me and Dad standing in front of a tree in Golden Gate Park.

"You were not a fat child," he said.

"I look fat to me," I said. "Especially in those white shorts."

"That's ridiculous."

I found his scorn comforting. I studied the photo and had to admit that as little girls go, I wasn't as wide as I'd been remembering.

"The caption calls you Noodles," Ari said. "Your nickname, I assume."

"Yeah, it's from the Irish version of my name. They pronounce it Noola, but it's spelled N-u-a-l-a."

"I see what you mean about Irish spelling."

"It's fierce. I'm glad Mom Americanized my name."

"Yes, it's doubtless for the best." Ari pointed to the man in the photograph. "That must be one of your O'Brien uncles."

"No, that's my father. We all look alike, don't we? Very Irish."

Ari nodded and seemed to be about to say more when the landline phone rang—two rings, then nothing.

"There's my signal." I got up and went to my desk to fetch a notebook and pen. Ari watched me with a slight frown.

"How can you write if you're unconscious?" he said.

"I'm not really unconscious, that's how. Trance is different. My body automatically writes stuff down because it can see the notebook even if I can't."

Ari looked stricken, as he usually did when I admitted some truth about the way I operated.

"I'll just go into the bedroom," I said, "so I won't disturb you if you want to work."

The leopard women loomed large in the trance conversation, after Y and I had gone over the week's events. I wondered if their spectral appearances could be considered an attack or a spying mission to set up an attack.

"I've never even heard of leopard women before," Y told me.

"I was afraid of that," I said. "I've been wondering if Spare14 might be able to help. Would you object if I asked him?"

"Not at all." Y's image looked profoundly sour. "I suppose if we're going to be forced into liaison, we might as well begin getting used to it."

"Forced?"

"The higher-ups are extremely interested in his offer. That's all I can say at the moment. At some point we'll need to set up a face-to-face meeting."

I remembered Ari discussing command jealousies.

"Yeah, you will have to," I said. "His talents just aren't in the same league as yours. He'll have to talk with the exec board physically. There's no way that he could communicate in trance like you do."

Y smiled. He almost purred. He looked down at a notebook that materialized in his image's lap—his agenda for our meeting, I assumed. "One last thing. This business of chanting yourself into a full trance? Don't do that again without more research."

"Don't worry! I won't. What about the mirror procedure?"

"That does seem safer, but be very careful."

"I'm still not sure if the leopard women really exist, or if they're some kind of dream image."

"It could well be the latter. A great many strange beings live underwater in the river of consciousness. The Collective Data Stream flows from our deep, deep past, and upon it, in boats built of word and image, bob many a strange secret."

I felt my hand writing this bit of Y's philosophy down, not that I knew why.

"On the other hand," Y continued, "I'm remembering the report you filed about the attempted burglar. Didn't you say that he had black tattoos on his face?"

"Yeah, and so did the guy I saw."

I called up his memory image from the mirror work and extruded it so Y could see it, too. The leopard guy had spotted fur all around his male equipment, and black, tattoo-like blotches marked the pale, hairless skin of his stomach. Y studied the EI for a moment, then nodded.

"Definitely leopardine rosettes," he said. "Have you ever seen one of those hairless house cats? Some of them have patches of skin that are the colors their fur would be if they had fur. The calicos, in particular, are quite mottled."

"I hadn't realized that. The leopard women I saw in trance had rosettes on their necks and shoulders, too."

"Well, there we are. It's quite possible that those spots aren't tattoos at all, but natural markings, reminders of their evolutionary past."

I considered the memory image for a moment more, then replaced it with my memory of the burglar on our steps. Seeing the two images one after the other confirmed my feeling that the burglar had been the same guy, though a lot more modestly dressed. I sent both images back to my unconscious mind.

"The experience really scared me," I went on. "It made me wonder if I'm a Chaotic at heart or something."

"Of course you're a Chaotic. That's one reason you're so valuable to the Agency."

I felt my physical mouth drop open. My image mimicked it.

"Didn't you realize?" Y registered surprise. "It's something you share with your colleague, Jerry Jamieson, another true Chaotic. It's your very affinity with Chaos that allows you to spot it when it obtrudes into our world. Like the strings of a harp, you both vibrate when someone plucks the correct—" He hesitated. "Well, perhaps I should start over with that metaphor."

"Don't bother. I get it. But I've sworn to serve the Balance, and I will. I've dedicated myself to Harmony."

"Of course. I know that. Harmony is not a natural state, that balance point between Order and Chaos. We all must strive, each from where we begin, to reach the goal of true Harmony." He smiled briefly. "The Agency needs you, Nola, but you need the Agency as well."

With that we signed off. I collected my pen and notepad and returned to the living room. Ari was still studying the photo album. He shut it and tossed it onto the coffee table.

"All done?" he said.

"Yeah," I said. "Do you think I'm an essentially chaotic person?"

"Of course you are. It's part of your charm."

"Sweet, but seriously—"

"I meant it seriously. I suppose that I'd have to describe myself as standing on the Order side of the line. Maybe that's why we make a good pair. Opposites attract."

I tensed and waited for the M-word to appear.

"I've got work to do before we go to your aunt's." Ari got up. "I'll just take my laptop into the kitchen."

I relaxed. In the doorway he paused, glanced back at me, and said, "Marriage."

I yelped, he chortled. The scum!

CHAPTER 8

WE ARRIVED FOR LUNCH at Aunt Eileen's to find not only Al sitting in the living room, but Father Keith as well, wearing his friar's robe and drinking a small whiskey with Uncle Jim, who was drinking a large one. Al had restricted himself to mineral water. Brian was sitting on the floor near his father's chair with a bottle of cola. Since the house was overheated as usual, Ari took off his jacket and revealed the Beretta in its shoulder holster.

"What are you drinking?" Uncle Jim said to him.

"Nothing, thanks." Ari sat down in the last available chair.

All of the men looked so solemn that I felt like I'd wandered into one of those depressing movies about Ireland during the Troubles. In the next scene someone would rush in and announce that Sean and Michael had been arrested by the Black and Tans. I dismissed this thought as a stupid fantasy and hurried down the long hall to the kitchen.

Aunt Eileen, dressed in black toreador capris and a pink blouse, and Sophie, wearing jeans and one of Michael's black Giants T-shirts, were arranging a buffet on the round maple table. Sophie looked at me with red-rimmed eyes and sniffled.

"How are you holding up?" I said to her.

"Okay, I guess. I'm so glad Father Keith's here. He just makes me feel like things are gonna be all right."

"That's part of his job, yeah. Has he told you about the Hounds?"

"Yes, and I've met them." Sophie perked up considerably. "They're going to help me through the first change. I'm going to be part of their pack."

"Wonderful! I'm really glad to hear it."

She smiled, albeit wanly. I turned my attention to my aunt.

"I couldn't find the energy to cook." Eileen waved at the table. "I just hope it's not too scrappy a meal."

On the table I saw platters of fried chicken and sliced roast beef, to saying nothing of two thirds of a chocolate cake, a number of vegetable dishes, and two loaves of homemade bread.

"It doesn't look scrappy to me," I said. "It would look like a lot even to someone who likes to eat."

"Oh, good. Sophie, would you open that jar of pickles and drain them?"

I opened the silverware drawer and brought out forks and knives, then arranged them on the counter beside the stack of plates. Once she'd done the pickles, Sophie trotted off down the long hall to summon the others. Despite the atmosphere of gloom, the men descended upon the buffet like the proverbial horde of locusts. Sophie and I picked at some cold salmon and otherwise ate salad. Aunt Eileen busied herself taking empty plates away and, occasionally, eating a bite or two.

I was standing in the corner of the kitchen when Or-Something appeared. The little blue creature manifested in the entrance to the hallway and whined as it danced on its clawed feet. Sophie had seen it, too. She snagged a handful of potato chips from the table and hurried over, but before she could offer the chips, Or-Something gurgled, coughed, and vomited a wad of paper at her feet. Sophie dropped the chips and picked up the wad.

No one else had seen the critter or its delivery, of course. I made my way over to them as unobtrusively as I could. Or-Something scarfed up the last chip and disappeared. Sophie and I edged out into the hall without being noticed, then hurried down to the living room. Sophie began opening up the wadded paper with trembling fingers.

"It's from José, not Michael. Ohmigawd!" She looked up wide-eyed and shaking. "They've been kidnapped."

"Who? José?"

"No, no, Michael and Sean. The Stormers got them." She was trying to read and talk at the same time. Her mind refused to run in straight lines at the best of times. "Little Sam tried to stop them, and so did José, but they grabbed them and opened fire."

"Whoa!" I said. "Who opened fire? Who was the target?"

"No one, they were just shooting so the guys would run."

"But who—"

"I told Michael he had to watch out for them. He didn't believe me. It's the gates. There's so much money in them."

"Sophie, stop!" I hissed at her. "Sorry, but let's start at the beginning. Where are Michael and Sean?"

"No one knows. That's the problem." She held the notes out in my direction and began to cry.

It took me some while to straighten out both the notes and the story. Although José's mind was more organized than Sophie's, his spelling was terrible. Michael and Sean had been planning on returning home, but Mike insisted on spending one night in the BGs' camp. Somehow or other one of the Protestant gangs, called Storm Blue, learned about their presence. José suspected treachery and was taking steps, he said, to find the informer. When my brothers left in the morning, the Storm Blue gang pounced.

"I don't know why Mike didn't have some kind of premonition," I said. "This whole thing must have been really well planned. Or, look, do you think José would double-cross us and keep Mike a prisoner? So his gang could profit, I mean."

"Never!" Sophie radiated honest shock. "Michael's a BG, a brother. José would never betray a brother."

"Okay. I just had to make sure. These Stormers, what do you know about them?"

"They're the second-biggest blue gang. Their leader's

this old guy named the Axeman. He must be a lifer 'cause he's so old. Like maybe even fifty."

"A lifer? What's that?"

"Someone like the old guy who owns the gate house. Someone who lives to be old even with all the rads."

"Gotcha. Are these Stormers the police force?"

"No, no. The police are a separate gang. Sometimes they're called the Blue Force, but usually everyone just calls them the police. The Chief's their leader. His name is Jorg Hafner, but people just call him the Chief. You don't want to say his name too much. It's like talking about the Devil. He might drop by if he hears you. He's another lifer—the Chief, I mean, not the Devil."

"Okay. So Storm Blue guys are not cops. Where do they hang out?"

"A bunch of places." Tears flowed again. "If they hurt Michael, I'll die. I'll just die."

"No, you won't. Stop sniveling and start thinking! I'll need all the information you can give me."

Okay, it was mean of me, but it worked. She stopped.

Out of all the people in the kitchen, only Ari had noticed us leave. He strode into the living room just as I was straightening out the last note.

"What's happened?" he said.

Sophie sobbed and crammed the knuckles of one hand into her mouth.

"Utter disaster," I said. "Look, could you go get some more food? For the Chaos critter, I mean, and then join us upstairs in Mike's room. I want to send a note back to José, and I'll need some paper and stuff. I'll tell you privately what's going on. Tell Aunt Eileen and the assembled guys that I'm going to try running some scans."

Sophie and I went upstairs by the front staircase, and in a couple of minutes Ari and a plate of leftovers joined us in Michael's junk shop of a bedroom—a desk cluttered with schoolwork and dirty snack plates, clothes all over the floor, baseball posters and rock posters plastered on the walls, an unmade bed. Sophie perched on the edge of the bed while I took the desk chair. Ari paced back and forth, kicking clothes out of his way while I filled him in.

"Our two wandering jerks used the BGs' camp as their headquarters," I finished up. "It looks like they never made it to Dad's world level."

Ari muttered something foul in Hebrew. "Just as well," he said in English. "We'll have an easier time getting them away from a gang than we would from legitimate police."

"You'll try to get them back?" Sophie said.

"Did you think we wouldn't?" Ari said. "Don't be stupid!"

This statement brought another gush of tears. I waited until she sniffed them back.

"If I can possibly get there, I'll go." My stomach churned and twisted. "And so will Ari."

He nodded his agreement and patted Sophie on the shoulder, a quick touch such as you'd give to a dog—or a wolf, I suppose. Under the clutter on Michael's desk I found a spiral-backed notebook and a couple of pens. I tore out some sheets, then gave the notebook and one pen to Sophie.

"Write down everything you can think of," I said. "Where this gang hangs out, who's in it, how they make their money, anything!"

I put the plate of food on the floor in the hopes of attracting Or-Something, then wrote some questions for José. I'd just rolled the sheet of paper up in a slice of roast beef when Or-Something appeared. It horked up another note, then set to chowing down. Ari put his hands on his hips and stared at the plate, where he must have been seeing food gradually disappear into thin air. I opened the note and read it aloud.

"The Storm Blooze want the Axeman to make cheef," José had written. "They gotta have munny for guns and shit. They musta takin Shawn to keep Mike unner controll. You cant keep a whirld walker prisoner real eezy."

"This is very true," I said. "I supposed the thinking is that if they threaten Sean, Mike'll have to follow orders. At least, I hope he will."

"Of course!" Sophie looked up in brimming indignation. "Mike would never let them hurt him. He'd never do anything dishonorable."

I decided against mentioning all the dishonorable things my baby brother had done lately. "What does make cheef mean?" I said instead.

"Get to be Chief of Police," Sophie said. "That means they gotta get rid of the Chief in power now, the Hafner guy I told you about. And that means they need lots of money to buy guns and stuff on the black market."

"I see," Ari said. "Politics by other means."

"The real problem," I said, "is finding another world-walker. We can't rescue Mike and Sean unless we can get there."

"True." Ari stopped pacing. "Which means we need to go home. I'll send Spare14 another e-mail."

"Why? He won't be able to pick it up if he's on Inter-change."

"He might be able to access the TWIXT system from there."

"TWIXT has its own system? Separate from Interpol, I mean?"

Ari winced. "I must be worried. I shouldn't have let that slip."

"Nola?" Sophie said. "Should we tell Eileen all this?"

"No," I said. "Don't tell Al, either. They're both worried enough. If we can find a way to go after the guys, I'll tell them then. I—" I stopped, because I felt an ASTA stab my guts like a hot knife. "Danger!" I whispered. "Ari—"

Ari drew the Beretta and crossed to the window in two long strides. With his free hand he pulled back the curtain and looked out.

"God help us," he said. "It's your mother."

Sophie shrieked. Or-Something whimpered and disappeared. My ASTA faded away.

"That's all we need!" I said.

"To make it a perfect day, yes," Ari said. "I don't want you upset any more than you are already."

"Well, look, we can wait till she goes into the kitchen and then sneak out the front door. Sophie, if Or-Something comes back with more notes, copy them out, then try sending it and the original notes to me. I don't know if it'll re-member where I live, so you'd better copy them first."

"Okay, but I bet it remembers. We fed it there. That's what seems to count." Sophie glanced down at the notebook in her lap. "I'll send you all the stuff I can remember, too."

We heard the front door open and Deirdre calling out, "Where is everyone?" I began an SM:P and followed her mentally as she walked down the hall to the kitchen.

"Let's go," I whispered to Ari. "Hang in there, Sophie! I'll call you later."

Ari and I crept out of Mike's bedroom to the head of the front stairs. "These creak," Ari whispered. "She'll hear."

"Just wait."

Sure enough, in about forty-five seconds the argument started in the kitchen. Uncle Jim bellowed at my mother, Mom bellowed right back. I could hear Father Keith yelling for peace, and Aunt Eileen trying to sound rational. Ari and I trotted down the creaking stairs without anyone noticing.

"We've got about three minutes before Mom leaves in a huff," I said. "Grab your jacket, and let's run!"

Our cowardice got us safely out. As we hurried down the outside stairs to the street, I realized that Mom had probably seen our gray Saturn parked near the house. As long as she didn't see us, I was fine with that.

When we got home, Ari took his laptop directly into the kitchen. I had just hung up my jacket and purse in the closet when he joined me in the bedroom.

"Very good news," he said. "E-mail from Spare14 was waiting for me. He's on his way back. I've been given a temporary clearance as a TWIXT officer under his direct supervision. This should prove helpful."

"Yeah." My hands shook out of hope, not fear. "Very."

"Let me do a little looking around. While I have the clearance, I also want to find your father's records." He hesitated. "If that's acceptable."

"Of course," I said. "In fact, please do."

"And I believe there's a file on SanFran. Let's hope it gives me more data on the gang situation."

"Yeah, that's exactly what I need to know, at least to start with."

"Nola, it's classified information."

I batted my eyelashes at him.

"Don't start that!"

"Start what?"

Ari growled, a sincere rumble of gathering rage.

"Spoilsport!" I took the wad of paper out of my jeans pocket. "Here are the original notes José sent. Make sure I haven't missed anything, and maybe Spare14 will want to see them, too."

Ari grabbed them and stalked off to rejoin his laptop. I tried to concentrate on running scans, but as I'd feared, I could pick up no trace of either Michael or Sean. If I'd known the chant and color associated with Interchange, I would have risked that procedure, but I had neither piece of information.

Spare14 called not long after, much earlier than I ever could have hoped. Once he'd received Ari's e-mails he had hurried back to our world, where he'd found my phone message waiting.

"Very bad news about Michael," Spare14 said. "TWIXT will step in. The unit was founded to handle just this sort of case."

"Wonderful." For a moment I had trouble speaking. "Thank you."

"But beyond that, I could have sworn I saw two of your brothers on Interchange, not just the one. The family resemblance is striking."

"You did, most likely," I said. "They were both there, hunting for gates. Sean's the name of the other brother. The Stormers have him, too."

"You have another world-walker in your family?"

I considered telling Spare14 that Sean had gone along as protection only. The danger threatening them both prodded me toward truth.

"No, Michael took him along to help search," I said. "Sean is a finder."

"I see." Spare14's voice brightened. "How very interesting!"

"Neither of them should have gone there."

"Quite true, sadly. Now, I've received authorization to allow you and Ari to join me in the search."

The thought of going to Interchange, of spending time there—I took a deep breath to chase away the terror.

"I'm up for that," I said. "Totally."

For a moment all I heard was a puzzled silence.

"I mean," I went on, "I'll be glad to assist."

"Splendid! I need to requisition another world-walker. I shall get back to you as soon as I can."

My hands were shaking so badly that it took me three clumsy tries to hang up the landline receiver. I began pacing up and down the living room floor while I struggled to focus my mind. Why did I find Interchange so frightening? Yeah, the place screamed danger, but something had to lie beyond the normal reaction any sane person would have had to it.

I was afraid that I was going to die on Interchange. I felt an ache in my chest where the bullet would enter. The question became: overactive imagination or premonition?

Someone walked into the room behind me. I turned around, expecting Ari, only to see myself, or a version of myself, wearing tight jeans and a black top. She looked like the image I saw in the mirror, except her hair was short and spiked with wax. She wore black eyeliner applied way too heavily and bright red lipstick. The deep V-neck of her sleeveless top revealed a tramp stamp tat on her left breast: a skull with a rose in its teeth like Carmen.

"Look, bitch," she said, "I already died there, *sed non omnis moriar*."

She vanished. An IOI? Maybe. Something weirder? Likely. "But I'll not wholly die" meant that whatever she was, she'd read the Roman poet, Horace. I was still trying to puzzle out this new apparition when Ari brought me the final catastrophe of the day. He sat down next to me on the couch and took a page of handwritten notes out of his shirt pocket.

"I found the file for a person who must be your father," Ari said. "He was born in the province of Hibernia on Terra Five, in—" He hesitated briefly. "That would be in 1955 according to the calendar that we use here. Convicted in 1997 of transporting himself for purposes of illegal immigration across world lines, along with two members of a banned political group of Hibernian rebels. One of the rebels was wanted for the murder of two Britannic soldiers, but she was never apprehended."

I looked away and considered this surprise. "She" was never apprehended? Maybe Dad had never fired those shots, then, that had killed two men. He might merely have witnessed a sight that fear and anger had burned into his memory. If so, to psychics like me and Aunt Eileen, the experience would read as his own.

"Something rather upsetting turned up, too," Ari said. "When I searched for Flann O'Grady, I found nothing."

"I've often wondered if that was his real name, yeah."

"The closest match I found was this fellow, Flannery Michael O'Brien. The file notes that he was married on Terra Four—that's here—with seven children. It gives their names: Daniel, Maureen, Sean, and so on, all of you in the correct order. So I'm assuming this is the right man."

I heard an ache in his voice. I slewed around on the cushion and stared at him. He gave me a sad little smile.

"What's wrong?" I said. "You can't mean the novelist."

"No, no, he lived much too early." Ari looked down at his notes. "Here's the hard part. I hate to say this, but Flann had a twin sister named Deirdre, and older sisters named Eileen and Rose, and brothers Keith, Harry, and one more older sibling who died in infancy."

"Wait a minute," I said. "What was his father's name?"

"Daniel. His mother's name was Nora."

I winced.

"Those are your grandparents' names, aren't they?" Ari said.

"Yeah." For a moment more I tried to hide behind confusion. "What are you getting at?"

"Can't you see it?"

The truth pushed forward and slapped me across the face. It rested on more than the identical names. I found it hard to speak at first. Ari waited, watching me.

"I'm afraid I can see it," I said eventually. "Genetically, he must be my mother's brother." I caught my breath with a gasp. "Her brother. Oh, my God." I turned half-away, turned back. "No wonder my family has the wild talents we do, huh? Inbreeding." I glanced at Ari. "No wonder you thought he was my uncle."

"Yes, the pictures in the family album were the first clue," Ari said. "It's fairly obvious if you look at them with an open mind. Now, the Deirdre on Terra Five died when she was six years old. It's not as if your father was raised with a doppelgänger of your mother."

"Still, he must have recognized her. Dad, that is, he had to know who this Deirdre was. Is. Oh, God, I'm getting so confused!"

"It's quite confusing. I'm assuming he missed his twin sister badly. They were only fraternals, of course, but still, she was his other half, suddenly gone."

"Her death must have hit him hard, yeah, if he was old enough to realize what had happened."

"At six? Yes, certainly old enough to know what death means, especially living where he did. The Britannics there have a great deal to answer for."

I refused to be distracted by politics, tempting though being distracted was. "His file won't tell you if he knew," I said. "But I remember stuff, odd stuff, words and hints that we could never say in front of Father Keith or Aunt Eileen." Memories crept back into my mind like whipped dogs. "He would never celebrate his birthday, for one. Birthdays were only for kids, he told us."

"If he had told you, it would have been the same as your mother's. Someone in the family might have wondered."

"Exactly. Ah, crap! A whole 'nother layer of secrets we had to keep. I bet he knew." I started shaking, first my hands, then my whole body, but this time, fear had nothing to do with it. I had to force out the words. "I just bet he did."

"The real question is, does your mother know?"

"I can't say for sure, but what do you bet this is why she's so damn determined to pretend we're all normal?" I laughed, one harsh bark. "And her such a good Catholic lady."

The bitterness in my voice seemed to poison the air in the room. Ari stared at me.

"Sorry," I said. "I've got reasons for being so mad, but let's not go into those now."

"Yes, let's," Ari said. "I can understand that you'd be angry, but let's look at this calmly."

"Calmly? How can I be calm about it?"

"Stop and think!" Ari plowed grimly on. "Their genetic relationship really doesn't make a tremendous difference. Your parents were never raised as brother and sister. Your Deirdre never even had a twin brother. They come from different worlds, different cultures, different countries, even. I don't suppose any legal system would consider—"

"It's got nothing to do with anyone's lousy laws." I found myself craving the claws and fangs of the leopard women. "It's what I know. That I know! My mother and my father— sister and brother. I don't care how they were raised. They knew, and they married anyway. All of us, my family—we're not legitimate, are we? Bastards, all of us, in the eyes of the damn Church! And my family, they mean the world to me, and how can I tell them?"

"Nola." Ari laid a heavy hand on my arm. "Calm."

"Oh, shut up!" I jerked my arm away. "You're not the one who's going to have to live with this rotten secret."

"Of course I am."

"It's not the same for you." I stood up. "This is personal. Let it lie."

The room seemed to have grown very large and distant. I took my cell phone from my pocket and started to edge around the coffee table. "Excuse me," I said. "I have to call my mother."

Ari got up fast and grabbed me from behind.

"No," he said. "You need to calm down first. You'll say things you'll regret."

"I don't care. Let me go."

He released his hold just long enough to grab me again, this time with leverage, and yank me around to face him. Since I was still holding the cell phone, I had to struggle one-handed. Even with rage boiling in my blood, even with Qi pouring out of me, Ari proved stronger. He threw his left arm around my waist, hauled me in, and caught my wrist with his right hand. He pressed nerve against bone with his thumb and forefinger. I yelped. My traitorous hand dropped the cell phone. He let me twist away. I turned to face him.

"You son of a bitch," I snarled. "You used the Vulcan nerve pinch!"

"Ah, that's better." Ari grinned at me. "You're yourself again."

I stood panting for breath and rubbing my wrist with my other hand. Ari stooped down and picked up the cell phone, then stood and put it into his shirt pocket.

"As your Aunt Rose might say," Ari said, "the female of the species is more deadly than the male. I don't know what's so wrong between you and Deirdre, but I'm not going to aid and abet it."

"You just did."

Ari sighed and set his hands on his hips. My blouse had gotten disrupted during our tussle. For anger management rather than modesty, I pulled it down and smoothed it, then ran my hands through my hair to get it off my face.

"Look," I said, "when I was a teenager, something happened that made my mother kick me out of the house just when I needed her the most. I ended up living at my aunt's. Without Eileen, I would have ended up on the streets, probably. Mom has been self-righteous and self-justifying ever since." I felt the anger rising in my blood. "And all the time she—"

"Hush!" Ari laid a hand on my shoulder, but he'd softened his voice. "Nola, please! I'm trying to understand, so please, sit down."

I sat, and he joined me on the couch. "Understand what?" I said.

"What was so wrong between you and your mother."

"Oh, okay! I got pregnant. There. Now you know." The memories rushed back and threatened me with tears. I shoved them away again.

"That's not Michael, is it?"

"No! I was ten when he was born."

"A bit young, yes. Well, it's none of my business, actually."

"Really? Most guys would think it was their business, if they'd been badgering some girl to marry them, and then they found out."

"I'm not 'most guys.'"

Now that I never would have denied. I turned slightly so I could see his expression: solemn, but not overly so. I could read sympathy in his dark eyes.

"It wasn't my child," Ari went on, "so it's none of my business. But—" He hesitated. "I take it you didn't carry it to full term."

"How do you know that?"

"I've been in a position to tell." He turned a faint pink. His accent grew more British by the word. "Rather a lot of times now, actually, over the past few months."

It took me a moment—well, a couple of moments—but I finally understood what he meant.

"Oh, I get it," I said. "You've had affairs with married women who did have kids. They had stretch marks, but I don't."

"Only one!"

"Only one woman or only one kid?"

"Only one married woman and only one child. But that's true about the marks on her stomach."

The pink on his face turned to red. We sat in silence considering each other's sins. Finally Ari sighed. His color had returned to normal.

"Um, that affair?" he said. "It was some years ago, when I was still in the army. Long since over."

"Ooh, you must have looked really sexy in a uniform. I bet the women were all over you."

I was expecting a blush, but he merely smiled. Smugly.

"One last thing." The smile disappeared. "I'd prefer not to think of my professions of undying love for you as 'badgering some girl.'"

"Okay. I'll just think of it as 'badgering me,' then."

He rolled his eyes and caught my closer hand in both of his. I had the SPP feeling that we were on our way back to normal, whatever normal meant in a relationship like ours.

"You put up with a lot from me," I said.

"I'm glad you recognize my sacrifices." He gave me one of his genuine smiles, neither tigerish nor ironic. "Do you want to hear my news? What I was about to tell you just before the storm."

"Sure. Why not?"

"Your father was paroled some weeks ago. Since he's out, Spare14 and his supervisor at TWIXT see no reason to waste his talents when they need world-walkers so badly. They're going to help us bring him home."

At that moment, I never wanted to see Dad again. The irony of it made it hard to breathe. I'd get what I wanted just as I no longer wanted it.

"What's wrong?" Ari said.

"The thought of seeing Dad makes me feel sick."

"You might change your mind, you know. People can get used to the most appalling things, given a little time."

"You have a point. Everyone else still wants him home, anyway, whether I do or not."

Michael and Sean, of course, I did want to see, my poor brothers, children of incest, like we all were. It occurred to me that I needed to find a favorite insult to replace "bastard." I was in no position to call anyone else that.

"What about Michael and Sean?" I said.

"I told Spare about the kidnapping. He's on his way over to discuss the problem."

"Oh, yeah." I took a deep breath and let it out slowly. "I already knew that. I told him about it, too. I'd forgotten for a minute there."

"This information really upset you. I'm rather surprised."

I opened my mouth to berate him. He clapped a hand over it. I nearly bit him.

"Sorry," he said. "My shortcoming, not yours." He took his hand away. "You're usually so at home with unusual phenomena that your reaction took me by surprise."

"Oh, okay, then." I took another deep breath. "The Church gets you so young, Ari. You can't imagine how deep their claws sink in. For a minute there I was the good Catholic schoolgirl again, seeing her parents damned by the doctrine, seeing herself as an outcast, sinful and guilty as hell."

"That *is* hard to understand."

"There's this guy, Ignatius Loyola, who founded the Jesuits. He said, 'Give me a child till he's seven, and I'll make him mine for life.' They call him a saint." My hands clenched into fists. I made them relax. "But he might as well have bragged about pulling the wings off butterflies."

I would have said more, but the doorbell rang. Ari took the remote from the coffee table and flicked on the TV's security channel. Spare14 stood on the porch outside our front door.

"I'll just go let him in, assuming he's not being used as a shield by an enemy." Ari drew the Beretta in his usual pleasant way of greeting someone. "We can discuss religion later."

Gun in hand, Ari hurried out of the room. I leaned back into the couch cushions and wished that I had a good stiff drink.

CHAPTER 9

SPARE14 ARRIVED WEARING his baggy khaki slacks, a white shirt, and a slightly scruffy navy blue blazer with an embroidered patch on the chest pocket. I recognized the abbreviation "Oxon." Although I had no idea which particular college the patch represented, Oxford University apparently existed on his home world. He carried his trans-dimensional briefcase, which he set down next to his armchair. Ari and I took the couch.

"So," Spare14 began, "Michael gets his world-walker genes from your father. Your family becomes more and more interesting."

I winced. Spare14 tilted his head to one side and blinked at me.

"Sorry," I said. "I've got a sore wrist, and I just tweaked it."

"That's a pity." Spare14 looked properly sympathetic. "Now, your father's name on his home world was actually O'Brien. It's certainly a common Hibernian name. Irish, I mean."

"Yeah, it is, and it can be spelled a bunch of different ways." I managed to keep my voice steady and change the subject. "This thing about Hibernia. Is that what they call Ireland on my dad's home world?"

"It's a province of Britain," Ari put in. "A much smaller version of the British empire still exists there. It no longer holds India or much else, really, except for Hibernia and Palestine." His voice twisted into bitterness on the last word.

"Quite so," Spare14 said. "I see you've been studying the online material for the exam, Nathan. Very good." He turned his attention back to me. "I see no reason why we can't get your father's terms of parole modified."

"Wonderful! I take it you've looked at his file."

Spare14 blinked several times and smiled. He was hiding something, but before I could confront him, he said, "Of course, this does depend on his willingness to cooperate."

"Cooperate?" I said. "Collaborate with TWIXT, you mean."

At my choice of verb, Spare14 stiffened in his chair.

"Dad's been in prison for thirteen years," I went on. "How do you think he's going to feel about law enforcement generally and specifically about the operation that put him there in the first place?"

"How did you know—" Spare14 began.

"Simple logic," I said. "What other agency would have jurisdiction over this sort of crime?"

"Um, well, er." Spare14 glanced away.

"You've been telling me for some time now that TWIXT has police capability," I continued. "Peacock blue uniforms, right?"

"How do you know that?" Spare14 sounded annoyed. "It's not even in the material Nathan's been given to study."

"She's good at this," Ari muttered. "Ferreting things out, I mean."

"I received information from an eyewitness to another arrest," I said. "There's nothing mysterious about it."

"Oh." Spare14 deigned to look at me again. "I have to agree, O'Grady, that your father's first reaction is going to be reluctance. Being released from the StopCollar and allowed to come home might be enough of a consideration to change his mind."

"This StopCollar thing," I said. "What exactly is it?"

"Consider how Nathan's interference generator scrambles listening devices." Spare14 tented his fingers and considered me over the arch. "The collar works in a somewhat similar way. It prevents the exercise of psychic talents by generating a supra-magnetic barrier field."

"So it causes countercurrents in the aura. Does it suppress all of the person's talents?"

"Yes, I'm afraid so. It's a nasty bit of work, really. On Terrae One and Five it can legally be used only on world-walkers and polyshifters—the two classes of the talented who might escape justice without it."

Polyshifters? The term was a new one on me.

"If the effect is anything like the procedure the Agency calls a Shield Persona," I said, "then Dad's miserable."

"No doubt. That's why its use is so restricted."

"What's the collar made of?" Ari leaned forward. "Some sort of metal, I'd assume."

"Yes, primarily platinum, but it's an alloy with silver. It has a nickel coating of some sort as well. The most common shape is a narrow torus. They all lock on."

A kind of necklace, like the one Aunt Eileen had seen Sean wearing in her dream? It was possible, I realized, though why the gang would collar Sean instead of Michael puzzled me. I listened to the technical details with only half a mind. I needed to sort out my reactions.

Whether Sean was wearing one or not, we knew that Dad was. I was furious with my father. At the same time, the thought that he was living a tortured existence thanks to white gold locked around his neck made me furious as well, just in a different direction. My deduction: although I could never forgive him, I still loved him under the rage.

I realized that Spare14 had just asked me a direct question.

"Sorry," I said. "Could you ask that again?"

"I was wondering if any other members of your family were finders. If so, perhaps one could accompany us."

"No, unfortunately. Sean's the only one. I'll need to bring my crayons instead."

Spare14 gave Ari a furtive glance, as if he was perhaps wondering if I were crazy.

"For an LDRS," I said, "Long Distance Remote Sensing. Automatic drawing is a part of it, and the crayons are an easy way to add color."

"Oh." Spare14 smiled in deep and evident relief. "Yes, by all means, bring whatever you need." He let the smile fade. "Now, we have a problem that concerns you, a complication, we might call it. A woman who must have been one of your doppelgängers was quite an important personage in the city. She was the mistress of the current chief of police."

"Was?" Ari said.

"Yeah, she's dead," I said. "She told me so earlier today."

Both men stared at me. Spare14 took off his glasses and rubbed his forehead as if it hurt.

"Well, she did." I shrugged. "It took me by surprise, too. Especially since she knew Latin."

"Nuala?" Spare looked up and peered with glasses still in hand. "Latin? Hardly! Are you sure—"

"She had short spiked hair and too much makeup, but otherwise she looked just like me."

"That must have been her, then." Spare14 put his glasses back on. "But Latin? No. She really did rise from the streets, poor girl. Some say she could barely read English."

Very interesting, I thought. Someone or something masquerading as Nuala had given me a tip. The question: could I trust it?

"So, this problem," I continued. "What if someone sees me and thinks I'm Nuala who's not dead after all. Is that it?"

"Precisely. At the moment, the Chief of Police has no idea who murdered his woman. The circumstances were very odd, and her body was never found. Or at least, not all of it."

"What do you mean, not all of it?"

"Just that. Someone put a woman's leg, wrapped in Nuala's bloodstained clothing, on the Chief's doorstep one night. They have no way of doing DNA testing in SanFran, so a positive ident was impossible, though apparently the leg seemed to be hers. She had tattoos, you see. When I read over the file, it seemed clear that the murder was meant as a slap at the Chief. The poor girl meant nothing in herself."

"They play for keeps over there, huh?"

"Yes, it's really not a very nice place."

"I've noticed. How did this chief guy take it?"

"Badly. He seems to have been honestly fond of her, odd, really, for a man like that, but I suppose even the worst of us have our good qualities. Be that as it may, what if word reaches him that she's been seen alive?"

"Will he want her, I mean me, back?"

"Possibly. Unless he feels that she's somehow double-crossed him, or pretended to die to get away from him, or some such thing. If so, he's likely to want you killed."

Ari growled.

"Quite," Spare14 said. "He's really a very suspicious fellow, I gather. Uneasy lies the head that wears the crown and all that. He's surrounded by armed guards at all times."

"And this is the job that the Storm Blue head guy wants," I said. "Is he crazy or something?"

"The Axeman?" Spare14 paused for a look of faint disgust. "That's what he calls himself. It's a joking reference to a taxman. His actual name is Allan Moore. What? O'Grady, you look so shocked."

"You can't mean this gangster is Alan Moore's doppelgänger. You know, the guy who wrote *Swamp Thing*."

Both Ari and Spare14 stared at me in some distress.

"And *Watchmen*." I was trying to be helpful, but I got the same stares. "Uh, you don't know, do you? The Alan I mean is an author. A comic book writer."

"Oh." Spare14's voice stayed polite out of sheer will power, or so his SPP told me. "I doubt it very much. The Terra Three Allan Moore is not the creative sort, except perhaps when it comes to extortion."

"Comic books again." Ari looked at me with eyes loaded with reproach. "Nola!"

"You don't need to be such a snob about it. You're the one who's culturally deprived."

We glared at each other.

"Um, well," Spare14 broke in, "let's move along, shall we? The gangster Allan Moore is also known as the Moore of SanFran. He's rather fond of ghastly puns."

"He's read *Othello*?"

"Yes, he comes from an educated background of sorts, not that education seems to have improved his character. He runs a protection racket among other nefarious activities. He comes to my office regularly." Spare14 shuddered at the memory. "I pay him, of course. Otherwise his assistant might set the office on fire, quite possibly while I'm inside it."

"Right," Ari said. "He knows you'll pay up because of your supposed numbers racket."

"Yes, exactly." He shuddered again. "I'll reach my radiation limit soon, and then a younger man will take over the SanFran office. I shall be very glad to leave it behind."

"Yeah, I bet," I said. "Um, about this radiation—"

"I'll make sure that you each have a standard TWIXT radiation badge. We'll leave if the levels become dangerous. There is medication for excessive dosages, but it has rather painful side effects, I gather. I'd prefer that none of us verify that from personal experience."

"So would I. I just hope we can get Michael and Sean out of there before they need the meds." A worse thought occurred to me. "And before the radiation causes permanent damage."

Ari winced. Spare14 looked grim and nodded his agreement. Rather than brood on the worst-case scenario, I returned to the Nuala problem.

"It's too bad I've got this real dark hair. If I try to bleach it, it'll just turn that weird orange that screams 'fake' to every woman around. And I'll need a new name. Nola's too close to Nuala. How about Rose? That's my middle name."

"Very good, yes." Spare14 grinned at me. "On Terra Three I'm afraid I'm known as Sneak."

I laughed. Ari merely smiled.

"Should I take a new name?" Ari said. "Are there any Jews in SanFran?"

"Some, yes, though I doubt if any member of any religion is very observant. I think you'd best pretend to be a relative of mine. We have similar accents. Everyone thinks I come from Jamaica."

"Jamaica?" I said. "Why Jamaica?"

"The disaster that created Interchange destroyed Great Britain along with the rest of northern Europe. That was back at the end of World War One. Just as here, there was a British colony in Jamaica, and quite a few refugees arrived to swell the ranks. Ever since, the colony's clung to the old ways. They sound more British now than the actual British ever did."

"Got it." I glanced at Ari. "So you need a British-y sounding name."

"What about Eric Spare?"

"Very good." Spare14 nodded at him. "Now all we need is the world-walker. I do hope the Head Office can send one soon."

I considered mentioning Dad's set of boxes but decided against it. For all of Spare14's relentlessly avuncular persona, I didn't quite trust him where my father was concerned. The boxes, I figured, might come in handy later if I needed to strike some kind of bargain.

For a while that afternoon, we continued to discuss strategy for our move onto Interchange. We needed to have everything in place before our transportation became available. Thanks to the demand, TWIXT agents had only a brief window to use a world-walker's services before the psychic had to move on to the next job.

"We'll go directly to my office," Spare14 said. "We'll be safe there. It's a lovely irony, in a way. Since I've paid the Axeman, no one will dare attack us on the premises. His gang would retaliate. He's quite reliable, really, in his way."

As he was leaving, Spare14 paused to ask me, "I don't suppose you have any news for me concerning the liaison offer?"

"I do, yeah. The higher-ups are extremely interested. They're thinking in terms of holding a face-to-face meeting as a next step."

Spare14 smiled and followed Ari down the stairs.

I was going to boot up my desktop and file a report to the Agency, but I heard a claw-clicking noise in the kitchen and hurried in to look. Sure enough, Or-Something was pacing back and forth on the tiled counter. At the sight of me, it gurgled and produced two large wads of paper. I opened the refrigerator and found some moldy slices of pizza, half a can of tuna fish, and a plastic bag of arugula. When I put out the pizza, the critter wagged its long scaly tail and hunkered down to eat.

One wad of paper came from José, and the other from Sophie. I glanced through them, saw that they contained a lot of useful information, and put them on the coffee table to read later. I went into the bathroom to consider how to change my look. Although I never wore much makeup, I kept some in a drawer of the vanity. I was going through my stash when an image formed in the oval mirror over the sink. I could see Nuala standing behind me, her hands on her hips, her head tilted a little to one side as she worked on a piece of chewing gum.

"Okay," I said, "who are you really?"

"Define really," Nuala said.

"Cute. We don't have enough time for me to stumble around trying to pin down reality. Are you Nuala's ghost or not?"

"What do you think?"

"Not, that's what."

"What the hell else would I be?"

"A projection via the squid machine. An IOI carryover from someone who's my genetic double. An angel in disguise. A demon in disguise. Is that enough possibilities for you?"

"None of the above."

"The real Nuala never took a multiple choice test in her life." I played my trump card. "Besides, you gave yourself away when you used Latin. She didn't know any."

The Nuala image snarled, then snapped her gum and disappeared.

"A bitch, that's what," I said. "Right answer, but it doesn't help."

I heard footsteps in the hall. In the mirror Ari's image appeared in the bathroom door. When he walked in, I turned around and stroked his chest with both hands just to make sure I was seeing actual flesh and blood. He grinned. I was.

"I must admit," he said, "that I'm glad you're not going to bleach your hair."

"Me, too. It would end up feeling like straw. I've got to do something about changing my look, though."

The words "changing my look" began to repeat and reverb, echoing around the tiled room. I heard Ari swear and felt his hands catch me by the shoulders.

I walked into the gray library where the bookshelves shot off multidimensionally. The angel with the pince-nez was standing at the lectern, but instead of a book, he was staring at a laptop screen. He looked up and smiled.

"You really might ask about those polyshifters," he said.

The library began to sway back and forth. The bookshelves swung around me like the flaccid arms of a drunk, but not a single book fell.

I blinked and saw the hallway floor drifting under me. Ari had slung me over one shoulder, caveman style, and was carrying me into the bedroom. He took me to the bed and flopped me down with my head on the pillow.

"Thanks," I said.

"You're back? Brilliant! If you'd hit your head on the porcelain or the metal pipes—"

"Yeah, I know."

Ari sat down on the edge of the bed and turned to face me. "What was it this time?"

"The library and the angel again. He prompted me to ask a question." It occurred to me that my beloved darling might be holding out on me. "Ari, do you know what a polyshifter is?"

"No. I've been wondering ever since Spare14 mentioned them. Something like a werewolf, I'd suppose, but worse."

His SPP made it clear that he honestly didn't know.

"Yeah, that's my guess, too," I said. "Someone who can change into more than one shape. If they can do it at will, they'd be really tricky to deal with, and I suppose that's why they can be collared legally."

I considered the possibility that the Nuala I'd seen was a polyshifter, but she was basically insubstantial, an image, not flesh. No one could put a platinum collar on an apparition.

"But that reminds me," I went on. "Don't you have a data file on SanFran on that educational online location?"

He froze.

"You do, don't you?" I said. "And you don't want to tell me because it's classified information."

He merely stared at me.

"You're incriminating yourself with silence," I went on. "You might as well admit it."

"There are times—" Ari punched his left hand with his right fist, though not as hard as usual. "I suppose you're going to make my life miserable again, wheedling it out of me."

"Your life? Last time it only took ten minutes before you cracked."

"That's very unfair of you."

"I've got need to know. I want that file."

"Nola! I've decided I want to join TWIXT. I don't want to jeopardize my chances by giving you access that you're not entitled to have."

"Last time—"

"Last time I didn't know if I wanted to join or not. The issue wasn't as important."

"Hah! Then it's your career you're worried about, not the ethics of the thing."

"I don't see why that has anything to do with the matter."

"You keep sounding more and more British. That means you know you're on shaky ground."

He growled at me. When I ran a quick check on his Qi, I felt frustration and annoyance, but not his core rage.

"Let's see," I said. "We could do the handcuffs and the garter belt again, and I suppose I really do deserve a spanking for this."

His Qi level rose, but not high enough. I thought of various inducements, all of which I'd disliked in the past, but with Ari as a partner, it was possible that I'd enjoy them. I sat up and smiled at him.

"Or you could tie me down this time, not just use the handcuffs," I said. "To the bed, I mean. Ankles, too. Spread out. You know?"

His Qi spiked. He stared at me in sad-eyed, droop-mouth martyrdom.

"I've been an awfully bad girl, Ari," I said.

He groaned, leaned over, and kissed me. I made him print out the SanFran file before we went any further.

When I got around to reading it, much later that afternoon, I found three pages of background and twenty pages of crucial detail. It listed the most important people and families, noted the prominent buildings, named the important public officers. It also described the existing neighborhoods and gave them a danger rating, most of which were high. Although the information was far from complete, I had a few details of my own to fill in some of the blanks, thanks to the most recent notes from José and Sophie. I collated their information as I read the stuff from Ari.

Politically speaking, two top dogs ran SanFran. The elected mayor—and he did seem to be elected the old-fashioned way—was in charge of the hilltop enclaves of the wealthy, both middle class and outright rich. The big prize in the underworld was the job of Chief of Police, currently held by the leader of the top gang, the Blue Force as they called themselves. The Chief dominated everything and everybody else. As long as he kept the general population under control, the mayor and his kind paid him well.

Where was all this money coming from? Gold. On Terra Three the big mines in the Sierra had never been picked clean. Individuals still panned and prospected in the mountains. Over in the East Bay hills, in a world where no one thought in terms of parks, green belts, and ecology, a few small mines still leaked mercury into the Bay and gold into the pockets of investors. All of the gold, and a little silver as well, came through SanFran, where some of it kept the rich rich and the Chief of Police employed.

Getting that top job for the Axeman, the Storm Blue boss, was going to mean a gang war as well as a lot of bribe money changing hands. A world-walker could command high fees from all the people who wanted out of SanFran and off of Interchange for good. Sophie was right. The kidnapping was all about the money.

I was still reading when Ari wandered in from the bedroom. He'd put on his jeans and a blue T-shirt, frayed around the neckband with age. White Hebrew letters marched across the chest in two peeling rows.

"What does that say?" I said.

"Microsoft Windows. I got it free at a trade show in Tel

Aviv." He paused for a yawn. "Tzaki was visiting, and he insisted we go."

I'd fallen into one of my standard mistakes: thinking of Israel as the biblical land of ancient mystery. Ari sat down at my left on the couch and put an arm around my shoulders to draw me close. I slid the printout under the cushion to my right.

"I'm not going to grab that from you," he said. "Don't you trust me?"

"After what I just let you do to me, how can you even ask that?"

"Point taken." He hesitated on the edge of embarrassment. "Er, you weren't just pretending to um, well, enjoy all that um, well, kind of sex, were you?"

"No, I sure wasn't." Much to my surprise, I'll admit, I'd found it intensely pleasurable. "You know, it made me think about things. There are times when I really feel Chaotic. Like I could spin out of control. Sometimes I do go over that edge."

"Such as those walking trances? And the leopard women?"

"Yeah, exactly. Mostly I can keep it together, when I'm working or with my family. But other times—" I hesitated because I disliked the insight I was facing. "I'm really serious about serving Harmony. I hate feeling like a Chaotic."

"And so you feel safe when I take charge of you in bed. Safe enough to really let go, I mean."

I winced. Even though I tried, I could not bring myself to look at him. "Yeah," I said eventually. "That's it."

"It's fine with me, mind. I'm hardly complaining."

"That was obvious, yeah."

He chuckled under his breath. I rested my head on his shoulder and wondered if I was blushing. If so, he never mentioned it.

"I have to admit," Ari said, "that when you announced you wanted that data, my first reaction was to wonder what you'd offer me for it."

"You bas— I mean, you creep!"

"I was rather ashamed of myself."

He sounded so sincere that I ran an SPP. Yes, he was ashamed, though not very.

"Which reminds me," I said. "I take it you told Spare14 what you knew about my father's criminal offenses."

"No, actually, I didn't. He probably looked up the file before he came over. Given his position in TWIXT, I'm sure he has access to whatever intel he needs."

"Then please forgive my suspicious mind," I said. "You know, neither of us are nice people."

He sighed. "True," he said. "I love you anyway."

"Is that an insult or a compliment?"

For an answer he kissed me.

Although I debated, I finally decided to call Aunt Eileen and tell her that we were going to Interchange. She'd only dream about it, and I wanted her to have clear information. She was pleased to learn that Interpol had what I termed "resources" to help us. As usual, she was too tactful to insist on more information.

"I suppose," I said, "there's no use in telling you not to worry."

The only answer I received was a long drawn-out sigh.

"I thought so," I went on. "Well, do your best, okay? And feed Sophie tranks if you have any."

"I do have some. I got her a prescription when she started displaying the symptoms. You know. For the other problem."

"Right. I'd almost forgotten that. Lycanthropy seems so ordinary now."

Aunt Eileen laughed with only a bare trace of hysteria. I had to admire her self-control.

"Will you call Al for me?" I said. "Tell him that we're on our way to get his domestic partner back home."

"I'll do that. He'll be so relieved." She hesitated. "I just hope you can find them and be safe yourselves."

I dredged up every bit of confidence I possessed and put it into my voice. "I'll call you the minute we get them back home."

I could only hope the confidence was justified.

While Ari put together a scrappy dinner, I called my

second-in-command, Annie Wentworth. I told her that Ari
and I would be following a case out of the area and that
she'd be in charge until we returned.

"Just stay on Chaos watch, basically," I said. "I'll file a
report with the Agency later tonight and tell them what's
going on. I'll copy it to you. You'll need to stay in touch
with Y."

"All right," Annie said. "Do you think you'll be gone
long?"

"I hope not. If we're not back in ten days, say, ask Y for
temporary help from Washington."

"I'll do that. Do you want Jerry to come stay in your
flat?"

"No. Ari's already taken care of that. His friend Itzak's
going to keep an eye on the place."

After we ate, Ari and I drove to a local chain drugstore,
one of those where the actual drugs are hard to find among
the kids' toys, snack foods, cooking equipment, cosmetics,
and whatever else they can cram in. While I loaded up on
beauty supplies, Ari wandered off, probably, I figured, to
find an aisle displaying more manly goods. I went looking
for him and finally saw him thumbing through magazines at
the front of the store.

Just as I turned down the aisle and started pushing my
cart toward him, the goddess Diana materialized between a
bin of on-sale Easter candy and stacks of soft drinks.
Dressed in a white hunting tunic and high boots, she glowed
with a silver light that came from her chalky white flesh. In
her hands she carried a bow, and a quiver of arrows hung at
one hip.

"Seek me," she said. "Remember this well: seek me."

She vanished before I could ask for clarification. I continued on down the aisle and fetched up next to Ari, who
was leafing through an issue of *American Rifleman*. He
smiled at me and returned the magazine to the shelf.

"Ready to go?" he said.

"Yeah. I just had a visitation from another goddess."

He sighed, deeply and in some distress. "I'd best be the
one to drive home, then," was all he said.

When we got back to the flat, I found a message from

Spare14 on the landline, saying that he'd heard from the "personnel department about the temporary help." I called him immediately.

"Tomorrow at ten AM," Spare14 said, "the world-walker's due to arrive in my office. If you could be there?"

"Promptly," I said. "Where's the gate we're going to use?"

"Reasonably close by, actually—to my office here, I mean. Unfortunately, it debouches a good distance away from my office there." He emphasized the word "there."

"I take it you don't want to use the gate in my aunt's house."

"The Axeman's gang must be keeping a watch on the BGs and their territory. They may even suspect that the house gate exists."

"Ah, I get it. If they do, and we come through it, they could be waiting for us."

"Exactly."

"One last question. Is there somewhere safe to leave Ari's car?"

"Oh, yes. Here, let me speak to him, and I'll fill him in on that sort of detail."

I handed the phone to Ari, then took the drugstore bags into our bedroom. I shut the drapes, turned on the light, and spread the things I'd bought out on the bed. I was organizing the various items when Ari came in.

"What is all that?" Ari asked from behind me.

"My disguise," I said. "In the morning I'm going to be a SanFran sex industry worker, and you're going to be my pimp."

He said something in Hebrew.

"Look, Ari, I know you don't like this idea, but we're going to a place where there are other psychics all over the place. What if someone spots me as a foreign influence? I might have to run a Shield until we get to Spare14's office, which means I'm going to feel drunk out of my mind."

"True. But what—"

"So I'll be a working girl that you've strung out on drugs. That's normal for there. Can you think of a better cover story? If you can, we'll go with that instead."

He shoved both hands into his jeans' pockets and contemplated the floor for several minutes. "No." He looked
up with a shrug. "It's the logical choice for our destination.
Although, given the radiation levels, instead of drunk you
could perhaps pretend to be brain-damaged. That would
take less effort, too, since it would come to you naturally."

He stepped back fast before I could kick him.

"Very funny. Ha ha. I hope I can avoid putting up the
SH. I'll feel crummy enough until we get my brothers
back."

"Assuming we can."

"Yeah." I turned cold. "Always assuming that."

Chapter 10

OUT OF SHEER ANXIETY I WOKE at dawn and crawled out of bed to take a shower. By the time I finished, Ari had dressed, started the coffee, and was stumbling around in the kitchen boiling granola in milk to make his version of oatmeal. When he insisted, I choked down a bowlful. Once we'd eaten, I concentrated on getting ready to go. Since Nuala apparently wore a lot of black, I wore tight jeans, a white sleeveless top with a low-slung cowl neckline, and a pink hoodie. I packed some clothes, my crayons, and other psychic supplies in Ari's sports bag

"Do you want to take your Agency laptop?" he said.

"No," I said. "It'll be okay in the wall safe."

"Very well. I can't risk leaving mine here, safe or no safe."

Probably not, I figured, considering all the quasi-legal things he did with it.

There remained the job of hiding me. I went into the bathroom and got to work with the curling iron on my hair. I made the curls just tight enough to spread out and fall gracefully like a halo around my face. Heavy bronzing powder on my hands and lower arms, my face and neck, my ankles—any skin that might show got darkened. With brown lip liner I created a fake shadow around my mouth to make it appear more prominent. I blended the edge into the bronzer with a cotton swab. I set the powder with theatrical makeup spray, something I normally hate, but in this case, I could put up with the lacquered feeling.

The end result? I looked vaguely mixed-race, a kind of genetic scramble that said "Interchange" to me. Ari looked me over and grinned.

"Too bad I don't own a pair of leather trousers," he said. "A high-class whore like you should be keeping me in expensive clothes."

I kicked him. He laughed.

Before we left, I put Chaos wards on every possible entry point. Ari set the alarm system on high and shunted the message capability to Tzaki's cell phone. As a final measure, I called Annie and told her we were leaving. She and our other associate, Jerry Jamieson, would be on strict Chaos watch until I returned.

Spare14 had rented an office just off Bryant Street, appropriately near the Hall of Justice. Ari double-parked in front of a narrow stucco building that housed a bail bondsman's shop on the ground floor and Spare14's unlabeled office above. When Ari unloaded the luggage, I carried the sports bag, and he took the suitcase. We hurried up the narrow stairs to the second floor.

Spare14's office door opened to a nondescript room, painted white, that he'd furnished with cheap pressboard furniture, also white, and a turquoise rug. When we walked in, Spare14 looked me over in surprise, then smiled with a small nod of approval. He was wearing baggy blue slacks with a garishly printed flowered shirt, his Sneak the Numbers Runner attire, I figured.

"I'll leave Nola with you," Ari said to Spare14. "I'll just take the car around to the garage."

"Very well." Spare14 handed him a plastic card. "Here's the parking pass. It goes in the machine by the entrance."

Spare14 escorted me into an inner room, also painted white, but with blue furniture: a short sofa, a pair of padded chairs that lacked arms. An uncurtained window looked across the narrow street to yet another bail bondsman's office. I walked over to the window and glanced out. Ari had already driven off.

I turned around and saw a person sitting opposite me on the sofa. I hadn't heard anyone walk in while my back was turned. I could have sworn that she hadn't been in the room when I entered, because she was a hard person to miss, a tall, heavyset African-American woman wearing an assortment of ragged clothing: black miniskirt over a pair of bike shorts, a dirty purple cardigan over a blue tank top over a green shirt with a deep tear at the dangling hem. Beside her on the floor sat a mesh shopping bag crammed with bits of cloth, topped with a black purse with a broken strap. She must have noticed me staring at her outfit, because she grinned at me.

"My work clothes," she said. "You don't want to look prosperous, not in the town we're going to."

"Yeah, so I've heard," I said. "I'm Nola O'Grady, by the way."

"Ah, yes. You've not met before," Spare14 said. "Nola, Willa Danvers-Jones, our world-walker for this trip."

We smiled at each other and nodded. I heard someone knock on the door in the other room. Spare14 had just turned in that direction when Ari strode in to join us.

"Good lord!" Spare14 said. "I must be getting old. I thought I'd locked the outer door."

"You did." Ari held up a thin piece of wire. "Sorry." He passed his hand over a pocket of his jeans, and the wire disappeared.

"I see." Spare14 smiled in a sickly sort of way. "Never mind, then. As I was about to say, I've got some good news. Javert has returned to SanFran. He's waiting for us in the bay at Aquatic Park. The travel tank gets rather oppressive."

"It must," Willa said, "but what's he doing back on Three?"

"He wants to link up with O'Grady." Spare14 looked my way. "Javert is far and away the most psychically talented agent TWIXT has. He thinks that if you two work together on this case we can solve it quickly. We'll need to. When missing persons cases drag on, they tend to become dead letters."

"I see." I could taste fear like acid in my mouth. What if

I never saw my brothers again? "I'm real grateful he'd lend a—well, a tentacle."

"We're taking this case quite seriously, I assure you. The Storm Blue gang have reached beyond their own world. We at TWIXT prefer to discourage criminals from doing so." His voice, normally so quiet, snapped on the last few words. "It's one of our primary missions."

"So we have backup," Ari said. "Good."

"Yes. Another TWIXT agent will join us at my office there, Hendriks from the Netherlands. He's a crack shot like you, Nathan. Just in case we run into some difficulty."

Some difficulty. Gunplay. I felt my stomach clench at the thought. Ensorcellment wears off after a while. Death by gunfire, not so much.

"Is something wrong?" Willa leaned forward on the couch. "O'Grady, are you okay?"

"Yeah." I forced out a smile. "I'm picking up odd vibes, I guess. Just in general."

Everyone looked at me, all of them concerned, questioning. I realized that I was mostly frightened, which I didn't care to admit, but also insecure about my talents for the first time in years. Would I be able to read a deviant world level properly? What if I couldn't, and we never found Michael and Sean? *Dead letters*. The words rose to taunt me.

"We'd best get on our way," Ari said.

"Quite." Spare14 took radiation badges out of his shirt pocket and handed them out. "Do wear these, and I have potassium iodide pills in the office on Three. They protect the thyroid gland, or so I'm told by the medical staff."

The badges looked kind of like the X-ray films dentists use, a two-inch square of film surrounded by white plastic, but these had a pin on the back, and the film looked more like a bright pink gel. Ari attached his to his shirt under the sweater, and I put mine on a bra strap.

"Do you need one?" Spare14 said to Willa. "You shan't be there very long. I'm sure you've somewhere else to go."

"I always have somewhere else to go." Willa paused for a grin. "Way somewhere else." She hauled herself up from the couch. "I'll meet you down at South Park."

"Is that where the gate is?" I said.

"It's not exactly a fixed gate." She glanced my way. "We call it an 'area of overlap' in the trade. Lots of underground vitrification around there, from the Oh-Six fire, y'know. I've got my focus orbs with me."

"Orbs?" I took a step toward her. "The kind you throw?"

"Oh, better'n that! These are the reusable variety. You'll see." She picked up her shopping bag. "Worth their weight in gold. Maybe more."

The orbs, I supposed, lurked under the junk in the bag. I wanted to ask more questions, but she shuffled off to the door, mimicking a homeless woman, old and broken, who would attract no attention whatsoever on the street. The so-called decent citizens would just turn their heads and refuse to look her way.

Spare14 put on a hideous sport coat—linen-colored polyester with gold threads scattered through it—and led us out of the office. He locked up, then gallantly carried the sports bag for me, leaving the suitcase for Ari. By the time we reached the street, Willa was nowhere in sight. When a cab glided by, Spare14 hailed it.

The drive was a short one. The cab let us out where Jack London Alley debouches onto South Park Avenue, a narrow street that runs around the well-kept oval of grass and trees that makes up the park. This particular neighborhood always reminds me of the French Quarter in New Orleans. Wooden flat-front buildings from the early 1900s sit cheek by jowl. Some have shops or restaurants on their ground floor, but even with the residences, their front doors open right onto the sidewalk. Most have fire escapes hanging on their upper floors instead of fancy balconies, but the general effect's the same.

Spare14 paid the driver, and we walked into the park, past the children's playground and through the trees to the east end. Willa was sitting waiting for us on a clean wooden bench, painted green, in the shade. She could travel as fast as Michael, I gathered, faster than we could drive, for sure. As we hurried over, she rummaged in her shopping bag and brought out a blue sphere, about the size of a billiard ball.

"Blue signifies the world you call Interchange," Spare14 said to me.

"Its real name is Terra Three, right?"

"We call it that, yes, but you must always remember that the world levels include the entire universe, not just this planet or even this solar system. When the universe generates its copies, it copies the entire thing, all the galaxies, all the stars."

"That's a real hard concept to wrap my mind around."

"I have a great deal of trouble with it myself. It's only clear to a few astrophysicists, I should think."

"So when you say Terra Three, you're really saying Universe Three or our tiny little bit of Universe Three."

"Precisely. The numbers mean very little, actually. With the usual human vanity, the scientists on my home world call us Terra One and number the rest from there according to some arcane formula. Your world, for instance, is Four, but it's really much closer to Six than to Five." Spare14 shrugged. "I can't pretend to understand why."

When we reached her, Willa smiled in greeting and waved her free hand at the bench. "Come sit down," she said. "It'll be a squeeze, but you'll all fit, I think."

A squeeze it was, until I sat on Ari's lap to make room for the luggage. Willa held up the sphere and contemplated it. She said nothing, did nothing that I could see, but the world twisted around me. I nearly vomited as the park wrenched ninety degrees, then shuddered slowly back to its original position. Ari's hands tightened on my waist, then relaxed.

"Here we are," Willa said. "Now, you all be careful. I'm heading back to One. Going to pick up Hendriks there."

Ari eased me off his lap. I stood on wobbly legs and looked around the park, thick with underbrush between spindly, unpruned trees. Instead of asphalt, red bricks paved the street. The houses across from the park needed painting and lacked fire escapes. The sky above swirled with yellow mist. When I turned to speak to Willa, the bench, made of warped gray wood and dotted with bird leavings, stood empty.

"Shall we go?" Spare14 picked up the sports bag. "We've got a bit of a walk ahead of us, I'm afraid."

"Wait," I said. "Last bit of my disguise."

I rummaged in the sports bag and brought out an economy-sized tube of petroleum jelly, which I slipped into the back pocket of my jeans. I made sure that the label emerged, though, so passersby could see what it was. Spare14 quirked a questioning eyebrow.

"For unnatural acts," I said. "Cost you extra, mister."

Spare14 blushed. A couple of young men, dressed in baggy black slacks and blue Dodger T-shirts, were strolling down the walk toward us. Ari laughed and slapped me on the behind.

"Don't, Eric!" I put a whine in my voice. "Be nice for a change."

The Dodger guys grinned and walked on by. Ari watched them go, then shrugged out of his leather jacket. Under his gray sweater the shoulder holster made an obvious bulge.

"Could you carry this? I've got to keep one hand free." He held the jacket out in my direction. "I want to let this world know I'm armed."

"You won't be the only person who is," Spare14 said. "But O'Grady, I'll take the jacket. We have a bit of a walk ahead of us, and you look decidedly unwell."

"Yeah, I don't feel right." I paused, to let the impressions of this foreign world filter into my consciousness. "The lines of psychic force are kind of skewed or maybe moving around. I don't really understand it."

"It stands to reason that things will be difficult at first," Spare14 said. "My talents are very limited, but when I first went to a deviant world, I felt a distinct unease."

"Unease is a good word for it, yeah." I paused again. "Let me try something before we go."

I conjured up a mental image of Sean and Michael, then tried running an SM:P. Nothing. When I cut it back to focus on Michael, I picked up only the traces of a void, a complete lack of everything, a sense of so utterly nothing that I could assume Michael must have gone through a gate into a deviant world level.

With the next SM:P I tried searching for Sean. Epic fail! as Michael would have said. Just as I felt a trace of Sean's Qi, I took a belly flop into a psychic swimming pool, a hard smack into something hostile, hard at first, then rebounding, a pain that flooded my body and mind.

"Crud!" I gasped, took a step, and nearly fell.

Ari grabbed one arm and Spare14 the other. I could hear them speaking as they lowered me onto the bench, but the words refused to make sense. A red glare danced in my eyes, just as if I'd looked straight at the sun. I shut them, then put my hands over my eyes as well. In the welcome dark the glow faded. I spread my fingers to allow a small amount of light through and peered between them. I could still see, though small black flecks, ringed with gold, drifted in my field of vision.

"What happened?" Ari said. "Are you all right?"

"I will be in a minute." I spread the fingers a little wider, realized that the flecks had disappeared, and let my hands drop to my lap. "I tried looking for Sean. Something hit me in the guts, something psychic, I mean."

"I thought it must have been something like that." He sat down next to me on the bench and stared into my eyes. "Your pupils aren't dilated. Good. I was afraid you'd been concussed."

"I'm not getting a headache, not in the usual way, anyway."

"Er, can you walk, O'Grady?" Spare14 hovered nearby. "We really had better leave. This park is Blue territory."

"And we're as Orange as hell, yeah," I said. "I'll be okay. Let's go."

As soon as I stood up, I knew I was making a mistake by moving, but staying meant danger. Mostly I felt confused mentally and tired physically, a bad combination in enemy territory. I put part of the blame on the failed SM:P, but beyond that I could perceive a web of psychic talents, hundreds of them, all of them conscious, in use, accepted. Their presence, so openly recognized and displayed, overwhelmed me.

It was like listening to loud static through headphones glued to your ears. You twist your head this way and that, but you can't escape the buzzing of a million bees.

We headed off north toward Market Street. For the first few blocks the neighborhood looked oddly familiar despite

being so shabby. Beat-up old houses shared the cracked
sidewalks and rutted streets with small commerce — a sheet
metal shop, a plumbing supply, a couple of run-down liquor
stores. I realized that I was remembering how this area in
my world had appeared when I was a small child, before
they built the new ballpark down by the Bay and brought
gentrification wholesale to the SoMa neighborhood.

Market Street, on the other hand — I'd never seen it in
such bad shape, full of potholes and, oddly enough, creased
by six pairs of streetcar tracks instead of the usual two. Pedestrians strolled along the sidewalks or dodged the occasional automobile as they jaywalked across the wide street.
When I looked west toward Twin Peaks, I saw no radio
tower on top of them, no houses, either. A glance east, and
I saw the Ferry Building, painted a peeling beige. Boards
covered half of the top-floor windows.

As we made our way across at Second Street, I realized
that none of the buildings lining Market stood more than
five stories high. Black with soot, they were all built in a
crumbling Beaux Arts style, heavy with urns and statuary
that would rain down like missiles in the next big quake.
Possibility Images of this disaster flooded my mind. I kept
looking up in sheer terror to reassure myself that yes, I was
only receiving PIs.

About halfway across I stumbled over a set of streetcar
tracks that ran on a strip of asphalt laid over bricks. Ari
caught my arm and steadied me. I pulled free and stopped
walking to fight against the noise buzzing and hissing inside
my mind. The number of bees had shrunk to maybe half a
million by then, but they still dominated my consciousness.

"Come along!" Ari said. "You've got to keep moving.
We're in the middle of the sodding street."

Dimly through the noise in my brain I heard a clanging.

"Tram," Ari snapped. "Walk!"

He yanked me by the arm and got me walking again, just
as the yellow streetcar whizzed past behind us. I decided it
was time to stop pretending bravery and raised a Shield
Persona, an SH as the Agency calls this function. The hiss
and buzz stopped, but deprived of my extra senses and talents, I felt staggering drunk. By the time we reached the

opposite sidewalk, I was panting for breath. Ari guided me
to the cool stone wall of a building and let me lean against
it to rest. Spare14 stood guard between the passing crowd
and us.

"You need Qi," Ari said. "Take what you can from me."
He leaned over me and kissed me.

I sopped up his energy like a wad of paper towels in the
rain. He kissed me again and let me feed for a long minute.
I forced myself to pull away. "I don't want to drain you," I
whispered. "But thanks."

Ari straightened up, started to speak, then turned
around fast when a female voice beat him to it.

"You need to get her to a doctor, not into bed."

I glanced around and saw a tall, square-shouldered
white woman elbowing Spare14 to one side. She wore a
long-sleeved black dress with a double set of buttons down
the ruched front. Maroon piping emphasized every seam. A
black scarf wrapped like a wimple around her head, but
stray wisps of gray hair had escaped to cling to her cheeks.
She set her hands on her hips and looked me over with cold
dark eyes.

"I'll be okay," I mumbled.

"No, you won't." She turned on Ari. "Listen, you! I know
what your kind is like. If this girl dies, what are you going to
do for cash? You might think about that even if you don't
care about her."

Ari opened his mouth, made a stammering noise, and
shut it again. She snorted and turned back to me.

"What drug did he give you?" she said. "Glory seeds?"

"No," I said. "He didn't give me nothing."

"Oh? Then what did you take on your own?"

I let my mouth hang open and stared at her.

"I beg your pardon!" Ari finally found his voice. "Just
who might you be?"

"My name is Major Grace. You can ask about me over at
the mission later. What counts now is getting this girl some
help."

Major grace for minor sins? I giggled over my mental
nonsense. Spare14 was hovering behind her and making
anguished faces. If he hadn't been so burdened with the

leather jacket and the sports bag, he would have been waving his hands in sheer despair. I remembered that we had to keep moving, had to get to his office. Give her what she wants, O'Grady!

"Look, Major," I said. "I'll be okay. I'm coming down. Honest. It was something in the drink, y'know? The john gave it me. I don't know what was in it. That was like at midnight. Long time ago now." I laid a hand on Ari's arm. "Don't be so down on him. He's all I got in the whole world."

"Probably so," Major Grace said. "More's the pity."

Ari snarled at her. Major Grace considered him with her head tipped a little one side. Her expression oozed contempt. Ari looked down at the ground.

"All right," she said. "But I want to see you two over at the mission later. Let her sleep it off, then bring her. We'll have a doctor on duty this afternoon. I persuaded him to come over a couple times a week. He donates his time. Won't cost you a penny."

Ari hesitated, looked up, then flashed her a grin. "Very well. And thanks."

Major Grace allowed her scowl to disappear. "Maybe there's hope for you yet."

She turned on the heel of her sensible black shoes and marched off. Ari let out his breath in a sigh of relief.

"Major?" Ari said to Spare14. "Well, she should be commanding an army unit."

"She is," Spare14 said. "That's who runs the mission she referred to—this world's version of the Salvation Army. They do what they can for anyone who comes to them."

The idea that compassion existed even here in SanFran gave me courage. As an experiment I dropped the SH. Most of those virtual bees had flown off. The buzzing, hissing sensation from the presence of my fellow psychics had faded to the level of mild tinnitus—annoying, certainly, but not disabling. I began to feel the psychic "magnetic force lines," to use a metaphor, of this new world. They tangled together in an odd pattern of knots and snarls, but at least I could sense them.

"Let's go," I said. "I can walk again."

We left Market through an archway. Over the side street,

a curved structure built out of crumbling black wood hung
between two stone pillars. I could just make out faded yellow letters that said "International Settlement." I had trouble figuring out if we were on Kearny, Stockton, or some
other street because over here everything looked different
from the San Francisco I knew.

Instead of glass towers and marble facades, low buildings lined the street: nightclubs, cheap hotels, some stone,
most red brick, a few stucco, interspersed with lunch coun-
ters, liquor stores, and tobacco shops. During the whole
walk north I saw only a few dozen cars go by instead of the
usual downtown traffic, and they were squat, ugly things
pieced together from random parts. Instead of trucks, horse
teams drew delivery wagons, though they double-parked
just like at home. All the streets were paved with red brick,
not asphalt.

Thanks to the low life expectancy here, everyone we saw
looked under forty, most even younger. People hurried
along the sidewalks—some well-dressed men in suits, some
women in flowered dresses, fitted coats, and little hats. The
rest were riffraff like us. A lot of people were smoking ciga-
rettes; the stench made me cough whenever I got a faceful
of smoke. On some of the corners we saw young boys selling penny newspapers, none thicker than a few printed
sheets.

Finally, we turned onto a broad street that ran at a di-
agonal to the grid behind us. Columbus Avenue—that I
recognized, because we might as well have walked into an
Italian city, judging from the street and business signs and
the talk of the passersby. I could smell sausage and garlicky
sauces, dark-roast coffee and pastries, as we passed restaurants and markets. Distantly, church bells rang out—Saints
Peter and Paul in Washington Square, I figured, where one
of my cousins had been married in my world's version of
the church. I smiled at the memory and felt a trace of Qi
recharge.

"Here we are," Spare14 said.

His office sat above a nightclub in a garbage-strewn alley off Columbus, or I should say, above a business that
once been a nightclub called The Purple Shallot. Boards

covered the big front window. The sign hung at an angle from a broken metal support.

"They didn't pay up," Spare14 said. "Late one night a small crowd of alleged drunks destroyed the interior."

Spare14 took a ring of keys out of his slacks' pocket and began to unlock a metal grate over a side door. I looked around. At the corner stood a bookstore, La Venezia rather than City Lights, but the name didn't matter. I finally knew where I was. Overhead, the sky was turning gray with wisps of fog. The sweat on my face began to dry in the cool wind. Qi flowed to me, more energy than the change in temperature would account for. I felt a presence, looked up at the encroaching fog, and saw the familiar gray Fog Face, about three feet high, floating above the building.

"Javert!" I sent a silent message. "Thanks!"

The face nodded at me, smiled, and disappeared. He left behind another waft of Qi, which I channeled into my lungs to flush out the smell of that gross tobacco smoke. I climbed the stairs to Spare14's rooms without any trouble.

Although Spare14 had referred to the place as his office, it turned out to be a small apartment. We walked into a front room with a tattered gray-and-green carpet, a sagging green couch shoved against the dirty white wall, and a pair of mismatched wooden chairs. Near a window stood a dark wood desk with a landline phone and a coffee mug full of pens sitting on its varnished top. I could see through an open door into a tiny kitchen done in cream-and-black tile.

"There's a bathroom of sorts on the far side of that." Spare14 pointed at the kitchen. "Do sit down, O'Grady. You look utterly exhausted."

"I was," I said. "I'm getting on top of things now."

Ari set down the suitcase and helped me to the couch. I sank into the plush cushions and rested my head on the padded back. Ari bent over me and kissed my forehead.

"Try to rest," he said.

"Okay. I kind of need to."

Spare14 put the sports bag down next to the suitcase and draped Ari's jacket over it. Ari knelt and opened the suitcase. He took out a small square gadget that looked something like an old-fashioned light meter.

"Going to check for bugs?" I said.

"Yes, why take chances? This Axeman fellow, who knows what sort of high-tech goods he can buy on the black market?"

I watched Ari run the detector around the baseboards. When he finished with those, he started on the window frames and the doorways. Spare14 sat down at his desk. He took out his key ring and unlocked one of the drawers. He reached in and pulled out his briefcase, the same one, I was willing to bet, that he carried in my home world. I had no idea how it had gotten into this desk on another world.

Ari finished scanning the room. He sat down next to me and put an arm around my shoulders.

"Think you can sleep?" he said. "Maybe you'll dream about Sean or Mike."

"Good idea. The conscious part of my mind's a wreck, but the rest of it's probably still functional."

"The rest of—" Ari sighed and gazed upon me with extreme reproach. I knew he was thinking about insurance adjusting. He got up, drew the Beretta, then strode over to the window. He pulled one of the heavy gray curtains open just enough to allow him to peer out. I lay down on the couch with his bunched-up sweater for a pillow, let my breathing slow, and shut my eyes. Trance or sleep, it didn't matter. I imaged my two brothers and let myself drift off into the warm dark.

The tinnitus turned into the soft splash of waves on sand. I was standing on a beach—somewhere, a long stretch of featureless sand, sea, and foggy sky. I turned and looked around me, but I saw no distinctive landmarks, just a rise of dunes topped with long strands of sea grass. In the far distance, to my right as I faced the sea, I could just make out what appeared to be a hill or enormous rock either in the water or looming over it. If the coast I stood on was the Pacific coast, and I assumed it was, then the bulge on the horizon lay to the north.

I started to walk toward whatever it was. Overhead, gulls gathered and cried, wheeling over the waves. The cries turned into human voices, and I woke.

Ari was standing by the door with Spare14 and a man I'd

never seen before, tall and on the portly side, with dark hair, receding at the temples, cut very short. He wore a pair of brown slacks, a white shirt, and a loosely cut tweed sport coat that hung open in a way I'd come to recognize. He was wearing a shoulder holster under that jacket.

When I sat up, the three men turned toward me. The third guy smiled briefly—very briefly. He had a full, round face with brown eyes behind brown-rimmed glasses.

"Agent Jan Hendriks," Spare14 said. "He's an expert on gang activity with links to psychic crime. We're lucky to get him."

"You flatter me," Hendriks said to him, then nodded at me. "You must be our psychic, Miss O'Grady. How are you feeling?"

"Better, thanks," I said. "I think I'm getting used to the aura field here."

Both Hendriks and Spare14 nodded as sagely as if they'd understood me. Hendriks glanced at Spare14. "You told me in e-mail that Javert has a theory. Javert always has a theory. Wait!" He held up one hand flat. "Let me guess. Our perps are somewhere on the beach."

"They are," I said. "I'm just not sure where on the beach. I couldn't see any clear landmarks."

"She's usually right," Ari put in, "when she says these things."

"What?" Hendriks said. "I take it you had some sort of vision."

"I wouldn't call it that. An objectified trance clue is more like it. Something links my missing brothers to the ocean."

"If you're right, this means I owe Javert a salmon." Hendriks smiled, a little ruefully. "We have a long-standing bet, you see, about his theories. A large raw salmon, to be precise. I hope they're in season."

"I have no idea," Spare14 said. "But I'm sure we can find some sort of large fish for sale down at the wharf."

"I've seen Javert," I said. "Or his projection, I mean. I need to get close enough to him to communicate."

"Where is he?" Hendriks said.

"Aquatic Park." Spare14 waved vaguely at the north-facing window. "Just down the hill. They've disguised his travel tank as a milk wagon, or so Personnel told me earlier today, but I believe he's out in open water."

I considered my memory of his projected image. I felt, very distantly, an impression of his physical presence and realized that he'd made a link between us when he'd transferred Qi. "Not anymore," I said, "the fishing fleet's coming in. Too dangerous. If they spotted him—"

Spare14 turned pale. "I'd not thought of that. Yes, what a tragedy that would be!"

"Quite," Ari said. "A query. When we find the kidnappers, do we have the authority to make an arrest?"

"Oh, yes," Spare14 said. "TWIXT has an arrangement with the Republic authorities. The California Republic, that is. The United States no longer exists here in any real sense."

In some dim way I'd known that piece of information, a logical development from the disaster that had afflicted Interchange, but still, hearing it voiced brought tears to my eyes. My country. Gone. None of the three men noticed when I wiped my eyes on the sleeve of my hoodie. None of them were Americans.

"If we do make an arrest," Hendriks told Ari, "we tell the local authorities that we're removing the suspects to Sackamenna. It will be true in its way. It merely won't be this particular Sacramento. Terra One holds jurisdiction over psychic crimes on spheres where such go unrecognized by the local legal codes." He hesitated. "Or on deviant levels, I believe you call them in English."

"Quite so," Spare14 said. "Now, I don't know if we can find a raw salmon, but we do need to acquire some human food. Hendriks, if you'll come with me for a bodyguard, I have a supply of this world's currency. We can leave Nathan here to protect O'Grady."

"Of course." Hendriks smiled and patted his shoulder holster. "My pleasure."

As soon as Spare14 and Hendriks left, Ari drew the Beretta and returned to his position next to the north-facing window. His eyes turned cold and distant as he scanned the street below.

"Is someone out there?" I said.

"I'm not sure. A couple of loiterers. They may be legitimate. Then again, I think I saw one of them on Market. A tall bloke, potbelly, wearing a blue-and-white shirt under a gray jacket. Odd coincidence, if he merely happened to come this way."

"Yeah, it sure would be. Let me run a scan."

As soon as I tried the SM:D I felt the threat.

"I'm getting a general sense that something real wrong could happen real soon," I said. "I can't tell if it involves that guy outside or not."

"He's moving on now. So's the other fellow."

I waited, watching him wait, Beretta in hand. Finally he shrugged, let his shoulders relax, and lowered the gun.

"They're gone," he said.

"Good." An idea occurred to me. "Hold on a minute."

I brought up the memory of blue-violet and focused my mind on Miss Leopard-Thing. I received a trace impression of her, but faint, a hint, that somehow something connected her to this world rather than her actual presence. I shook my head in an improvised CEV.

"Receive anything?" Ari said.

"Not enough to draw any conclusions. I'll try again later, when I'm not so tired."

"I wish you weren't here. If someone sees through your makeup and decides to sell the information that Nuala's returned—"

He let the sentence dangle. I shuddered. "Oh, yeah! Bad news," I said, "but you can't find Mike and Sean without me, so don't even think about sending me home."

Chapter II

"**H**AVING A TRUE PSYCHIC ALONG is going to make it much easier to exchange details with Javert." Hendriks paused to wipe his hands on a napkin. "I've always been able to communicate general thoughts, but this way we can plan."

"Well, I'm no telepath," I said. "I hope I can translate what he says."

"Don't worry. Javert is remarkably talented that way. In you, he'll have the receiver he needs."

Ari and Hendriks turned in their chairs and looked at Spare14, who was sitting at his desk and talking on his antique black landline phone. Although he was speaking English, he was using so much code that I had no idea what he was actually saying.

"Well, it's a seventeen fifty four," Spare14 said. "Yes, yes, and you'll need a twelve and a sixteen." He paused.

I noticed Ari and Hendriks exchange a glance and a small nod of understanding.

"Very good," Spare14 resumed talking. "At oh thirteen, yes. I have a thirty-six here twice." A long pause. "Good. I'll consult with you later." He hung up and smiled vaguely at us. "Running a numbers racket is quite convenient at times. If anyone were eavesdropping, they'd think I was speaking with a client."

Neither man smiled in return. Ari got up, tossed the waxed paper that had wrapped his sandwich into the paper garbage bag, and paced over to the window. He drew the Beretta again and eased the curtain back a few inches to keep watch.

Spare14 and Hendriks had returned with a small feast of Italian deli food, most of which the three men had eaten. I'd managed to avoid more than a handful of veggies.

"We need to consider how to proceed with this investigation," Spare14 said. "When O'Grady ran a psychic scan for her brothers, it had very unfortunate results."

"Tell me about that." Hendriks turned my way. "Can you remember what happened?"

"Yeah. When I tried scanning for Sean—he's the finder—I hit a wall. I felt it physically. I received no data. The aftereffect was a sound like the worst tinnitus in the world. It lasted for a good hour, maybe more."

"Very odd." Hendriks picked a bit of pepperoni off his shirtfront and delicately dropped it into the garbage. "I went over the files on the Axeman and his gang this morning. As far as we know, none of his gang members have more than the most rudimentary talents. The defense you describe requires major abilities."

"That's what I thought, yeah." Now that my mind had mostly cleared, I could remember some significant details. "Some evidence indicates that the kidnappers put a Stop-Collar on Sean. Is it possible that they'd own one?"

Hendriks glanced at Spare14, who nodded a yes. "The black market here is quite robust. The Axeman would have the money to buy an item such as that." Spare14 paused for a sigh. "Even the best police forces are vulnerable to corruption. And of course, the police force here is not one of the best. Some officer might well have stolen the equipment, in this case, if he had some desperate need for cash, and sold it to Chief Hafner's rivals through a fence."

"And could a StopCollar produce the effect I felt?"

"Possibly," Hendriks said. "It depends on which type, the torus or the band. The flat band can amplify certain vibrations. Amplify them enough, and you'll get distortions that the talented then perceive in various ways—sound, light, or in one case that I investigated, a persistent smell of rotted meat."

"These aren't manifested phenomena, are they?"

"No, no, just an activation of the appropriate center in the brain. The distortions fool the appropriate neurons into seeing or hearing."

I searched my memory and found Aunt Eileen's dream of Sean wearing a "modern necklace."

"I think this could be the flat band."

"That would be a major setback," Hendriks said. "Could the Axeman know that his hostages have a sister with talents?"

"It's real likely. The entire gang knows about me — Mike's gang, that is, the BGs. One of them's been ratting out all sorts of data."

"Then it's likely the Axeman's set up a defense against you. The BGs, hmm? Very small beer, that gang. Certainly not worth TWIXT's time."

"I'd always hoped so, considering my little brother runs with them now and then."

"The world-walker? He's a juvenile, correct?"

"Yeah, not quite seventeen. And out of control."

"He's not a bad kid." Ari turned from the window. "Fatherless boys like Michael tend to go through a wild phase."

"Oh, yeah," I said, "but a wild phase with wild talents is a lot worse than some kid stealing a car or smoking dope."

"True. He's buggered things up good and proper this time."

I winced in agreement. "Look, we know that a direct scan's too dangerous, but I'm willing to try an LDRS."

"No," Ari said.

"Good idea," Hendriks said simultaneously.

"It's up to O'Grady, I should think."

Spare14's opinion won. While Ari glowered, I got out my crayons and a pad of paper from our luggage. I sat down on the floor near but not in front of the open window, put the pad in my lap, and spread the crayons out next to me. Spare14 and Hendriks moved out of my line of sight. Ari took a seat on the couch where he could keep an eye on me without being too distracting.

When I thought of Michael, I picked up nothing but darkness and the faint sense that he was still alive — reassuring, but not useful when it came to finding him.

"I think Mike's asleep somewhere on this world level," I said. "I'm concentrating on Sean now."

My hand darted into the spread of crayons and picked out burnt sienna. It sketched in what appeared to be part of a wooden wall, then tossed the burnt sienna back in favor of marigold. It scribbled over the wall, dropped the yellow, grabbed the black, and drew black spots on the yellow smears. I stopped the procedure, but I smiled. Oh, yes. Something — or rather someone — very directly connected to Miss Leopard-Thing was here on Interchange.

"No go," I said. "Someone is interfering."

I heard Spare14 sigh. He got up and walked into my field of view.

"Do you have any idea who?" he said.

"What do you know about leopard people?" I said. "Sapients evolved from leopards the way we are from apes, that is. Fairly civilized with metal tech and developed talents."

I thought Spare14 might choke. He stared at me open-mouthed and narrow-eyed, made an odd couple of guttural sounds, then covered them with a cough. Hendriks laughed, one whoop of high amusement.

"Very sharp, this psychic, so you might as well tell her." Hendriks paused for a grin. "Sneak."

Spare14 pursed his lips and scowled at him, then smoothed out his expression.

"He's right, I'm afraid," Spare14 said. "Very well. They exist on one of the rather more puzzling world levels, Terra Two."

"Puzzling how?"

"Two should be very close to One, according to the formula our scientists have developed. But it's extraordinarily different. The solar system there — Venus is quite pleasant, with large oceans, not the hellhole it is in every other version we know. It has a large moon like Earth's, which I gather does partly explain the better climate."

"Oceans, huh? Warm? Covering a large part of the planet?"

"I see that I might as well admit that it's Javert's home world."

I smiled; he smiled.

"Now, as to your question," Spare14 continued, "the leopard people dominate the Earth on Terra Two. Their actual species name is *pardus sapiens*. Some people call them 'Spotties,' but that's a racial slur, really. The proper common name for them is Maculates."

"As opposed to Immaculate, huh? But then there was only one of those, and she lived a long time ago."

The men stared at me in bewilderment.

"It's a joke," I said. "Never mind. Do go on."

"Very well." Spare14 paused to clear his throat with what I considered unnecessary drama. "Terra Two is the only world level of our local cluster in which they exist. There are other anomalies in that solar system, but I'd really prefer not to go into those."

"Fine with me," I said. "But I have need to know about the Maculates. They've contacted me several times now."

Spare14 shut his eyes for a moment, as if he were engaging in silent prayer. "You might have mentioned them before this."

"You made it clear that certain kinds of information were off-limits. I saw no reason to share intel one-way."

"My apologies. I should have been more forthcoming."

"Especially since she knew about them all along, eh?" Hendriks said.

Spare14 shot him an evil glance, then walked back to his desk to sit down. While I told him about my contacts with the Maculates—I left out the effect on my love life—I put away the crayons and the pad of paper, then sat down next to Ari.

"So," I finished up. "I wonder if the guy is working with Storm Blue. I'm pretty sure he's the person I saw in the visions. I don't see why he'd interfere with my LDRS if he weren't hiding the gang's HQ."

Hendriks and Ari nodded.

"So," I said, "we can conclude that he must have some psychic talents."

"Most Maculates do." Spare14 drummed his fingers on

his desktop and thought for several minutes before he went on. "Well, if you can't find your brother by psychic means, then I suppose we'll have to fall back on gathering information in more usual ways."

"How far away is Major Grace's mission?" Ari said. "I suspect she knows a great deal about what goes on in this city."

"You could well be right." Spare14 drummed his fingers on the desk again while he thought. "It's not far at all, just down on Sackamenna Street. Eight or nine blocks, perhaps. O'Grady, are you well enough to make the walk?"

"Sure, if it's safe."

"It should be. We're on the edge of the respectable districts, where the Chief's mistress was never well known."

"You know," I said, "who could really help us is the BGs, but their camp is way away from here, over in the Excelsior district—well, whatever it's called here. Southeast side of town."

"We really can't risk that. Transportation is such a problem with the lack of vehicles."

"Couldn't we go back to Four and then reenter through the Houlihan gate?" Ari said.

"That could present fatal problems if Storm Blue's waiting. We cannot just shoot our way through. On the other hand, if we could determine that the gate's not being watched—let me just run this by the liaison captain."

"In any event," Hendriks put in, "we'd have to wait for another world-walker to become available."

"Javert's is here, surely?" Ari said.

"He is, but there are regulations," Hendriks said. "He can't possibly leave Javert unattended. Bringing his tank with us would be impossible."

Spare14 took a digital tablet, some brand called a Dasher5, out of his trans-dimensional drawer. I noticed that he left the drawer open and wondered if he had some kind of world-transversing router in it. I figured it would be rude to ask. When he finished, he locked the tablet into that particular drawer, then unlocked the drawer below. He took out two sleek squares of black plastic, about two inches on a side and maybe half an inch thick. On one side sat two rows of tiny buttons; on the other, a screen area.

"Hendriks, I assume you have yours," Spare14 said. "O'Grady, Nathan, these are how we at TWIXT keep in touch."

As Spare14 explained how the communicators worked, I realized that linking up with TWIXT would bring the Agency benefits far beyond police support. They had technology to offer as well as information.

"One last thing," Spare14 handed Ari something that looked like a leather card case. "Some proper ID, though of course it's not for TWIXT itself. The California Bureau of Investigation issues these to our agents. I had one made for you because I know I can trust you to use it judiciously. It's valid on several world levels."

Once we left the office, Ari took up the rear guard while Hendriks walked a few steps ahead of Spare14 and me. He set a pace slow enough for our two gunmen to keep an eye on everything that was happening around us.

We walked down the alley to Grant Avenue, where I received a genuine shock. Chinatown did not exist in this SanFran. Grant continued downhill as an ordinary street, narrow, dirty, cluttered with brick buildings and the occasional wooden flat-front house. Here and there as we walked along I saw a business run by persons of Chinese descent—an herbal medicine store, a restaurant—but these commercial ventures were few and housed in ordinary architecture, not the wonderful Asian styles and bright colors I knew from my home world. Spare14 noticed my surprise.

"The main wave of Chinese immigration never happened here," he told me. "The disaster that created Interchange caused horrific loss of life in Asia. They say that the death rate reached ninety percent."

Even back in those days, that figure meant millions of deaths. For a moment I felt so sick that I could barely speak. "That's really terrible! What caused the disaster, anyway?"

"No one's sure. The scientists on One do know that an enormous burst of radiation was responsible. It stripped off part of the ozone layer and ionized the atmosphere by something called an electromagnetic pulse. Do you know what that is?"

"Only kind of." I remembered my vision, which matched this explanation. "But a nuclear war would produce that kind of pulse, right? Which is probably why the people here think there was a war."

"Exactly. There would have been enormous lightning bolts, all sorts of magnetic disturbances, and a rise in the level of background radiation."

"But what caused the original burst of radiation, I mean the thing behind the pulse?"

"No one knows, though of course there are theories. The current best hypothesis is an abnormally large solar flare, although, if I understand this correctly, such a natural phenomenon should have happened on all the closely-bound levels, not just the one." Spare14 shrugged. "Well, TWIXT has a research team working on the problem. I certainly don't have the scientific education to understand it."

We left Grant and turned down Sackamenna. On the corner of that street and Joice stood a coffeehouse, where Hendriks and Spare14 decided to wait. The Salvation Army workers might get suspicious, Spare14 feared, if Ari and I arrived with an escort. Our destination stood right across Sackamenna, close enough for Hendriks to keep a watch on it through the shop's front window.

Major Grace's mission turned out to be headquartered in the building I knew as the Donaldina Cameron House. At home, it functioned as a museum and tribute to its founder, the formidable Presbyterian reformer who had rescued young Chinese girls from lives of forced prostitution. Back at the turn of the twentieth century, Chinese immigration was strictly limited by travesties of justice called the "exclusion laws," but pimps and other dealers in human misery always know the angles. Apparently, Cameron's doppelgänger had rescued girls from the same situation here on Terra Three, at least up until the disaster, because a bronze plaque on the front door commemorated her work.

The cubical brick building must have had a fierce karma of its own to attract Major Grace and her unit. It looked like a fortress, painted a stone gray, with small windows

covered on the lower floors with iron grates. At the front
door a tall, muscled young man with a shaved head and a
maroon-and-black military-style uniform looked us over.

"Major Grace asked me to bring her down." Ari jerked
a thumb in my direction. "She's been sick."

"Okay. The doctor's set up right at the end of this hall."
The guard gave us a genuine smile. "You're in luck. He just
opened up, and there's no line yet. Welcome to Mission
House."

"Welcome" set the tone of the pale dusty-rose foyer. A
floral display of oddly misshapen irises and ferns sat on a
small table just inside the door. As we walked on down the
long corridor, we saw framed colored prints of what I
thought at first were standard religious paintings—Abraham
and Isaac, Jesus healing the blind man, the parting of the
Red Sea, Jesus preaching the Sermon on the Mount.

At the end of the hall, on the wall beside a staircase up,
a four-foot-high oval print, matted in pale green, displayed
a woman with strong features and wavy black hair. She
wore long robes, elaborately embroidered in bright colors,
and a necklace of silver coins. A white glow streamed out
from behind her head. The caption called her, "Jesus' sister,
Sophia, the Light of the Earth." I whistled under my breath
in surprise.

"I wonder if these people come from this world level." I
kept my voice soft. "Terra Three should have the same beliefs that our Four does. The two didn't separate till 1919,
according to that printout you gave me, anyway."

"This poster indicates a different belief, certainly," Ari
said. "Even I know that your Jesus didn't have a sister."

"Not one that counted for anything, anyway. These people must be Gnostics."

The doctor's office turned out to be a plain square room,
painted pale blue and furnished with two chairs, a rickety-
looking oblong table, and a wooden dresser. On top of the
dresser the doctor had spread a blue-and-white-checked
dish towel and set out various supplies: bandages, swabs,
and an old-fashioned apparatus for taking blood pressure
with a rubber bulb and a metal dial. I saw no digital anything anywhere. He was a youngish white guy with blond

hair and a thick mustache. On his white coat he wore a hand-lettered name tag that said only Dr. Dave.

"So," Dr. Dave said to me. "What's the matter?"

"I don't know if anything is," I said. "Major Grace wanted me to see you. She saw me when I was coming down from some crap a john put in my drink."

"Here. Sit down." He became all business.

I took one chair; he pulled up the other and sat close. Ari leaned against the wall by the door and watched with his arms folded over his chest. The doctor stared into my eyes.

"No more dilation," he said. "Do you have any idea what the drug was?"

My memories of Sean's wild teenage years returned to help me fashion a good lie. "It made my heart beat real fast, and I heard this roaring in my ears. I kept seeing weird stuff, but it wasn't glory seeds. I didn't puke or nothing."

"Okay, some kind of hallucinogen laced with strychnine. What was he trying to do, get out of paying you?"

"Just that, yeah. Didn't work, though. I wasn't that stoned."

"Good." He scowled. "Men like that—" He looked Ari's way. "Next time check out the customer better, will you?"

"I shall, yes." Ari peeled himself off the wall and managed to look guilt stricken. "I'm sorry now that I didn't work him over."

"That wouldn't have solved—well, I take that back," Dr. Dave said. "It would have made him think before he pulled this stunt again." He considered Ari for a moment. "You must be from Jamaica."

"Yes. Kingston, actually."

Dr. Dave nodded, then turned back to me. "Let me take your vital signs. You'll be okay, but for crying out loud, maybe you could think of another way to earn your living?"

"I dunno, and what does it matter? I'll be dead soon enough."

"You can't know that." Dave smiled at me. "You might be one of the lifers. They're getting more and more common. What if you had thirty years ahead of you? What then?"

I arranged an idiot stare: eyes narrow, mouth half-open. "Never thought of that," I said. "I dunno."

"One last question. Why the bronze stuff all over you?"

"Some johns like it darker, that's all."

"Okay." He shrugged as if to say "whatever." "Let's see how your heart's doing now."

He did a pretty thorough job of checking me over with the limited equipment he had available, listening to my heart rate and lungs with a stethoscope, taking my blood pressure. He'd just finished when a skinny young Black girl, dressed in a baggy maroon tunic, appeared in the doorway of the office.

"Major Grace wants to see you guys," she said to Ari through a wad of chewing gum.

"She does? Where is she?"

"Upstairs." The girl blew a gum bubble, then retracted it. "The office door is open."

She turned and trotted out again. The doctor watched her go, then glanced my way.

"One of the mission's orphans," he said in a quiet voice. "She's not going to live to grow up, poor kid. Blood cancer."

My stomach clenched, but I put on a show of indifference. "Too bad, yeah," was all I said about it. "Say, thanks, Doc. Okay?"

"Okay. Send in the next people on your way out, will you?"

Sure enough, when we walked out we saw more patients, all of them dirt poor, judging by their much-mended clothes, most of them mothers with children. The line stretched all the way out to the foyer. Some of the mothers looked no more than fifteen or sixteen. One pregnant girl looked even younger than that. I did notice several grown men: a young guy, painfully thin, with red hair and a horrible cough, and a guy of maybe thirty, tall, potbellied, wearing a blue-and-white shirt but no jacket.

We climbed the stairs. On the landing Ari paused.

"Did you see that guy?" I murmured.

"Oh, yes. Same one. His being here might explain why he was in the neighborhood earlier."

"Might."

Ari smiled with a quick flick of his mouth. "Yes. Might."

We continued up. We had no trouble spotting Major Grace's office, which was only a few short steps from the head of the staircase. The door stood open, and I could see the Major herself, sitting at a big oak desk in the middle of a small yellow room. She was writing something by hand in a black book, ledger-sized, with a fountain pen. She glanced up, saw us, and smiled.

"Come in," she said. "And shut the door."

We did. She gestured to the pair of wooden captain's chairs in front of the desk, and we sat down.

"Are you all right now?" she said to me.

"Yeah," I said. "The doctor said there was strychnine in the crap the john gave me. Couldn't have been much. It didn't kill me."

"And thank God for that." She leaned back in her chair and considered us over tented fingers. "May I ask your name?"

"Rose. Just Rose. I don't have no last name."

"I assumed that." She glanced at Ari. "And you?"

He hesitated for just the right interval before saying, "Eric Spare."

"You're both new here in SanFran, aren't you?"

"What makes you think so?" Ari leaned forward in his chair.

"I saw the way Rose kept looking around her as you crossed Market." Major Grace smiled at him. "Gawking, I think we may call it. You were carrying a suitcase. Nothing more unusual than that. And of course, there's your Jamaican accent. It's none of my business, but I'm curious why you came."

"I'm looking for my brother," I said. "Everyone says he ran away from home, but I think someone kidnapped him. He's a super-handsome guy, black hair, big blue eyes. He's not real smart, and he gets into trouble all the time, trusting people."

"I see." Major Grace sat up a little straighter and turned a little grimmer. "What makes you think he would have come to SanFran?"

"Where else was he gonna go? Ain't nothing much else around once you leave Sackamenna."

"That, unfortunately, is quite true. Huh." She picked up the black ledger and put it into a drawer of her desk. From another drawer she took a red ledger, then retrieved her fountain pen and twisted off the cap. "Let me write this down. His name? Age? Last seen?"

"Sean, and he disappeared just a couple days ago. He's like in his twenties, but he don't act grown up." I was allowing for the effect of the StopCollar. "He acts like he's still a kid or maybe drunk, but he don't drink. He's just not real smart."

She thumbed through the red ledger, then opened it and flipped through. I could see that the pages had other names and descriptions on them. She started a fresh page with Sean's name and wrote down what I'd told her. I could pick up the last words even though they were upside down, "probably retarded."

"Oh, dear!" She looked up. "Well, I won't lie to you, Rose. This doesn't sound very hopeful. But let me see what I can find out. You never know. Our regulars hear things."

"Thanks." The quaver in my voice was real. "I really—I mean, thanks. I'm kinda surprised, that you'd help someone like me."

She smiled. "You're older than sixteen, aren't you?"

"Sure. Lots. Why?"

"Then there's nothing I can do about your choice of occupation. You're still a human being. You might even change your mind about all this one day."

I let my mouth drop open and stared at her. Ari stood up and held out a hand in my direction.

"Come along," he said. "We'd best leave now."

"Oh, for heaven's sake, Eric! Sit down! What do you think I'm going to do, convert her away from you? I promise you, I'm not going to do anything of the sort. All right?"

Ari hesitated, then sat, but he crossed his arms tightly over his chest and glared at her.

"In your own way you do love her, don't you?" Major Grace said. "It seems obvious to an old lifer like me. Rose, I'm glad you've got your Eric. No one's going to steal you the way they may have stolen your brother. I won't lie to you. This is not likely to turn out well."

"Yeah, I was afraid of that. You hear so much crap about the big gangs. I guess they're all bad, huh?"

"Yes, and the small ones aren't much better."

"Someone saw Sean talking with this guy who was bragging he belonged to Storm Blue. Is that a real gang, or was he just blowing hot air?"

"Let's hope it's not true. The Storm Blues are the worst." She fixed me with a narrow-eyed stare. "If anyone from that gang approaches you, do not go with them." She turned the stare on Ari. "Most of the missing persons in my book were last seen with Storm Blue men. I don't care how much money they offer you. Don't take it."

"I won't," Ari said. "I'd rather not lose her."

"Good." She smiled briefly. "Now, Rose, come back tomorrow, and maybe I'll have something to tell you. You're also welcome to come here for a meal. We serve lunch at noon and dinner at sunset every night."

"Thanks. I mean, really, thanks." I glanced at Ari as if I were asking his permission. "Maybe, huh?"

Ari shrugged, glanced at the Major, shrugged again. "I'll think about it." He stood up. "But, yes, thank you."

This time, when he held out his hand, I got up and took it. He pulled me close, a little roughly, and marched me out of the Major's office just like a real Eric the Pimp would have done. We went downstairs and walked out past the long line waiting to see the doctor. There was no sign of the tall guy with the potbelly. He'd been too far back in line to have already seen Dr. Dave and legitimately left.

We said nothing until we'd gotten outside and walked some distance from the guard at the door. We paused on the corner and looked across the street to the coffeehouse. I could just see Hendriks and Spare14 in the window. Hendriks saw us, waved once, and got up. Spare14 followed, and they headed for the door.

"Storm Blue again," Ari said. "I wonder what they do with those stolen children."

"Sell them, probably. That file you showed me talked about a slave trade, remember."

His flare of rage burst into my mind and made me tremble. I felt it as danger, not aimed at me, but danger nonetheless, as raw and impersonal as an earthquake or tornado. If a Storm Blue gang member had walked by at that moment, Ari might have drawn and shot him.

"Calm down, Eric," I muttered. "This place is crawling with people with talents."

"Right." He took a deep breath, then another, looked this way and that, laid a hand on my shoulder. The rage slowly blew away like dead leaves in the wind. "Tomorrow we'll see what Major Grace can tell us."

"Yeah. Jeez, she's quite a lady, huh? It hurt to lie to her."

"You have a conscience?" He smiled. "I learn something new about you every day."

I was tempted to kick him but refrained because Hendriks and Spare14 were crossing the street to join us. As we walked back up Grant, Ari told them what little we'd learned. I gave them my impressions of Major Grace.

"I must see if TWIXT can offer her assistance in some way," Spare14 said. "The gang lords must hate her."

I shivered in a sudden SAWM. "Yeah, I just bet they do."

"She needs someone in the mission to keep an eye on things," Ari said.

"A good job for one of our undercover men." Hendriks glanced at Spare14. "When we return to the office, perhaps you can make a suggestion to the liaison captain?"

When we reached the office, Hendriks and Ari went into the kitchen to finish off the remains of the lunch, while Spare14 sat at his desk and talked in numbers to his landline phone. I flopped down on the couch. I wasn't precisely tired, more overwhelmed by the tangled lines of psychic force on Interchange and the strangeness of it all. The tinnitus rang a little louder than before.

I found myself thinking of Major Grace, a grand example of the Harmony I sought for myself. She must have had strict principles to join the Salvation Army in the first place, which would have made her an exponent of Order, but her compassion had kept her from fossilizing into a one-person judge and jury like so many Order-bound people did. Had we put her in danger by visiting her? Only if someone in Storm Blue had not only seen but recognized us.

I ran an SM:D, then an SM:L, for Mission House. The threat persisted as a constant background, like the hum of traffic near a freeway or the sound of waves on a beach. When I remembered Sophie's story of the Peacock Angel missionaries who'd been driven out of town, I realized that all the missionaries, not just Major Grace, lived in danger from the gang lords. The hatred had threatened them long before we'd ever dropped by, just as Donaldina Cameron and her helpers had lived in constant peril from the men who'd made money off the girls she rescued. Like her, these missionaries must have known the danger and decided that it would never stop them. They'd set up an island of Harmony in the midst of Chaos.

Spare14 finished rattling off numbers and hung up the phone. "There." He gave me a firm nod. "Things are moving in the right direction. Allow me to apologize once again, O'Grady, but I'd best not give you any details about procedures at this time. Once we have our official linkage, I can be more forthcoming without breaking regulations."

"I can understand that," I said. "Not a problem."

Ari and Hendriks returned to the living room, snacks in hand. Ari handed me a bottle of orange juice and glared. I drank a couple of mouthfuls and handed it back.

"O'Grady," Spare14 said. "You need to rest. There's a bedroom of sorts here, just a mattress and pillow on the floor, I'm afraid, but better than nothing. I have a reputation as a binge drinker to maintain, you see. Whenever the Axeman is due to come round, I place a few empty gin bottles on the furniture in here and then stagger out of that room to greet him. Quite convincing, apparently. When in Rome and all that."

The bedroom turned out to be narrow, bare, and almost unfurnished. A mattress, two blankets, and a pillow lay on the wood floor near an uncurtained window. Nearby stood a wooden orange crate full of empty gin bottles, Spare14's props. Before Ari let me lie down, he examined the room minutely with two different gadgets. As he left, he shut the door behind him. I got comfortable on the mattress and went into trance.

I was hoping for images of Sean and Michael. Instead, I saw a grotesque white woman—fat, dressed in a garish striped blouse and blue jacket, with red lips and dyed hair. She was laughing hysterically and bobbing up and down from the waist, over and over. I tried to move away, but in my trance-bound state every step I took brought me back to the woman. I spoke to her and got only the laugh for answer. Behind her, I saw mirrors that reflected nothing, not even her back.

I heard Ari's voice, saying, "They can move quite quickly when they want to."

I broke the trance. I lay still, sweating, panting for breath, and decided that I'd cross trance exploration off my list of procedures for the moment. I allowed myself to fall asleep in hopes of some sort of meaningful dream, but the only clue I received was one I knew already: the sound of the sea, murmuring as I went under.

Chapter 12

LIGHT FLOODED MY EYES and woke me. Ari had turned on the bare bulb of the overhead fixture. I sat up, flung an arm up to shield my eyes, and muttered a few choice words. When he turned the bulb off again, I realized that night had arrived. A pale light glimmered through the uncurtained window from a streetlamp outside. Ari knelt down on the mattress next to me, and I sat up.

"Tell me something," I said. "I need your first fast response to a sentence. Don't try to think about it. Just tell me what it means off the top of your head."

"Very well."

"They can move quite quickly when they want to."

"TWIXT. My new ID, my position as an agent recruit—cutting through a great deal of red tape."

"Huh." This meaning seemed to have no bearing on anything. "I heard a message, but it must have come from someone else's subconscious mind, not yours."

We got up and returned to the living room, lit by a cheerful yellow glow from a brass floor lamp with a satin shade and a pronounced lean. Spare14 was sitting at his desk, eating cold ravioli, while Hendriks sat on the chair by the window, drinking a bottle of dark beer.

"Agent Hendriks," I began.

"What? Call me Jan, please."

"Okay, sure. I need your quick response to something I heard in trance."

Jan, fortunately, had experienced the process with another psychic, as had Spare14 when I ran the AH procedure with him—that's Audio Hallucination, as the Agency slang goes. Both responded much as Ari had, which left me believing that the sentence I'd heard might indeed pertain to TWIXT. Why and what it meant continued to baffle me.

Ari went into the kitchen and came out with a white carton in one hand and a spoon in the other.

"Can I get you to eat something before we go?" Ari said.

"Depends on what it is."

"Gelato. Dark chocolate."

"No problem. Hand it over."

He grinned at me. "I assumed that it was something you couldn't turn down and that you could keep down."

"You're right." I took the spoon and carton. "On both counts."

Jan rolled his eyes. "Tsk, Nathan," he said. "You act like her father."

Ari gave him an icy look that made him wince, but I smiled. That's it! I thought. I sat down on the couch and started in on the gelato while I thought things through. I felt so conflicted that I lost track of how many calories I was consuming. The last person I wanted to confront at the moment was my father, but on the other hand, we had to find Michael and Sean fast.

"Okay," I said. "What the trance statement meant is a reference to my father. We need a world-walker. He's one. How fast can TWIXT move on getting Dad out of that lousy collar and here? If they remand him to your custody—"

"Just so." Spare14's voice rang with excitement. "We'd have the team member we badly need. Let me see what I can do. It's quite true that TWIXT can move quickly in a crisis. As I said before, a world-walker in criminal hands certainly qualifies as a crisis."

So I sat on the couch eating ice cream while Ari and Jan checked their respective Berettas and Spare14 made phone calls across various world levels. He spoke mostly in numbers, although now and then I heard a reference to O'Brien,

Flannery M. The scene struck me as so surreal that I began to wonder if I was caught in a trance vision. The cold gelato reassured me that I was awake. I'd finished about half of it when Spare finally got off the phone.

"I've gotten in touch with several higher-ups," he said. "We should have news in the morning, one way or another."

"Very good," Jan said. "Javert will be glad to hear it, too. It will mean that his person can stay with him at all times. Javert suffers from anxiety when he loses his world-walker. It's being in the tank, you see, that disturbs him. He's fearless in the open sea."

"Speaking of whom," Spare14 said, "we need to get down to the water."

"Right," I said, "but before we go, I've got to repair my makeup. Too much got rubbed off when I was sleeping."

After I did the necessary maintenance, we left. When we walked outside into a chilly wind, I was glad I'd brought a jacket to go over the thin hoodie. Fog covered the sky but stayed high in a silver dome. The streetlights at the corners shone yellow with a glow much paler than the illumination I was used to. The houses we passed were mostly dark and shuttered.

Occasionally, we walked by a restaurant or bar that had already closed. I was thinking that I must have slept late, maybe even to midnight, but we passed a grocery store with a clock, dial glowing green, visible through the iron bars over the front window. Only nine in the evening—apparently no one trusted the night in this neighborhood.

We hurried over to Mason Street. Down the middle of the brick pavement ran the gleaming metal slot for the cable. The clanks and buzz of the vibrating line sounded impossibly loud thanks to the lack of normal traffic, or I should say, the lack of a level of traffic that I considered normal.

"Should be a cable car along soon," Spare14 remarked.

In a few minutes his prophecy proved correct. Ringing its bell, the little wooden car slid up the hill and stopped in the intersection when Spare14 hailed it. We swung aboard the outside seats, and Spare14 paid everyone's fare. The gripman clanged the warning bell. We started off with the familiar lurch and hum.

As the cable car crested the hill and started its rackety plunge down, I got a good clear view of the Bay. I stared, goggled, shook my head, and stared some more. There were no bridges. To the west the stretch of water where the Bay met the ocean stood unspanned: no Golden Gate. To the east, a dark Yerba Buena Island rose out of the water with no Bay Bridge in sight. Far to north, where I'd normally see a chain of lights that marked the Richmond Bridge, I saw nothing but mist rising from the water.

Lights did gleam, however, out on Alcatraz, long regular rows of lights, in fact, in the prison buildings. I could guess that the local authorities still kept inmates out there. From that general direction I heard foghorns, a low slow note followed by two higher, quicker sounds. As the car clanged and clattered downhill, I stared out at the Marin headlands, where I was used to seeing the headlights from traffic winding up the highway from the bridge. None shone or moved in this alien night.

At the terminus we left the cable car and walked fast down the dark sidewalk toward Aquatic Park, a semicircular harbor that backs up to the Fisherman's Wharf area. Hendriks and Spare14 went first; I followed, while Ari took up the rear guard. In the pale light from sparse streetlights the park looked utterly strange to me. No concrete bleachers lined the eastern crescent, though I did see a few wooden benches. At the shallow water line, a dirt path and weeds replaced the sidewalk and the trim lawns I knew at home.

On the western edge a tangle of trees stood some feet back from the water's edge. When we reached it, Hendriks drew his gun. I glanced back and saw that Ari had done the same. My heart pounded briefly, but I talked myself into staying calm. As we walked past, I heard rustling in among the trees and overgrown shrubbery.

Ari touched my arm and murmured, "Alert." I did a quick SM:L.

"Two people in there," I whispered. "A man and a woman."

"Danger reading?"

"No." I felt Qi oozing from the thicket. "They're having sex."

We walked on. The milk wagon stood a good distance beyond the trees, half-hidden by more shrubbery. Rather than a horse-drawn wagon, the big white tank rode on an actual truck, but it looked as jerry-rigged as all the gasoline vehicles in SanFran seemed to be. It had six wire-spoked wheels with narrow tires, protected by mismatched bumpers. The hood that covered the engine hung at an odd angle. Along one side ran the logo, "Albany Farms" in hand-painted blue letters. Yet when we walked up, I could hear the quiet whisper of a perfectly tuned generator and the soft bubbling sound of the aerator that kept the water inside oxygenated.

A young man opened the driver's side door and jumped down from the truck's cab. In the dim light from Spare14's flashlight I got only a general impression of him: skinny, ill dressed in faded jeans and a sweater, a mop of straight dark hair.

"Police," Spare14 snapped. "Do you have a permit to park here, or is this a Section Fourteen violation?"

"I do, sir," the guy said. "My name is Russ Davis, and the permit's number seventeen fifty-four."

"Very good." Spare14 smiled at him. "How have things been going?"

"Okay. Javert's getting real antsy, though, in this smaller tank. Can't say I blame him."

"This is O'Grady, the psychic." Spare14 nodded in my direction. "Can she speak with him?"

"Sure. He'll be glad to meet her, I reckon." Russ turned and opened the passenger side door of the truck cab. "Climb in, Miss. The view window's right behind the seat. Just pull the curtain to one side. Javert'll turn on the light when you do."

I climbed into the cab, which smelled like pepperoni, probably from the world-walker's supper, and followed instructions. As soon as I reached for the curtain, I felt Javert's mind touch mine. Light flashed on behind the circular view port. I knelt on the seat cushions and peered through glass into pale greenish water.

I'd been expecting Javert to be large, not kraken-sized, no, but comparable somehow to a human male. In actuality, he was about four feet long, not counting his two extensible tentacles. Those, I found out later, he could whip ahead of him for another six feet. While he looked squidlike, he had some features in common with cuttlefish, too. It was obvious from the moment we met that he belonged to a species as different from calamari as we were from lemurs.

Overall, Javert had the shape and silvery color of a torpedo, fronted by a cluster of short tentacles, but his actual head appeared nearly spherical from the large brain inside it. His eyes were huge and pale yellow. They sat forward on his face rather than lying on either side of his head as those of the lower orders of squid do. I assumed that he had binocular vision. The two long tentacles curled up like Princess Leia braids next to his cheeks.

All down his back ran a structure sort of like a fish's fin, though it lacked bones. About four inches high, it waved gently in the water. When we began conversing, the fin was a silvery-blue color. I say we conversed, but words had little to do with it. Javert's people certainly had language, and at times he made various sounds that I could dimly hear through the glass. Mostly, however, we exchanged images and feelings punctuated by the words I thought to him in English, which he understood as long as I kept the thoughts simple.

Javert began by sending me a wave of sympathy over my missing brothers. Because of the Qi transfer earlier, he'd been able to pick up my anxiety. I thanked him aloud. He managed to ask me, after a few attempts at making his meaning clear, if I was sure that Michael and Sean were still alive—still swimming in the ocean of life, is how he phrased it.

I'd know if they had died.

He radiated his belief in what I'd told him.

I had a vision earlier. It seemed to link them to the ocean.

I sent him an image of the beach and distant rock or hill that I'd seen in trance. His fin color brightened to green, and he waved his short tentacles in what I took as excitement.

You think this means they're near the ocean, too?

He sent back: YES. A WHERE ON COAST.

I was so shocked by receiving actual words that it took me a moment to understand. I eventually made a guess: *You mean a place on the coast somewhere?*

YES.

The California coast is kind of long.

He sent a feeling of sad agreement.

Still, I bet they're near the water somewhere. Hendriks owes you a salmon. Don't let him forget.

Javert's fin changed to yellow with a ripple of green dots. I could feel his good humor. He spread his short tentacles to give me a glimpse of his circular mouth, ringed with triangular teeth, then bunched them again as he beamed me the concept, DELICIOUS.

I grinned. *By the way, Hendriks is here.*

Javert showed me an image of Hendriks climbing into the cab.

I leaned out the open door. "Jan," I said, "he wants to talk with you."

I slid over and scrunched myself up against the steering wheel to allow Hendriks the room to clamber into the truck. He bumped his head on the roof, swore in a Germanic language that I took to be Dutch, then knelt on the seat and arranged himself reasonably comfortably in order to look through the view window. He put both hands up to his mouth and wiggled his fingers like tentacles at Javert, who responded in kind. They both laughed, each in their own way.

I supplemented with images what Hendriks said and translated Javert's images and feelings in turn. Eventually, we came up with a plan.

Since the fishing fleet had tucked itself up for the night in the harbor, Javert could safely return to the bay. There he'd be able to draw upon the vast reservoir of water Qi, which he could transfer to me as necessary to ward off the effects of the StopCollar.

I'd been wondering how we were going to get Javert into the bay without attracting the wrong kind of attention. Jan and I left the truck and joined Ari and Spare14. The four of us walked down to the water line at a darkish spot between two streetlights. Davis backed the truck with its tank up to the water as close as he dared with those thin and rickety tires and wheels to consider. He killed the engine and joined us on the ground.

"Someone watching," he said to Spare14.

I turned around and saw a man and woman standing halfway up the slope of lawn behind us. Ari drew his gun and took a couple of strides toward them.

"Hey, suckers!" he called out in a credible SanFran accent. "Want to join the stiff in the water?"

"No, sir!" the man said. "Just passing by. Sorry. Don't shoot!"

She kicked off her high heels, bent and grabbed them, then ran in a zigzag pattern up the slope to the street above. The guy backed away, hands in the air, then spun around and raced after her. From their Qi, I got the impression that they were the couple we'd passed in the thicket.

"Charming place." Ari holstered the gun. "I just told them we were dumping a corpse, and it made a good cover story."

Davis walked around to the back of the truck. He fiddled with a handle, then opened a tiny door to reveal a keypad. When he punched in code, I heard a lock click and a door creak deep inside the tank. I sensed Javert's words inside my mind.

"He's ready," I said.

A door snapped open. A mechanism hummed and extruded a long tube of flexible material similar to a fire hose but much wider. Javert streaked out of the tube's mouth in a jet of water. He landed in the bay with a splash and ripple about ten feet from shore. I felt his profound relief at being out of the travel tank as he jetted out into deeper water. Davis punched in more code and retracted the tube.

"When we bring him back in," Davis said, "it'll suck up some fresh water along with him to replace what we just lost."

"Brilliant," Ari said. "By the way, where did he pick up the name Javert?"

"Oh, he saw some old movie version of that French

book. I reckon he had a different take on it than most folks, though."

I walked down to the water's edge and leaned against the side of the tank. Out in the bay, Javert circled around and jetted back in my direction. He stopped some distance away, where, or so he indicated, the water was deep enough for something he called "a good hover." He spent a few minutes harvesting Qi, then signaled that I could begin.

I ran an SM:P for Michael. I sent my mind out and right away picked up a trace of him, a clear signal that led me to move in closer. Javert funneled Qi my way, which I sucked up and stabilized. An image appeared in my mind. Javert signaled that he, too, could receive it.

I saw as if I were looking through a peephole into the crowded, brightly lit room where a couple of dozen people were throwing a party. I could hear nothing, but in one corner a couple was dancing to what must have been rock music, judging from the way they twisted and turned in rhythm. Michael was lounging on a sofa with a nearly naked blonde girl draped across his lap. One of his hands rested on her bare midriff, and the other held a bottle of beer.

You little snot! I was only thinking to myself, but Javert "overheard," as it were. I felt his puzzlement.

My brother has a girl back home who's devoted to him, and here he is, messing around with someone else.

Javert radiated amusement but "said" nothing.

Nearby in an armchair sat a big bear of a man with gray hair, a sparse mustache, and gray beard. Although he smiled at my brother, his blue eyes were as cold and sharp as shards of ice. Every now and then he glanced unsmiling over his shoulder, maybe making sure that no one was creeping up on him.

CELEBRATING? Javert beamed.

Yeah, I thought in return. *Sure could be.*

Michael felt my presence. I sensed him go tense, then grin, then cover his reaction by swigging from the bottle. He looked slantwise at the man in the armchair, then repeated the gesture twice. The Axeman, I thought—not that Michael could hear me think the word. Our mental overlap only went so far.

I shifted focus, looking for Sean, and finally found him, sitting on the floor in the opposite corner from the dancers. He was wearing nothing but a pair of jeans and a necklace, a thin flat band of polished white gold that had to be the StopCollar. The idea, I supposed, was that even if he somehow managed to get away, he wouldn't get far without shoes and a shirt in the foggy night.

Although I could see Sean, I could pick up not the slightest trace of his mind or aura. From his slumped posture and the way he kept closing his eyes, only to jerk them open again, I could see that he was exhausted and maybe severely depressed.

I felt the sudden touch of another mind on my own. The ASTA alarm started ringing.

OUT! Javert yelled—well, a psychic yell, but a yell nonetheless.

I pulled back fast and shut down the SM.

GOOD! QUICK ENOUGH. NOT FOLLOW US.

Real good, yeah, I sent in return. *I gotta talk to Jan about this.*

I called the TWIXT team over to the side of the tank. In the dim light from the distant streetlamps I could read nothing from Hendriks' face, but an SPP told me that he was both surprised and worried by the news that Storm Blue had a psychic watchman. He thought hard and long after I explained what had happened.

"I need to check in with HQ," Jan said. "Obviously, our data on Storm Blue has become out-of-date. Huh. I wonder if they've kidnapped other psychics?"

"Or simply recruited some," Ari said.

"Recruited one, anyway," I said. "His mind felt familiar. I can't be one hundred percent sure, but I'd bet big money that it's the Maculate again. The guy who broke up my LDRS, the guy we saw on our steps."

Ari swore.

"If so, our Spottie may have overplayed his hand." Jan considered this for some seconds longer. "Nola, tell me. What sort of danger reading do you get from this situation?"

"Severe."

BIG THINGS IN MIND. PLANS.

"Javert thinks that Storm Blue might have big things in mind, some kind of master plan."

"Let us hope not! But he might be right. Tell him we'd better find out."

I did. Javert expressed satisfaction.

After a brief conference, Javert and I decided that running another scan might present more dangers than benefits. So that Jan and Ari could guard the operation, we stayed in the park until Davis returned Javert safely to his tank.

"We'll be heading back to One," Davis said to Spare14. "We'll come back here tomorrow, but I think we'll settle somewhere down by the ocean. Javert'll tell O'Grady where, when we find a good spot."

Davis hopped back into the truck and started the engine. They drove off west, following the curve of the water line, with the truck bouncing and jouncing on the uneven dirt road. No wonder Javert hated the tank! I received the impression that he was thinking of ejecting his stomach contents before they finally reached a paved area that led up to the smooth street.

"We'd best get back," Spare14 said. "The last cable car runs around eleven-thirty."

We caught a car down at the Fisherman's Wharf terminus with no trouble and rode safely back to our stop on Mason. We headed down Broadway, a strangely silent street of shabby apartment houses. After a few blocks I received a SAWM, distant at first, stronger when we reached Columbus.

"Something's wrong," I said. "Someone may be waiting for us."

Ari and Jan both drew their Berettas. Ari drifted forward, Jan drifted back, and Spare14 laid a hand on my shoulder and guided me to stay in the middle with him. My stomach clenched in a fear that had nothing to do with psychism. I was thinking of Nuala, shot and dismembered just to challenge the man who loved her.

We walked past the bookstore to the mouth of the alley. I could see someone leaning against a wall about halfway down. The SAWM doubled. I stopped walking and glanced behind me. Jan turned around to keep watch from the rear.

"Bad news," I whispered.

Ari fired, one quick shot into the plaster wall next to and about the level of the lurker's ankles. The person screamed, danced away from the spray of plaster chips, and threw her hands in the air—a young woman, I realized from the sound of her voice. In one hand she was clutching an object that gleamed like metal.

"Drop the weapon!" Ari called out.

In the building behind her, a light flashed in an upstairs window, then went right out again. By the brief flare I saw a woman dressed in a short skirt and a tight jacket.

"Ain't got no gun," she said. "It be a flashlight."

"Drop it anyway."

She bent her knees in a half squat and placed the flashlight on the ground. I got the impression that it was too expensive to risk breaking. She raised both hands again and stood up. When Ari gestured with the Beretta, she walked toward us with hesitant little steps on high heels.

"Hey," she said. "Why you so uptight? Can't a girl turn a trick in peace?"

"Do you expect me to believe that?" Ari paused to look her over. "How many johns come down this alley?"

She wrinkled her nose in a pout, then lowered her arms and set her hands on her hips. I placed her age at around fifteen.

"A flashlight, is it?" Ari went on. "Trying to get a good look at someone?"

I could see her tighten like a strung wire.

"Yeah," I said. "That's exactly what she was trying to do."

The girl swayed a little to one side to look around Ari. "Shit," she said. "You ain't Nuala."

"Damn right," I said. "Who thought I was?"

"Lot of people, honey, just a lot of people wondering. Chief Hafner, he pay big money to get her back."

"He can raise people from the dead?"

I laughed. She laughed as well, a creaky little sound.

"Who paid you?" Ari said. "I gather you wanted to shine

the light in Rose's face for a look, then run back to your boss."

"I ain't gonna tell you nothing more. It'll cost my life if I rat."

Ari glanced at me. "She's telling the truth," I said.

"Then pick up your flashlight and go," Ari said. "And tell whoever it is that Rose's Jamaican pimp wants him to sod off."

She laughed, quite naturally this time. "I will, good-looking," she said. "That's pretty damn funny."

She minced off, paused to grab the flashlight, and headed out of the alley. Spare14 let out his breath in a puff of relief. He took out his key ring and used his own flashlight to find the locks on the two doors. I ran an SM:L on the apartment: no one was lurking there. I'll admit to feeling more than a little relieved once we got safely upstairs. Spare14 drew the drapes over the window before he turned on the floor lamp.

"Well," he said. "That was a bit upsetting."

"Just a bit?" Jan said. "Ah, you Jamaicans! So fond of understatement!" He paused to turn in a slow circle and look over the living room. "But not fond of beds for over-night guests, I see."

"Quite the contrary," Spare14 said. "Agents use this apartment now and then. I have several air mattresses for those occasions. I suggest we allow O'Grady and Nathan to have the privacy of the bedroom, such as it is. Did you bring a bag?"

"Yes, I stowed it in the kitchen." Jan paused to yawn. "It seems obvious that you never cook, and so I assumed it would be out of the way there."

I decided to interrupt the banter. "One question. Ari just put a bullet into someone's house. What's going to happen about that?"

"Nothing," Spare14 said. "If the householders are wise, at any rate, and I suspect they are. You noticed, I'm sure, how quickly the light went out again."

"In SanFran," Jan put in, "you don't question men with guns."

"I see. Okay, I just wondered. I think I'll clean up a bit."

I washed off my itchy makeup in the bathroom sink, dried off with a fraying towel, and did other necessary things. When I finished, Ari and I carried our gear into the bedroom. Ari opened the suitcase and brought out a small glass cube—a travel lamp. It provided the only light in the bedroom besides what came through the window from the street. I knelt on the floor and straightened out the blankets on the narrow mattress.

"It's a good thing I love you," I told Ari. "We don't have a lot of room on this."

"True. You can have the pillow." He hesitated, then sat on the floor opposite me. "You're holding back something about Michael, aren't you?"

"What is this? You're suddenly psychic, too?"

"No. I just know your moods by now."

I considered, but I was too tired to lie.

"Is this room bugged?" I said.

"No. I've been all over it, and frankly, I don't think Spare14 would eavesdrop on one of his agents."

"Let's hope not." Still, I kept my voice low. "Michael seemed to be having entirely too much fun at that party. I'd like to believe it was all an act to put the gang off their guard, but the girl on his lap seemed to think it was real enough."

"Ah. You didn't mention the girl before."

"Damn right I didn't, not in front of the others. She was wearing a miniskirt. Nothing else, not even a bra."

"Mike is sixteen, almost seventeen now, yes, but still. At that age, he's going to take whatever a girl offers, no matter what the circumstances are."

"I suppose so. You would have, huh?"

"Quite right." He grinned at me. "And don't tell me you're shocked." He let the grin fade. "I think we can trust him to do the right thing when we come to get him out of there, wherever that is. He wouldn't have smiled when he sensed you if he'd truly gone over to Storm Blue's side."

"You're right, aren't you?" I felt relieved, at least about Michael. What troubled me still was the image of Sean, slumped and exhausted with that miserable collar around his neck. At least the gang was keeping him where he and

Mike could see each other. For that much I could be grateful.

I took off the top I'd been wearing and laid it into the suitcase. When I unhooked my bra, I examined the radiation badge by the light of the travel lamp. A thin blue line had appeared on the pink gel—a bad sign, I figured.

That night I dreamed about my family. I received no psychic messages, no clues, just fragments of memories, happy ones, mostly: running across lawns in the park, playing video games with Sean, taking care of baby Michael. In most of them my father appeared, smiling, good-looking in a macho kind of way, with better cheekbones than your average Irish guy has. Generally, he was patient with all of us, which, when you've got seven children, makes you a candidate for that first step on the road to sainthood. If you broke one of his rules, you got a hard slap for it, but that was always the end of the incident—one single slap, no recrimination, no taunting, no reminders. I had missed him bitterly for over thirteen years.

Yet I woke up remembering that he was also my mother's brother, genetically speaking, and that he must have known it all along.

Gray fog light shone through the uncurtained window. Ari had rolled off the mattress onto the floor, but he stayed asleep on his stomach, his head pillowed on his arms. I wondered if he'd slept that way on maneuvers with the army, lying right on the desert ground that had meant so much to his people for so long that he was willing to die for it.

I got dressed without waking him, then crept out of the bedroom. I could smell coffee. In the living room, I found Jan and Spare14 already up and awake. Spare14 turned his desk chair around and smiled at me.

"Great news!" he said. "Administration agrees that your father should be paroled. There are formalities, of course, but they're proceeding with all possible speed."

Both men were watching me expectantly, smiling a little, sure I'd be pleased.

"Wonderful!" I managed to stammer out the word. "How will he get here?"

"Davis and Javert will bring him when they come

through. I doubt if it'll be today, thanks to those formalities, but soon, very soon."

I tried to smile, but tears filled my eyes and spilled. I covered my face with both hands.

"Sorry," I stammered. "I'm just so glad to hear it."

I knew by their SPPs that they believed my lie, but even as I wept, even when I managed to choke it back and force a smile, I heard in my mind the grotesque laughter of the woman from my trance vision, laughing at my tears.

CHAPTER 13

TO HIDE MY FEELINGS I went into the kitchen and made more coffee. It took some effort to figure out how to use the weird metal coffee pot Spare14 had, a thing called a percolator. Whether it was me, the canned grounds, or the percolator, the brew tasted awful, but it was coffee. I took two mugs into the bedroom. Ari woke, sat up, sniffed the air, and held out his hand. I gave him one of the mugs and stood by the window to drink mine.

"Dad's going to be released," I said.

"How do you feel about it?"

"I don't know. I honestly don't know."

Ari let it go at that. There are reasons I love him. Once he dressed, we rejoined the others. Over a breakfast of left-overs, Spare14 gave me more details about my father's release.

"Once the courts approve, Davis will have temporary custody for prisoner transport. Your father is also still wearing a StopCollar. Davis will bring the code that releases them."

"They don't trust Dad, huh?" I said.

"Of course not." Spare14 paused for a wry smile. "They do assume that once he sees you, he'll know that we're telling the truth about the danger his sons are in, and then he won't just walk away from us."

"You mentioned formalities."

"Yes, a court hearing, entering data into the system, and checking him out of the halfway house where he's been staying. That sort of thing. Once he's free, Davis and Javert will go to Five to fetch him."

"How long will all this take?"

"Normally, at least a week, but we're trying to rush it through as an emergency. At the most, I hope, two days. Much depends on whether there's a magistrate of the right sort available." Spare14 paused to think. "I suppose he or she would be roughly equivalent to a superior court judge in your system."

The wait meant time for Ari and me to return to Mission House. I made sure my makeup looked convincing before we left. Thanks to a bloated orange sun punching holes into the yellow mists, the day was hot and humid. Ari took off his sweater and substituted a beaten-up old denim shirt, worn untucked, that hid the shoulder holster from casual glances. Anyone who meant trouble, however, could spot it if they were careful and back off. If they weren't careful, Ari would deal with them.

As we walked down to Sackamenna Street, Ari warned me that my father would have changed in disturbing ways.

"It's not just the passing of time," he said. "Prison does things to men. I'm afraid that with your talents, you're going to receive a painful impression."

"I've read about it, but yeah, that's not the same as experiencing it."

He caught my hand and gave it a comforting squeeze.

At Mission House a formidable young woman, tall and muscled, wearing black pants, maroon tunic, and the black headscarf, stood just inside the door. When we told her we wanted to see Major Grace, she told us to go right up.

"May God and Sophia bless you," she said.

"Well, may they bless you, too," I said.

"Oh, they already have." She smiled, a thing of pure joy, like a small child's grin when she sees a Christmas tree all lit up, utterly caught by the moment of delight. I envied her, but only briefly. Faith: the best drug in the world.

We walked on down the long rose-colored hallway, cool

and shadowed after the hot sun outside. A hand-lettered sign on the closed door to Dr. Dave's clinic room gave the times that he'd be present. At the foot of the stairs, Ari paused and glanced around him. I ran a quick SM:L.

"No one's nearby," I said. "What—"

"Hush." He took something out of his shirt pocket. He slid a small square of clear gel under the framed portrait of Sophia. When he took his hand away, the square stayed behind.

"Safety precaution," he murmured. "Tell you later."

We proceeded up the stairs. Major Grace's office door stood half open. I could see her crouching down in front of a wooden filing cabinet while she stowed papers in the bottom drawer. When we walked up, she heard us and rose, smiling, to toss the last few papers onto her desk. I noticed that she'd left the drawer open. She had nothing to hide, I figured.

"Ah, Rose and Eric," she said. "Well, I do have news for you, and it's not as bad as it could be."

"That's something, huh?" I sat down in a chair facing her desk, but Ari stayed standing. He leaned against the wall just inside the open door, next to a framed poster of the Ten Commandments.

Major Grace sat down behind her desk and took the red ledger out of a drawer. She flipped through it, then opened it at Sean's page.

"I asked around at dinner last night," Major Grace went on. "As I suspected, some of our regulars heard things. Your brother is in the hands of Storm Blue, which is the very bad news. However, he's still alive, which is good, and even better, one woman who has dealings with the gang says she's sure they won't kill him or sell him. She doesn't know why he's valuable, but she says that he is. She thinks that one of the men in the gang may have taken a fancy to him, but that's only her guess."

"That don't surprise me if it's true. Sean's like that with guys." I was expecting her to have some reaction, but I saw none. "I guess she don't know where he is, huh?"

"No. Storm Blue has a couple of safe houses, but if your brother's valuable, he's not likely to be in one of those.

Mostly they use them to sell drugs. No one knows where the Axeman himself lives. Some say it's down near the beach, but that covers a lot of ground." Major Grace took a piece of scrap paper from the wastebasket beside her desk. "I'll give you the addresses if—" She paused. "Eric, you're leaning against the Commandments. They're not hanging straight anymore."

"Sorry. I'll just fix that."

Ari turned around to fiddle with the picture frame. While he did, Major Grace wrote down the addresses. She held up the scrap of paper.

"Rose, before I give this to you, you've got to promise me you won't just go barging into these places. I don't want you to end up in the same predicament as your brother."

"I won't. I know it's real dangerous. Maybe Eric could, like, pretend to want to make a buy. He's kinda dangerous, too."

"No doubt." Major Grace rolled her eyes toward heaven. "I don't want to know, actually, what Eric may do."

Ari grinned at her. I took the scrap of paper from her and secreted it in my bra.

"Thanks," I said. "But I feel sort of hopeless."

"So do I." Major Grace considered me with sad eyes. "I'm sorry, but you probably won't be able to get him back, not without a great deal of help from Above, and I don't mean Chief Hafner."

"Yeah, I figured. I just want to know what's happened to him. I don't got enough money to buy him back."

"If they're even willing to sell. I'm sorry."

I let my eyes fill with genuine tears, then brushed them away. "Thanks," I whispered. "I'm sure grateful."

"You're very welcome. I'll pray for him."

"Thanks. If anything'll get him out, that will, I bet."

Major Grace smiled and raised her hand to bless or dismiss us, I wasn't sure which. I thanked her again, and we left.

I waited to ask Ari about the gel square until we were several blocks from Mission House. Or squares, I should say, in the plural, because I could guess that he'd slipped another one under the Ten Commandments.

"Listening devices," Ari told me. "They'll pick up noises of a certain volume, like a scream or an argument with raised voices, and relay it to Spare14's office and my comm unit." He patted a jeans pocket. "By helping us, Major Grace has upped her danger quotient considerably. I don't like that."

"Neither do I. Where did you get those things? From Tzaki?"

"No, from Spare14. TWIXT is so far ahead of us technically that I'm amazed. They can set the nano-mechs in those squares to respond to a number of stimuli and report in to a variety of devices. The gel that holds the nano-mechs can match any color and be placed anywhere, nearly invisible."

"It's amazing, all right. And dangerous."

A puzzled Ari glanced at me.

"What if the police want to spy on their own people? Big Brother's watching you. I wouldn't want to live under that kind of surveillance."

"You have a point, I suppose." He sounded unconvinced. "Depending on the government in question. Most people would value the safety the surveillance offers."

I baa'ed like a sheep. He gave me a dirty look but argued no further.

We returned to the apartment to find Jan reading a newssheet on the couch and Spare14 at his desk talking on his landline phone, mostly in numbers. I sat down on a chair near the door while Ari went to the window, drew the Beretta, and began his stone-faced watch on the street below. Spare14 hung up the phone.

"That's step one completed. The court has approved the modification in your father's terms of parole."

I tried to smile and failed.

"You must be very nervous," Spare14 went on. "It's quite understandable, O'Grady. No need to be embarrassed." He swiveled his chair around to look at Ari. "Any new intel?"

"Oh, yes." Ari turned from the window. "We need to discuss a possible operation."

Jan tossed the newssheet aside and sat up straight to listen. I dug into my bra, retrieved the paper with the addresses, and handed it to Spare14. While Ari explained about the safe houses, I fetched a pencil and my pad of oversized paper from the bedroom. Ari broke off what he was saying to the other agents.

"Nola, you shouldn't be—"

"I'm not going to try a scan. I just want to diagram out the IOIs and other clues I've gotten. Sometimes I can see a data pattern that way."

"Very well, then. Wait for Javert's backup before you run procedures."

"That's what I'm doing." I may have snarled. "Waiting."

Ari winced and let me be.

I let myself sink to the edge of trance to work the pattern. On one sheet of paper I jotted down all the psychic clues I'd received since Sean and Michael had gone off. I'd had some big scores, such as the vision of Diana in the drugstore and the Maculates, as well as some minor mental twitches. I numbered each of them, twelve in all, not that the numbers ranked or did anything but identify them. For the second sheet, I shut my eyes and began letting my hand put numbers where it wanted.

When I finished, I studied the sheet and realized I'd put down fourteen numbers instead of twelve. Number thirteen I grasped immediately; it referred to Javert. I looked up and saw Spare14 watching me while pretending not to.

"Okay, Sneak," I said, "what are you holding back?"

Spare14 turned scarlet. Jan laughed—one mocking whoop.

"Oh, very well." Spare14 sounded like a man with a bad sore throat. "The Axeman either has a doppelgänger on Terra Six or a gate in his possession that leads there."

"A gate he couldn't open until my brother fell into his hands?"

"If it *is* a gate, yes." Spare14's color slowly ebbed back to normal. His voice eased as well. "We are honestly not sure. Either he or a doppelgänger has been spotted on Six."

"Does Javert know about this?"

"Oh, yes. He doubtless would have let it slip sooner or later."

"Ah, a bit of consolation for you, eh?" Jan said.

Spare14 refrained from answering. I couldn't blame him. I scribbled this information under 14 on my list, then returned to the pattern. The more I studied it, the less sense it made. The goddess Diana and the Laughing Woman sat right in the middle with the other clues arranged around them in what seemed like a random scatter. I got up and put the papers away in the suitcase. If I let my unconscious mind and the Collective Data Stream process the pattern, it might make more sense later.

My conscience nagged at me. I'd sneered at Spare14 for withholding intel, but I was doing the same to him. After seeing Willa at work, I knew what lay inside that set of brightly colored boxes I'd found in Dad's desk. I did a quick Search Aura Field:Links and realized that no matter which type they were, the orbs had a profound significance for the matter in hand. I returned to the living room.

Spare14 and Jan were discussing where to buy lunch. When they saw that I was waiting for them to finish, they both stopped talking.

"Is there any chance," I said, "of getting a world-walker to take us back to Four? I've got to go to my flat to retrieve something we need."

"Oh?" Spare14 said. "What, if I may ask?"

"A set of world-walking orbs. They belong to my father."

Spare14 made a small choking sound. Jan goggled and fanned himself with the news sheet as if he felt faint. Ari allowed himself a brief smile.

"I wondered," Ari said, "when you'd remember those."

"When they became relevant," I said, "and they have."

Spare14 reached for the telephone. "Let me just put in a four-oh-two request. That's the second highest possible urgency level. The highest only applies if someone's in danger of injury or death."

About twenty minutes later Spare14 announced that Willa Danvers-Brown would meet us at South Park. Ari and I went alone on the theory that two ragtag individuals would attract less attention than four. Since my mind had adjusted to the local lines of psychic force, and I wasn't reeling from a botched Search Mode:Personnel, I figured that the trip should go smoothly.

Although we walked fast, we did our best to blend in with the people on the street. Every now and then we paused to look in a shop window or to listen to a newsboy crying the headlines. No one seemed to pay any attention to us. I received no ASTA or SAWM until we reached the overgrown oval of South Park, version 3.0, and even then the warning felt muted and distant. I glanced around and saw a couple of teen boys in Dodger T-shirts sitting on a patch of lawn some twenty feet away. They had their backs to us, but they were the only possible source of the threat.

Fortunately, we were leaving. Willa, dressed in her bright patchwork of torn clothing, was waiting for us on the dirty gray bench. When we sat down next to her, she took a blue-green orb out of her junk-filled shopping bag.

"Nice to see you again," she said. "They told me I'm supposed to stick with you once we hit Four."

"Good," I said. "I need your opinion about something."

As before, the trip through the gate nauseated me, though Ari's stoic expression never changed. From his SPP, though, I could tell that he was merely good at hiding how lousy he felt. What Willa experienced I had no way of perceiving without being hopelessly rude to a fellow psychic. The journey felt shorter, this time through, maybe about ten seconds in all. It brought us right back to South Park, version 4.0.

"Let's find a cab," Ari said, "and go pick up the car. I still have the parking card Spare14 gave me."

"I'm shocked." Willa grinned at him. "Old Sneak usually keeps that kind of thing clutched tight in his little fist."

"He probably thinks he does have it. I gave it back to him, then retrieved it again without his realizing it."

"You're going to go far in TWIXT, Agent Nathan. I just have this feeling about you."

So Ari had other skills consistent with his ability to pick locks. Funny how you can live with a guy for a while and not notice details like that. They didn't improve his driving any, of course. The whole way out to our flat Willa kept clutching her chest with one hand as if she feared a heart attack.

My own moment of fear came when we pulled up in

front of our building. The door to the upstairs flat stood slightly open. I ran a quick SM:L.

"Someone's in the garage," I said.

"Stay in the car!" Ari snapped.

He slid out and drew the Beretta, took a couple of steps forward, then stopped. He laughed and holstered the gun just as a damp Itzak Stein walked down the driveway. I let out my breath in a gasp, which was the first evidence I had that I'd been holding it.

"Are you guys back already?" Itzak said. "I was just washing some crap graffito off the front."

"What made you come out here?" Ari said. "Did someone break in?"

"Someone tried, but I called the police when the alarm tipped my phone. More of that lousy Q wave, whatever it is." He looked down at his wet white shirt. "You need to get a new hose. The old one leaks."

Willa and I got out of the car. I introduced her, and we all trooped upstairs. The alarm, Itzak told me, had signaled an attempted break-in on the lower flat, not the upper.

"This time, though, we got a picture on the front camera," Itzak went on.

"I didn't know we had a security camera," I said.

"That's one of the things Ari and I installed on Sunday. When LaDonna was here." He sighed and looked forlorn for a couple of seconds. "Anyway, let's take a look at what's on the hard drive."

The camera recorded to a DVD. The DVR linked to the TV in our living room. Willa, Itzak, and I sat on the couch, but Ari stood, pacing back and forth, while Itzak scanned through the stored images with the remote control.

"Here!" He froze an image onscreen.

Even in the gray-scale picture, I recognized whom I was seeing: Miss Leopard-Thing herself, in her long skirt and a human jacket, two sizes too big across the back to accommodate her three pairs of breasts in front. At her throat the silver chain necklace gleamed.

"The Maculate psychic," I said. "She came herself this time."

"The what?" Itzak snapped.

"We'll explain later," Ari said. "Run the recording."

Itzak followed orders. Ari stopped pacing and concentrated on the screen. In flickering images the Maculate tried the door handle, then laid her claw-tipped fingers on the wood. I suspected that she was erasing the wards I'd put on the door, or trying to. All at once she pulled her hand away and spun around, glancing this way and that.

"The alarm must have gone off," I said.

"It's silent." Itzak paused the recording and looked my way.

"That wouldn't matter. She'd still know."

Itzak started to speak, then merely shrugged and pressed play on the remote. Onscreen, the psychic ran down the stairs and out of camera range, but a few frames later a flare of light turned the screen white. The flare slowly receded to reveal the empty porch.

"Illegal transport orb, what'll you bet?" Willa said. "She ran right back to her den on Two."

"What?" Itzak said. "Nola, will you please tell me what's going on? I won't waste my breath asking Mr. Closed-mouth Nathan over there."

I debated, then decided that the simplest possible explanation was the best. "She's a were-leopard," I said. "She wants the stuff we've come back to get. She thinks it's in that desk in the lower flat."

Itzak heaved a sigh worthy of grand opera. On the screen the recording continued to display a view of empty porch. Itzak hit fast-forward. We all watched the long sequence of next to nothing until at last a police officer bounced into the fast-forwarded view. Itzak shut the recording off.

"I arrive a few minutes later," he said. "Nothing more to see. Move along, folks. Et cetera." He put the remote onto the coffee table, then turned to me. "Now look, don't you think I deserve some kind of explanation? Sorry, but I don't think 'were-leopard' really fills in the data fields."

Willa shook with suppressed laughter.

"Has LaDonna told you about the job offer yet?" I asked Itzak.

"Yeah. What does that have to do with anything?"

"Everything, that's what. Are you going to take it?"

"I'm seriously considering it, yeah."

"Then you know about the Agency."

"I wouldn't call it knowledge in any certain sense. I'm inclined to believe what LaDonna told me. She doesn't strike me as crazy, but you never know with mathematicians."

"She's telling the truth," Ari said.

"You might as well join up, Tzaki," I said. "Because by watching that recording, you've learned too much for the Agency to let you go." I glared at him. "We have ways of making you forget. None of them pleasant."

"Oh, come on now," Willa said with a snort. "That's not true!"

"Well, yeah, but it was really fun to say."

"I should have known better than to go out to dinner with you and Ari," Itzak said. "I should have realized that LaDonna was an evil temptress, too." He grinned at me. "Not that I mind being tempted. We skype each other a couple times a day, by the way."

"I'm glad to hear it." I returned the smile and stood up. "Ari, why don't you fill Tzaki in? Tell him more than what you think he should be allowed to hear. Willa, come with me, okay? There's something I want to ask you."

As we walked down the hall to the bedroom, I took a good look around. The only things out of order were Itzak's suit jacket and laptop lying on the kitchen table, where he must have put them when he'd arrived.

Although I had a paranoid moment before I got the wall safe open, I found the set of boxes where I'd left them. I brought them out four at a time and set them on the bed while Willa made assorted noises of shock and delight.

"Sixteen!" she said when I finished. "Oh, my God, I've never seen a full set of sixteen before. Are these transport or focus?"

"I'm hoping you can tell me that. I do know they belong to my dad. My brother, the one who's missing, has seen them. They have a real affinity for him. They sang when he touched them."

"May I try?"

"Sure. I don't think we should open any, though."

"I agree. I just want to touch the box. Ah, here's the blue-green. That'll be the safest, because we're here on Four already."

Willa touched the box with the tip of her index finger. No note sounded, but she nodded in satisfaction. "Focus orbs," she said. "Tuned to your dad and his son, from what you just told me." She took her hand away. "You need to be real careful with these. They're worth a fortune. Maybe two fortunes. How did your dad get them?"

"I don't know, but I think he swiped them. The Maculate told me they were stolen property, anyway. Hers, I guess."

"Not legally. Maculates are expressly forbidden to own orbs."

"They are? By some kind of treaty?"

"No, by us, the Walkers Guild on One." Willa grinned at me. "The Maculates don't agree, of course. Now, this spotted lady must have transport orbs, which means a supplier for them, because you can only use those once."

"No wonder she wants this set, then."

"Yes, but unless she knows how to retune them, they're not going to do her one damn bit of good. What have you got to carry these in?"

I rummaged through the closet and found a black backpack, but when I brought it out, Willa shook her head.

"That's got Giants logos all over it. We're going to land in Dodger territory."

More rummaging brought me a shabby brown shoulder bag that had once carried my laptop, back when laptops were four times as thick and a lot heavier than they are now. The boxes just fit inside. The whole thing weighed far more than it should have, given the weight of the boxes themselves. When I slung it over one shoulder, I staggered. I flopped the bag onto the corner of the bed. The mattress groaned and sank an inch or so under it.

"They think you're stealing them," Willa told me. "Better let Agent Nathan carry that."

"He'll have to. I'll never get up the hill to Sneak's office hauling that around. Will they keep getting heavier and heavier?"

"Nah, I doubt it. Usually they only have a single setting on the theft protection app."

I managed to haul the bag and the orbs down to the living room. As Willa and I reached the doorway, I heard Itzak say, "You wouldn't lie to the bosom buddy of your boyhood, would you?"

"Tzaki," Ari said, "I don't have enough imagination to invent all this."

They shared a grim laugh. I brought the carrier bag in and placed it on the coffee table with a grunt. Ari quirked an eyebrow.

"The boxes," I said. "They can manipulate gravity."

"They what?" Itzak snapped. "Nothing can do that!"

"These can."

Ari picked up the bag in one hand, winced, and set it down again. "Apparently true."

"They access the curled dimensions. The ones beyond the macro four we see and move in." Willa tried to be helpful. "On the quantum level, the gravitons emanate from one of the hidden seven spatials, you see. That's why normal gravity's so weak compared to other basic forces."

Ari and I stared at her like the pair of idiots we were.

"I get it," Itzak said. "So they can induce a flow of gravitons when they need to."

"Yes." Willa smiled at him. "The associated AI chip holds the danger parameters that activate the effect."

Ari sighed his insurance adjuster sigh. I wondered if I should have been one, too.

"Nola," Ari said, "you did remember to lock the wall safe, didn't you?"

I turned around and hurried back down the hall. Sure enough, I'd left the safe standing open. I shut the door, then twirled the lock and replaced the Monet poster. Before I left the bedroom, I changed into clean underwear. When I changed the radiation badge over to the clean bra, I noticed that the blue line on the gel had spread over a third of the surface. I longed to take a proper shower. The shower in Spare14's office had mold in all the corners. Unfortunately, I hadn't brought my makeup with me. Washing off what I was wearing would put me at risk.

I started to return to the living room. As I passed the kitchen door, I heard a whimper. Or-Something materialized on the counter and gazed at me with piteous eyes. Its snaggly brown teeth spoiled its attempt to look cute.

"Hungry?" I said. "Okay, let's see what I've got."

I found half a can of tuna and some ancient salads in the fridge and put those out for the critter. While I watched it chow down, inspiration struck. Aunt Eileen had given me a special pad of paper for grocery lists—not that I ever remembered to use it. I found it and a pencil and wrote a note to José, asking for his help. Telling him the address of the office, however, would put Spare14's cover story at risk.

"I need to talk with you, but I can't get out to BG territory. Can you tell this critter to find me in your SanFran? I'll be in North Beach off Columbus in a little while."

I wrapped the note in stale pita bread and held it out.

"José," I said. "Take it to José."

Or-Something snatched it, gobbled it down, note and all, and disappeared into Interchange, or so I hoped.

Which was where we needed to go, even though I loathed the thought. I wondered if the Maculate could discern that the orbs had left the premises. I hoped she could, so she'd stay away. I could imagine her trashing the flat in a fit of temper. When I voiced the problem, Itzak offered to stay until we got back.

"I might as well start composing my resignation letter for the bank," Itzak told me. "It's obvious I'm in too deep to get out now."

"Well, hey, I was just kidding. No one will do anything to you if you turn down the job."

"Oh, I know that. I'm intrigued, is the problem. I want to know more about these deviant worlds and Qi talents and all the rest of it. I'll skype LaDonna later and tell her."

The rest of us were just about to leave when the landline phone rang. Since I received no mental overlap from any of my family members, I let the answering machine pick up.

"Miss O'Grady, this is Mr. Singh, the realtor. I have gotten more complaints from the neighbors about firecrackers on the sidewalk and strange persons wearing cat costumes. I have explained to them that you are not at fault, but they do not seem placated. Please call me at your next convenience." He clicked off.

"I don't have the slightest idea when my next convenience will be," I said. "Poor guy. We're probably taking years off his life. But that reminds me. Tzaki, that graffito — what was it?"

"Just some dirty words."

"Good. Look, if you see a black circle with arrows coming out of it, leave it alone. I'll take care of it when we get back."

"Another mystery." Itzak rolled his eyes. "Well, good luck on wherever it is you're going. And I hope you get back."

"Yeah, so do I. I sure hope we do. All of us."

CHAPTER 14

WILLA RETURNED US TO INTERCHANGE, then departed for her next job. The afternoon shadows had lengthened, and the entire sky blazed orange and red with sunset. On Market Street, when we reached it, a jumble of streetcars and patched-together automobiles honked and clanged. A uniformed policeman stood in the intersection with Second Street and directed traffic with a whistle and hand signals. He wore big white gloves like a cartoon character. Thanks to this legitimate function of Chief Hafner's police force, we made it across safely and started up the hill toward Spare14's office.

Ari had slung the shoulder bag containing the boxes bandolier-style across his body in such a way as to leave his gun hand free, but the strap would interfere with a smooth draw of the Beretta should he need it. I had such a bad case of nerves that I gathered Qi for an ensorcellment reserve. I felt the same distant warnings I'd felt down in South Park, but they never grew any stronger or more focused, merely persisted like an ugly whisper in my mental ear.

As we made our way uphill, I noticed that well-dressed people outnumbered the scruffy. They all walked fast, mostly downhill, looked straight ahead, and traveled in pairs or little groups. Workers, I figured, heading home for the evening, and very aware that the nights in this city belonged to the underclass, not to them. Some of the best-dressed women walked with beefy young men whose grim expressions and obvious shoulder holsters marked them as bodyguards.

In all the blocks up to Columbus, I saw only one person who looked older than forty, a lifer with big money, I figured, from his beautifully tailored gray suit and his bodyguard. In the warm day, and thanks to the close crowd, I realized something else about Interchange. No one used deodorant.

Now and then we came across beggars with radiation-caused birth defects: a man with no legs sitting on a square of wood with wheels, a woman blind because she had no eyes, only flesh where they should have been. Some of the well dressed dropped coins into their laps as they hurried on by. Others swung wide to avoid them.

We passed a few street people who paused to give me the once-over. Some stared; others glanced sideways, trying to hide their attention. I picked up SPPs that told me they were wondering about something and longing for something. Logic filled in the blanks: wondering if I were Nuala and fantasizing about the Chief's reward money. Most lost interest and turned away as my disguise held. Two, however, a woman on Market Street and a newsboy as we crossed Sutter, stared a little longer and looked a little deeper. Their SPPs seemed to say, "could be her, could be her." I hoped I was only being paranoid.

We reached Spare14's office to find the metal grate and the door behind it locked. Ari took his piece of wire out of his jeans pocket. I stood between him and the alley while he picked both locks. He held the door for me, then followed me inside.

"We could have just rung the bell," I said.

"I know, but I want to give Spare14 something to think about. If I can work these locks, a professional would have the doors open in no time at all."

"I'm glad you don't consider yourself a pro."

He chuckled under his breath. At the top of the stairs Jan stood waiting with his gun drawn. "Oh, it's only you," he said. "I thought so, but Sneak here is ready to transmit the panic code."

"I am not." Spare14 stepped into view. "Nathan, I do wish you'd ring the bell like a normal person."

"I was just proving my earlier point. You should get better locks on those doors."

"Ari?" I broke in to what looked like a brewing argument. "I'll take that bag."

I braced myself for the weight. Ari unslung it and handed it over. It weighed only a reasonable amount, as if the anti-theft app had turned its gravitons off, or whatever it is you do with gravitons.

"It's much lighter now," I said.

"Yes, I noticed that the moment we touched down on Interchange."

Spare14 quirked an eyebrow. Ari crossed his arms over his chest and said, "About those locks."

I left the men arguing over Ari's criminal tendencies and carried the set of boxes into the bedroom. I laid the satchel in the bottom of the suitcase and piled our clothes over it. I returned to the living room to find Spare14 sitting at his desk and Ari standing at the window, keeping watch. Jan nodded my way to acknowledge that I'd come back into the room.

"Things have gone quite nicely on Five," Spare14 said to me. "Your father should arrive here tomorrow."

My heart pounded for a few beats, so loudly that I was surprised no one else heard it.

While we'd been on Four, Spare14 and Hendriks had laid in a supply of deli food, including some green salad that I could actually eat. It also provided leftovers to feed Or-Something when it showed up with a note from José.

"Want to talk too. Tomorroh Leftys' Hoffbrow on Eddy just up from Market 3 o'clock. Can you be thair?"

Along with some pasta in pesto, I fed the Chaos critter a note saying yes, Ari and I would be there. It gobbled everything down, burped with a waft of garlic, then vanished on its way back to the BG camp.

That evening the three TWIXT officers spent a long time arguing about what to do next as well as how far their authority to do anything extended. Although the SanFran justice system was utterly corrupt, it had been officially des-

ignated an indigenous cultural expression derived from local conditions. According to TWIXT regulations, agents
thus had no right to meddle with it, as Spare14 pointed out.

"Yes, of course," Jan said with some exasperation. "But
the gang we're dealing with has no respect for the trans-
world legal system. Law and order mean nothing to them."

"As far as I can tell," I said, "we're dealing with an essentially Chaotic world level, worse even than my home
world."

"True," Ari put in, "but we're here to represent the
forces of Order, as your agency would have it, not to in-
crease the Chaos. If TWIXT embodies anything, it's the
principle of Order."

"Ah, but remember, I'm not part of TWIXT. That makes
me a wild card in this poker hand."

All three of them stared at me for a moment. Jan seemed
to be suppressing a smile.

"Besides," I went on, "if TWIXT should respect the indigenous system, and if that system's Chaotic, then you really should act in a Chaotic manner yourselves."

"You're having a joke on me, aren't you?" Ari said.

"No, I'm being logical." I grinned at him. "Just like
you've taught me."

Ari growled. Jan laughed, and even Spare14 looked
amused.

"O'Grady has a point." Spare14 leaned back in his chair
and tented his fingers. "Our problem, as I see it, is twofold.
The police here have no respect for the rule of law, and Interpol doesn't exist on this world level. On another world
level, we could introduce ourselves to the local police and
work with them."

"You've all got your CBI IDs, don't you?" I said. "Or do
the police here see the CBI as a rival gang?"

"Unfortunately, they do. We'd have to find some reason
for them to join our operation, and then be very careful
what we told them. They might want to maintain custody of
the world-walker themselves. Because of the money he
could make them, of course."

"Nothing would be easier for this lot," Ari put in, "than
to frame Michael on some false charge."

We sat in a gloomy silence for some minutes.

"I'm thinking," Jan said eventually, "about Storm Blue. At the moment they hold the strong position. What we need to do is weaken it."

"Easier said than done," Ari muttered.

"But look," Hendriks went on. "Nola handed us a weapon with those two addresses. If Chief Hafner learns that the Axeman is trying to oust him and take over, won't the Chief take action? If nothing else, shutting down those safe houses would serve notice on his rival."

"It would also siphon some of the Storm Blue gang's strength," I said. "The police would probably arrest anyone they could catch."

"Or shoot them," Spare14 said with a sigh. "Doubtless for resisting arrest, and it might even be true."

Ari turned from the window. "How do we get Hafner the information?"

"He must have informers," I said. "Maybe even a network of them. Huh, I wonder if the BGs can help us there? I've already set up a meeting with José. He might know where to place the information."

"It's certainly a possibility," Spare14 said. "Though I'd prefer to find O'Grady's brothers before a shooting war breaks out, and one might over this."

"Umph." Jan looked dour. "Very good point."

"I'm not dismissing your idea," Spare14 went on. "We merely need to pick the correct time. Having the O'Grady boys killed in a crossfire would be counterproductive."

"Extremely so," I said.

"Still." Spare14 reached for his landline phone. "Let me just see if I can reach the liaison captain. She should still be up at this hour."

"Is that Valenzuela?" Jan said.

"No, Kerenskya."

"Oh, good! She doesn't mind taking a risk or two."

I hoped that the risk would be to the regulations, not my brothers.

Spare14 dialed, listened, smiled, and began to speak in halting Russian larded with English numbers. Ari glanced my way and rolled his eyes, probably at Spare14's accent.

Neither Jan nor I understood a word of the Russian, though I assumed that both men knew what the coded numbers meant.

"Very well," Spare14 said. "About Hendriks' idea of manipulating the Chief of Police? The liaison captain agrees that it has merit, but it would be best to proceed slowly."

"Rumors first," Jan said. "Vague ones."

Spare14 nodded. "I could contact some of my clients. Sneak makes the occasional book as well as running numbers. I could offer odds on there being a new police chief soon. Leave it quite vague, never mention Storm Blue—in fact, I could hint that one of the major Orange gangs might be considering a move. Just to keep things inchoate, as it were."

"I like that," Jan said.

"Very well, then," Spare14 went on. "What would you say for the odds, ten to one against? The current chief holds four aces, to continue O'Grady's poker analogy."

"Yes, but those odds are too high to arouse much interest," Jan said. "Seven to one, I'd say." He glanced at Ari. "What do you think?"

"I don't understand odds, because I never gamble."

"What, never?"

"Never. It's too easy to lose, and I prefer not to lose at anything."

"Wise of you, Nathan," Spare14 said. "Seven to one sounds reasonable to me. Now, I carry accounts for some trustworthy customers, but occasionally they cut in people I don't know. If anyone drops by tomorrow to put down money, I'll have to ask everyone to hide in the bedroom. Except Eric, I think. My nephew, after all. I'll feel more secure with a Jamaican gunman close at hand."

Spare14 scribbled some notes on a piece of paper, then began working the phone. He called only a dozen people—my best marks, he called them—but judging by his end of the conversation, they were all intrigued.

"There," he said when he'd finished. "We'll see how that rumor spreads. If it reaches the Axeman, he may drop by. Which could be interesting."

Spare14's prediction came true the next morning. We'd

just finished breakfast when the doorbell rang. Although
Ari stayed sitting on the couch, Jan and I retreated to the
bedroom to hide. I left the bedroom door open a crack and
arranged my makeup mirror to give me a tiny, partial look
into the living room. As soon as I heard the downstairs
door open, I received a mid-level ASTA: situation dangerous, no immediate threat.

I whispered the news to Jan, who drew his Beretta and
stood to one side of the door. "Just in case," he murmured.

I heard voices come into the living room, Spare14 and
two other men.

"My nephew," Spare14 was saying. "Eric is another refu-
gee from Jamaican high society."

In the mirror I saw a sliver view of the Axeman. I recognized him from my earlier vision, the round face, the curly
gray beard, the icy blue eyes. Behind him, I could just discern a second white guy, on the short side, thick around the
middle, black hair—not much of a view, but I picked up his
SPP easily enough. Psychotic and not real smart summed
it up.

"Hello, Scorch," Spare14 said to him. "I paid up already
this month."

"We know that, Sneak." The Axeman had an oddly
pleasant voice, the mark of the guilt-free criminal. "I came
to ask you about the odds you've put out. What's the big
idea?"

"I heard rumors. I have to raise enough cash to pay you,
don't I?"

"Rumors, huh? I don't suppose you'll tell me where you
heard them."

"I don't think it matters, really. Just here and there, and
none of them were in the least conclusive. Hence the high
odds against. I did overhear one Orangeman talking when
I went to buy a bottle of gin. He shut up as soon as he realized someone else had come into the store."

"You and that damned gin!" The Axeman laughed and
shook his head. "You've got to stop those little trips to
Dreamland via Geneva. You're a good customer. I'd hate to
lose you to a bad liver."

"Well, it's not as if I indulge constantly."

"Yeah, but when you do, you damn near drown in the stuff." He turned slightly. "Eric, you need to speak to your uncle about these binges."

"He won't listen," Ari said. "My father's been trying to sober him up for years."

"That's one reason why I left Jamaica." Spare14 sounded convincingly annoyed.

The Axeman chuckled, then went on. "Anyway, okay, so rumors are going around, no hard facts. What I really want to know is, have you heard the names of the gangs that are going to make this move? Or I should say, supposedly make the move."

"I've heard two, yes. The Inquisitors and the Riordan Boys."

"Huh!" Scorch had a husky voice, as if he'd breathed a lot of hot smoke. "The Riordan Boys ain't got what it takes."

"The Inquisitors do," the Axeman said. "But only barely."

"What if they joined forces?" Ari put in.

"That's an interesting idea, young Eric! Two Orange gangs? Between them, they could squeeze a lot of juice."

Spare14 groaned at the pun.

"It's giving me the seeds of an idea," the Axeman continued. "What if they joined forces, indeed?"

"Always thinking," Scorch said. "That's you, Boss."

"So what if they did?" Spare14 said. "Once they took over from Hafner, the real fight would just be starting. I can't see either La Rosa or Sullivan turning down the top job just to be polite."

"Especially not La Rosa with Celia to spur him on. He may call his gang the Inquisitors, but she's the one who knows how to apply the hot irons, and I don't mean on his shirts." The Axeman paused for a laugh. "The question would be whose orange would get squeezed the hardest? Neither of them would have much juice left by the end. The end result: a chance for the right person to step in."

"Ah, I begin to catch your drift," Spare14 said.

"If, of course, the rumors are true." The Axeman paused. "In this town, who knows? It's enough to drive a man to drink, all right."

"It provides a temporary escape, at least."

"True, although I've had a vision lately that might lead to a permanent escape."

"You've been chewing glory seeds?"

"Don't get smart with the boss," Scorch said.

"Down, boy!" The Axeman laughed again. "Life looks hopeless to most of us. No way out except the one no one wants to take. But you never know. There are other worlds out there."

"A lovely idea. Getting there, however—"

"Yeah, not so easy. Well, thanks for the information. Come on, Scorch. We've got a few more social calls to pay."

In my mirror I saw Spare14 follow them to the head of the stairs, then start down after them—to lock the doors behind them, I assumed. Jan holstered the Beretta. We waited until Spare14 returned before we joined him and Ari in the living room.

"Well done," Jan said to Spare14. "I admire how calmly you deal with criminals like him."

"It's all show." Spare14 made a sour face and laid one hand on his stomach. "Inside, I'm a quivering mass of terror. Be that as it may, let's hope my ruse worked. He's got to believe that I don't know he's the one behind the current rumors."

"And I also hope that Javert gets back here soon," I said. "I have to agree with Ari. I need to wait for backup before I run more scans, but I really need to run some."

I got my wish an hour or so later, when the landline phone rang. Spare14 answered and said, "Davis! Good. You're all back safely, I take it." He paused, listening. "Very well, if you're sure that's safe." More pause. "Yes, of course, you're right. Fine. We'll see you soon." He hung up the phone. "Your father's with them."

"They're coming here?" Ari asked.

"Yes. They came through the South Park overlap, you see, so they're not far. They'll drop off O'Grady's father, then drive around the edge of the bay to the ocean. Davis has an idea about where they can hide the milk wagon."

I combed some of the curl out of my hair and left my bronze makeup off. Angry or not, I wanted my father to recognize me. In San Francisco, that drive across Market and up to Columbus would have meant a long trek through traffic. In SanFran, Davis called again in ten minutes.

We all went down to the alley, although I hung back in the doorway at the bottom of the stairs and let the TWIXT officers go ahead to the sidewalk. For days I'd been brooding about meeting Dad, knowing what I knew, but I still had no idea of what I was going to say to him.

We heard the fake milk wagon growling along, coming closer and closer. It turned into the alley and stopped with a wheeze of brakes. Davis opened the door and jumped down. He trotted around to the passenger side and helped a thin man, dressed all in blue denim, his hair a solid steel gray, climb down from the cab. Prison clothes, I thought: jeans, blue chambray shirt, jeans jacket, and the jacket had numbers stamped in black across its chest pocket.

I appreciated Ari's warning when I realized that yes, I was seeing my father. Since he'd always worked construction, mostly outside, I was used to seeing him tanned and muscled. Now he was dead pale and painfully thin. He looked gray—not only his hair, but all of him, his face, his skin, his aura—washed out, used up, dangerously low on Qi. He took a step and staggered, then leaned back against the tank and shook his head as if he was trying to clear it. I could see the white-gold torus gleaming at the neck of his denim shirt. He stared down the alley with his mouth slack, simply stared in that one direction.

"Let's have that collar off," Spare14 said. "Davis, you have the code?"

"Yessir, right here." Davis took a slender tube out his shirt pocket. He tapped one end. "Code Twelve. Activate." He waited a few seconds, then nodded. "Okay, I reckon we're ready to go. It's safest for someone with no talents."

Everyone looked at Ari, who allowed himself a brief smile and took the tube.

"Touch it to the collar anywhere," Spare14 said.

When Ari held the code tube up, I could see that it looked something like an old-fashioned glass thermometer. Numbers ran down one edge. A green line pulsed inside.

"Mr. O'Grady?" Ari said. "Allow me."

Dad turned his head slowly and looked him over with a slight frown, puzzled rather than angry.

"I assume you'd prefer to use the name O'Grady," Ari said.

"Yes." Dad sounded exhausted. "Thank you."

Ari cupped a hand, held it up close to the StopCollar, and touched the metal with the code tube. The collar snapped open, lurched forward, and fell into his hand as a straight rod. Dad caught his breath in a gasp and smiled, but the smile struck me as weary, as gray as the rest of him. He started to raise his hands to his neck, then hesitated. He looked at Ari as if he was asking permission.

"By all means," Ari said. "That thing must have been irritating beyond belief."

Dad nodded and rubbed his neck with both hands. He tipped his head back and smiled up at the sky. Ari handed the dormant collar to Spare14, then turned back to my father.

"Someone's here to meet you." Ari stepped out of the way.

Dad glanced around and saw me. "Nola?" He wept, two thin trickles of tears. "Noodles. You're all grown up."

I felt the secret, the wrong he'd done to the heart of my family, like a monster crouching between us. He'd lived a lie with my mother, lied to all of us for years and years, and worst of all, made us lie all unthinkingly to the world around us. I hesitated, sobbed once, then kicked the secret out of the way and ran to him.

What the hell, he was still my dad.

He hugged me, held me tight, and we wept together. He pulled back, caught me by the shoulders, and gazed into my face. "Is it true what they've been telling me?" he said. "About Sean and Michael?"

"It is. This isn't the way we wanted to welcome you home, but I'm sure glad you're here."

He managed a real smile at that. For a few seconds the grayness enveloping him lifted like fog, only to close back in again when he noticed the huddle of TWIXT officers standing nearby.

"It's quite a welcoming committee," Dad said. "A fair number of guns, and then The Squid himself."

"That's because of the kidnapping. Michael's a world-walker like you, Dad. Didn't they tell you that?"

He muttered something under his breath and shivered. "They did not. A world-walker, and he's part of some gang? No wonder we're getting the reception we are." He focused his gaze on Spare14. "That's what you get for taking me away. How was I supposed to raise the boy right?"

Yep. Still my dad. Spare14 stammered, then forced out a smile but said nothing.

"Nola," Ari said. "Let's get you and your father off the street. Davis needs to take Javert down to the ocean."

"Good idea, yeah. Dad, come on."

Ari lingered to speak to Davis. We left the TWIXT officers standing by the tank and climbed the stairs up to the apartment. Dad walked into the middle of the living room and stood looking around him with a slight smile.

"Uh, Dad? There's something I should tell you right away. The guy who took the collar off you is my boyfriend, and he's Jewish, and we're not married, but we live together."

He raised a hand. I ducked. I heard the truck outside start up, and footsteps on the stairs. "A cop?" Dad said. "You're living with some damned Britannic cop?"

"He's not Brittanic! He just learned his English there. He's Israeli."

"Oh. Well, then, that's a bit better."

"You don't care that he's Jewish?"

"Hell, no! The Palisteenis have always been good friends to us Hibernians. We're in the same boat with the damned Brittanics and all. But a cop?"

At that precise moment Ari walked in. He opened his mouth, but I shot him a glance that kept him silent. Dad crossed his arms over his chest and glared at both of us impartially.

"Well, I'm kind of a cop, too," I said, "but this isn't the time or place to tell you about the Agency I work for."

"All right, I'll wait for the bad news. What do you mean, you're not married?"

"Well, we're not. Come on! You know damn well that times have changed. Couples live together all the time."

"I don't care what other people may do or why. You're my daughter, and I tried to raise you right."

"You mean by the rules of that lousy church, don't you? Well, I don't—"

I stopped because Dad shut his eyes and hissed a sigh from between clenched teeth. I remembered the gesture all too well, the calm before a storm of tirade. I also remembered the secret and felt my rage-fueled Qi rising to match his.

"Hey," I snarled. "You're a fine one to get down on me, after what you and Mom—"

His eyes snapped open, two dark blue pools of fear. I'd never seen him frightened before. The gray fog swirled thick around us both as he brought his Qi back under control and I squelched my own rage.

"Well, Mr. *O'Brien*?"

"You know."

"Yes, I do."

"Do the rest of them know?" His voice shook.

"No. Only Ari." I gestured Ari's way. "That's Ari."

More footsteps sounded on the stairs, and I heard Jan's voice, telling Spare14 some story about Javert.

Dad let out a puff of breath and unfolded his arms. "You're right enough. I'm not one to look down my nose at anybody." He glanced at Ari. "Sorry."

"Quite all right," Ari said. "I've never been in prison, but I can see how you'd feel that way about us."

They considered each other, both wary, both silent, until I felt like a bone between two dogs.

"What counts now," I said in desperation, "is finding Michael and Sean."

"Quite right," Ari said. "I'm sure we all realize that."

"No matter what else we'll all fight about later?" I managed to smile at my father. "Dad, now you know you're really back."

"So I do." He glanced at Ari. "I see that one thing hasn't changed in my family. We're not ones for peace and quiet."

"I've noticed," Ari said. "Believe me, sir, I've noticed."

Spare14 and Jan walked into the room to intensify the awkward moment, even though they both kept their facial expressions perfectly neutral. Jan carried a gray duffel bag. When he set it down by the couch, I noticed black letters printed on it, "O'BrienFM H-Block 814." Ari and Dad never looked away from each other. I decided that screaming to break the tension would be a bad move.

"Dad," I said instead, "I've got your set of orbs. They're here." I gestured in the direction of the bedroom. "Want to check them out?"

His smile broke through the fog. "Thank God," he said. "I've been worrying about those for thirteen years, wondering if you mother would sell the damned desk with everything still in it."

"Not likely! She's kept all of your clothes, everything you ever touched." I realized that there was a thing he must want to know, and badly. "She never remarried, either."

For a moment I thought he might weep again. He curbed his Qi and followed me into the bedroom.

As soon as I closed the door behind us, the boxes sounded their notes in a scramble of chords and dissonances. Dad knelt down by the suitcase and tossed its contents onto the mattress to reveal the set. In the dim room the bright-colored boxes seemed to glow. I sat down on the floor next to him.

"Michael said they remembered you," I said.

"He's right."

As Dad touched each box, the orb inside sang out, one pure note. Each lid snapped open for a few seconds, too, so I could glimpse each one and see that their colors matched their boxes.

"Good. They're still functional." He looked up, abruptly solemn. "Speaking of Michael and the family, the releasing magistrate warned me that Pat was dead. Spare14 must have told her."

"Yeah." I heard my voice catch. "He was murdered. It was because of the lycanthropy."

"He did develop that, then, did he? That's another thing I've been worrying about."

"He was shot by a nutcase who hated werewolves on principle."

Dad winced, shook his head, and looked away. "Did they ever catch the murderer?"

"Yes. I helped track him down. He resisted arrest. He was armed, and so Ari shot and killed him."

Dad considered this in a long troubled silence. "Well," he said eventually, "maybe you've made a good choice for your man, after all." He looked at me and scowled. "Why won't he marry you?"

"He wants to marry me. I keep saying no." I felt my Qi rising, a hot point of pure rage. "How can you lecture me about marriage when—"

"I know! Peace, peace, Nola! Don't you think I realize what a rotten, sinful thing we did, your mother and I?"

"Did she know?"

"Eventually. Not at first. I knew." He caught his breath with a sob. "Can you understand? We were both so damned young at the time. She was so beautiful, and so like the Deirdre I'd lost." He glanced my way. "I had a twin sister, you see, back home on Five. I watched her die one night of a fever."

In a silence as thick as winter fog, we locked our gazes on each other. My anger trembled just beyond my reach. Listen, O'Grady! I told myself. Stop judging and listen!

"And there she was again, grown up and beautiful and not truly my sister, not in any real sense. Can you understand that?"

"Not really, but I'll try."

He winced again.

"Dad, why didn't you tell her the truth?"

"Oh, but I did. Finally. She was still living at home, and so I went over to take her to a movie, or so Dan and Nora thought. Instead we went to the park to talk. I was going to tell her everything and end the affair and then throw myself off the bridge. The trouble was, she had something to tell me first." His eyes drooped, weary with memory. "She was pregnant— with Dan, that was—and so there we damned well were."

Everything I thought I knew about my mother dissolved like fog in hot sunlight.

"She'd make love with you," I said, "but no birth control?"

"I should think not! Piling one sin on top of another would have done us no good."

I decided that I could save that hurricane-force argument for later, much later. Like, never. I knew without being told that my mother never would have had an abortion, legal or not. I remembered her contorted face, her pure animal rage, when I admitted that I'd been to the clinic and had the procedure. No wonder—I'd taken the way out of my trap, a way closed to her for all kinds of reasons.

"I had some stupid idea," Dad went on, "that we could marry, have the child, and then live apart in the same house as brother and sister. You can guess how long that lasted."

I nodded. Maureen had been born sixteen months after Dan.

"And in time, in a way, we forgot. That I suppose you won't be able to believe, that we both grew so used to everything, my work, our babies, our normal life, being treated just like any other young couple, that we pushed the damn secret out of our minds."

"Until TWIXT came for you."

"Until then, yes. I never thought they'd hop so many levels to get me. The Brittanics put pressure on them, probably. That's what they do, the arrogant bastards, act as if they still own half the damned world." He gave me a wry smile. "I got careless, that night, and didn't take an orb with me, so I couldn't get away when the cops ran my truck off the road. I tried to jump out of the cab and get clear enough to—" He hesitated, then finished the sentence. "—to just walk fast. I suppose you must know what that means. There were too many of them. I couldn't get free of them."

"What if you had gotten away? They still would have been after you. You'd have been on the run. We still would have lost you."

"At least I'd have been able to come home one last time and say good-bye."

"That would have helped, yes."

"Did you ever get the letter I sent?"

"Yes. Reb Zeke got it to me before he died."

"He's dead?"

"Yeah. Long story. Let's see, I bet you'd like to hear all the family news. Dan's in the army. They just sent him to officer school or whatever they call that."

I ran through the last thirteen years, though I deleted a few facts, like Sean being gay. Dad was troubled enough by Maureen's divorce. While he listened, Dad began picking up the clothes and other stuff he'd tossed out of the suitcase to get at the boxes. He put them back one thing at a time, folding the clothes, shaking his head over the carton of ammunition Ari had brought along, until he came to my pad of paper.

"And what's all this?" He gestured at the notes.

"Psychic information I've picked up over the past few days. Stuff relating to Michael and Sean's disappearance. I don't understand all of it, like that bit about the Laughing Woman. I saw her in trance, and she creeped me out."

Dad held the pad out at arm's length to read the note. He's nearly sixty now, I thought. His vision's changed.

"Huh," he said. "You wouldn't remember this, most likely, not with the front of your mind, anyway. That's Laughing Sal from the old Playland amusement park. You must have been what?—six or seven—and for your birthday we went to that museum of mechanical toys under the Cliff House. She scared half the life out of you. You didn't believe me when I kept telling you she was just a big wind-up doll."

The memory flooded back: the enormous automaton, bobbing and swaying, her horrible mechanical laugh, and the way I cried until Dad picked me up and carried me away from her. With the memory came a stab of knowledge.

"She gave generations of children nightmares, I'd wager," Dad was saying. "A damned ugly thing she was."

I laid a hand on his arm and interrupted. "Playland! It was down by the beach, wasn't it?"

"Practically on it. Now, it was long gone by the time I arrived in San Francisco, but there were pictures with the exhibit."

"That's where Mike and Sean must be, in Playland, or

the place in this world level that corresponds to where Playland was in Four. Or maybe Playland's only where we should start looking. I don't know exactly, but it's a crucial clue."

He whistled under his breath. "We'd best go talk to dear old Inspector Spare14. Huh, he's come up in the world since I last saw him."

"Wait a minute! Was he the one who arrested you?"

"Oh, yes. He led the team. He was just an ordinary cop, back then, but that's one reason the magistrate on Five listened when he asked for me. She figured he'd know if I was a safe release or not."

And was that why Spare14 had gone looking for me back on Four, when I was hunting down Belial? He must have known all along that my father had a big family, and that at least some of us were bound to have talents. Sneak. He could be that, all right. I decided that I could confront him later. We had more pressing problems to solve.

"I see," I said. "Before we join the others, can I ask you a question about the orbs?"

"Of course."

"Where did you get them? A Maculate woman's been telling me that they're stolen property."

He laughed, just softly and briefly. "No doubt she sees it that way. My guild on Five confiscated them from the Maculates. They attuned them to me when I passed my apprenticeship. Huh! It's taken her long enough to find them—no, wait." He paused to count something up. "The spotted hag that owned them originally must be long dead by now. I suppose this one learned about them some way or another and set about tracking them down."

"Why do the guilds keep them away from the Maculates? Or is that a secret?"

"No real secret at all, though I'm not sure who knows about it. It's something I learned in prison." His voice trailed away, and for a moment he looked out at nothing. "You hear a lot of strange stuff inside. Some of it's even true." He forced out a smile. "But I believe this particular story. Some of the Maculates hunt for ape. It's their favorite food. Not many apes are left on their home world, so they have to hunt elsewhere. The meat fetches a very high price on the black market back on Two."

"Black market?"

"Well, the Maculates are civilized. Most of them would never eat a sapient species. But there are always a few, you know, in any race, who like crossing the lines. Eating ape gives them a thrill, I suppose."

"Sapient?" I turned cold when I remembered the meat locker I'd seen in the mirror-vision. Chimp and gorilla parts? I only wished. "You mean us, don't you? Human beings."

"Yes." He smiled, but it wasn't a pleasant smile. "I'm afraid I do."

I scrambled up from the floor. "There's something I've got to tell Ari right now."

"Oh? About Playland?"

"That, too. But we left his buddy guarding our flat back home, and two of the Maculates have already tried to break in."

Chapter 15

"YOU CAN USE THE TRANS-WORLD ROUTER in my desk," Spare14 said. "Do you think you can reach your friend that way?"

"Let's hope," Ari said. "Let me just get my phone."

Ari strode across the living room and charged into the bedroom. Dad and I sat down on the couch. Jan drew his Beretta—on general principles, I supposed—and took up a watch at the window while Spare14 fussed with the equipment in his desk drawer. I concentrated on banishing Possibility Images of a half-eaten Itzak.

"I could take your Ari back to Four," Dad said, "not that I want to face your mother just yet or Eileen and Jim, either."

"You wouldn't have to," I said. "There's an overlap area in South Park. The vitrification, you know."

"Ah. I used to know where other gates were here in San-Fran. The entire level is full of them." He smiled. "Like a Swiss cheese. But it's been a long time since I walked round this city."

Spare14 glanced our way and pushed out a sickly smile that might have been an apology. He returned to working on the router. Ari strode out of the bedroom with his laptop in one hand and his cell phone in the other.

"Come sit down," Spare14 said to him. "I've set up a separate password for you."

"Thanks," Ari said. "Let's hope I can reach his phone. I've got no idea how often he picks up e-mail."

"If he's skyping LaDonna," I put in, "he's bound to be online a lot."

"If he's doing what?" Dad muttered.

I did my best to fill him in on thirteen years of digital progress while Ari and Spare14 fiddled with the router and the cell phone. They swore now and then in several languages. At last Ari smiled and held his phone to his ear.

"It's ringing," he announced.

We all fell silent, staring at Ari, until he grinned and spoke in Hebrew into the phone. I only recognized one word, "Tzaki." It was enough, especially since they switched to English after a few exchanges.

"No, I'm not having a joke on you," Ari said. "You saw the footage, didn't you? Well, that's one of them . . . Yes, with the claws . . . What? . . . I have no idea if they'd cook you or eat you raw, but I'd rather we didn't find out . . . Stay away from the flat. We don't care if she claws the furniture . . . Yes, by all means tell LaDonna everything."

At that point Ari lapsed back into Hebrew, and I assumed that Tzaki was doing the same. In a few minutes he clicked off and sighed in profound relief.

"There," Ari said. "He won't go near the place unless the alarms sound, and if that's the case, the police will be there ahead of him. I don't suppose our spotted harridan will risk meddling with the police. They're armed if she does."

"Oh, great," I said. "A dead Maculate on our steps— that's all we need! I wonder what the neighbors will say about that to Mr. Singh?"

"Let's hope it doesn't happen." Ari turned to Spare14. "Do you have any idea where they're finding the transport orbs?"

"I don't, no." Spare14 looked faintly mournful.

I felt my father's impulse to speak, quickly stifled, and turned to look at him. He looked blandly back, as innocent as the morning dew, to use one of his favorite phrases. Neither Spare14 nor Ari had noticed. Jan, however, quirked an eyebrow and gave Dad a pointed glance. I decided to change the subject.

"You know," I said, "I've been thinking about what happened to Nuala, the girl who was the Chief's mistress. You told me that all they found of her was one leg, right? I wonder if the rest of her ended up in a Maculate's stomach?"

Talk about a successful ploy—the others forgot orbs and looked as sick as I felt. Spare14 cleared his throat several times with a little gulp.

"Good God," Spare14 said. "I surmised she'd been murdered by a rival gang." He cleared his throat again. "But it never occurred to me that she might have been eaten."

Jan went dead pale and wiped sweat from his forehead. Ari appeared utterly unmoved, but I could feel the cold Qi of rage pouring out of him.

"That renegade Maculate with Storm Blue," I continued, "the one that broke into my LDRS. He must have transport orbs at his disposal. I'm sure he's the guy we chased off our front steps."

"Wait," Ari said. "If he's a world-walker, and he's in the gang, why would they need Michael?"

"You don't have to be a world-walker to use a transport orb," Dad broke in. "You trigger it by shattering the outer shell."

For instance, I assumed, by throwing it hard onto a sidewalk.

"Thank you." Ari nodded his way, then turned back to Spare14. "We can use this. When Hafner finds out what happened to his mistress, no doubt he'll be willing to help us."

"A sudden change of heart," Jan muttered, "about the CBI."

"Let me think." Spare14 drummed his fingertips on his desk. "We need to decide how to approach him. Perhaps we should let the rumors circulate before we do. When are you meeting the leader of the BGs—José, isn't it?"

"Yes, that's his name," Ari said. "At three o'clock. Soon, in other words. I agree about waiting to bring in Chief Hafner. For one thing, I don't think we should try to follow up on the Playland tip till after I've spoken to José."

"I agree, too," Jan said. "We need all the advance information we can get before we move into the ruins. Especially if Storm Blue have an ape-hunter in their ranks." He glanced at me. "You don't think he's a professional, do you?"

The memory of the meat locker rose in my mind. What I'd thought were chimp parts might well have been the remains of children. I nearly gagged but steadied my voice. "He could be a pro, yeah. If he is, what do you bet he comes here to hunt? The cops don't care what happens to people who don't have money and who do have physical problems. The outcasts, in other words. He can get away with murder."

"Oh, yes." Ari's voice was quiet and steady, but I could pick up his rage. "The helpless always make good victims."

The psychic atmosphere in the room turned morbid. And Miss Leopard-Thing, then, could sell his kills back at home. No wonder she could afford all those silver chains.

Before we left, Spare14 gave Ari a wad of local currency and a pair of keys to the front door, a compromise, I supposed, to keep him from picking the locks again. I repaired my makeup and put more curl in my hair. I also told Dad to call me Rose, not Nola, and explained why.

"All right." Dad glanced Ari's way and made a snorting sound. "My *wild* Irish Rose, eh?"

"I've asked her to marry me a hundred times," Ari said. "In any sort of ceremony she'd like."

I'd never heard him sound defensive before. It had a certain charm.

Dad turned my way and looked at me with a gimlet eye worthy of Aunt Eileen. "I see that we'll have to all sit down and discuss this later."

I felt a dark cloud of lawful wedded doom hovering over me.

Rather than stay in the company of two TWIXT officers, my father came with us when Ari and I went to meet José. Getting to walk down a street with family, being outside without the StopCollar—it was all a grand luxury to him, he told me, even if we were on Interchange.

I was too aware of the Chief's bounty on Nuala to enjoy anything. Some of the people we passed stared at us openly, although I realized that most were looking not at me, but at my father's gray hair. He looked poor, and he was a lifer—not the usual combination in SanFran. Still, every now and then I noticed someone studying me. I could practically hear them drooling at the thought of Chief Hafner's reward.

We walked over to Mason, then caught a cable car down to Market. We sat on the outside bench and clung to poles like the apes we are. I was painfully aware that I sat between father and boyfriend; occasionally they glanced across me to each other but never smiled. After a few uncomfortable blocks of this, Dad leaned back against the wooden bench and studied the passing view as if he were memorizing it. At the Sutter Street stop, he turned to me.

"About those transport orbs," Dad said, "it's Wagner the Fence we'll be wanting to see—that is, if he's still in business. His establishment used to be just down the street from Lefty's."

"Uh, Dad, you know this guy?"

"I did a bit of business with him years and years ago." He frowned, thinking. "The old man might well have passed on by now. Well, we'll see."

The shop had indeed survived where Dad remembered it. *Wagner and Son, Used Books* filled the ground floor of a soot-stained brick building a few blocks up from Market. A big sheet of orange cellophane covered the front window. Through the orange glow I could see stacks of books, piled any which way on top of a table. A small brass plaque on the door read, "Mitch Wagner, proprietor."

Before we went in, Ari unbuttoned his denim shirt to reveal the shoulder holster, then held the door for me. It took my eyes a few minutes to adjust to the gloom. Dust motes drifted in the orange light from the window. Strands of cobwebs hung from the ceiling and swayed in the draft from the door. Dad went straight to the back of the store, well, as straight as anyone could walk in there, because books crammed the entire small store, on shelves up to the ceiling, in piles on the floor. Ari followed Dad, but before I could join them, St. Maurice appeared in the crowded aisle.

"*Libri,*" he said. "*Abest TTT. Specta, stulta!*"

He disappeared. Books, right, full of information in a place that had no Tela Totius Terrae, that is, no World Wide Web. I looked around as ordered, saw a shelf marked "Local History" and went right for it. I riffled through the decaying volumes and pamphlets fast. Even though my hands got filthy and itchy, I found treasure: *Playland As We Knew It*, a crumbling volume with blurry pictures, but pictures nonetheless. I hurried after Ari, who was standing at the back of the store with my father.

They were facing the counter, talking with a guy who looked around thirty. At first I thought I was seeing Itzak Stein. Mitch was a short guy, kind of stocky but by no means fat, with the same sort of looks as Itzak, neither handsome nor unattractive, with thinning hair cut real short. But the smile—not Itzak's charming grin—was a predatory twitch of his mouth, and his dark eyes stayed narrow behind his wire-rim glasses. He wore faded jeans and a long-sleeved shirt that once upon a time had been white.

The son, I assumed. As Dad had suspected, the old man must have died. I picked my way through the narrow aisles between bookcases and dodged around unstable stacks of books. Mitch was standing behind a counter scattered with magazines. An old-fashioned mechanical cash register sat at one end, a gooseneck lamp at the other.

"Remember me?" Dad said to him. "You were little more than a boy, the last time I was in here."

"Not real well, but yeah, you look familiar. A friend of my father's?"

"A customer of his, anyway. Years ago now, I bought some rare books from him."

"I think I do remember you." Mitch smiled briefly. "You took a couple of items from the occult list."

"I did, the ones in Irish."

When I joined Dad in the pool of light, Mitch looked up and caught his breath. He went pale around the mouth.

"Nuala," he said in a less than steady voice. "Oh, my God! Nuala."

"What?" I put a snap in my voice. "What's with this Nuala crap? My name is Rose, you sucker."

Mitch leaned over the counter and took a good long look at my face. "Shit," he said eventually. "Yeah, you're not her. Sorry. You've got to be related to her somehow."

"Maybe I am. None of your business, is it?"

"None!" Mitch held up one hand like a Boy Scout and glanced at Ari. He focused a terrified gaze on the Beretta. "What is this? A heist?"

"Not if you're a good boy." Ari patted the shoulder holster. "Jamaicans aren't known for their patience, however, so I suggest you cooperate."

"What do you want from me?"

"Information. You've been selling transport orbs to a Spottie, haven't you? I know an organization that'll pay me for a rat-out. Ever hear of TWIXT?"

Mitch began to sweat.

Dad joined in. "You don't want to go inside on Five. Take it from me. I hear that slam on One is worse."

Mitch gulped, but he never looked away from Ari's gun hand. "What do you want to know?"

"Who's the Spottie, and what's he doing here?" Ari said.

"I don't have a name for him. He wouldn't tell me, would he? He comes in with cash, a lot of cash. I'm not about to ask him where he gets it, either. I don't want a faceful of claws. Get it?"

"Don't get stroppy with me, Mitch." Ari stepped closer to the counter. "Unless you want a faceful of what I have on offer." He drew the Beretta.

"Okay, okay! He calls himself Claw. That name's probably a pseudonym, though."

"Gosh gee," I said. "Ya think?"

Mitch made a sour moué in my direction. "Whatever. He's got to be a renegade from Two. I don't know if he works the meat market or not. I'd guess he does."

"Why?" Ari snapped.

"He wants orbs that'll take him to Two and then back here. He must have some reason to go back and forth."

"That makes sense. Does he ever ask for orbs to other worlds?"

"Yeah, just lately he wanted a couple to Four. I had some, luckily."

Our world. Dad and I exchanged a knowing look.

Ari kept after Mitch. "Is Claw Orange or Blue?"

"Blue all the way. He came in here the first time with Scorch the Torch."

"Scorch vouched for him?" Ari holstered the Beretta. "So he's linked to Storm Blue?"

Mitch nodded.

"Where are you getting the orbs?" I said. "From the cops?"

"Not from any of Hafner's men. If this guy's a cop at all, he's from some other force. I don't know where he's from or what he is. He'd kill me if I tried to pump him."

His SPP radiated truth and terror. "I believe you," I said. "He's not a pleasant customer, huh?"

"No." Mitch laughed in a high-pitched giggle. "Not pleasant at all. He comes in every couple of months, usually has a pair for sale. When I told him I had a steady customer for trips to Two and back, he started bringing those pretty much exclusively. I pay in cash. Honest to God, I don't know his name."

"That I'll believe." Ari picked up the questioning again. "And then you get the word to Claw? How?"

"I don't do anything. He knows somehow. He told me once that the orbs call to him."

Ari glanced at Dad. "They could," Dad said. "Which means he's got talents of a sort. Most Maculates do. That's what makes them such good hunters."

Ari considered Mitch for a moment. In a swift strike he reached across the counter with both hands and grabbed the fence by the shirt. Magazines plummeted to the floor. Mitch squealed and flailed, but Ari dragged him half onto the counter until they were face-to-face.

"If I find out that you've told Storm Blue we were in to see you, I go straight to TWIXT with the tip." Ari's voice stayed perfectly calm. "Do you understand? They'll take you off this level so fast you won't have time to shit your trousers."

Mitch made a gurgling sound that amounted to "Yes." Ari let him go. Mitch slid off the counter, got his feet under him, and began fussing with his torn shirt. I noticed Dad watching Ari in admiration. The dark cloud of doom crept closer.

"I want to buy this." I waved the Playland book in Mitch's direction.

Mitch merely stared at me as if I'd spoken in Latin. For a moment I wondered if I had. Ari took a dollar bill out of his jeans pocket and tossed it on the counter.

"There," Ari said. "Shall we go have lunch?"

"A fine idea," Dad said. "I might be back another day, Mitch, to look at that occult list again."

Mitch forced out a smile, grabbed the dollar, and gibbered an "Okay, yeah, swell."

So this was where Dad had gotten the Hisperic document I'd found in his desk drawer. As we left the store, I was thinking about how normal he'd appeared, back when we were all children, the hard-working construction foreman, the father of a typically large Catholic family, a superior sort of ordinary blue-collar guy. No wonder his sudden disappearance had baffled everyone for so long!

"Dad," I said, "you sure know how to keep secrets."

"I've always had to." He gave me a quick smile. "I'll tell you about Hibernia sometime." The smile disappeared. "It would explain a number of things."

Lefty's Hofbrau catered to the Orange side of SanFran. Orange-and-black leather upholstered the booths. Giants' memorabilia plastered the dark wood-paneled walls: pennants, photos, game programs, and bits and pieces of uniforms. I noticed a Willy Mays jersey, lovingly framed under glass, and saw a couple of gloves signed by pitchers I'd never heard of. Both doppelgängers and individuals unique to the world level must have made up the team.

In the front a cafeteria setup featured indeterminate animal parts in gravy and lots of potato dishes. The smell of heavy food made me gag.

"I can't eat any of that disgusting stuff," I said. "You guys get what you want."

Dad shot me a sharp glance. "You're not pregnant, are you?"

"No. Dad, please!" I turned away to look the place over. "I don't see José anywhere. They'll probably be late."

They were, and the minute they walked in, I knew why. José was dying. Skinny, bald, dead pale except for the thick crust of growths that covered half his face, he walked slowly and kept turning his head to see out of his one good eye. The two guys he'd brought with him watched every step he made, and they kept their arms out away from their bodies, ready to catch him if he fell.

When I'd last seen José, about a month earlier, I'd noticed that the wartlike growths had crept toward one eye. They'd reached it and filled in the socket. His rock-bottom Qi level told me that they were sending tendrils into his brain. I recognized one of his two friends: Little Sam, who stood well over six feet, a barrel-big and barrel-solid teenager missing half his teeth. The other guy I'd never seen, almost as tall as Sam but slender, with dark curly hair and dark skin. His right hand looked normal. Where his left should have been he had only a smooth stump of wrist, too smooth to be due to an injury.

When they sat down in the oversized booth we'd snagged, José introduced him. "This is Orlando. He's going to take over the BGs when I'm gone. That'll be in a couple weeks probably, maybe a month."

I had to admire the way he refused to hide from the obvious. I figured he didn't want sympathy, either.

"Okay," I said. "You know Ari, and this is my father, and Mike's, too, of course—Flann O'Grady."

"Pleased to meet you, sir." José held out a six-fingered hand in Dad's direction. "Looks like you've been inside."

"Yeah, on Five." Dad shook hands with him. "I don't recommend the experience."

Everyone laughed except Ari, who smiled.

"Lunch is on us," Ari said. "Let's go get in line, but I'm paying."

"We'll get stuff for José." Orlando had a pleasantly dark voice. "Sam, try not to eat the man into bankruptcy, okay?"

Everyone laughed again as they got up and trailed after Ari, but as soon as we were alone, José let out his breath in a long sigh.

"Hey," he said, "sorry you have to see me like this, BG Sis. Wanna ask you, how's Sophie? She okay?"

"Yeah, if you mean her health, but she's developed lycanthropy."

"Jeez! And I thought I had problems!" He started to laugh, coughed, coughed harder, and grabbed a napkin from the table. He hid what he spat up, but I could guess that it was blood.

The growths, I assumed, were also putting down roots into his throat. I slid a glass of water across the table. José grabbed it and drank.

"That's better," he said. "So our little Sophie's a werewolf? I guess it goes to show. You think you know someone, and here you don't know shit." He grinned. "Don't look so sad, Nola. I'm glad I'm checking out of here. Why do you think we call old people lifers? This place is worse than any jail I ever heard of."

"I never put that together, about the lifers, I mean. But, crud! Your eye—it must hurt."

"When it gets too bad, we'll have a little good-bye party, and then Orlando will solve the problem for me." José pointed a finger at his head. "Bam." He picked up the glass again and had another drink of water.

I managed—barely—to keep from crying. This guy had saved my brother's life once and was going to help us do so again, but I could do nothing for him. When I'd first signed up with the Agency, they'd warned me that I was going to face more misery than I could fix. They'd been right.

"Anyway," José went on, "I owe you an apology. We did a lousy job of protecting Brother Mike and Brother Sean, didn't we? Shit, I shoulda known Storm Blue was up to something before they moved in. We shoulda gone with the guys when they walked down to the gate. Figured it was safe. Done it a hundred times. Ya know how that goes."

"I do, yeah, and I don't blame you for anything."

"Thanks." He meant it sincerely. "So, what do you need the BGs to do?"

"Spread rumors," I said. "Let the grapevine tell Chief Hafner that someone wants his job. Mention that Storm Blue's getting the money together to take the job. By the way, how much can the Axeman charge for a trip out of here?"

"Two thousand a head."

I thought back to the currency section of the TWIXT file. You could buy a three-piece tailored suit downtown for fifty. Steak dinner, two or three bucks, depending on the ambience.

"That's plenty of bribe money, all right," I said.

"And guns, yeah." José paused and turned slightly in his seat, as if he were getting comfortable, but I noticed that he turned his good eye toward a nearby table. He leaned forward and murmured. "You know, there might be a couple people in here now who are straining their eardrums. Don't look. You'll spook them."

"Okay." I spoke a little louder. "Did you know that there's a renegade Maculate in Storm Blue?"

"A Spottie?" José grinned and mimicked my increased volume. "Now that's interesting! I can sell that piece of news."

"Can we all guess what happened to Nuala? I wonder what the Chief would think if he knew."

José laughed, a burst of black humor that ended in a coughing fit. I risked a quick glance around and saw a woman in a tight black dress watching us. She looked away fast when she caught me looking at her. José wiped his lips on the napkin in a bloody smear and looked contrite.

"You and Mike gotta be related to her somehow," he said. "Shit! Sorry if I was heartless."

I realized that while he knew about world levels, he'd missed the concept of doppelgänger. "It's okay," I said. "A distant cousin, that's all. But that's why I'm wearing all this makeup. I don't want anyone drawing the wrong conclusion."

The others returned, balancing laden trays. Although José and I both picked at the food, the other men chowed down with a vengeance, even my father. Prison food, I supposed, had been meager and lousy. The barman appeared and brought two pitchers of beer and glasses all round to the table. I noticed that Ari and I were the only ones not drinking. Dad caught my glance and grinned.

"I never did get to drink that six-pack," he said. "The one I went to the market for that night."

The night when he'd been arrested, he meant.

"I don't know what happened to that," I said. "But Uncle Jim bought your truck. It's up on blocks in storage somewhere. He was sure you'd want it when you got back."

For a moment I thought he'd weep. Instead, he saluted me with the glass and had a long swallow of beer.

With the food we received a flood of useful information about Storm Blue and the way that the police chief worked in general. The BGs were a small gang, hustling for whatever they could scrounge, but their very position near the bottom of the hierarchy meant they heard everything worth knowing. Since they presented no threat to the top gangs, no one bothered to watch their mouths around them.

"How many men are there in Storm Blue?" Ari said at one point. "You mentioned the twenty captains."

"Each captain, maybe ten guys under him?" José waved his fork vaguely in the air. "But not all of those are gonna be in town at once. Some are mules, and some of them are gonna be out in the valley picking up shipments to bring in. Some are runners and diggers."

"And girls," Little Sam put in. "Some of those guys are girls. Working the streets, ya know."

"Right. Not all of the guys have guns, either." José paused for a bite of his pot roast. "Maybe fifty gunners." He glanced at Orlando. "Sound about right?"

Orlando nodded his agreement and continued sopping up gravy with a chunk of bread. My stomach clenched. Facing fifty armed men was better than facing two hundred, but still the odds were hopeless.

"Diggers?" Ari said.

"Guys who go through the old dumps, looking for good stuff. Car parts, pieces of radios." José shrugged. "They don't find much anymore. Most of the real loot got found a long time ago, but I guess down in the ruins of L.A. you can still pull up some good shit if you don't mind the rads."

"Ah. I see."

"Now look, when the shit hits the fan, we wanna be there," José went on. "I can give you five guys plus me."

"Not you," Ari said. "With vision in only one eye you

won't be able to see clearly enough. You'll be nothing but a target."

"Yeah," Little Sam put in. "You tell him!"

"Maybe I'd rather go fast than just sit around and wait." José shrugged one shoulder.

"I can understand that." Ari's voice hinted at sympathy. "But if we can do this at all, we're going to need to work with the cops. You and the BGs don't need to be around for them to notice."

"That's true," Orlando said. "But Mike's a BG, and that means some of us gotta be there."

"I can understand the feeling, but if the cops move in on BG territory, it won't do Mike or you any good."

"He's got a point," José said. "I worked too damn hard building us up to let us get torn down in one raid. Listen to the Jamaican! He's thinking."

"Okay, okay," Orlando said. "You're still the boss."

"Damn right." José picked up one of the pitchers and refilled his glass. "I'll drink to that."

Dad, Ari, and I returned to Spare14's office in a somber mood. When we walked in, Spare14 was talking on his landline while Jan sat on the couch with a stack of newssheets in his lap. Spare14 hung up and turned around his chair.

"Well?" he said.

"Fifty gunners," Ari said. "At least. Without help from the police, there's little we can do."

"Just so." Spare14 sounded exhausted. "Unless we can get a Tac Squad from headquarters. I doubt if the liaison captain will agree to a large-scale operation. It would require too much forbidden technology, and even then, the risk to TWIXT agents would be considerable."

"Very high, yes," Jan put in. "Not that we wouldn't run that risk to rescue kidnap victims—if we had a decent chance at success."

"It's too easy for a rescue to go wrong." Ari glanced my way in explanation. "Killing the hostages as well as the rescuers."

"Yeah, I understand that."

"What we need to do, then," Spare14 said, "is to assemble more information before we make our case to Hafner.

The question is whether he'll work closely with a team from the CBI. Us, I mean."

"Hafner's own men would be running a considerable risk, too," Jan said, "if they join us in the Playland part of the operation."

"What about Playland?" I held up the book I'd found. "This'll show us what it was like back in the 1920s. What's it like now? Back in San Francisco it's gone."

Back on my home world, a real estate developer, a man nicknamed "the Golden Rat" had razed Playland-on-the-Beach and built condominiums in its place. Here on Interchange, or so Spare14 told us, the amusement park had shut down one ride or concession at a time until nothing remained but crumbling ruins behind a rusting fence.

"No one would ever have suspected that the Axeman has a hideout there," Jan put in. "A dismal sort of place, and I gather it's swarming with vermin."

"Maybe including some of the two-legged kind," I said.

"Nola," Ari said, "must you keep repeating lines from bad films?"

I ignored the question with as regal an air as I could manage.

"We don't have the men and body armor to shoot our way through a rubble field," Ari continued.

"Exactly," Jan said. "If we can find the precise location of the hostages, the odds of freeing them improve, and our odds of surviving the operation do as well."

"And that," I said, "is where Javert and I come in. If we can find the entrance—"

"Entrances." Dad laid a hand on my arm to interrupt me. "They won't be keeping important hostages in some place that lacks a back door. We'd best make sure we've stopped up all the holes before we set the dogs on the rats."

The others nodded sagely. I realized that someone had come into the room behind me and turned around to see a man with antlers growing out of his head. Distantly, I heard hounds baying.

"Actaeon!" I said. "Run for your life!"

He gave me a sad smile and disappeared.

I was sitting on the floor, propped up in my father's

arms. He was kneeling behind me, and Ari was kneeling in front of me.

"I'm okay," I said. "I was just getting a reminder that I'd forgotten Diana. The goddess, you know, that I saw in the drugstore."

I heard Jan giggle, and Spare14 sigh. Ari got up, then leaned down and offered me a hand. Between them, he and Dad got me on my feet and over to the couch. I sat down next to Jan.

"What's all this?" Dad said. "I saw the name Diana on your list, but I didn't realize it came from a vision."

Even though he hadn't seen me in thirteen years, he still understood me.

"I saw an image of the goddess, yeah. She told me to seek her, but she didn't say why." I brought up the memory image and extruded it, pale white like marble, just like St. Maurice.

Dad considered it for a long minute or two. "I wonder if she meant the Diana statue up in old Sutro's gardens. On the big hill up above Playland, that was, if I'm remembering it rightly."

"An interesting location, that," Ari said.

Dad smiled. I banished the MI.

"But we'd best not go up there just yet," Spare14 said. "I don't want to tip our hand. Perhaps Javert and O'Grady can find some information on that as well. Er, Nola, I mean. We have two O'Gradys now."

"Two O'Gradys and a squid," I said, "and that's almost as good as an army."

CHAPTER 16

IN SANFRAN THE SUNSET DISTRICT turned out to be a long stretch of sand dunes, sea grass, and scrub brush except for the areas bordering streetcar lines. The city had already finished the Twin Peaks tunnel before the worlds split and the disaster occurred on the newly-born Terra Three, but no one had had the capital to build up the district. With the low population, there hadn't been much need for tract housing, anyway. The city had put in four streetcar lines, among them an L Taraval line, the one that gave my Uncle Jim so much trouble back home. Here the L ran out to a small version of the San Francisco Zoo. Davis and Javert had chosen their hiding place near its terminus, right by the beach, a safe distance away from the ruins of Playland.

I spent the afternoon studying the Playland book, because we waited till after dark to go join them. When the time came, Spare14 split our group up, because, or so he told us, a group of five people traveling together at night would have aroused suspicions. He and Jan took the streetcar. Ari and I went with my father. Dad had spent some time studying the paper map of the city. He'd refreshed his memory about certain "overlaps and access points," as he called them. We gave Spare14 and Hendriks a head start, then started walking northwest along Broadway.

"The theory of fast walking's quite complicated," Dad told us. "I never had a chance to study it properly, you see, thanks to being so involved with the IRA. But I do know the rudiments of the practice."

I abruptly realized that we were no longer on Broadway. Somehow or other we'd crossed half the city and were heading straight west up Laurel Hill. A few small cottages dotted the slopes rather than massed apartment buildings. No 1950s glass-and-steel office complex loomed at the top. Instead, a low stone wall and trees crowned the hill.

"We'll just nip into the cemetery here," Dad said. "See the marble arch?"

The arch in question glimmered in the light of a streetlamp. Two weeping angels lurked in the shadows to either side, so realistically sculpted that it took me a moment to realize that they were marble, not IOIs. Dad led us through to the sound of lions roaring. We were walking down Sloat past the Zoo, miles away from Laurel Hill. Ari muttered something in Hebrew.

"Ah, the Lord's original tongue!" Dad said.

"You're enjoying yourself, aren't you?" I said. "And showing off."

Dad laughed and slipped an arm around my shoulders to hug me. "Right you are. It's been a long time since I could walk so freely."

"How did they keep in you in prison? Did you have to wear that lousy collar the whole time?"

"No, or I would've been stark mad by now." The laughter died in his voice. "They built the H Block right beside a power station, a huge thing, and the cables ran right overhead. Pylons all round to carry the power lines, too." He shook his head. "Invisible chains, is what they were."

"Supra-magnetic fields."

"Just that. They had half a regiment guarding the damned station, too, in case the IRA tried to bring it down." He shrugged. "Ah, well, that's behind me now. But I'll tell you something, my darling, and this is why I'm showing off, as you put it. When you younger kids were all small, I looked forward to the days when you'd start developing your talents. I thought I'd be there to help you and take you through the process, like growing a splendid garden. Never happened, did it? But at least I can show you what I know."

I choked back sudden tears. "Yeah, but Mike still needs you. Real bad."

Dad hugged me again and let me go. "Then it's a good thing I'm here."

During this conversation, Ari had been walking just a step or two behind us, listening, I supposed, but also keeping watch. I felt his SPP as poised and ready for danger.

"Let's stop for a moment," Ari said. "The street's ending."

About half a block away Sloat petered out into a streetlight and a scruffy lawn, a strip maybe ten yards wide. Behind that a slope rose, thick with trees and underbrush, and dark. I glanced up and saw a quarter moon riding the edge of incoming fog, a light soon to be dimmed.

"Can you get a fix on Javert?" Ari said. "I'm not keen on blundering around in the dark. What if someone else is waiting for us?"

I ran two careful scans. "I don't feel any danger in there," I said, "except for a couple of skunks. We don't want to upset them, though."

When I ran an SM:P for Javert, I felt the touch of his mind and a waft of Qi from above. Over us, hovering maybe twenty feet off the ground, Javert's Fog Face projection formed.

HERE! FOLLOW!

I pointed it out to the two guys, but neither of them could see it. I'd expected that of Ari, but I was surprised about Dad. I was also, I admitted to myself, pleased to find that I had a talent he lacked.

Okay, I said to Javert. *Lead on!*

He took us to a narrow dirt path that skirted the skunks' territory at a safe distance. After a couple of hundred yards I saw something white glimmering ahead, the milk wagon. Davis slid out of the cab and hailed us. In my world the truck would have stood right beside the Great Highway in a very public parking lot where hang gliders and surfers

came to practice their sports. On Interchange, Davis had
parked on a dirt road in the middle of unclaimed land,
near-wilderness.

"Where's Spare14?" Davis said.

"Coming with Hendriks on the streetcar," Ari said. "He
wanted to stop at the liaison captain's station for some reason."

I GO. BRING. Javert in his Fog Face suit drifted off
again, heading back toward the Zoo.

When Jan and Spare14 arrived, some twenty minutes
later, they brought the reason for their stopover with them:
sandwiches and a supply of currency for Davis, and a large
raw salmon for Javert, tidily wrapped in white butcher paper.

"She ordered one from the local fishmonger for me," Jan
said. "Very kind of her."

Davis stowed the huge salmon in the cab. "The inspector
won't want to eat that in the tank, I reckon. It's kind of a
messy job, the way he eats. But he'll want a good swim later,
anyway."

YES! Javert confirmed it. LATER.

First, however, we needed to do our psychic reconnaissance. Like mine, Javert's talents worked best on an empty
stomach.

We all went down to the beach. Davis drove with
Spare14 in the passenger seat and Jan on the running board,
clinging to the cab with one arm through the open window.
Dad took Ari and me with him on a fast walk. On the beach
pale surf gleamed in the moonlight. I could see the ocean
moving and swelling, a dark mass that stretched out to a
silver horizon.

"Do you sense any danger?" Dad asked me.

"No. Just a distant warning about the city as a whole, but
we already know it's dangerous."

We walked down to the tide line and waited there for
the truck. When it arrived, Jan jumped down and Spare14
got out to join us. I did an SM:Location while Davis backed
the vehicle up to the water's edge. He climbed down from
the cab and hurried to the back of the tank.

"No one around," I said.

Davis worked the mechanism and released Javert into the surf. He jetted out into deeper water in a burst of relief and sheer joy.

Together we summoned Qi and got to work. I found Michael easily. He was asleep in a wood-paneled room with the blonde girl clasped in his arms. From the ease with which they both slept, I could deduce that he was well treated, one of the gang, hardly a prisoner at all—except for the hold over him that Sean gave the gang.

Where was Sean? Javert and I decided to leave searching for him to the last, just in case the psychic sentinel shut us down before we'd finished scanning out the location. We started from Michael's room and began to widen our view—not that we saw precisely or clearly. What we received were impressions, better than nothing but by no means as clear and detailed as a map. I could see Michael because he was my brother. If Sean had been collar-free, I could have seen him, too. Anyone or anything else—no.

First, a hallway led to stairs at either end. Opposite Michael's door, another door, leading to hallways and enemies, where distantly I could perceive another psychic mind, prowling around, wide awake—a Maculate. No go there, then. Up one stairway to a narrow room, cluttered with junk: rusty machinery, slabs of wood, tangles of electrical wire. Up the other stairway to an enormous room. I got impressions of a long floor-to-ceiling rise of metal, of a curved wall nearby, of littered trash and odd little walls just standing around, unconnected to anything. Finally, we saw a detail. Leaning against a wall stood a huge wooden sign painted with a faded, cracking clown face. From the picture in my book, I knew this had once hung on the Fun House.

Javert pumped me more water Qi. We floated through the big room and saw a right-angle crack in the ceiling: a hatch, a metal hatch. We pulled back to our bodies, then returned to the site, but above ground this time. We found the hatch near the concrete foundations of a ruined building. The psychic mind prowled closer and went on alert. Closer still—a nocturnal being, Claw for sure.

LEAVE!

As much as I hated to cancel the search for Sean, staying risked giving our presence and the game away. We sped away from the ruins and returned—I to the group around the water tank and he to the ocean. My stomach growled. So, apparently, did Javert's.

EAT FISH! PLEASE.

I relayed the message.

"Did you want one of these here sandwiches, Miss?" Davis said. "The captain sure sent me plenty of 'em."

"No, thanks. I—"

"Yes, she does!" Ari snapped.

Rather than fight with him about it, I took a cheese-and-lettuce sandwich. It smelled so good, and I was so hungry by then, that I did eat most of it.

While I ate, Davis unwrapped the raw salmon. He cradled it in his arms and waded out into the surf. Javert came jetting back in. In the dim moonlight I could see little, but I got the impression that his extensible tentacles shot out, grabbed his dinner from Davis' arms, and stowed it on top of his head. He jetted out again, and I withdrew the link between us. I had the feeling that watching him eat would have been both rude and kind of disgusting. Davis came dripping out of the surf.

"You'll catch cold," Spare14 remarked.

"Nah, I'm used to it. I think I'll have me one of those sandwiches while I dry. We should be safe enough out here if you all want to go home."

"I can walk Spare and Hendriks back to the streetcar stop," Dad said. "Won't take me but a minute or two, and then I'll come back for my daughter and her intended."

I felt like growling at the word but giggled instead, helplessly.

Thanks to Dad's help, we all returned to the apartment without trouble. As soon as we got in, Dad sat down on the couch and fell asleep. I retrieved my pad of paper and crayons from the bedroom. While the Playland reconnaissance was fresh in my mind, I made as much of a map as I could of what I'd seen. By the time I finished, Ari's watch read nearly midnight.

"We need to make some decisions about sleeping arrangements," Spare14 remarked. "It appears that the senior O'Grady has claimed the couch."

"I spotted a hotel just about half a block away," Ari said. "That's where Nola and I are staying tonight."

"Very well," Spare14 said. "Just be careful on your way there. Get back here by nine o'clock."

Ari grabbed his sports bag, and we left the apartment. We walked down a silent, dimly lit Broadway—no cars, no strip joints, and the only bar we saw had the shabby look of a haunt for elderly alcoholics. It smelled like one, too, when we passed it, a fug of beer and sweat and tobacco smoke.

We turned into a narrow alley that dead-ended at the hotel in question, three floors of wooden firetrap, or so it looked on the outside. The front door opened to a tiny lobby, papered in peeling green paisleys, that smelled of smoke with an undertone of vomit.

The registration desk stood beside a stairway leading up. Behind it sat a fat woman with short gray hair and bright red lipstick, a lifer, judging by the deep wrinkles around her mouth. Her upper arms bulged out of a tight white sleeveless shirt. She lowered the newssheet she'd been reading and looked us over.

"An hour or all night?" she said.

"All night," Ari said. "How much?"

"Five bucks, since you brought your own girl." She laughed, wheezing, at her own joke and held out a mottled hand.

Ari handed her a five and received a room key in return. Apparently, this establishment scorned the idea of guest ledgers. We climbed up to the second floor, found the room, and went in. It contained a double brass bed, a wooden chair, and a nightstand. A bare light bulb hung from a chain in the middle of the ceiling. The air, however, smelled reasonably fresh, as did the sheets when I pulled back the blankets on the bed to check. Ari got out his travel lamp, set it on the nightstand, and turned off the overhead glare.

"Better than Spare14's floor, huh?" I sat down on the edge of the bed and kicked off my shoes.

"Tolerable, yes." He drew the Beretta, crossed to the window, and looked out. "No one followed us."

"I would have known if they had."

He holstered the gun and pulled down the window shade, which was mottled with the brown splotches of leaked rain. He turned back into the room and considered me without speaking. His SPP had changed to sullen.

"Okay, something's wrong." I took off the pink hoodie and tossed it onto the wooden chair. "What is it?"

He shrugged and crossed his arms over his chest. To give myself a moment to think, I picked up the pillows on the bed and checked under them for bedbugs. Nothing moved, and the wall above the bed lacked the telltale stains of bugs squashed by previous patrons.

"I guess this place is clean enough." I put the pillows back in place. "Ari, what's wrong?"

Again the shrug. I was in no mood to play guessing games. From his SPP I could untangle a few strands.

"It's because of Dad, isn't it? What's wrong, an ex-con isn't good enough for you?"

"What? That's got nothing to do with it. To be honest, from what I know of the Brittanic Empire, I have to admire him. Any decent man would fight against it."

"Then what the fuck is wrong?"

"That's more like the woman I love."

This reply totally confused me. Ari uncrossed his arms and walked over to sit down next to me on the bed.

"When your father's with you," he said, "you act like you're sixteen years old. You even giggled a couple of times. It was rather nauseating, actually."

I stared, caught between anger and insight. The insight won. "Crud," I said. "I'll have to watch that. I guess it's because I was a teenager last time I saw him."

"That, too, I'm sure."

"What else?"

"He brings it out in you. I've never seen a man establish control over an adult child as quickly as he did. It took him what? A couple of hours?"

I remembered Sean saying that I was living with a man much like our father. "Control that you want for yourself."

"That's quite unfair," he snarled, which reassured me that I was right.

"No, it's not. You love being in control, in bed or out of it. Why else are you always harping on getting married?"

"Most women want to be married."

"Maybe in Israel they do. I don't."

His Qi twisted around us, sharp as thorns. I went tense, ready to stand up and put distance between us. His scowl made me realize that we'd just driven onto a collapsing bridge. I could escalate the argument, say just the right thing that would make him slap me hard enough to bruise. Our affair would be over, and Dad would have me all to himself again. I turned the metaphoric car around and drove back onto safe ground.

"Ari, please, can't we drop this for now?"

His metaphor: rage as a vicious dog on the loose. He grabbed it by the collar and chained it up again. "Yes, of course. We're both tired."

"Yeah," I said, "and stressed to the max."

"True." He took a deep breath and got up, walked over to the window again and pulled up the shade to look out. Anger management. I could feel his Qi easing. He lowered the shade and turned around to look at me from the safe distance.

"Come to bed," I said. "It's been too long."

He stared and stayed where he was. I pulled off my top and threw it onto the hoodie.

"Oh," he said. "That."

"Yeah." I unhooked my bra, slipped it off, and tossed it onto the heap. "This."

He came back, sat down, and pulled me close. When he kissed me, he laid one hand on my breast. The Qi began flowing again, but smoothly, and in the right direction. We both stank of sweat, but the smell fit the sleazy room and became oddly erotic.

Yeah, brass beds do creak. A lot. Afterward, I hoped no one was trying to sleep in the room below us. Ari yawned once and fell asleep. I did the same in his arms.

I woke early the next morning to a generalized sense of danger, too weak to be a full-blown SAWM or ASTA, but too insistent to be ignored. I got out of bed and dressed in my jeans and a blue-and-white striped shirt—clothing I'd picked as things Nuala would never have worn. I badly needed to use the bathroom, but the room lacked one, and prowling around the hotel alone in search struck me as a bad idea, especially with that free-floating danger signal hovering around me.

I decided that I'd better wake Ari up. I stood about three feet from the edge of the bed and said his name over and over. Shaking him awake would have been dangerous. Eventually, he turned over with a grunt and sat up.

"What?"

I explained the problem. He laughed.

"There's probably a chamber pot under the bed."

"You're kidding!"

He got out of bed, knelt down, and pulled out the utensil in question. It came covered with a flimsy towel, once white, now much stained though recently washed.

"You'd better take off those jeans," Ari said. "It's tricky for women until you get used to it."

It was, but I managed.

Returning to Spare14's crummy apartment felt like returning to civilization after that. Jan had already been out to a local bakery, and Spare14 had made a large pot of strong tea. I ruined some coffee in that lousy percolator while the others started in on the food.

Although both Dad and Ari nagged me to eat breakfast, all I could get down was a cup of coffee and some shreds of a sweet roll. For the first time I could admit to myself that maybe I did have an eating disorder. I knew I needed to eat, I wanted to eat, but my throat seemed to close up as soon as I took a mouthful. I could barely choke anything down.

Jan snarled at both Ari and Dad. "You're only making it worse for her," he said, "and incidentally, I'm sick of listening to you."

Dad winced and shut up. Ari glared, but Jan glared right

back. Spare14 cleared his throat and broke up the macho staring match.

"I've been speaking with the liaison captain," Spare14 said. "She says to go ahead with any reasonable plan. She agreed with O'Grady. Fight Chaos with Chaos. I suppose things come down to that."

"Good," Jan said. "Kerenskya's a woman of courage. Unlike some of the others we've been saddled with."

"That's enough," Spare14 snapped.

"Quite right. I overstep." Jan grinned at him. "I am silent."

"I only wish." Spare14 turned to Ari. "We have to figure out how to beard the Chief in his den."

"Oh, I don't know," I said. "We've planted a lot of rumors, and I've seen a lot of people staring at me. I wouldn't be surprised if he turned up here."

I'm not sure if that was a premonition or a lucky guess, but the Chief, arrived soon after. I'd just gone into the bathroom to curl my hair and do my anti-Nuala makeup when I felt a SAWM like a stab of ice in my stomach. I heard the doorbell buzz and Spare14's voice, but I couldn't decipher his words. I put down the curling iron and began to summon Qi. Heavy footsteps came upstairs, four men from the sound of it. I began to spin the gathered Qi into a ball, ready to throw. Unfamiliar voices filled the living room. One baritone growl I heard distinctly.

"Where is she? In here?"

Someone flung open the bathroom door, and I found myself face-to-face with a man wearing a navy blue uniform and carrying a Colt.45 in his right hand. The nameplate on his shirt pocket read "Hafner." He stared at me with dark eyes, deep-set in his hatchet-sharp face.

"Shit!" he said. "You're not her."

"No, sir," I said as calmly as I could manage. "I'm not, but how can you tell?"

"You don't smell like her."

The danger warning disappeared. I tossed the ensorcellment Qi over my shoulder and let it scatter. His statement made me suspect that he was a shape-shifter, a lycanthrope, most likely, judging by the silver at the temples of his thick black hair. He gestured in the direction of the living room with a wave of his gun.

"Come out, will you?" he said. "It's only hope that makes me so damn rude."

"I'm sorry." I put as much sympathy in my voice as I could muster. "I'm afraid she's really gone. I'm a psychic. I've seen her—well, I guess we can say ghost, though that's not exactly what I saw."

He stared at me for another long moment, then nodded. His entire body twitched as if it longed to deny the truth. "Okay," he said. "I don't suppose you know how—"

"I do, but please, let's get out of this moldy bathroom."

He laughed, a rueful sort of sound, and agreed.

The living room was full of cops: the three TWIXT men and three uniformed SanFran officers, one lieutenant and two sergeants, one of whom, a tall blond, looked oddly familiar. Hafner's command staff, I figured, and they'd drawn their guns. My father had turned dead pale and retreated to a corner of the room. He'd wrapped the gray fog around him again and pressed himself so tightly against the wall that I doubted if the police had even noticed him. Ari stood by the window, his arms crossed over his chest. When I joined him, he put his arm around my shoulders.

"Very well, gentlemen," Hafner said. "My apologies for the raid. I received some faulty information."

I could feel Ari's surprise at this admission. I was surprised, myself. Hafner was turning out to be very different than the monster of corruption we'd been expecting. Still, when I sampled his SPP, I sensed a heart of iron. He'd killed men to get the job he held, and he saw absolutely nothing wrong with that. He was also still holding his Colt .45.

Spare14 stepped forward. "We have a confession to make, Chief. The three of us are CBI men. Miss O'Grady here is a certified police psychic and a distant relation of your missing woman."

Hafner laughed with one quick bark. Werewolf—I was growing more sure by the minute. The other officers moved with a peculiar gliding walk to stand behind him. A pack of werewolves, actually—I remembered my glimpse of the moon from the night before. We had a week before they changed, and I thanked Whomever for it.

"We're tracking a renegade Maculate," Spare14 continued, "a professional ape-hunter." He sighed and softened his voice. "I'm afraid that—"

Hafner froze, staring at him. "No, please God, no, not that." He caught his breath with sob. "He didn't—"

"I'm afraid you see what I was getting at. I'm very sorry."

Hafner tipped his head back as if he were going to howl in grief, then shook himself. As he returned his gaze to Spare14, I sampled the Chief's Qi—iron heart, iron control, genuine grief. "I do see," Hafner said. "You're sure of this?"

"Very sure." Spare14 glanced my way. "O'Grady?"

"There's no doubt that she's passed over," I said. "As I told the chief, I saw my cousin's revenant." *I won't wholly die.* Nuala's remark took on a grisly new meaning. "She told me something that fits with the other evidence, the things we know that make the Maculate the most likely suspect."

Hafner bowed his head and stared at the carpet.

Ari stepped forward. "We have evidence that the Spottie's joined Storm Blue. We came here, actually, to search for two hostages that the Axeman's holding. We ran across the Spottie—he calls himself Claw—during the course of our investigation."

Hafner looked up. "Let me see your IDs."

All three of the men produced the little leather cases. Hafner checked them carefully, not that I blamed him. I glanced at the spot where I'd last seen my father, but he was gone, maybe into the bedroom, more likely a good bit farther away than that. I figured he'd return when he could be sure the police had left.

"Very well, gentlemen." Hafner holstered the Colt at last. When his officers did the same, the tension in the room eased.

"We've received some interesting information about this gang," Spare14 said. "Are you aware they're planning a strike on your position?"

"I've heard rumors but no real evidence. Is it true?"

"Very true. If you'd care to sit down, I'll explain. Oh, by

the way, Agent Nathan has discovered the addresses of their two safe houses."

Hafner looked at Ari and smiled, an expression that made him look more murderous than ever, thanks to his very white strong teeth. "Good job," he said. "I think we've got some planning to do. Assuming, of course, that the CBI will agree to a joint operation."

"We'd like nothing better," Spare14 said. "After all, Chief, this is your territory, not ours, though we would like to have custody of the Maculate." He paused and gave Hafner a glance loaded with meaning. "Should he survive the raids, that is, which may not be possible."

"If he survives, of course I'll remand." Hafner smiled again. "But I'm afraid these raids are a dangerous business."

"Understood." Spare14 nodded and passed a death sentence on Claw with the gesture. "Now then, would you care to sit down?"

The police contingent stayed for a good hour while Hafner and Spare14 planned out a complicated operation. Hafner and his lieutenant would lead coordinated raids on the two safe houses while the TWIXT team—or the CBI men as the Chief thought of them—would control the Playland operation. Hafner would supply extra officers, however, as reinforcements.

"Timing's everything," Hafner said. "We also need to plant a leak about the safe house raids in advance. We want to draw as many gunners off the Playland site as possible. I don't want any dead hostages."

"Neither do we," Spare14 said dryly. "I quite agree about the plant."

They returned to discussing details. While I listened, I continued to feel the sense of dread that had woken me. Yet it never coalesced into an ASTA or SAWM. I could judge, therefore, that I was in no particular danger personally, not at the moment, anyway. By concentrating, I managed to extend the field, as it were, to the men in the room. No, none of them were in danger, either, nor did it apply to my father. Who? I sat very still and let images rise into my consciousness.

Major Grace. I felt a cold chill around my heart when I saw a memory image of her open office door. Anyone could have been in the hallway when she told us about the safe houses.

I pulled myself back to the moment. The men had fallen silent to allow the tall blond sergeant to write notes. He sat at Spare14's desk, his head bent as he worked in a notebook with a fountain pen. Now that I was no longer terrified that the cops were going to shoot us all, I recognized him, a doppelgänger of Lawrence Grampian. Werewolves, for sure!

"You don't need a plant," I said. "Storm Blue already knows about the safe house leak. They've got a spy in Mission House." I turned to Ari. "They're going to send someone after Major Grace."

Ari swore in Hebrew. Jan laid an automatic hand on his shoulder holster. Spare14 glanced at his watch.

"Nearly noon," he said. "They'll be serving lunch at the mission. The doors will be open to anyone."

"I'll go over and warn her," Ari said. "If that's acceptable. I don't want to trust a phone call. The spy could be listening to her end of the conversation."

"Quite true, and she's a stubborn woman when it comes to trusting in her God. Very well. The Chief and I will finish up the last few details here. O'Grady, go with Nathan. You'll be able to persuade her of the danger better than the rest of us can."

As we walked over to Mission House, I gathered Qi. With every stride closer we took, the sense of danger increased. I began to wrap Qi around itself into a loose skein, ready to be tightened into a sphere once we stopped walking and I could concentrate.

At a side door of the grim gray building a line had already formed for the meal: mostly women and children again, but even the men were all thin, ragged, and oddly quiet. The children leaned against their mothers or sat down on the ground to wait. Few smiled. Neither did any of the adults.

"Can we go straight in?" I said.

"I'd rather not attract attention," Ari said. "Is she in immediate danger?"

I ran a quick Personnel scan. "No. She's in some kind of a meeting with other people around her."

We got in line just behind a handful of young men, all of whom looked ill: scrawny, pale, and exhausted. The sun shone in a flood of the orange light through the perennial dust clouds. In that glare everyone looked as flushed as if we'd been caught in an epidemic of fever. One of the men in front of us started coughing, a rasping deep cough that ended when he spat up into a scrap of cloth.

"That's blood," another guy said to him.

"Just a little," he said.

The other guy shrugged, and neither spoke again.

The side door opened. The line began to file into a long, low-ceilinged room crammed with oblong plank tables, each covered with clean butcher paper. At the far end stood a long cafeteria-style counter, where young men in the black-and-maroon uniform of their army were filling bowls with soup. Each person got a plate with a bowl of soup and a chunk of white bread. Everyone said thank you and looked glad to get it.

Ari and I exchanged a glance and stepped out of line. "Let's go upstairs," Ari murmured. "Is that where she is?"

I was about to agree when a door behind the counter opened and Major Grace walked out. The danger warning stabbed at me.

"No," I said. "She's right here."

We took a few steps away from the line and stood up against the cheerfully yellow wall of the dining room. I gathered more Qi, wound and wrapped it tighter and tighter. The young men who'd been in front of us went through the line and brought their trays to a table off to one side. The guy with the cough took a mouthful of warm soup and began to hack stuff up again. His friends ignored him.

The tables filled up with oddly silent diners. Occasionally, a child cried or called out. Even more rarely an adult said something to the person next to them. Major Grace walked through the room, stopping at every table to greet the diners, smiling at the children, conversing briefly with the adults she knew.

Eventually, she reached the guy with the bad cough. He'd finished eating and slumped down in his chair. When Major Grace stopped and spoke to him, he raised his head and tried to smile. The effort brought on the racking cough. He twisted, choked, and fell out of his chair sidewise onto the floor. Someone shouted. The Major called out for help. The diners at the nearby tables turned in their chairs to look. Several people rose to see what was causing the confusion. Behind her, I saw a man with a shaved head stand up and pull a knife from his boot.

I hurled the Qi like a fastball, overhand and straight into his chest. It hit with a flash of silver enveloping light. The knife flew into the air, then clattered on the floor. He screamed, twitched, gibbered, and fell forward onto his face. Women screamed, and children wailed in terror. The friends of the man who'd fainted grabbed him and pulled him out of the way. Ari ran to the Major's side with the Beretta drawn and ready.

I made my way through a thinning, noisy crowd, but I noticed that even as the diners pulled away from the tables where the incident had taken place, they carried their food with them. Ari lunged forward and grabbed a pale, heavy-set man by the collar. He swung him around and whacked him across the face with the Beretta. The guy howled in pain as blood spurted from his nose and lips. A second knife clattered to the floor.

Major Grace knelt by the man I'd rendered harmless and stared into his face. He smiled at her, the usual mindless gape of the ensorcelled. His wide-open eyes displayed less intelligence than your average sheep. His fingers twitched to some unheard rhythm, and he giggled. I knelt down beside her.

"All right," Major Grace said. "Rose, what are you?"

"A certified police psychic."

"That's not what I meant. Are you a human being?"

"Huh? Yes, of course I am."

"Can you tell me outright that you're not a demon? They have to answer when you ask them, or so I've been told."

"No problem." I made the sign of the cross for good

measure. "I am neither demon nor angel, only a human weirdo."

Major Grace managed a smile at that. "What did you do to this fellow to make him have that fit?"

"Ensorcelled him with extra Qi. You can call it 'life force,' if you prefer. Nothing more than that. He'll be back to normal in a couple of hours."

"Nothing more, hum?" Major Grace shook her head and laughed under her breath. "All right, if you say so." She gave me a wry smile. "Thank you. It was obvious what he had in mind."

"Yeah, he must be from Storm Blue. That's who we're tracking. Eric is a CBI agent. Or I should say, his name's not Eric. It's Ari Nathan."

"You two should be on the stage. I was totally taken in." She sighed and glanced away. "That's hard to do."

"I hated lying to you." Which was true, even though I'd just fudged a few more facts. "Storm Blue really is holding my brother Sean prisoner, if that's any consolation."

"It is, yes. Thank you."

We stood up. Ari had holstered the gun. He'd also bound the accomplice's hands behind his back with the guy's own belt and made him lie facedown on the floor. He stood nearby and talked into his TWIXT communicator. Major Grace looked the prisoner over.

"Jason, a new recruit," she said, "or so we thought."

With the incident under control, the diners in the room went on eating. No doubt they'd seen worse.

A small group of Army personnel rushed into the dining room. They clustered around Major Grace and all began to talk. One of the women was weeping with a run of silent tears down her face. I felt a trace of ASTA at the door and spun around in time to see a familiar blonde girl slipping out of the room. I'd seen her before, sitting in Mike's lap and sleeping in his bed.

"Ari," I said, "A Storm Blue girl just ran. The news is going to get back to the Axeman."

"Good." He slipped the communicator back into his shirt pocket. "We want the gang members off the Playland site, don't we? Defending the safe houses, running for their sodding lives, I don't care which." He turned to Major Grace. "Chief Hafner's on his way. He'll post a man as your bodyguard for the remainder of today and tonight. Maybe longer, if necessary."

"My dear Eric!" She smiled. "I mean, Agent Nathan. I appreciate the thought, but I have the best bodyguard in the world. And if He should decide that it's my time to join Him in the world of light, then I will, no matter who stands guard here."

"Maybe so," Ari said. "But I'd just as soon he had some backup."

The backup arrived in a few minutes when Chief Hafner and two patrolmen strode into the dining room. The few people who hadn't gobbled their lunch and left got up and hurried out. I looked the ordinary cops over carefully, but none of them displayed any lycanthropic tendencies. It seemed logical that the wolves would lead the hierarchy.

The Chief nodded at me and the Major to acknowledge us, then took Ari to one side. While they stood talking, the patrolmen took charge of the pair of would-be assassins. One cop substituted handcuffs for the conscious guy's belt, then hauled him to his feet and held him at gunpoint. The other patrol officer cuffed the ensorcellment victim.

"What happened here?" he said to me.

"He hit his head when he fell."

The cop glanced at Major Grace, who smiled in fake helplessness. "I had my back to him," she said.

"Okay. Hit his head will do, then."

Ari hurried over to join us.

"The Chief wants to speak with you, Major," Ari said. "O'Grady, let's go."

As we left Mission House, we met the police lieutenant, who told us that the Chief had ordered a wagon brought for our transportation out to the beach. He handed Ari the keys and indicated a black vehicle sitting at the curb. When we inspected it, we saw that it had been cobbled together out of several different trucks. Under its off-kilter roof it would seat eight people on tattered bench seats.

"Good, it's got an engine," I said to Ari. "I was afraid it would have horses." I started to say more, then realized that a smear of blood decorated the front of his shirt. "Are you hurt?"

"No." He glanced down. "That's where I cleaned off the Beretta."

"Right. After pistol-whipping that guy."

"No need to exaggerate! I only hit him once."

"Whatever. I'd better drive."

Ari glanced into the front seat. "It's a manual transmission."

"Damn! Okay, you drive, but please, try to not kill anyone on the way."

CHAPTER 17

WE RETURNED TO SPARE14'S OFFICE to find Sergeant Grampian and the two patrol officers still present, waiting with Spare14 and Hendriks. As soon as we walked in, Spare14 told me that Dad had never come back.

"He will," I said. "You can't blame him for not wanting to hang out with a bunch of cops."

Spare14 gave me an odd look. I could have sworn he felt guilty about having arrested my father in the first place, though I couldn't see why he would. I flopped down on the couch to grab a few minutes' rest. My Qi badly needed to recharge.

"Is there a long gun available?" Ari said. "I wish now that I'd brought mine."

"I have some in the kitchen," Spare14 said. "In that narrow little cupboard. I think it used to hold an ironing board."

Jan grinned and trotted into the kitchen. He brought back two rifles that reminded me of guns from Western movies. He handed one to Ari, who smiled and ran loving fingertips over the wooden stock. Spare14 opened one of his desk drawers, rummaged through it, and gave each man a leather sack of cartridges.

"Bolt-action Winchesters," Ari said. "Solid, but I hope they reload quickly."

"Let's hope you don't need more than six shots," Grampian said. "Hendriks, you and I need to get on the road. These two men—" he pointed at the regular officers, "—are staying with Agent Spare."

"Right," Jan said. "Nathan, you've got a chrono, I see."

They actually did coordinate their watches, just like the movies. I was impressed. The final plan required precise timing. Hafner's two squads would begin their raids on the safe houses precisely at 14:30, a time chosen to fall after the working people's lunch breaks but before rush hour. The safe houses were located on the stretch of Mission Street that ran parallel to Market, right downtown.

"We can't risk harming pedestrians and bystanders," Grampian said. "It's not our job to kill innocent people."

I would have been surprised by this attack of morality had I not remembered that wolves were the original breeding stock for herd dogs. Apparently, Hafner and his top level personnel were evolving toward domestication.

Jan and Grampian would move their men into Playland from the east side at 15:00 sharp. Ari, Dad, and I would sneak into the complex from the west five minutes later. With luck, I could find Michael and Sean immediately. Dad would walk them out of the hidden rooms. The Playland squads would meet in the middle of the ruins. With luck, again—lots of it. "Where is your father?" Spare14 sounded irritable. "I never even saw him leave."

"Right behind you," Dad said.

Spare14 yelped and spun around. None of us had seen him return.

"One good ambush deserves another," Dad said.

To give him credit, Spare14 managed to smile. "Only fair, yes. May I ask where you were?"

"Up in Old Sutro's front yard. I had a look at that statue of Diana." Dad grinned at me. "You saw something worth seeing, Noodles. She's guarding a gate."

"Ye gods!" Spare14 said. "A trans-world gate?"

I caught my breath with a hiss.

"Just that. Now, I don't know what lies on the other side of it. It's out of balance somehow. I'm not sure what's wrong with it, but since I wasn't sure I could get back, I didn't try it out."

"Wise of you. Very useful information, that. Thank you."

"Well, the Public Solicitor back on Five made the terms of my release clear enough." Dad looked at Spare14 with an unreadable expression. "I gave my word I'd help you with this. Damned if I'll break it."

Spare14's SPP oozed a peculiar kind of guilty feeling. Later, I reminded myself, I was going to ask both men what lay between them. At the moment we had a few other things to attend to.

"As far as I could tell," Dad continued, "there's some sort of tunnel been dug nearby, leading up to the statue's position. I don't have the talents for spying out that sort of thing, but I could hear the hollowness when I walked over it. Our Nola might be able to tell us more."

"Very well," Spare14 said. "We'll go have a walk around the gardens first. It's only thirteen hundred now. We have time for a look. That tunnel might lead us to the Axeman."

"It could also be his escape route," Ari said. "We'd best make sure it's blocked."

"Hang on a minute, then," Dad said. "I'd better collect an orb or two, just in case."

He hurried into the bedroom. I could hear him rummaging around in the luggage, but when he returned, he didn't seem to be carrying anything. I figured that the orbs could shrink or slide into one of those curly dimensions Willa had mentioned.

"Shall we go, gentlemen?" Spare said. "Nathan, if you'd drive—"

"No," I interrupted. "We don't want to turn into the Keystone Kops, do we? I think my father had better drive."

Ari shot me a scowl.

"I can get you there a bit faster," Dad said. "Especially with an orb right to hand."

"Quite." Spare14 looked rueful. "I tend to forget."

"Not too fast, though, Dad. I need to run a few scans."

The drive out on Geary went smoothly, at least on the mechanical level. Although Dad hadn't driven a car in thirteen years, the reflexes came right back to him. That we met barely any traffic on the street helped. My scans turned up nothing specific, but the closer we came to the ocean the more my feeling of dread grew. At the dirt crossroad that stood in for 19th Avenue, the dread crystallized.

"Sean's in big trouble."

Dad hit the accelerator. The wagon jumped forward. In a few seconds we reached a narrow street, partly paved, that would have been Point Lobos Avenue back on Four. He parked at the crest of an overgrown hillside that sloped down to the ocean beach below.

Once, here just as on my home world, Adolf Sutro's mansion, a huge house set in a terraced hillside garden, had existed as a masterpiece of American wealth, the showplace of a self-made man. His staff had created flower beds and little groves, long lawns and flagstone paths. Sutro had imported copies of the world's most famous statues, all of them made of the finest marble. I'd seen photos of the walks and stone parapets, the lacy white wrought-iron benches, and the utter bad taste of everything—the Venus de Milo stuck on a garden wall, a flower bed depicting an American flag.

When the Sutros died, both Sutro version 3 and Sutro version 4, they'd left the property to their respective cities. Neither city, San Francisco or SanFran, had the wherewithal to take care of it. Squatters moved into the mansion and inadvertently set it on fire one cold night. Vandals and decay gutted the gardens. At home, once the Great Depression began to lift, the San Francisco city government had hauled away the ruins and turned what was left into a tidy little park with spectacular views.

Not so here on Interchange, where depressions of all kinds had never ended. The area covered by the gone-wild garden looked twice as big as the park back home. From the street I could see the concrete foundations of the burntout mansion poking through the rampant shrubbery, a tangle of greenery that shouted "danger." Although the others piled out of the wagon, I sat for a moment and ran SM:Location scans. I picked up a distant trace of Sean, but the collar stopped me from pinning it down.

"Bad situation?" Ari opened the car door for me.

"You bet. Someone's in there. I'm not sure if they're waiting for us or not."

He swore under his breath. I got out of the wagon and took a good look around. A grove of trees, thick with underbrush, lined the street side of the gardens. In that riot of untended botany any number of enemies might have been lying in ambush.

"Here's something worse," I said. "I can't find the Axeman at all. We know he doesn't have the talents to hide himself."

"Damn!" Spare14 said. "Perhaps he's found some sort of interference device. Something that works like the Stop-Collar without having the drastic effect on the user."

"Perhaps," Ari said. "But I've got a bad feeling about this, and I'm not even psychic."

The men readied their weapons. I gathered Qi in a loose skein. Spare14 insisted that he take the point himself, the most dangerous position. Ari walked just behind him, rifle at the ready. Dad and I occupied the middle of the line, and the two patrolmen took up the rear guard.

It took some searching among the trees lining the street, but we finally found a dirt path in. We walked between a pair of headless marble lions, covered in graffiti, and under the twisted remains of a towering wrought iron gate, blood red with rust. Panels of scrollwork dangled precariously above us from sagging pillars. I heard a bird chirp twice, then silence. The entire entrance area, I realize, had fallen silent, much too silent.

As we walked through the gate, I heard a whistle off to one side and distant. Human or bird? I couldn't tell. We came out to a long view down the terraces. Eighty years of neglect had let the trees grow tall and shrubs and weeds fill in between them. High grass, clover, and wild mustard, all of it drying out here in early summer, had turned the flower beds into strips of meadow bordered with bushes and tangles of weeds. Everywhere I could see fallen statues, some smashed to pieces. Graffiti, most of it foul, covered every exposed bit of stone.

About twenty yards in, we came across a circular area

that once had been paved—a carriage drive, I guessed. The paving stones had kept down the weeds and formed a clearing of sorts. From it, graveled paths sloped down to overgrown lawns streaked with patches of tumbled stones and mud. In the troubling silence I could hear the distant murmur of the ocean far below.

"Someone's cleared these paths recently," Spare14 said. "O'Grady, do any personnel appear on your scans?"

I ran an SM:L. "Someone—something's in here," I said. "I don't read them as hostiles." I tried another scan and picked up half-formed talents. "Outcasts, maybe, people born with bad disabilities."

"Well, we'll do our best not to cause trouble for them." Spare14 spoke loudly and clearly. "We do not want to harm the harmless. We're only hunting a murderer."

I heard rustling among the nearby shrubbery, quick steps fading away, as if a person scampered deeper into the gardens. Distant whistles sounded. Although the silence felt as thick as ever, I sensed another person approaching. His SPP radiated a desperate hope mingled with terror.

"Hold up," I whispered. "A messenger."

Among the tangled bushes and brambles a human face appeared, topped with red hair as wild as the foliage, then a pair of hands in thick leather gloves. With a rustle and a grunt a little person, his body a classic case of dwarfism, he parted the tangle and stepped out. He wore patched-together clothes of old denim. I went down on one knee to look at him eye to eye. He smiled, and his terror began to ease into simple fear.

"What's wrong?" I said.

"Are you hunting the leopard man?" His voice was a pleasant tenor.

"Among others, yeah. Has he been giving you trouble?"

"He's murdered three of us."

I remembered the corpse in the meat locker that I'd mentally labeled as chimpanzee. Obviously, I'd been wrong. Miss Leopard-Thing traded in human flesh, all right. My stomach twisted.

"He comes from under the goddess," the messenger said. "He must have a tunnel."

"Is there a door?" Spare14 stepped forward.

"We've never been able to find it. If we had, we'd have blocked it."

"Quite so. Well, if we can, we're going to put a stop to it today."

"One way or another," Ari put in. "Thanks for the tip-off."

The little person smiled, then turned and slipped back into the foliage. His hands in their leather gloves parted the brambles as if he were swimming the breaststroke. I heard a rustling, a footfall cracking a twig, then nothing, yet I could psychically tell that he was still moving away from us.

"A tunnel, again," Dad said. "That must be where the gate is. I think we'd best hurry."

He led us to a terrace that still stretched level and solid, thanks to the stone wall that contained it. More broken statuary lay among the weeds. The remains of rusted fili-gree marked the location of the once-white benches. I nearly tripped over a huge marble head, stained with rust and bird droppings.

"This doesn't bode well for Diana," I said.

"Oh, she's not done too badly," Dad said. "You'll see."

Since he'd scouted it out, Dad took us straight to the statue. Near the concrete foundations of the long-gone mansion, Diana the Hunter in her tunic and tall boots stood on a high plinth. She was about to draw an arrow from her quiver. A hunting hound stood on its hind legs beside her, caught in the middle of a joyous leap. Her marble gleamed, clean and polished. Someone had clipped the grass all around the plinth. Someone had laid offerings at her feet: decaying roses, candle stubs, a chipped white bowl coated with the red scum of evaporated wine. "The little people's goddess," I said.

Dad walked over to the statue. He paused and looked up at her as if asking permission, then laid his hands on the base. When he swore under his breath, I knew he was con-firming Ari's bad feeling. I remembered the blonde girl again, slipping out of Mission House. If she was a fast walker or had a vehicle, she would have reached the Axe-man in plenty of time for him to escape.

"Someone's used this gate recently," Dad said. "In the past quarter hour, I'd say, but that's just an estimate."

"I suspect we know who it must have been." Spare14's voice ached with frustrated fury. "I just hope he didn't take the hostages with him."

"Let me just see about that," I said.

I walked a little way away from the group around the statue. A normal Search Mode: Personnel for Michael told me immediately that he existed on this world level and nearby. Ari hurried over to join me.

"I've picked up Mike," I said. "I think he's down under Playland."

"Good. That's one of them."

I held up my hand for silence. When I sent my mind out in a call for Javert, I felt him answer. He was jetting through open ocean, heading for Seal Rock, while Davis followed along onshore in the milk wagon.

"I'm waiting for Javert," I said. "When he's close enough, I'm going to try overriding the StopCollar to find Sean."

"Is that safe?"

"Of course not! Is it safe for you to go charging into Playland with that rifle in your hands? Are you going to do it anyway?"

"Of course I am." He hesitated, then shrugged. "Very well. You've made your point. Proceed as planned."

I felt Javert come online, psychically speaking, that is. He told me that he'd achieved a good hover despite heavy surf. The moment that we joined minds, I felt a surge of water Qi flooding into my aura. I sat down on the ground, leaned against a tree to support my back, and drifted into trance. I drew up Qi from the earth until the view before me danced and shimmered like a drug hallucination.

GO! Javert said.

At first the SM:P threatened to overwhelm me. I felt as if I were falling a long way down toward water, the same water that would turn hard and smack me senseless when I belly-flopped.

UP!

I flew. Skimmed the water, arched up into the sky. Below

me the earth spun and dipped. I sent out my mind for Sean and felt him clearly. My physical mouth opened without my conscious decision. Reflexively, I spoke aloud and told Ari what I was seeing.

"He's in a tunnel beneath the statue. He's caught there. Get Dad to walk him out before he suffocates."

BACK TO BODY! SPY KNOWS!

I followed Javert's orders and let myself glide down. I felt my body envelop me, warm and comforting as I came out of the trance. I heard Ari yelling the information at my father and returned my attention to Javert.

GOOD! I GO SOUTH. WAIT OFFSHORE.

Hey, I didn't expect you to wait on the beach.

Javert rippled with laughter and took himself off-line. When I staggered to my feet, Ari caught my arm and led me back to rejoin the squad at the statue. Spare14 stood with a pistol in one lax hand and stared at the Diana figure. The two police officers kept glancing around them, turning this way and that, utterly gob smacked. Dad had disappeared.

Dad reappeared—not precisely out of thin air, but close. One moment, no one stood at the base of the statue, but the next, he did. One officer yelped; the other stepped back fast. Dad had one arm around a weeping, shivering Sean, still half-naked, still bound by the white gold collar around his neck.

"What happened?" Ari said. "Does he know where the Axeman is?"

"He's not going to be able to give us a coherent story," Dad said, "until we get this damned collar off him."

Ari reached into his shirt pocket and pulled out a glass tube. "Code Twelve," he said. "Activate."

A green line pulsed along the edge of the tube. Spare14 made a choking sound.

"Where did you get that?" Spare14 said.

"Davis gave it to me the morning that O'Grady arrived," Ari said. "No one ever asked for it back."

Spare14 started to speak, then merely sighed. Ari held one hand up under the collar. When he touched the metal with the tube, as before it seemed to leap off its victim's neck into Ari's waiting hand. He handed Spare14 the collar and, this time, the code tube as well.

Sean sat down on the grass in a motion that just barely missed being a faint. Dad and I knelt down to either side of him. Dad stripped off his denim jacket and helped Sean put it on.

Sean steadied himself and gasped out the words, "Where's Mike?"

"I sensed him under Playland," I said.

"What the hell? Why doesn't he just walk out of there?" Sean leaned against Dad and kept on shivering. "He knows they don't have me anymore."

"I don't know why," I said. "I don't have that much overlap."

Sean shut his eyes and took a deep breath. "I just found him. Nola, this sucks. He's got a gun. He's hunting Scorch, and Scorch has a gun, and he's hunting Mike. Hide and seek with guns." He opened his eyes wide. "Mike's looking for something, too. I don't know what. Something important."

Ari knelt down in front of Sean. "What about the Axeman? Where is he?"

The two patrolmen and Spare14 crowded close to listen. Spare14 took out his communicator, ready to pass on the intel.

"I don't know," Sean said. "Some other world. Look, Mike had everyone convinced that he'd gone Blue. He was glorying in it, he said, being rich and important. He wasn't just the youngest O'Grady any more. The girls were all fighting over him, too. Nola, can our baby bro swagger! Even I believed him, but maybe that was just that fucking collar."

"Sean!" Dad snapped. "Watch your language in front of your sister!"

"Sorry." Sean flinched. "So this morning, the spotted dude kept saying something was wrong. Not about Mike, I mean, but the situation. Danger from wolves, Claw said, whatever the hell that meant, but the Axeman took it really seriously. When the news came back that the cops were planning a safe house raid, the Axeman figured that Hafner knew what was going on. He started getting some stuff together so he could bail."

"You're telling us he's escaped." Ari sounded quietly enraged.

"Yeah. Mike pulled a number on him, though."

Ari swore in English, this time. Dad cleared his throat loudly. "Sorry," Ari said. "Go on."

Sean did. "The Axeman lied to his guys. To his gang brothers, for crying out loud! He sent them down to defend the houses. 'I'll be coming after you,' he said, 'with some more gunners.' I heard him. He was lying through his teeth. But they went, the jerks. He told some other guys to go upstairs and keep watch for cops."

"Upstairs is above ground?" Ari said.

"Yeah, in the ruins. So that left him, me, Scorch, Mike, and the girls. Not the hooker girls, they live in the safe houses. The gang member girls. Ash—that's the girl Mike liked best—she'd been down in town trying to get a snitch killed. She came running back. That's when we knew you were on the move, Nola. This black-haired bitch ensorcelled the knife man, she said. Mike and I knew it had to be you."

I squalled but kept it short.

Sean went on, "So the Axeman said that's it. We're leaving through the gate."

"Where is Michael?" Dad said to me. "Should I go after him?"

"No," Ari snapped. "Too dangerous."

"I wasn't talking to you," Dad said.

They glared at each other while I ran a quick SM:P and found Mike, furious but alive, still underground, still searching. "I can't pin him down exactly," I said. "He's moving through too wide a space."

"Yeah, it's big, the complex, I mean." Sean continued his story. "Mike tried to get him to leave me behind, or at least take the collar off me, but the Axeman was a little too smart for that. So we all start up the tunnel to the statue. Scorch keeps shoving me along at the rear. So Mike opens the gate. The Axeman and the girls go through. Mike tells Scorch to go through, but he won't unless I go first. So Mike shut the gate. You should have heard Scorch howl." Sean paused for a twisted grin

"But," he went on, "It wasn't funny when Scorch pulled a gun. I had just enough brain left to turn around and knee him in the balls, and Mike grabbed the gun. Scorch got away. He ran back down the tunnel. Mike ran after him. He yelled something at me about the collar, getting something for the collar, but I couldn't figure out what he meant. I started down after them, but I heard someone fire a shot, and the ceiling started falling in. The gang dug the tunnel themselves, the jerks. It's just dirt, no beams, no nothing. So I went back up to the top and sat down to save oxygen. I knew you were on the way, Nola. Dad, you're just the biggest bonus in the world. I thought I sensed you, but I couldn't believe it. I was praying the air would last."

"And it did," Dad said. "I'll thank all the saints for that."

"Me, too," Sean said. "All of them. In alphabetical order."

"If the tunnel's collapsed," Spare14 said, "we can't use it for access. Damn!"

"Quite so," Ari said. "We'll continue with the operation as planned. Sean, how many men are left in the complex? Those guards you mentioned."

"I don't know for sure. With the collar on, I couldn't make much sense of anything. Maybe three, maybe four."

Spare14 had been relaying information into his communicator while Sean talked. He turned to Ari. "I just spoke to Chief Hafner. The raids went well. The safe houses are under police control. Oh, and there was no sign of the Maculate among the dead."

"Very well." Ari smiled with a twitch of his mouth. "Maybe we can rectify that down in Playland." He turned to me. "Can you find Claw?"

I concentrated hard on an SM:Personnel. I'd seen Claw once, dashing down our front steps. He'd also eaten my doppelgänger, and because of that, I could place him as a bundle of energy, a pulse moving along Geary Street.

"He's moving this way, as fast as he can." I paused and felt his energy more clearly. "He's desperate. There's something he wants real bad. I wonder if his transport orbs are still down in the hideout?"

"A good guess," Dad put in. "He may have made the same mistake I did."

"Sean," I said. "What's the underground like?"

"Well, for starters there's one huge room. It was part of Playland once. There are still walls and weird stuff down there, mirrors and games and stuff. One way down is this long metal slide. But there are stairs, too. When they brought us in, I was still trying to fight the collar. I couldn't tell where the hell I was."

Dad murmured, "I know what you mean," and laid a comforting hand on his shoulder.

"And then there's other underground rooms," Sean continued. "I guess where they fixed the machinery, the original Playland workers, I mean. The rooms look like workshops and storerooms. But the gang dug out some more hallways and rooms. They did a lousy job of it, too."

"It's a confusing mess. That's what you're telling me."

"Yeah. I'd better go with you."

When Sean tried to stand up, his legs gave way under him, and he sat down hard. I read his Qi as dangerously low and caught Ari's attention.

"The collar's drained him. He'll need time to recharge."

"I can go with you." Sean struggled up to a knee.

"No." Ari pushed him back down with one hand. "You'll only be a liability."

"Quite so," Spare14 said. "I'll stay here with Sean and guard. Do you want these two officers to go with you?"

"No," Ari said. "We need to move fast and quietly."

The patrolmen looked vastly relieved.

"Very well," Spare14 said. "And Scorch and the others might try to dig a way out through the tunnel. We'd best be here to greet them if so."

"True." Ari glanced at my father. "O'Grady, do you want to stay here?"

"Hell, no, not if you're taking Nola down there."

"And you're not leaving me behind," I broke in. "I'm not a finder like Sean, but Mike's my brother. I can keep track of him."

I turned and looked at my father, daring him to argue. He looked back, seemed to be considering an argument, then said, "I wouldn't expect anything different from you."

I smiled; he smiled. The three of us headed out.

We found a flight of precarious steps leading down through the broken statues and weeds and windblown trash. The gardens ended at the edge of the cliff. A stone parapet studded with broken chunks of sculpture did double duty as a retaining wall. The hillside fell away, a long steep way down, to the ocean, a view of dark wrinkled water edged with white on the pale beach. Off to the south, we could see the remains of Playland. Just beyond those lay a dark strip of wild green: Golden Gate Park. I could just make out the windmill.

I focused my attention on the ruins of Playland, turned by distance into a sketch map of ten acres of chaos. The layout struck me as far more haphazard than the Playland in San Francisco. In the book I'd found at Wagner's, the two amusement parks looked somewhat alike, each an arrangement of rides and concessions organized around two pair of cross streets like city blocks. After the split of worlds and the disaster, they had changed in separate ways. Here in SanFran the streets had disappeared into a confusion of shapes, as if booths and rides had sprung up wherever anyone felt like putting them.

Along the east side, back toward town, ran the dead roller coaster, a wooden skeleton like the spine and ribs of some sea creature picked clean by scavengers. Just west of it a big circle of concrete marked the location of the merry-go-round. On the southwest corner stood the crumbling stucco walls of a substantial building. Other than those landmarks, nothing came clear. I saw a jumble of shapes like the contents of a huge wastepaper basket spread out on a floor. Here and there the hazy sunlight picked out a gleam of metal.

I had no idea what shape represented what ride or location. Nothing matched my mental images of the map in the book or in the map Javert and I had sketched out. I sent my mind out to Javert and felt him come back online. I focused hard on my view of the ruins.

MESS. BROKEN CORAL. YOUR OCEANS. BOTTLES BAGS PLASTIC.

I took this as meaning the view reminded him of a dead coral reef. *Too true,* I replied. *Much too true.*

"Can you see the location of that hatch?" Ari said.

"No, not from here. I hope to God I can find it down there."

He winced. "So do I."

Behind us someone whistled. I spun around and saw the red-haired little person. He hurried over and pulled a big tangle of bushes and weeds away from the stonework. A clumsy-looking wooden door appeared.

"Stairs down," he said. "I'll close it after you."

"Thanks," I said. "Wish us luck!"

"Luck, and our prayers go with you!"

We all had to stoop and wriggle to get through the door. Once we stood on the stone stairs, however, in a few long strides Dad walked us down. Another few strides, and we reached the chain-link fence that surrounded the ruins. Here at street level the landscape—a junkyard—confused me even worse. Piles and heaps of boards, lumps of fallen stucco, twisted hunks of metal, tip-tilted walls, beams and girders that stuck up randomly through mounds of outright garbage—I had no idea what we were seeing. Javert informed me that he could make no sense of what my mind relayed. I wasn't surprised. Dad, Ari, and I moved along the fence until we found an entrance that someone had improvised with a pair of wire cutters. By then it was five minutes to three. Ari pulled his communicator from his shirt pocket and confirmed that Jan and his squad were waiting on the far side of the complex.

"They'll be moving in soon," Ari said. "Nola, any sign of Claw?"

I felt the Maculate's energy, a pulse like a beating heart, moving through the rubble. My mind objectified him as the stink of carrion.

"He's inside the fence. Either he can do fast walking, or he knows some secret entrance. He got past Hendriks' squad, anyway."

"Other Storm Blue men?"

"Yes. Three by the roller coaster. Personnel out in the street to the south. That's on Fulton. Between Playland and

the park." I refocused and got a better fix on a pulse of fading Qi. "Someone's dying. Another's trying to help. More
men than that. I think some of the men at the safe houses
must have escaped and gotten back here."

Ari said something foul and clicked the communicator
on. "I'm going to call down Spare14 and the others. The
situation's too dangerous for the three of us to handle."

"Okay, but make it fast. We've got to reach Michael before these guys get underground to help Scorch hunt."

"True. I—"

A burst of gunfire off to the south interrupted him. The
communicator beeped. With a flick of his thumb he answered, listened, then nodded and clicked off.

"Hafner's moving down Fulton Street," Ari said. "Cleaning up the stragglers. Very well. We'll continue as planned."

"I could just go in and start looking for Michael," Dad
said.

"I said, we'll continue as planned."

"You're in charge, then?"

"I should think that was made clear when we were discussing the matter back in Spare's office. If you'd been
there—" Ari left the rest unsaid.

They both looked my way. I felt a sudden sympathy for
King Solomon, he of the difficult judgments.

"Dad," I said, weaseling, "Ari was in the Israeli army. He
knows what he's doing."

"Umph," was all Dad answered, but he turned away and
began studying the rubble ahead. Ari smiled but mercifully
kept silent.

The next few minutes passed entirely too slowly. The sun
kept trying to break through the yellow fog. The day was
not precisely hot but unpleasantly humid. I became more
and more aware of the stink from the garbage just ahead of
us. The place doubtless lacked working plumbing. Somewhere there had to be dung heaps, my nose told me, just
like in the Dark Ages.

Ari and Dad both stood as still as if they'd been turned
to marble themselves. Neither looked the other's way. I felt
my heart pounding like a drum that urged me to dance. I
had to struggle to imitate them and stay still. Now and then

I heard gunshots and tried to persuade myself that the noise came from a long way away.

I was more frightened for Michael than myself. As Sean had said, Michael was moving through the underground complex, darting down tunnels, pausing to press himself against walls and listen, hunting Scorch even as Scorch hunted him. When I felt Javert ride into my mind on a wave of concern, I remembered that I had a powerful ally.

Can you tell Mike to just get the hell out of there?

I TRY.

I was aware of Javert sending the words that I lacked the talent to send. I felt Michael's mind shutting them out with a barrage of sheer anger.

HE THINKS TRAP LIE.

Crud.

Javert agreed. When I concentrated on Michael again, I could tell that his location lay somewhere to the north and roughly in the center strip of the ruins. He was moving too fast through too complex a space for me to be more precise. When I relayed this information to Ari, I whispered.

"I doubt if Scorch can hear you," he said.

Ari appeared to be on the verge of smiling. I couldn't believe that he could be so calm, until I remembered that his entire life had trained him for just this sort of operation. He glanced at his watch.

"Hendriks should be in by now. Let's go."

Javert, we're going in.

CAREFUL!

You bet.

In single file we picked our way through the break in the fence. Piles of trash had blown up against the chain links and stuck into a crazy quilt of papers and wet garbage. Flies buzzed around the stink and crawled on the trash, as thick as black mold. The gang had simply thrown all kinds of leavings out there, human waste as well as food scraps. I gagged but kept walking. A few yards brought us into somewhat cleaner air.

Directly ahead lay a six-foot-high tangle of metal chains around big wooden boards, streaked with faded pink paint, and some indeterminate hunks of concrete. Ari held up one hand for a stop, but while Dad and I waited, he picked his way around the pile. He paused to look ahead, then beckoned for us to join him. I followed him blindly. The visual disorder, the stinks, the scuttling sounds made by fleeing rats—I was losing my power to think clearly, losing even the ability to make sense of what I was seeing.

Javert, help! I'm drowning in Chaos. Clues, we had clues.
CLOWN FACE. REMEMBER CLOWN FACE.
Right! Thank God! We saw it underground.

"We want the fun house," I said aloud. "But I don't have any idea of where it is, not in all of this." *All this rubble looks alike.*

TOO TRUE.

Ari muttered in Hebrew. Even though I couldn't understand a word of it, the familiar sounds were oddly soothing.

We moved around that first pile of junk to find ourselves standing on what must have once been a street or wide path. All around us ruins spread out, stinking, heaped up, random, and inhabited by filthy small lives. Crumbling stucco walls, about shoulder high and black with graffiti, stood to our right, while on the left big shards of shattered glass lay in a rough square about ten feet on a side. We kept close to the wall and walked forward a few steps.

"Claw," Ari said. "Where?"

I let my mind roam through the aboveground wreckage off to the south—to our right, that is, at that moment. With Javert's help, I saw in vision the circular patch I'd noted from the cliffside. Beside it, something that looked like a huge metal broken umbrella hung at an angle from some kind of pole.

"By the remains of the merry-go-round," I said. "Working his way north toward us."

"Get down!" Ari pointed at a pile of rusty metal that once upon a time had been a bumper car.

Dad and I squatted down behind it. Ari went down on one knee with the rifle loose in his hands. I ran a second SM:P. The Maculate ducked and dodged behind heaps of rubble as he zigzagged through the ruins. Like Michael, he moved too quickly for me to pinpoint his location.

"He's changed direction," I said. "He's moving east now,

farther in, and no one's following him. He's given Hafner the slip."

I scanned for Michael: found him, standing in the dark in some indeterminate location below us in a narrow space, waiting, furious, listening. Another man, also furious, also underground, moving very slowly forward. Above ground: one human man running for his life. The stink that represented Claw to my consciousness intruded on the scan.

"The Maculate's stopped running," I said. "He's walking with a kind of purposeful stride."

"Is he armed?" Ari said.

"I don't know, but I bet he is. I can just pick up his vibrations. They're murderous."

"That I'll well believe."

Dad snorted. "You can believe anything she says," he remarked to empty air.

"Keep your voice down," Ari said, again to the empty air.

My stomach began to hurt. I focused on the job in hand. I was profoundly grateful that I had Javert as backup.

I FIND SIGN. SHOW YOU. ALSO CLAW.

An image presented itself to my mind.

Thank you! That's it, all right.

"I see the Maculate," I said aloud. "He's got a long gun. It looks weird. Behind him a rusty sign says 'Fun House this way.' There's an arrow." I raised my arm to point in the matching direction. "That's the way we need to go."

"To the south, then." Ari spoke quietly.

Dad nodded his agreement, not that Ari had asked for it. We got back to our feet. We turned around the corner of the stucco walls and began heading along a narrow path. It twisted and turned between piles of planks, faded signs, a broken stove, more thick chains, ruined by rust. Over everything lay a fine drift of trash and garbage. I had no idea of where we were in relation to the ocean or to anything else.

Ari smiled. I looked where he pointed and saw a three-foot sign about twenty yards away, hanging at an angle above a pair of sagging wooden walls. The arrow read "Fun House this Way" and indicated the east, deeper in.

"I hope that no one's turned the damn thing around," Dad said.

"So do I." Ari shrugged the problem away. "We'll find out soon enough if they have."

"A path's been cleared in that direction," I said. "I bet it's the right way."

By following that path, we reached the shelter of a decayed ice cream stand. Two walls and the metal counter still stood. A burst of gunfire sounded from the direction of the roller coaster.

"Down!" Dad grabbed me by the shoulders.

We fell more than knelt together behind the shelter of a heap of old metal signs. Ari squatted down nearby and took out his communicator. His SPP terrified me. He cared nothing about his own safety. He wanted one thing: blood, the deaths of those who threatened my family—his family too, now. The rage that he kept chained had broken free.

"Hendriks?" Ari's voice was perfectly calm, perfectly cold.

I could hear the faint sound of Jan's answer. "All okay here. Two dead Storm Blue men."

"Good."

"Has O'Grady picked up more personnel above ground?"

"Yes," I said. "One guy, trying to climb over the fence at the east edge."

Ari relayed the message, then said, "I'll be moving my unit to the entrance hatch."

Jan answered. "We'll pick off the fugitive and meet you there."

The path followed a set of rusted, twisted tracks, sort of like train tracks but much narrower. Here and there we passed overturned cars of some sort, bulbous things from a kiddie ride, most likely. The path stopped at a roughly oval-shaped patch of cleared ground. In the middle, lying flat, metal gleamed.

"The hatch," I said. "But Claw's still above ground. We must have gotten here ahead of him. We need to hide."

"He can smell us," Ari said. "He's hunting ape."

All three of us took what shelter we could behind a pile

of broken planks that lay against one of the kiddie-ride cars. Two huge red-rimmed eyes stared at us from the rubble. I nearly screamed before I realized that they'd been painted on the front of a kiddie-train car, this one shaped like a ladybug. I cursed all whimsy and ran more scans.

I could feel Claw's presence nearby, smell the stink of carrion growing stronger.

"He's coming closer," I whispered. "The Spottie, I mean."

Ari nodded to show he'd heard. He studied the nearby spread of garbage, then picked up a fist-sized lump of rusty metal from the ground. I had no time to wonder why.

I focused on Michael. Mike was moving down a long hallway toward the huge open space Javert and I had seen, but he paused and then darted sidewise into some sort of opening. I felt his flash of triumph as he grabbed a small object from a flat surface. He was so pleased to have it that I could finally identify what he'd been searching for. The code tube! He had no way of knowing that we'd already released Sean from the StopCollar.

Michael left the small room he'd been in and started inching his way along a corridor. The huge room loomed in front of him. I realized that he was approaching stairs, an improvised rickety-looking set that led up to the ceiling.

"Ari!" I whispered. "Mike's about to come up."

Ari made no answer. He was staring across the open space at a small gap between piles of rubble, just a few feet from the hatch itself. On the bigger of the two piles, a fallen wall lay across a hunk of metal girder. I caught a trace of movement. Dad laid a warning hand on my shoulder. I froze, barely breathing. In the still of the windless day, a clutch of paper bags, stuck against the girder, fluttered with a tiny rustle. I heard a low sucking sound like a very small pump.

Ari rose to a kneeling position and threw the chunk of scrap metal toward the sound. It landed with a thump. He dropped flat onto the ground. I never heard a gun fire, but something whistled through the air in the direction of the thump. Ari got up to a kneel again.

"He's got an air rifle," he whispered. "Clever bastard."

We waited. I heard another rustle, another pumping sound. The metal hatch shuddered and with a scrape and groan began to slide back. I heard a growl. The Maculate's head appeared from behind the rubble heaps. Claw had also risen to a kneel. He swung up the rifle he was carrying and aimed not at the hatch but straight at me. Ari shot first. Claw's head jerked around. He rose to his feet in what must have been a sheer animal reflex, because he fell in an instant. His body thudded onto the downed girder with a spray of red blood. His gun slipped from his flaccid hands and dropped onto the clutch of paper bags. The hatch slammed shut.

"Nola, don't look," Ari said. "He won't have a face left."

The force of his icy rage knocked the breath out of me. I gulped air and summoned Qi to steady myself down.

"Anyone else?" Ari said. "In the immediate vicinity, I mean?"

"No." I could hear my voice shaking. "Not between us and the east, where the roller coaster is. There are some people over there."

Ari's communicator beeped in his shirt pocket. He took it out. "Nathan here," he said. "Is that you, Hendriks?"

I could just hear Jan's answer. "Yes. We heard a shot."

"I took out the Spottie."

"Good."

"Can you get a fix on our position?"

"Yes. We're proceeding forward under cover."

"We'll wait." Ari clicked off the communicator and returned it to his pocket.

"Wait?" I said. "Michael—"

"Do you know if that was Mike opening the hatch or was it Scorch? Can you be sure?"

I realized that I didn't know, not with any certainty.

"Scan," Dad said.

I did. I picked up Michael right away, no longer triumphant, still simmering with rage as he pressed up against a freestanding wall. I also saw a muddled, fuzzy image of the open space in front of him: the big underground level to the Fun House that Sean had mentioned. Out on the floor a man paced back and forth. It wasn't Michael. I had a feeling that I could almost see the long metal slide behind him and some other tall structure as well. Nothing came clear.

"Okay, it was Scorch. He's got to be right under the damned hatch. Mike's watching from the side."

"I thought so. Scorch must be trying to prevent Mike from getting out." Ari paused, listening. "Here comes Hendriks and his squad."

I turned to speak to Dad. He'd disappeared.

Chapter 18

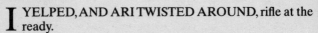

I YELPED, AND ARI TWISTED AROUND, rifle at the ready.

"What?" he snapped. "Your father! Where is he?"

"I don't know for sure, but I can guess," I said. "He's gone after Michael."

"A stupid move! Damn him!"

I choked back my impulse to snarl in my father's defense. When I ran an SM:P for Dad, I found him down in the complex below us. He was standing in the middle of a narrow corridor and turning his head back and forth, as if he was deciding which way to go. The sounds of footsteps crunching trash and men's voices brought my mind back to the upper air.

Shouting Ari's name, Jan led his squad—Sgt. Grampian and four street cops—out of the rubble. Ari called back, and we stood up to join them. I hung back, but the men surrounded the hatch, a square of metal three feet on a side. One edge sported a pair of handles, shiny from recent use. I drifted forward and ran an SM:L for the area immediately under the hatch—no one near it. Scorch and Michael must have moved away from the stairs to resume their deadly game. With Javert's help, I sensed them: Scorch hopeless and furious, Michael merely furious. I could find Dad, too, but his position kept changing, blinking, as he fast-walked through the complex, one minute here, the next there. I gave it up.

"Above ground's been cleared of hostiles," Jan said. "Where's our senior O'Grady?"

"Down under," I said. "He's trying to fetch Michael out."

Ari muttered something under his breath. From the tone I was glad I didn't understand it.

"You're the one with military experience," Jan said to Ari. "Should we wait?"

"It depends." Ari turned to me. "Is Scorch the only hostile in the complex?"

"Yes. He's not going to come out now. He's not deaf, and so he must have heard us up here."

"Then we'll open the hatch. Nola, stand back from the edge." Ari glanced around. "Grampian?"

"Acceptable, yes." Grampian looked around at his officers. "Follow his orders. The Jamaican knows what he's doing."

Ari and Grampian took up positions either side of the hatch. Jan moved back a few feet from the third side but stood where he could shoot anything coming out of it. All three held their rifles at the ready. Two patrolmen bent down and each grabbed one handle. They counted, one, two, three, and on three pulled the hatch up toward them like a shield. They stepped back and let it fall in their direction with a clang and a drift of dust. The opening appeared, dark against the pale dirt around it. I felt the stab of an ASTA and ran an SM:D.

"Scorch is waiting for someone to step on the stairs," I said. "He's behind the curved wall by the slide. I can feel his SPP. He wants to take some of you with him."

"Where's Mike?" Ari said.

"Around the other side of the big room. There's someone standing just under the slide, not Scorch—crud! I should have known. It's Dad. Mike's moving out into the room."

Shots. The twang of a bullet striking metal. More shots. I felt every one of them like electric shocks down my spine. I wanted to scream. My mouth had turned too dry to make a sound.

Dad's voice, echoing up, "You can come down now. He's dead."

Consciously, I never ran another search or scan. Adrenaline and Qi together flooded my mind and gave me a temporary power of vision. I could see the scene below like a picture painted on a vast piece of cloth that floated and wavered in the air in front of me. Dad was standing between the huge metal slide and the rickety stairs, staring across the room at a dead man lying facedown on the floor. Michael stood behind the body with a gun in his hand.

The sound of men pounding down the staircase jerked me away from the vision. Ari and Grampian had disappeared inside, while Jan was in the process of following them down. The patrolmen fanned out around the hatch and stayed up above, just in case, as one of them said to me. I was so stiff with tension that moving hurt, but I forced myself. I trotted over and went down the stairs.

When I reached the floor below, Dad ran over and joined me. A shaft of dusty sunlight fell through the open hatch and illuminated enough of the huge room for me to see what I needed to. On the other side, past the stairway and the slide both, Michael stood staring down at Scorch's dead body. He was still holding the gun. I could tell that he was fighting back tears. Ari called his name and waited until Michael looked up and saw him. He walked over and threw an arm around Mike's shoulders. Mike started trembling.

"Yes," Ari said. "It hurts."

Michael took a deep breath and nodded his agreement.

"You're one of us now," Ari said. "Never forget how you're feeling at the moment. It will keep you from killing someone when there's no need."

"I did need to, didn't I?" Michael was whispering. "Now, I mean."

"Oh, yes," Ari said. "This goes in the report as a justified homicide, an emergency measure when protecting an unarmed world-walker. That's who's standing with Nola. You *will* have to answer to the liaison captain at a hearing."

"Okay. Here." He held out the gun, and Ari took it.

"That's what I was waiting for," Dad said to me. "You

never want to startle a man with a gun in his hand, particularly when he's just used it."

Michael started to walk over to me and Dad. Halfway
across the room he stopped and stared. Dad took a step
forward. I could feel Dad's SPP, a tangle of feelings: pride
in his youngest son, relief at his own safety, regret that it
had taken a killing to keep him safe. Yet, most of all, I
picked up his joy at seeing Michael again.

"Dad?" Michael said. "Dad!"

"None other." Dad started toward him, then looked
back over his shoulder at me. "By the by, you're marrying
the right man, even if he is a cop."

He'd just made me a tremendous concession, but I had
ground to defend from that dark cloud of wedded doom.

"Dad," I said, "I am not marrying anyone."

"We'll just see about that." He nodded my way, then
strode to Michael's open arms.

Ari hurried over to me. "What are you doing down
here? I told you—"

"Oh, shut up!" I was snuffling back tears. "I had to see
them safe for myself."

Ari snarled and pointed at the stairs. I took another look
at Dad and Michael, who stood close together, face-to-face,
talking in soft voices. My gaze wandered to Scorch's body
and the pool of blood thickening around him. I decided
that, yes, I'd seen enough and headed for the stairs.

I'd gotten about halfway up when something came floating down from outside on a waft of air. Trash, I thought, and
swatted at it to knock it aside. I missed, got a better look in
the shaft of sunlight, and grabbed it instead. A peacock
feather, clean and whole. Despite the humid air, I turned
cold. I hurried up the rest of the way. For a change, the watery yellow sunlight, tainted with the dusty mist, struck me
as beautiful.

The patrolmen, all armed, had taken up positions around
the perimeter of the open space.

"Did anyone come by here?" I held up the feather. "Did
someone throw this down the stairs?"

"No, Miss," one of the street cops said. "We would have

seen them. There's probably a lot of junk left under there, from the old days, I mean, when this place still worked."

"Yeah, you're probably right." I knew he wasn't, of course, but I saw no use in pressing the issue.

Javert called to me. YOU OKAY NOW?

Yes, but. Peacock Angel cult—do you know anything about that?

He radiated puzzlement. HUMAN THING YES/NO

Yes. Religion.

Utter and complete puzzlement.

Never mind. It's okay. I can't tell you how much I appreciate your help.

WELCOME. I GO BACK TO TANK. A wave of disgust followed in the wake of that last word.

Okay. So long and thanks for all the Qi.

In a flood of squiddish laughter Javert broke the connection.

I was expecting the usual bureaucratic police procedures at the site and afterward. From the number of gunshots I'd heard, I knew that a lot of men had died both in Playland and out on Fulton. I doubted that the raids on the safe houses had been bloodless. Ari and Jan had just carried up Scorch's corpse when Hafner arrived, flanked with the men he'd commanded on the raids. Grampian hurried to meet him and report in. Hafner listened, nodding now and then to show approval.

"The Spottie's dead," Grampian told him. "Right over there. Nathan killed him."

Hafner walked over to the girder where the Maculate still hung, splayed out. Flies had already gathered for the blood. Hafner spat on Claw's body, then turned away and walked over to Ari. He shook Ari's hand and clapped him on the shoulder.

"Good job," Hafner said. "One less crook for you CBI men to take back with you."

Hafner walked off to rejoin Grampian. With a shake of his head, Ari came over to me.

"Won't there be some kind of inquiry?" I asked him.

He looked at me as though I'd turned into a blithering idiot. "Here?" he said.

"Oh. Right. Uh, how do you feel about Claw?"

He shrugged.

"You're going to have nightmares tonight, aren't you?" I said.

"Well, he may have been a sodding Spottie, but he was a—what do I mean?" Ari stared down at the ground and ran both hands through his hair. "An alien, but—"

"A sapient being," I said. "A conscious entity, even though he was a murdering criminal."

Ari nodded. "They wiped out the gang down at the safe houses. I doubt if anyone lived to stand trial."

When I laid a hand on his arm, he took a deep breath. "None of my affair, I suppose. We'll deal with all that later."

I watched the cops begin wrapping the dead Maculate in a sheet of heavy cloth. All I could see was a safely indeterminate shape, though a red stain seeped through the shroud. *Non omnis moriar*, Nuala's image had told me. As long as Claw lived, it had been true in a gruesome way. With him gone, she was truly gone as well. I allowed myself a small prayer to Whomever that she'd have some peace at last.

SPARE14 DROVE HIS SMALL squad, including my brother, down in the borrowed wagon. He dropped off the two patrolmen, had a few brief words with Hafner, then took the rest of our TWIXT contingent back to the apartment. When we arrived, he found a message on his landline phone that gave me some hope of seeing Order respected. The liaison captain, Anna Kerenskya, wanted full written reports from everyone involved with all the deaths, including Scorch the Torch and Claw, that were the direct responsibility of the TWIXT squad. I could tell from the snap in her voice—she spoke in heavily accented English—that she, at least, did not take a suspect's death lightly.

"We're in for it," Jan said. "Wait till she finds out about the man I dropped over on the east side. We'll all be raked over the coals at a full hearing."

"Tonight?" Ari said.

"No, no," Spare14 said. "It'll be convened in a week or

so. It takes time to organize this sort of thing. First we'll have to file our reports, all of us, even those of you affiliated with other agencies."

Me, he meant.

"Then they'll need to find four impartial officers with the time to sit with Kerenskya on the panel," Spare14 continued. "Since Michael is a juvenile, I'll need to interview him formally in my office back on Four before the hearing. I hope that he won't have to appear. Oh, and remind me to check your status, Nathan, and see how many credit points this operation will give you on the examination." He paused briefly. "I'm assuming you still want to apply for the TWIXT position."

"More than ever," Ari said. "The Axeman escaped. I count that as a failure, and I don't like failing."

Everyone looked at Michael. Dad was sitting in the middle of the couch, with Sean on one side of him and Mike on the other, a tableau of O'Grady men, all so much alike for more than one reason.

"I'm real sorry about that. Seriously," Mike said. "But he would have killed Sean if I hadn't opened the gate. He threatened it, and I knew he meant it. Epic gross!"

Sean nodded a confirmation.

"Then you doubtless did the best you could at the time," Ari said. "Where is the bastard?"

"On Six. That's where that gate leads. The Axeman talked a lot about his contacts on Six," Michael said. "He's been funneling money over there for years, whenever he could get a transport orb from a fence. He had this idea that he could start a commune or village or something, a place for people who got out of SanFran to live and work."

"My God!" Spare14 said. "Talk about your grandiose plans! He must have had some real connections over there. I don't suppose he mentioned their names?"

"No such luck. He never really trusted me." Mike hesitated. "Six is where Ash came from."

"She's the blonde, huh?" I said. "The hot blonde?"

Michael blushed scarlet, all the answer I needed. Dad turned his head to give him a sharp look that foretold a future lecture. He had never been a "boys will be boys" type of father. Michael cringed. I decided to let Dad learn about Sophie on his own.

"So they'll have allies, too," Jan said. "More's the pity."

"Work to be done," Ari said.

Spare14 nodded. "Six is a very difficult situation, I'm afraid."

"Do the people there know about talents?" I said. "And different world levels, too?"

"No, they don't." Spare14 tented his fingers and frowned at them. "There has to be a reason for this, but on the deviant levels that our scientists have labeled with odd numbers, at least some of the people know about the hidden side of things, the worlds, the talents. Those with even numbers, like your own world, O'Grady, do not. Two is the exception, of course. Two is always the exception."

"And no one knows why," Jan put in. "As we all know." He grinned at his joke, if you can call it that. "I remember a detail from when I was studying for a salary-grade exam. The scientific theory runs that the fractal splits between levels have a right and a left side. Those on the right do know about the multiverse, and those on the left, don't. But the cram book went on to say that the words right and left were only metaphorical."

"That makes no sense at all," Dad said.

"Quite right," Spare14 glowered at nothing in particular. "It doesn't. I do wish HQ would explain these things more clearly."

"Speaking of explanations," I said. "Sean, you're the older brother, aren't you? Not some teen boy? Like, you're grown up? Why did you ever go along with Michael's crazy idea?"

"Hey!" Mike began. "It wasn't—"

"You shut up." I turned all my attention and a scowl Sean's way. "What in hell were you thinking?"

"That we'd be back by morning," Sean said. "Hey, it wasn't our idea to get kidnapped, y'know. We were going to check out a couple of gates and come right back. Besides, I didn't want Mike going over here alone. It's dangerous, in case you haven't noticed."

"Brat! But you stayed over on Tuesday, too. That's what gave Storm Blue time to kidnap you."

"Yeah, I know." Sean winced and looked away. "That was because of José. It was Mike's last chance to see him."

My turn to wince. "Well, yeah. Okay. Next question. When you and Michael went through the gate, I picked up nothing. Neither did Aunt Eileen. I suspect there's a reason for that."

Sean shrugged as if he knew nothing about it. Dad turned a baleful eye his way.

"Oh, okay," Sean said. "What's the opposite of finding?"

"Losing," I said. "Are you telling me that you can hide yourself when you pull dumb stunts like this one?"

"I wouldn't put it exactly like that, but yes, I can. Claw knew it, too. He's the one who insisted they collar me."

"So Claw knew a lot about talents?"

"You bet. He gave me the creeps. He wanted to kill and butcher me, but the Axeman wouldn't let him." Sean went pale at the memory. "He had a girl back home, he told us, Claw, I mean, not the Axeman. When he brought her enough dead apes, she'd let him get her pregnant. I don't know how many apes he needed, but I sure as hell didn't want to be one of them."

"He talked about having kids a lot," Mike put in. "I called them 'cubs' once, and he took a swing at me. The axeman had to break it up."

Jan and Spare14 exchanged a significant glance.

"This is going to be an interesting set of reports," Spare14 said. "HQ will doubtless want follow-up, and I suppose I'll be postponing my holiday leave yet again. At least I'll be vacating this wretched office soon. I'm sincerely pleased about getting away from Three."

"I hope to God," Jan said, "that they don't tap me to take your place."

"I'm nearly at the radiation limit," Spare14 said. "You've got a long way to go, so you're no doubt right to worry. Which reminds me. O'Grady and Nathan—or I should say, all you O'Gradys and Nathan, there's no reason for you to stay here tonight, but I'll collect any radiation badges before you leave. The medical staff will need to check them and record the readings."

Words could not express my feelings at the thought of getting out of SanFran. Sheer joy would be a good start. We wasted no time in collecting our luggage. Before we left, however, I did have one last thing to ask Spare14.

"Earlier this year, when I was hunting Belial," I said. "You were scanning for me. Why? I know you wanted contact with the Agency, and that Nathan's report gave you a lead. But you were spying on me, not the general situation."

Spare14 briefly dithered, then said, "Well, to be honest, it was due to my guilty conscience. The Brittanic officer who was pursuing the case against your father never told us he had a family. So we never made any attempt to contact your mother."

"Dad," I said, "why didn't you say something?"

"I was hoping the bastard didn't know I did. I was afraid of reprisals. The Brittanics are known for that, taking rebellion out on a man's family."

I stared, gape-mouthed.

"They're not like the British here," Dad continued. "Never make that mistake." He looked straight at me and emphasized each word. "They are not like the English you know."

Ari glanced at Spare14 as if asking for confirmation. Spare14 nodded his agreement and sighed.

"So I found out about the family long after the trial." Spare14 glanced my father's way, though he couldn't quite bring himself to look Dad in the face. "I'm sorry. We would have made some provision for the children had we known in time."

Since he had talents enough to hide his SPP, I wasn't sure if I believed him or not.

"At any rate," Spare14 continued. "When I was assigned to Four, just a few months ago now, I remembered your family and thought I'd see what had happened to the children. When I realized that you worked for the Agency, you became the logical place to start my inquiries." He turned to Dad again. "I'm also the one who told the releasing magistrate about your son Patrick's death."

"And I'll thank you for that," Dad said. "I had a chance to digest it that way. It would have been a bitter shock if I'd gotten all the way home before I found out."

"So I thought."

"There's another thing I'll thank you for, not lying when Major Newcombe demanded it of you."

"There was no evidence you'd shot anyone, none." Spare14 turned to me. "I felt at the time that the Brittanics wanted your father hanged and were willing to bend justice till it broke in order to do so. I refused to go along with it. They did have evidence of his being an accessory to the killers' escape, and they made the most of it."

"Thank you." My voice choked on tears. "Thank you from the bottom of my heart."

Spare14 smiled at me, then held out his hand to my father. Dad hesitated, then shook it in farewell.

With Dad and his set of orbs along, returning home to Terra Four that evening presented no problems. The first thing I did when we reached our own world's version of South Park was get out my cell phone and call Aunt Eileen.

"You're back," she said. "News?"

"Michael and Sean are safe and right here."

She caught a liquid breath that told me she was fighting back tears. "I'll call Al right away." She sniffed heavily. "Ah, here's Sophie. Hang on."

I heard her speaking, then Sophie's high-pitched shriek. Aunt Eileen returned to the phone.

"She's dancing around the kitchen, and honestly, I feel like dancing myself."

"Call Al before you do, okay?" I had to smile. "Oh, and there's another call you need to make—to Mom."

"Yes, I certainly do! She'll be so relieved. I know she blusters and natters, but she does love all of you children."

"Well, most of us, anyway. We're coming straight over, and we've got a surprise."

"Don't tell me it's true, then! I dreamed last night that you'd brought Flann home."

I should have known. "Yeah," I said. "He's here, too."

Aunt Eileen began to cry, big sobs of relief and joy.

"I'll let you go," I said. "Ari's flagged down a cab. We'll pick up our car and get over there as soon as we can."

By the time we parked in front of the Houlihan house, the sun hovered low in an orange blaze of incoming fog. Uncle Jim came out on the front porch and stood with his hands on his hips to watch us unload the cramped Saturn. Dad got out first. Michael and Sean pried themselves out of the back seat and stood stretching on the sidewalk.

Jim yelled down the steep flight of brick steps. "Jesus H, Flann! Where the hell have you been?"

"Hell," Dad called back. "Tell you about it over a drink."

With a shriek Sophie came bounding down the steps to throw herself into Michael's arms. Sean stood smiling at them off to one side. I had just gotten out of the car when I saw Mom barge through the front door onto the porch. She was wearing a black jacket over a demure gray dress and swinging her handbag, obviously leaving in one of her usual huffs. On the top step she turned back to snarl at Uncle Jim.

"I am not going to stand here and listen to nonsense," Mom said. "I can't believe you thought I'd—"

"Deirdre!" Dad called up. "Open your eyes, will you?"

She stiffened. Her back arched as if she'd felt an electric shock. Slowly, very slowly, she turned and looked at him, merely looked, stared, said nothing, never moved.

"It's really me," Dad said. "Here, I'll just come up."

He sprang up the stairs two at a time while she continued to stare, never moving, never speaking. When he reached the porch, she raised one hand and laid it alongside his face. At the touch of solid flesh and blood she began to weep. He threw an arm around her shoulders and swept her into the house. For a moment I saw a vision of them as they looked in old photographs, young and beautiful, both of them, besotted with each other, and so much alike that I wondered how I'd ever missed seeing their secret.

Hand in hand, Michael and Sophie walked up the stairs

to disappear inside as well. Ari opened the trunk and tossed
Dad's duffel bag to Sean. Sean carried it up the steps and
hurried into the house after Uncle Jim.

"Shall we go home?" Ari said.

"Please. I want a real shower."

"I'll take one with you."

We shared a grin and drove off. I don't think anyone noticed. As we turned onto Silver Avenue, we passed Al's car.
He honked, I waved, and Ari nearly drove into the oncom-
ing number 44 bus. It took me a minute before I could
breathe well enough to talk.

"I've got to find out who sent me that hallucination in
the park, so I can take over the driving again."

"Now I know we're really home. Let's hope the flat's still
there and free of Maculates."

I ran a quick SM:L. "Yeah," I said, "it is. But you know, I
bet that the Maculate woman who's been bugging me isn't
going to stop. Claw was her mate, not just her supplier."

"Supplier of ape meat, you mean? She'll be furious
when she finds out he's dead."

"The apes fight back!"

"If she causes trouble for you, she'll have me to deal
with." Ari laid on the horn and swerved around a pedes-
trian, who screamed.

"Never mind that now! Just drive."

When we got home, Ari called Itzak, and I called Annie.
After I went through the flat to renew the Chaos wards, Ari
and I had our shower, and its logical aftermath, then went
out to a late dinner at the Japanese restaurant like a normal
couple. That night, though, around three in the morning,
Ari had the nightmare. I woke up to hear him barking orders in Hebrew, telling the Palestinian boy to stop where he
was. In his sleep he flinched with a quick groan. He'd fired,
I supposed, and killed the suicide bomber yet once again. I
sat up and turned on the nightstand lamp.

"Ari," I said, "sweetheart, darling, Ari, it's okay, you're
just dreaming." I repeated this litany a couple of times before he woke with a jerk of his whole body.

He sat up and looked at me, but it took a good minute
for him to recognize who I was. His hair stuck to his face

with sweat. I held out my arms. He turned to me and let me
hold him while he trembled.

"There isn't any end to this, is there?" he said.

"End to what, darling?"

"I don't know. The guilt, I suppose. And just the sight of
it, the things you've seen, the things you've done. They
come back up like vomit."

The trembling eased, then stopped. He pulled away,
tried to smile, failed, and ran both hands through his
sweaty hair. "In the heat of the moment," he said, "there's
nothing wrong with killing someone. That's the hell of it,
Nola. In the moment, you have to fire, and you do, and it's
perfectly justified and right. It takes time before the memory blows up in your face. Then there's no way back or
out."

"That's true about everything. There's never any way
back, whether it's a good thing or a lousy one."

"True." He lay back down with a sigh. "Unfortunately."

When I lay down next to him, he rolled into my arms. I
left the light on and held him, just held him, until we both
could sleep.

We'd just gotten up, around 11:30, and Ari was making
coffee in the kitchen, when a hoarse Aunt Eileen called me
on my landline phone. I sat down in my computer chair to
talk.

"What's wrong with your voice?" I said. "Are you getting a cold?"

"No, I was just on the phone for hours last night, telling
everyone that Flann's home." She paused for a dry cough.
"Dan and Maureen and Kathleen, of course, and Father
Keith, and Rose and Wally, and the Donovans—well, you
get the picture."

"Let me guess. You're throwing a party."

"Yes, tomorrow afternoon. I hope you and Ari are coming. Your mother has to be there, of course."

"Of course. Well, I'm tempted to say we can't come, but
damn it, it's my family, too."

"Exactly, dear. I'll speak to her about things. After all,
you're the one who brought him back."

"Will that really cut any ice with her?"

Aunt Eileen sighed. I heard a sound that implied she was drinking some kind of liquid.

"I hope so," she said eventually. "You know what the problem is, don't you?"

"Sure. My abortion when I was a teenager."

"Not just that. I mean, she was honestly upset about it. We all were, especially you, but I really don't think she'd have acted so horribly about that alone. She would have made your life miserable, but she never would have thrown you out of the house. It gave her the excuse she needed, in a nasty way."

"Excuse for what?"

Eileen hesitated before she continued. "The sad thing is that you were always Flann's favorite child, very, very favorite, really, though he tried not to show it in front of the other children. I suppose it's because you're the most like him in so many ways. Deirdre was so jealous. It was when you were nine, I think, that I saw it. We were having a picnic in the park, and I was watching Flann teach you how to kick a soccer ball. The way Deirdre looked at the two of you curdled my blood. Right after that she started in on you about your imaginary fat."

I was stunned. There I was, the psychology major, Miss Psychic Talent herself, so proud of my insights into everyone else, but I'd never realized that my own mother was jealous of me.

"That's where the eating disorder comes from, I bet," I said.

"Yes, and I'm so glad you can finally admit you have one."

"I could see the dust fleck in someone else's eye, but not the splinter in my own."

"You're not the only one, dear." Eileen paused for a long moment to have another couple of swallows of whatever she was drinking. The pause gave me time to wonder: did she know about my mother and father's marriage? Had she dreamed the truth but kept the secret for all these years?

"Sorry," Aunt Eileen said. "I made myself some herb tea and honey for my throat. Anyway, do you think Deirdre will ever admit that she's jealous of her own daughter?"

"No. I guess she still is, huh?"

"Probably more so than ever, now that he's back. I'm about to call her. If she says one word to Flann about your pregnancy, I'll strangle her with my own hands."

And yet, of course, Eileen would never strangle anyone, and Mom knew it. I doubted if she could resist the chance to drive a permanent wedge between me and Dad. Maybe not right away. She'd probably enjoy thinking about it, savoring the prospect, but sooner or later the subject would come up. I could imagine the fake sorrow in her voice as she dropped the bomb on our relationship.

"Why don't you and Ari come over for lunch today?" Aunt Eileen said. "We can talk more then. We need to come up with a strategy for dealing with Sean's problem."

"Sean's—oh right. What Dad's going to say when he realizes Sean's gay."

"Exactly. Sean and Al are willing to hide it for a little while, but eventually Flann will just have to face facts." She paused to sip more tea. "Do come over. I'm honestly sick of talking on the phone."

"You? Sick of talking on the phone?"

For a reply she coughed.

"We'll be glad to come over," I said. "That way I won't have to eat whatever Ari cooks."

What Aunt Eileen was cooking was a wonderful chicken soup and blueberry muffins. I found the soup easy to eat, but the muffin stuck in my throat, even though it was delicious. I could not stop my mind from counting calories, worrying about fat content, and all the rest of the compulsive details that had obsessed me for so long. I did manage to get most of a muffin down, but it was a struggle.

"You should eat more," Ari began. "You—ow!"

Aunt Eileen had kicked him under the table. "One step at a time, dear," she said. "How about some fresh coffee?"

Ari sighed and reached down to rub his shin. She got up, poured coffee all round from the carafe on the stove, then sat back down.

"I don't know where Michael and Sophie are," Aunt Eileen said. "It's probably just as well, too. I—" She hesitated at a sound from outside.

An ancient truck came clanking up the drive. Aunt Eileen got up and looked out the window over the sink. "It's Jim," she said. "I wonder what he's doing home?"

He enlightened us as soon as he got in. "I took the afternoon off," Uncle Jim said. "Flann and I are going to go get his truck out of storage. They should be here any minute." He looked at me, hesitated, and sighed. "I should have called home first, honey. Sorry. Deirdre's going to be with him. She took the week off work, he told me."

I stood up. "It's okay, Uncle Jim. You didn't even know we were here. Ari, let's go."

We weren't fast enough. Another car trundled up the drive and parked behind the truck.

"I'll head them off at the pass." Uncle Jim fled the kitchen through the back door.

Ari and I ran for the front door, but just as we reached it, my mother opened it. She was wearing jeans and a gingham shirt, the first time in thirteen years, I figured, that she'd dressed so casually. Her Qi, too, flowed around her smoothly, quietly, in a way that I remembered from my childhood. She was looking back over her shoulder and talking to someone behind her.

"I must have left it in the living room," she was saying. "I'll just see."

She turned. What she saw was not whatever her missing item was, but me. We stared at each other for a long, cold moment.

"I'm surprised you'd show your face around here," Mom said eventually. "Aren't you afraid of what your father will think of the things you've done? He must know about the live-in boyfriend. But I bet there are other little matters you haven't mentioned."

"I know what you mean. Have you told him?"

"No, not yet."

I felt pure rage build at the implied threat in that "yet." I squelched what Qi I could and looked her straight in the face.

"You know, Mom, we both have secrets to keep, don't we? You keep mine, and I won't tell the rest of the family yours."

"And just what do you mean by that?"

"How you're twice an O'Brien, by birth and by marriage."

My mother went pale. Even through her makeup I could see the pallor form. Her hands shook so hard that she nearly dropped her handbag.

"I know it's been hard on you," I went on. "Waiting and wondering if Dad was dead or alive. You risked damnation twice over to marry him, didn't you? More than twice. With every child you gave him, you risked it again. Well, he's back, and he's yours." I paused for emphasis. "All yours. A little peace and quiet would be nice now, right?"

I tensed and waited for the explosions to start. None came. She took a step backward and caught her breath with a little ladylike gasp. I took a step forward.

"Does he have to know everything that happened when he was gone?"

"No." Her voice shook. "It would only cause trouble in the family."

"A lot of trouble."

I smiled. She tried to smile.

"Okay," I said. "Subject closed—forever, as far as I'm concerned."

My father came walking around the corner of the house and joined us on the porch. He started to say something, then paused to look back and forth between us. His eyes narrowed, just slightly.

"Is something wrong?" Dad said.

Mother forced out a smile. "Oh, no," she said. "Nothing at all."

That's when I knew that I'd truly won. He put an arm around Mom's waist and pulled her close. She rested her head against his shoulder, and he smiled, not at anything in particular, just perhaps at her touch.

"Coming to the party tomorrow, Noodles?" Dad said.

"You bet," I said. "It should be a really good time."

"Maureen and her children will be there, Jim tells me. She has children! I'm a grandfather. How did that happen?"

"You don't look it, Dad. You're too young to be a grandpa."

Dad grinned and gave me the thumbs up sign he'd always used to show approval. Together, snuggled close like teenagers, he and Mom walked past us and went inside. Aunt Eileen had come into the living room to wait for them. I caught a glimpse of her expression—a horrified fascination, as if she were watching *King Lear* or some other tragedy play out—before she smoothed the expression into a welcoming smile. She knew, all right. She must have known from the beginning. She'd said nothing, no matter how it must have tormented her, given her deep faith in her religion. Now I was going to follow her example and share the burden. I promised myself and the family that I'd never say a word.

Mom and Dad headed across the living room toward the kitchen. Why shouldn't they be together now? I thought. They've both been through hell already, thirteen years of it. That's when I realized that I'd forgiven them for the marriage. As for forgiving Mom for other events between us, that would take me a while more. I turned around and found Ari smiling at me.

"Brutal," Ari said, "but effective."

"Thank you, darling."

"Do you want to go home?" he continued. "You still look tired."

"I am tired. Yeah, let's go before Dad starts in on me about getting married." I summoned a heartfelt scowl. "Dad and, of course, you."

"I've been thinking about that. I know you don't want to marry. I should stop badgering you about it."

A ploy if I ever heard one! I stayed silent.

"But," Ari continued, "I doubt if your father's going to stop. So why don't we just get engaged? Formally, I mean. And then we can just keep putting off the date for the wedding. Our jobs, you know. Much too busy. Important government affairs."

He meant it. I finally heard what his SPP was trying to tell me: he was being sincere.

"That's a thought," I said. "A thought I'm surprised you had, but a good one."

"Nola, I want you to marry me because you want to marry me, not because you're sick and tired of saying no."

If that was a ploy, it was the best one ever, but again, I knew he meant it. I put my hands on his shoulders and reached up to kiss him.

"Okay," I said. "Consider yourself engaged."

Agency Talents
and Acronyms

AH Audio Hallucination
ASTA Automatic survival threat awareness
CDEP Chaos diagnostic emergency procedure
CW Chaos wards
CDS Collective Data Stream
CEV Conscious evasion procedure
DEI Deliberately extruded images (visible only to psychics)
DW Dice walk
E Ensorcellment
FW Fast Walking
HC Heat conservation
IOI Image Objectification of Insight
LDRS Long distance remote sensing
MI Manifested indicators (of chaos forces)
PI Possibility Images
SAF Scanning the aura field
SM Search mode
SM:D Search mode: Danger
SM:G Search mode: General
SM:L Search mode: Location
SM:P Search mode: Personnel
SAWM Semi-automatic warning mechanism
SH Shield persona
SPP Subliminal psychological profile
WW World-Walking

Katharine Kerr
The Nola O'Grady *Novels*

"Breakneck plotting, punning, and romance make for a mostly fast, fun read."   —*Publishers Weekly*

"This is an entertaining investigative urban fantasy that sub-genre readers will enjoy...fans will enjoy the streets of San Francisco as seen through an otherworldly lens."
    —*Midwest Book Review*

LICENSE TO ENSORCELL
978-0-7564-0656-1

WATER TO BURN
978-0-7564-0691-2

APOCALYPSE TO GO
978-0-7564-0709-4

Diana Rowland

Secrets of the Demon

978-0-7564-0652-3

"Rowland's hot streak continues as she gives her fans another big helping of urban fantasy goodness! The plot twists are plentiful and the action is hard-edged. Another great entry in this compelling series." —*RT Book Review*

"This is an excellent police procedural urban fantasy that like its two previous arcane forensic investigations stars a terrific lead protagonist... Kara is fabulous as the focus of the case and of relationships with the Fed and with the demon as the Bayou heats up with another magical mystery tour that will take readers away from the mundane to the enjoyable world of Diana Rowland."

—*Midwest Book Reviews*

And don't miss:

Sins of the Demon

(January 2012)   978-0-7564-0705-6

To Order Call: 1-800-788-6262
www.dawbooks.com

P.R. Frost

The Tess Noncoiré Adventures

"Frost's fantasy debut series introduces a charming protagonist, both strong and vulnerable, and her cheeky companion. An intriguing plot and a well-developed warrior sisterhood make this a good choice for fans of the urban fantasy of Tanya Huff, Jim Butcher, and Charles deLint."

—Library Journal

HOUNDING THE MOON
978-0-7564-0425-3

MOON IN THE MIRROR
978-0-7564-0486-4

FAERY MOON
978-0-7564-0606-6

and new in paperback:

FOREST MOON RISING
978-0-7564-0710-0

To Order Call: 1-800-788-6262
www.dawbooks.com

DAW 70

Gini Koch
The Alien *Novels*

"This delightful romp has many interesting twists and turns as it glances at racism, politics, and religion en route. Darned amusing." —*Booklist* (starred review)

"Amusing and interesting...a hilarious romp in the vein of 'Men in Black' or 'Ghostbusters'." —*Voya*

TOUCHED BY AN ALIEN
978-0-7564-0600-4

ALIEN TANGO
978-0-7564-0632-5

ALIEN IN THE FAMILY
978-0-7564-0668-4

ALIEN PROLIFERATION
978-0-7564-0697-4

ALIEN DIPLOMACY
978-0-7564-0716-2
(Available April 2012)

To Order Call: 1-800-788-6262
www.dawbooks.com

Seanan McGuire
The October Daye Novels

"...will surely appeal to readers who enjoy my books, or those of Patrica Briggs." —*Charlaine Harris*

"Well researched, sharply told, highly atmospheric and as brutal as any pulp detective tale, this promising start to a new urban fantasy series is sure to appeal to fans of Jim Butcher or Kim Harrison."—*Publishers Weekly*

ROSEMARY AND RUE
978-0-7564-0571-7

A LOCAL HABITATION
978-0-7564-0596-0

AN ARTIFICIAL NIGHT
978-0-7564-0626-4

LATE ECLIPSES
978-0-7564-0666-0

ONE SALT SEA
978-0-7564-0683-7

To Order Call: 1-800-788-6262
www.dawbooks.com